WAR OF LANKA

Amish is a 1974-born, IIM (Kolkata)-educated banker-turned-author. The success of his debut book, *The Immortals of Meluha* (Book 1 of the Shiva Trilogy), encouraged him to give up his career in financial services to focus on writing. Besides being an author, he is also an Indian-government diplomat, a host for TV documentaries, and a film producer.

Amish is passionate about history, mythology and philosophy, finding beauty and meaning in all world religions. His books have sold more than six million copies and have been translated into over twenty languages. His Shiva Trilogy is the fastest-selling and his Ram Chandra Series the second fastest-selling book series in Indian publishing history. You can connect with Amish here:

- www.facebook.com/authoramish
- www.instagram.com/authoramish
- www.twitter.com/authoramish

Other Titles by Amish

SHIVA TRILOGY

The fastest-selling book series in the history of Indian publishing

The Immortals of Meluha (Book 1 of the Trilogy)

The Secret of the Nagas (Book 2 of the Trilogy)

The Oath of the Vayuputras (Book 3 of the Trilogy)

RAM CHANDRA SERIES

The second fastest-selling book series in the history of Indian publishing

Ram – Scion of Ikshvaku (Book 1 of the Series)

Sita – Warrior of Mithila (Book 2 of the Series)

Raavan – Enemy of Aryavarta (Book 3 of the Series)

INDIC CHRONICLES

Legend of Suheldev

NON-FICTION

Immortal India: Young Country, Timeless Civilisation

Dharma: Decoding the Epics for a Meaningful Life

'[Amish is] one of the most original thinkers of his generation.'
— *Arnab Goswami*
(Senior Journalist and MD, Republic TV)

'Amish has a fine eye for detail and a compelling narrative style.'
— *Dr Shashi Tharoor*
(Member of Parliament and Author)

'[Amish has] a deeply thoughtful mind with an unusual, original and fascinating view of the past.'
— *Shekhar Gupta*
(Senior Journalist and Columnist)

'To understand the New India, you need to read Amish.'
— *Swapan Dasgupta*
(Member of Parliament and Senior Journalist)

'Through all of Amish's books flows a current of liberal, progressive ideology: about gender, about caste, about discrimination of any kind... He is the only Indian bestselling writer with true philosophical depth – his books are all backed by tremendous research and deep thought.'
— *Sandipan Deb*
(Senior Journalist and Editorial Director, Swarajya)

'Amish's influence goes beyond his books, his books go beyond literature, his literature is steeped in philosophy, which is anchored in bhakti, which powers his love for India.'
— *Gautam Chikermane*
(Senior Journalist and Author)

'Amish is a literary phenomenon.'

— *Anil Dharker*
(Senior Journalist and Author)

—◆ **RAM CHANDRA SERIES BOOK 4** ◆—

WAR OF
LANKA

AMISH

HarperCollins *Publishers* India

First published in India by HarperCollins *Publishers* 2022
Building No 10, Tower A, 4th Floor, DLF Cyber City, Phase II,
Gurugram – 122002
www.harpercollins.co.in

2 4 6 8 10 9 7 5 3

Copyright © Amish Tripathi 2022

P-ISBN: 978-93-5629-509-4
E-ISBN: 978-93-5629-154-6

Typeset in 11/13.7 Adobe Caslon Pro at
Manipal Technologies Limited, Manipal

Printed and bound in the UK using 100% renewable
electricity at CPI Group (UK) Ltd

Om Namah Shivāya
The Universe bows to Lord Shiva
I bow to Lord Shiva

To my father, the late V.K. Tripathi,
And to my young son, Neel.

I used to reach up and hold his hand, to learn how to walk,
I reach down to embrace him, for it makes my heart soar.
I used to ask him questions, for he schooled me best,
I give him books to read, to expand his horizons.
I strove to make my father proud of me,
I strive to be worthy of emulation to my son.
Blessed am I,
With among the most sacred of bonds,
Which stretches across generations.
The one with my father, the one with my son.
And the soul will forever reverberate with these beautiful words.
When a father told his son:
I am proud of you, my boy. Always was, always will be.
And a son told his father:
I love you, dad. Always have, and always will.

Death may be the greatest of all human blessings...

—*Socrates*

In fact, the greatest blessing is when you never have to die again.
When you attain Moksha or Nirvana,
Liberation from the unrelenting cycle of rebirths.

Do good.
Help others.
Perform positive karma.
Lead a worthy life.
And earn that greatest blessing for yourself:
A death to end all deaths.

List of Characters and Important Tribes
(In Alphabetical Order)

Akampana: A smuggler; one of Raavan's closest aides

Arishtanemi: Military chief of the Malayaputras; right-hand man of Vishwamitra

Annapoorna Devi: A brilliant musician who lived in Agastyakootam, the capital of the Malayaputras.

Ashwapati: King of the northwestern kingdom of Kekaya; father of Kaikeyi and a loyal ally of Dashrath

Bharat: Ram's half-brother; son of Dashrath and Kaikeyi

Dashrath: Chakravarti king of Kosala and emperor of the Sapt Sindhu; father of Ram, Bharat, Lakshman and Shatrughan

Hanuman: A Naga and a member of the Vayuputra tribe

Indrajit: Son of Raavan and Mandodari

Janak: King of Mithila; father of Sita

Jatayu: A captain of the Malayaputra tribe; Naga friend of Sita and Ram

Kaikesi: Rishi Vishrava's first wife; mother of Raavan and Kumbhakarna

Kanyakumari: Literally, the Virgin Goddess. It was believed that the Mother Goddess Herself temporarily resided in the bodies of carefully chosen young girls, who were then worshipped as living Goddesses.

Khara: A captain in the Lankan army; Samichi's lover

Krakachabahu: The governor of Chilika

Kubaer: The chief-trader of Lanka

Kumbhakarna: Raavan's brother; also a Naga

Kushadhwaj: King of Sankashya; younger brother of Janak

Lakshman: One of the twin sons of Dashrath; Ram's halfbrother

Malayaputras: The tribe left behind by Lord Parshu Ram, the sixth Vishnu

Mandodari: Wife of Raavan

Mara: An independent assassin for hire

Mareech: Kaikesi's brother; Raavan and Kumbhakarna's uncle; one of Raavan's closest aides

Nagas: Human beings born with deformities

Nandini: A good friend of Vishwamitra and Vashishtha from their days in the Gurukul. She was from the land of Branga.

Prithvi: A businessman in the village of Todee

Raavan: Son of Rishi Vishrava; brother of Kumbhakarna; half-brother of Vibhishan and Shurpanakha

Ram: Son of Emperor Dashrath and his eldest wife

Kaushalya; eldest of four brothers; later married to Sita

Samichi: Police and protocol chief of Mithila; Khara's lover

Shatrughan: Twin brother of Lakshman; son of Dashrath and Sumitra; Ram's half-brother

Shochikesh: The landlord of Todee village

Shurpanakha: Half-sister of Raavan

Sita: Daughter of King Janak and Queen Sunaina of Mithila; also the prime minister of Mithila; later married to Ram

Sukarman: A resident of Todee village; Shochikesh's son

Sursa: An employee of the trader Naarad. She was passionately in love with Hanuman, despite his vow of celibacy.

Suryavanshis: The descendants of the Sun God. This dynasty of kings and queens was founded by Emperor Ikshvaku.

Vaanars: The Vaanars were the powerful dynasty that ruled the land of Kishkindha along the Tungabhadra River.

Vali: The king of Kishkindha

Vashishtha: *Raj guru*, the *royal priest* of Ayodhya; teacher of the four Ayodhya princes

Vayuputras: The tribe left behind by Lord Rudra, the previous Mahadev

Vedavati: A resident of Todee village; Prithvi's wife

Vibhishan: Half-brother of Raavan

Vishrava: A revered rishi; the father of Raavan, Kumbhakarna, Vibhishan and Shurpanakha

Vishwamitra: Chief of the Malayaputras; also temporary guru of Ram and Lakshman

Note on the Narrative Structure

If you have picked up this book, then in all probability you have read the three earlier books of the Ram Chandra Series. And hopefully, have liked them!

Thank you for your continued love and support.

More so, thank you for that most precious gift to an artist: your time. I hope this book lives up to your expectations.

As some of you may know, I have been inspired by a storytelling technique called hyperlink. It has also been called the multilinear narrative, in which a connection brings many characters together. The three main characters in the Ram Chandra Series are Ram, Sita and Raavan. Each has life experiences which mould their characters. Each life in this story is an adventure with a riveting backstory. And finally, their stories converge with the kidnapping of Sita.

The first book explores the tale of Ram, the second the story of Sita, and the third burrows deep into the life of Raavan. And the three stories merge from the fourth book onwards into a single narrative. You hold in your hand this combined narrative: the fourth book of the Ram Chandra Series.

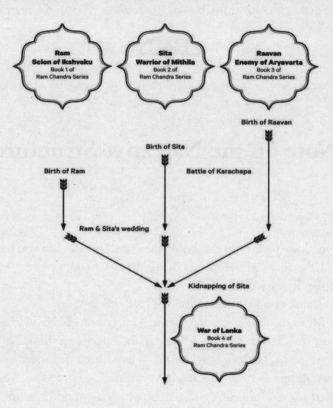

I knew that writing three books in a multilinear narrative would be a complicated and time-consuming affair, but I must confess, it was thoroughly exciting. I hope it is as rewarding and thrilling an experience for you as it was for me. Understanding Ram, Sita and Raavan as characters helped me inhabit their worlds and explore the maze of plots and stories that illuminate this great epic. I feel truly blessed for this.

Since I was following a multilinear narrative, I left clues in the first (Ram–*Scion of Ikshvaku*), the second (Sita–*Warrior of Mithila*), and the third books (Raavan–*Enemy of Aryavarta*), and most of them are unveiled in the fourth, *War of Lanka*.

I hope that you enjoy reading *War of Lanka*. Do tell me what you think of it, by sending me messages on my Facebook, Instagram or Twitter accounts given on the first page.

Love,
Amish

Acknowledgements

Life is what happens when you are planning other things. And it has led me to now having 4 jobs, simultaneously. Firstly, I work with the Indian government cultural diplomacy corps. Secondly, I also host TV documentaries, and am, in addition, co-producing a movie based on one of my books. Notwithstanding, writing remains the core pursuit. Truly, it keeps me going, even when life is difficult and hard. I'd like to thank all those who help me in my writing, for they are the buttresses to my core.

The three men I look up to: My father, the late Vinay Kumar Tripathi; my father-in-law, the late Dr Manoj Vyas; and my brother-in-law, the late Himanshu Roy. They look upon me from *pitralok* now. I strive to make them proud of me.

Neel, my young son. The purpose of my soul, my supreme joy, my greatest achievement, my deepest love. I strive to be worthy-of-emulation to him.

Usha, Bhavna, Anish, Meeta, Ashish, and Donetta - my mother, my siblings and my sisters-in-law, for all that they do.

They read the first draft, usually as each chapter is written. More importantly, we all know that we will always be there for one another. We have each other's back. Always.

The rest of my family: Shernaz, Preeti, Smita, Anuj, Ruta, Mitansh, Daniel, Aiden, Keya, Anika and Ashna. For their consistent faith and love.

Aman and Shivani, who run all my work and life. They are family to me.

The team at HarperCollins. My editor Swati, the marketing team Shabnam and Akriti, the sales team Gokul, Vikas, and Rahul, and my publishers Poulomi and Udayan, led by the brilliant CEO of HarperCollins India Ananth. This is my first published book with them. And I am enjoying this new journey immensely. Looking forward to many more.

The CEO of my previous publisher Gautam, my editors Karthika and Deepthi (who edited the first draft of this book), the marketing manager Neha, and the rest of the Westland team. We may have parted ways in unfortunate circumstances, but they will always be family to me.

Vijay, Shubhangi, Padma, Divya, Anuj, Yukta and the rest of my office colleagues. They look after my business work which frees up my time to write.

Hemal, Neha, Rohan, Hitesh, Shikha, Shriram, Vinit, Harsh, Akshata, Sarah, Prakash, Sujit and Team OktoBuzz. They have produced most of the marketing material for the book, including the awesome cover, and much of the digital activities. I have worked with them for many years. Like fine wine, they age well!

Mayank, Deepika, Sneha, Naresh, Vishaal, Paridhi, Gunjan, and the Moe's Art team, who have supported media relations for the book. Calm and wise, they are among the best media managers I have ever seen.

Sangram, Shalini, Shrey, Pawan, Rohan, Priyadarshan, and Team *Think Why Not*. An awesome agency which drove the marketing of my work, from my 2nd book to my 6th one. It's great to have these geniuses back to drive the AR and new-age marketing agenda for this book.

Ashish Mankad, a brilliant designer, and more importantly, a thinker, who helps guide and drive the art for my books. He also designed the new website.

Satya and his team who have shot the author photos that have been used on the inside cover of this book. He made a rather ordinary subject appear easy on the eyes.

Preeti, a publishing industry wizard, who works on the international deals for my books.

Caleb, Kshitij, Sandeep, Akhil, and their respective teams, who support my work with their business and legal advice.

Mrunalini, a diligent Sanskrit scholar, who works with me on research.

Aditya, a passionate reader of my books, who has now become a friend and a fact-checker.

Sanjay, Archana, Olivier, Pranjulaa, Sandeep, Ravichandran, Vineet, Somnath, Kanwarpreet, Jaseena, and Naseema - my team at Nehru Centre, London, for their love and support. And I want to acknowledge a former Nehru Centre team member we lost recently, the late BV Narayana, a gem of a man who is sorely missed.

And last and most eminently, you, the reader. Your consistent affection, support, understanding and encouragement keeps me going. Thank you so much. May Lord Shiva bless you all.

Chapter 1

3400 BCE, India

Raavan, the king of Lanka, was bleeding profusely from wounds all over his body.

He was running hard. Calling out the name of the woman he loved. The only woman he had ever loved.

'Vedavati! Vedavati!'

He was finding it difficult to breathe. The ever-present dull pain in his navel had suddenly become excruciating. Tears streamed down his eyes. He could hear wild animals – the howling of wolves; vultures screaming; bats screeching. He could not see them, though. It was pitch dark as Raavan sprinted through the deserted streets of Todee village.

'Vedavati!'

He saw a torch flaming bright at a distance.

Raavan raced towards it.

'*Vedavati!*'

A sudden explosion of light from a hundred torches lit simultaneously. Raavan screamed in agony as he stopped and covered his eyes with one hand. As his irises adjusted to the brightness, he removed his hand to see a mob gathered under the blinding light of the torches.

Raavan ran towards the light, lithe and swift.

'*Vedavati!*'

In the crowd were his men. Kumbhakarna. Indrajit. Mareech. Akampana. And his soldiers.

Something wasn't right.

Kumbhakarna looked old. Haggard. He was crying. He raised his arms towards his elder brother. *'Dada ...'*

Raavan looked over the shoulders of his beloved younger brother. Towards the hut he recognized only too well.

Her house.

He heard a scream. A loud wail of pain. Of terror. He knew the voice. He loved that voice. He worshipped that voice.

'*Vedavati!*'

Kumbhakarna tried to stop Raavan. 'Dada ... don't ...'

Raavan pushed Kumbhakarna aside as he ran towards the hut. To the door that stood ajar like the hungry mouth of a demon.

Vedavati's husband, Prithvi, lay on the floor. On his back. Lifeless. Eyes open wide in shock and terror. Brutal knife wounds all over his body still oozing blood. A blade was buried in his heart. The kill wound.

Raavan looked up.

His Vedavati.

Sukarman, the wayward son of the local landlord, was holding her up by her neck. His face was twisted with anger. His hands were squeezing her throat brutally. His biceps bursting with malevolent strength. Her body was sliced all over by a knife gone mad. Muscle and sinew were weeping red tears. Her clothes were bloodied, her beautiful face swollen and covered by wounds. A pool of blood collected at her pristine, unblemished, uninjured feet.

NOOO!

No sound escaped Raavan's mouth. It was as if he had been paralysed by a great demonic force. He could do nothing. He just stood there and watched.

'Where is the money?' screamed Sukarman. His voice was like thunder. Monstrous.

Despite the pain she was in, Vedavati's face was calm. Gentle. Like the Virgin Goddess, *the Kanyakumari that she was. She answered softly, 'It's Raavan's money. He has given it to me as charity. It's his chance to discover the God within him. I will not give it to you. I will not part with it.'*

Give it to him, Vedavati! Give it to him! I don't care about the money! I care about you!

'Give me the money!' growled Sukarman. He increased the pressure on her throat with his left hand. A slow squeeze. He raised his right hand, the one that held the bloodied knife, and brought it close to her face. 'Or I'll run this through your eye!'

Give him the money, Vedavati! Give it to him!

Vedavati's answer was simple and calm. 'No.'

Sukarman grunted like a beast as he brutally stabbed Vedavati's left eye, leaving the knife buried. Blood burst forth, spraying Sukarman's face. He brought his right hand back, opened his palm, and banged the back of the scabbard. Hard. The knife dug through her eye socket and pushed into her brain.

NOOOOO!

Raavan was crying. Shouting. But only he could hear himself. His voice remained buried in his throat, echoing miserably within him.

He could not move.

Suddenly, he heard the cries of a baby. Wailing loudly.

And the fiendish paralysing hold on his body was released. He looked down.

The baby was lying on the ground. Wrapped in a rich red cloth with prominent black stripes.

'Raavan ...'

He looked up.

It was her.

His obsession. His great love. The Kanyakumari. Vedavati.

Sukarman was no longer there. But she remained.

Her right arm was twisted at a strange angle. Broken. She had been knifed at least twenty times. Most of the wounds were on her abdomen and her left hand was on her belly, blood gushing through the gaps between her fingers. It flowed down her body and congealed around her, on the ground. A knife was buried deep in her left eye.

But her face was still and serene. Like it had always been. Like it always would be.

'She's my little girl, Raavan. Promise me that you will protect her. Promise me.'

Raavan looked down again. At Vedavati and Prithvi's baby. Sita.

He looked back up. At Vedavati. He was crying helplessly.

'She's my little girl, Raavan.'

'Dada ...'

Raavan realized he was being shaken. He opened his eyes groggily and stumbled out of his dream to see Kumbhakarna peering down at him.

The king of Lanka was strapped to his chair in the *Pushpak Vimaan, the legendary Lankan flying vehicle.* He was clutching his pendant in a tight grip—the pendant that always hung from a gold chain around his neck. Created from the bones of Vedavati's two fingers, the phalanges carefully fastened with gold links. They had survived the cremation of her body. They now served as crutches, supporting him through his tormented life.

He looked around, still unsteady from his disturbing dream. The ever-present pain in his navel was much stronger. Throbbing.

The *Pushpak Vimaan* was shaped like a cone that gently tapered upwards. The portholes at the base were sealed with thick glass but the metallic window shades had been drawn down. The sound of the rotors winding down reverberated in the air. The *vimaan* had just landed in the grand Lankan capital of Sigiriya. Around ninety Lankan soldiers stood at attention inside the craft, waiting for their liege to disembark.

Kumbhakarna unstrapped Raavan and helped him to his feet.

And then Raavan saw her.

Sita.

She had been untied, and was being held tight by four Lankan women soldiers. She strained furiously against their vice-like grip.

Raavan stared at the warrior princess of Mithila. The wife of Ram, the king-in-absentia of Ayodhya. The Lankans had succeeded in kidnapping her.

Sita. Thirty-eight years of age. Born a short while before her mother and father were killed. She was the spitting image of the woman who had given her life.

Raavan couldn't tear his eyes away from her face. The face of Vedavati.

Sita was unusually tall for a Mithilan woman. Her lean, muscular physique gave her the appearance of a warrior in the army of the Mother Goddess. Battle scars stood out proudly on her wheat-complexioned body. She wore a cream dhoti and a white single-cloth blouse. A saffron *angvastram* hung from her right shoulder.

A shade lighter than the rest of her body, her face had high cheekbones and a sharp, small nose. Her lips were neither thin nor full. Her wide-set eyes were neither small nor large. Strong brows arched in a perfect curve above creaseless eyelids. Her long, lustrous black hair had come undone and fell in a disorderly manner around her face. She had the look of the mountain people from the Himalayas.

Her face was thinner than her mother's. Tougher. Less tender. But it was still almost a perfect replica of the original.

'You may as well kill me now,' growled Sita. 'I will never allow Ram or the Malayaputras to negotiate with you for my release. You have nothing to gain.'

Raavan remained silent. His eyes brimmed with tears of grief and misery.

'Kill me now!' shouted Sita.

She's my little girl, Raavan. Promise me that you will protect her. Promise me.

And Raavan whispered his answer to that noble soul he had loved his entire life. An answer that travelled across the wide chasm of time. A chasm that can only be crossed by the relief that is death.

A whispered answer, audible only to him. And Vedavati's soul.

'I promise.'

—JF J5D—

The Sun God had begun his journey across the horizon and a new dawn was breaking. A new day. A tragically melancholic new day.

Ram stood silently, looking at the conflagrations as they rose high above the funeral pyres. Unblinking. The quivering flames reflected in his pupils. Sixteen pyres. Consuming the bodies of the brave Jatayu and his Malayaputra soldiers. Brave men who had made the ultimate sacrifice while battling to protect his wife Sita from being kidnapped by Raavan.

His younger brother Lakshman stood beside him, his gigantic, muscular body hunched by a sagging spirit. They looked at Lord Agni, the God of Fire, resolutely devouring the bodies of their noble friends. The brothers drew tortured comfort by repeating the powerful chants from the sacred *Isha Vasya Upanishad* that filled the air.

Vayur anilam amritam; Athedam bhasmantam shariram.
This temporary body may burn to ashes; But the breath of life belongs elsewhere. May it find its way back to the Immortal Breath.

Ram's face was blank. Devoid of expression, as it always was when he was enraged. And right now, he was beyond furious.

He looked at the rising sun.

Ram was a *Suryavanshi*, from the *clan of Surya*. As had been the tradition in their family for centuries, the day began with a prayer to Surya, the Sun God. But Ram was in no mood to pray. Not today.

His ragged breath and clenched fists were the only sign of the furious storm that raged within. The rest of him – his body and his face – was eerily calm.

He stared at the sun.

Return my wife to me. Return Sita to me. Or I swear upon the blood of my ancestors, I will burn the world down! I will burn the entire world down!

Suddenly his instincts awoke with a warning. He was being watched.

Ram was instantly alert, unclenching his fists that had been compressed into tight balls just moments ago. He regulated his breath. The steely training of a warrior kicked in.

Ram glanced at his brother without turning his head. Lakshman was staring at the funeral pyres, tears streaming down his face. He was clearly unaware of any threat.

Ram looked down. His bow and quiver were a few feet away. Not close enough.

He looked at the pyres, and beyond them. Into the forest, behind the treeline. Into the darkness.

Someone was there. He could sense it. Clearly, whoever it was, was a very good tracker, for they had made no sound; no mistakes which would send out a warning.

Why haven't they shot us yet?

And then it hit him.

He spoke loudly. 'Lord Hanuman?'

Hanuman, the Naga Vayuputra, emerged from the darkness behind the trees. Gargantuan, yet moving as weightlessly as a feather, sure as a shadow. He was dressed in a saffron *dhoti* and *angvastram*. The outgrowth from his lower back, almost like a tail, followed behind him like a silent companion. It swished in constant rhythm, as though it watched his path. Hanuman was massively built, with a sturdy musculature, and was unnaturally hirsute. His awe-inspiring presence radiated a godly aura, and his facial features were distinctive. His flat nose pressed against his face and his beard and facial hair encircled its periphery with neat precision; the skin above and below his mouth was silken smooth and hairless; it had a puffed appearance and was light pink in colour. His lips were a thin, barely noticeable line.

It almost seemed as if the Almighty had placed the head of a monkey on a man's body.

Thirty Vayuputra soldiers followed him with soldierly discipline. Their complexion, features and attire made it clear that they were from Pariha, a land beyond the western borders of India. The homeland of the previous Mahadev, Lord Rudra.

Parihan Vayuputras.

Hanuman walked with his mouth slightly open, the fingers of his right hand pressed against his lips. Tears fell freely from his grief-stricken eyes. He stared at the two brothers from Ayodhya and then at the funeral pyres.

Lord Rudra have mercy.

Ram and Sita had often met Hanuman during their exile in the forest. Sita had known Hanuman since she was a child, and treasured him as an *elder brother*. She called him Hanu *bhaiya*. She was the one who had introduced him to Ram.

Lakshman had never met Hanuman formally. He had seen the Naga Vayuputra twice when he was a child. When Hanuman had come in secret to meet their Guru Vashishtha in their *gurukul*. Little Lakshman had been suspicious. To this day, he harboured the same prejudice that almost every Indian felt against the Nagas. 'Naga' was the term Indians used to describe those born with deformities. Now, his long-held suspicions were instantly triggered again.

Lakshman quickly picked up the bow lying at his feet and nocked an arrow.

Ram leaned across, pushed Lakshman's hands down and shook his head.

Lakshman growled, 'Dada …'

Ram whispered, 'He's a friend.'

Ram walked around the funeral pyres and towards Hanuman.

The mighty Vayuputra sank to his knees and covered his face with his hands as Ram approached. He was crying now, his body shaking with misery.

Ram immediately understood. Hanuman had assumed that Sita had been killed and her body was being consumed by fire now, in one of the funeral pyres. Hanuman had cherished Sita as his younger sister.

Ram went down on his knees and hugged Hanuman. He whispered, 'Raavan has kidnapped her …'

Hanuman looked up immediately, stunned but relieved. He turned to the pyres. His gaze had altered. He now beheld the warriors who had met a most glorious end.

Jatayu. And his fifteen Malayaputras.

Hanuman was a Vayuputra, the tribe left behind by the previous Mahadev, Lord *Rudra*, the *Destroyer-of-Evil*. The Malayaputras were the tribe left behind by the previous *Vishnu*, the *Propagator-of-Good*, Lord Parshu Ram. These two tribes worked in partnership with each other, even if differences cropped up on rare occasions, for they represented the Gods that had once walked this earth.

Hanuman slowly balled his fists with resolve. 'Jatayu and his Malayaputras will be avenged. And we will bring Queen Sita back.'

Chapter 2

'Dada!'

Shatrughan rushed into the training hall. Many Ayodhyan soldiers had gathered, as they often did, to watch their regent Bharat practise with his spear. On his deathbed, Emperor Dashrath, their father, had proclaimed Bharat the crown prince. But Bharat had spurned the coronation and instead placed his elder brother Ram's slippers on the throne of Ayodhya, and announced that he would administer the empire as Ram's regent, till such time that his elder brother returned to rule his kingdom. The youngest among the four brothers, Shatrughan, had opted to stay with Bharat in Ayodhya. Shatrughan's twin brother Lakshman had accompanied Ram on his fourteen-year banishment to the forest, a punishment for the unauthorised use of a *daivi astra*, a *divine weapon*, in the Battle of Mithila.

Bharat ignored his brother's voice. No distraction. He remained focused on his battle practice.

The spear he held was normally used as a projectile, to hit enemies from a distance. Or by the cavalry to mow down the opposing army. But Bharat was reviving the ancient tradition of using the spear as a weapon of close combat. It increased a warrior's reach dramatically as compared to a sword. It was a two-in-one weapon, and the wooden shaft at its gripping end could be used as a stick-bludgeon, while the knife-edged metallic end was a sharp blade. It was a fearsome weapon that was difficult to wield, but Bharat was good with it. Very good.

'Dada!'

Bharat didn't stop as he smoothly transferred his weight to his back foot and swung the shaft-side of the spear, smacking his adversary on the head. Before his opponent could steady himself, Bharat went down on one knee and swung with the other side of the spear, pulling back just in time so as not to cause actual damage. But the message was clear. Bharat could have disembowelled the soldier duelling him.

The audience of battle-hardened soldiers broke into loud applause.

'Dada!'

Bharat finally turned to look at Shatrughan. He did not express his surprise at finding his diminutive, intellectual brother in the battle-training gymnasium, a place he rarely visited.

One look at Shatrughan, and Bharat knew that something was disastrously wrong.

—JϝＪⅫD—

'I have sent the message to Hanuman, Guruji,' said Arishtanemi. 'But …'

Arishtanemi, the military chief of the tribe of Malayaputra, was with Vishwamitra, the formidable chief of the Malayaputras, in their capital city, Agastyakootam. The previous day, Arishtanemi had given Vishwamitra the shocking news that Sita had been kidnapped by the villainous king of Lanka, Raavan. She had been recognised as the seventh Vishnu—the *Propagator-of-Good*—by the Malayaputras. Vishwamitra had not seemed at all perturbed at all by the news. In fact, he had expressed joy.

'But what?' asked Vishwamitra.

'I mean, Guruji ... Who am I to question you? And you know everything.' Arishtanemi was not being facetious. Just the previous day, he had discovered that Vishwamitra had known for more than two decades that Sita was the daughter of Vedavati, the love of Raavan's life. Raavan would never hurt Sita and therefore, the Malayaputra plan was still plausible. Raavan – villainous and evil according to most Indians – would be destroyed by Sita, which would cement Sita's image as the saviour of the land. That Vishwamitra had envisaged and plotted this over such a long period of time seemed inconceivable to Arishtanemi. 'But Hanuman ... I mean ...'

'Speak it,' growled Vishwamitra. 'Speak your mind.'

'Well, Hanuman is a friend of Guru ... I mean the other ...' Arishtanemi knew better than to utter the name of Vashishtha, once Vishwamitra's closest friend and now his arch-enemy. Very few knew the details of how the antagonism had begun, but almost everyone knew the toxicity of it.

Vishwamitra softened his voice to an ominous whisper. 'Say it.'

'I mean ... Hanuman is loyal to Guru Vashishtha ... Will he listen to us?' Arishtanemi blurted.

Vishwamitra leaned back and took a deep breath. He closed his eyes and composed himself. Hearing that name always had a strange effect on him. His friend-turned-foe. A flurry of emotions flooded his heart. Hatred. Anger. Resentment. Melancholy. Pain … Love.

Nandini.

When he opened his eyes, Vishwamitra was calm again. Unruffled. As someone who believes he carries the fate of Mother India on his shoulders must be.

'Why do you think I did what I did with Annapoorna Devi?' Vishwamitra answered the query with another question.

Arishtanemi knew that Vishwamitra had used Annapoorna Devi and her strained relationship with her estranged husband, Surya, to leak the information to Kumbhakarna that the Malayaputras had recognised Sita as the seventh Vishnu. Vishwamitra had bet that it would only be a matter of time before Kumbhakarna's elder brother, Raavan, would think of kidnapping the Vishnu to exercise leverage over the Malayaputras for the medicines that both he and Kumbhakarna needed to stay alive. And his bet had paid off.

'Because, for all your love and respect for Annapoorna Devi,' answered Arishtanemi, 'you love and respect Mother India more.'

'Exactly,' said Vishwamitra. 'I will do what must be done for what I love and respect most. Hanuman may be loyal to that snake Vashishtha. But he is more loyal to Sita. He loves her like a sister. He thinks that Sita's life is in danger while she's in Lanka. Hanuman will do what we tell him to do, because he will think it is the only way to save Sita.'

Arishtanemi nodded. 'Yes, Guruji.'

— ᒍᖴ ᒐᔆᗞ —

Sita had been imprisoned in the famed Ashok *Vatika*. A stunning and massive *garden* citadel, it was built five kilometres from the Lankan capital city of Sigiriya. The plush garden was atop a tabletop hill, surrounded by thick, well-bastioned fort walls. Two parallel walls, each twenty-five metres high and four metres thick, stretched outwards from Sigiriya. Both walls were dotted with watch towers that allowed for easy scouting and defence. The path nestled between them opened into the citadel of Ashok Vatika. The garden spread over one hundred acres and contained trees sourced from all corners of the world. Floral beds spread their aroma and attracted life around them, from colourful butterflies to elegant ladybirds. Peacocks danced in splendid isolation on verdant flats and rolling grass-covered, man-made hillocks. Their preening vanity snatched pride of place in this effusion of life. Known as the favourite of Lord Rudra, the peacock added a touch of elegance and grace to this place of extravagant beauty. Luxurious cottages in the centre of the garden were well equipped for comfortable living. The grand cottage in the heart of the garden had been allocated to Sita.

The name, Ashok Vatika, was itself resonant with both fact and symbolism. A profusion of Ashok trees, especially around the cottages in the centre, established the literal intent of the nomenclature. But there was more. The old Sanskrit word for *grief* was *shok*. Hence, *ashok* meant *no grief*. This garden, this Ashok Vatika, was an oasis of happiness, joy, even bliss. But Indians are philosophical by nature; therefore, naturally, they also have a penchant for digging deeper. And *ashok* can also mean 'to not feel grief'. Some are cursed by fate to experience misery that becomes the foundation of their very being. They are inured to the vicissitudes of life. Nothing can hurt them any more, for they have already been hurt beyond endurance. Fresh drops of grief cause no ripples in their ocean of anguish.

It was an *ashok* Kumbhakarna who walked into the Ashok Vatika, having left his horse at the citadel gate.

Raavan had decided that Sita would be kept in protective custody in the garden, away from Sigiriya. A mysterious plague had ripped through the city over the last too-many years. He would not have Sita put at risk. Well-trained women soldiers had been stationed in the garden and at the citadel walls to ensure that Sita did not escape. Food, books, musical instruments and anything that Sita might need to keep herself occupied had been provided. But Sita was not in the mood to distract herself with any of these pretences at normalcy.

'I know you are only following orders,' she said politely. 'But I will not eat this food.'

She was sitting on the veranda outside her cottage. Soldiers had placed before her bowls filled with the finest gourmet food in Sigiriya, cooked by the royal chefs in Raavan's personal kitchen.

A soldier officiously opened a lid. 'This food is not poisoned, great Vishnu,' she said, confused but still deferential. 'If you so order, I will taste each dish right now and dispel your concerns.'

Sita laughed. 'Why would Raavan poison my food? He could have killed me several times over by now. With complete ease. I know it is not poisoned. But I will not eat.'

'But ...'

'I will not allow Raavan to negotiate with my husband or the Malayaputras for my life.' She pointed with her thumb at the cottage behind her. 'In there, and around here, you have removed every possible means for me to kill myself. All I can do is refuse to eat. I understand you are only following orders, and I hold nothing against you. But I will not eat.'

The nervous soldier began pleading. 'But, My Lady… Please listen to me. We cannot let you die. We will be forced to make you eat.'

Sita smiled. 'Try it.'

Kumbhakarna had been hiding behind an Ashok tree, watching the interaction. He stepped into her line of vision now. Instantly, the polite Sita was gone. She stood up, fury stiffening every muscle in her body.

The soldiers turned around and, upon seeing Kumbhakarna, went down on one knee in respect to the Lankan royal. He dismissed them and they left immediately.

Kumbhakarna stared at Sita. It was beyond astonishing. She was almost a replica of Vedavati. Almost, but not entirely. For Vedavati was calm and gentle while Sita clearly could be aggressive and combative. It was time to check if she possessed her mother's compassion and sense of fairness.

'You don't have to eat if you don't want to, great Vishnu,' said Kumbhakarna politely as he walked up to Sita. 'But may I request you to look at this?'

Sita looked suspiciously at the rolled-up painting that Kumbhakarna was holding out.

'Why?' snarled Sita, wary.

'What harm can it cause, looking at a painting, Queen Sita?'

Sita stepped back from the giant Kumbhakarna, raised her hands in combat position, and said, 'You unroll the painting.'

Kumbhakarna nodded gently, stepped back to increase the distance between Sita and him, held up the rolled-up canvas horizontally, and slowly, deliberately, unrolled it.

Sita was stunned.

It was her. It was a portrait of her. But younger, around twenty-one or twenty-two years of age. Her clothes were a soft violet: the most expensive dye in the world and the colour favoured by royalty. The face, the body, the hair, everything was exactly like her. To be fair, *almost* exactly. For there were subtle differences. In the portrait she was calm and gentle, almost like a *rishika*. She was curvaceous, full and voluptuous, unlike Sita in real life. She was more feminine. Less muscular. Less lean. None of Sita's proud battle scars found expression in the painting.

It wasn't as if a thirty-eight-year-old Sita had been altered into a much younger version in the painting. Instead, a warrior Mother Goddess had been transformed into an achingly attractive celestial nymph.

There was something ethereal about the painted lady's beauty. Her face. Her eyes. Her serenity. Sita had never imagined herself so full of beauty.

And then it hit her. This painting was a labour of love. Every brushstroke was a caress. It was prayer. Devotion. The passion, the longing was palpable. This painter was deeply, madly and heartbreakingly in love with the object of the painting.

Bizarre.

She took a step back and growled in anger. 'What the bloody hell is this? What are you trying to do? Who painted this?'

Kumbhakarna's answer was simple. 'My brother Raavan.'

'Why in Lord Indra's name would Raavan paint this? I had never met him before the day you kidnapped me. And certainly not when I was that age!'

'I didn't say that he's met you before.'

'Then what the hell are you two trying to do? What mind games are these? Some stupid good policeman–bad policeman routine? Do you really think I'll fall for this nonsense?'

'We are not trying to make you fall for anything.'

'Tell that demon brother of yours that he can keep painting me for as long as he wishes, but he will not sway me! I will starve to death! I swear on the holiest of them all, Lord Rudra!'

Kumbhakarna's eyes were moist as he said softly, 'This is not you. This is not your portrait.'

Sita was silenced. For only a moment. And then she gasped as her expression changed dramatically. From anger to shock. Almost like she knew what the next sentence would be. But it couldn't be … It could *not* be …

Kumbhakarna continued, 'This is your mother. Your birthmother.'

Chapter 3

'Ram,' said Vashishtha, 'I don't think you understand.'

'No, Guruji,' said Ram, unfailingly polite. 'I do understand. And I am not changing my mind.'

The *rajguru* of the Ayodhya royal family tried hard to control his irritation. Ram could be extremely stubborn once he made up his mind. Almost nothing could sway him. Not even the *guru* whom he respected as a father.

Hanuman, Ram and Lakshman had quickly marched northwards to the sacred Tapti River, along with thirty Vayuputra soldiers. Tapti was one of the only two major rivers in India that flowed from east to west along its entire course; the other one being the holy Narmada River. Indians, who saw a divine plan in everything, deeply loved this river, which moved in the same direction as the sun. Hence the name: *Tap* means *heat*, especially that of ascetism and meditation. The *Tapti* River, the *one fired with the heat of ascetism*, was dotted with *ashrams* along its banks, which had been established by great *rishis* and *rishikas* for people who sought ascetic knowledge. Vashishtha had waited for Ram, Lakshman, Hanuman and the Vayuputras at one such *ashram* – the abode of the pious saint Changdev.

The convoy had left the *ashram* after seeking the blessings of Rishi Changdev. They now sailed down the Tapti River towards the Gulf of Cambay – which was a part of the Western Sea – from where they intended to head northwards. The Gulf of Cambay was an inverse-funnel shaped inlet of the Western Sea, sandwiched between the Deccan peninsula to the right and Saurashtra to the left. They would sail through this funnel towards their ultimate destination, the port city of Lothal, a few hours away.

'Listen to me, Ram,' said Vashishtha, deeply troubled by Ram's decision. 'I don't think this will work. I don't think Hanuman can do it alone.'

'I disagree with you, Guruji,' cut in Hanuman. 'It can be done. And I will not be alone. The Malayaputras know Lanka, they know the secret entrances into the Sigiriya fort. And I know the Malayaputras. We will do it.'

The plan was simple. Hanuman would steal into Sigiriya along with some Malayaputras whom he knew well. They would find Sita and escape with her, making a quiet getaway. A surgical strike. It would be far more effective than open war. Many lives could be saved.

'Do you really think he will just let this happen? So easily?' asked Vashishtha. 'You don't …'

'My sincere apologies for interrupting you, Guruji,' said Hanuman, his hands folded together in contrition. 'But you needn't worry about Raavan. Kumbhakarna, you know, owes me his life. And he is an honourable man. He will not deny the debt he owes me. I will get Sita out of Lanka, alive and unhurt.'

Vashishtha took a long breath and then let it out in a rush. With frustration. 'I am not talking about Raavan. He is not in control of this situation.'

Ram and Hanuman understood who he was talking about.

His friend-turned-mortal-enemy. Vishwamitra.

They remained silent.

'Guruji,' Ram said finally, with polite boldness, 'I request you to not allow your prejudice ...'

Vashishtha interrupted him with a raised voice. 'Ram, are you calling me prejudiced? I assure you I know that ... that ... man. I know him better than anyone else. Better than even he knows himself.' Vashishtha paused and composed himself. 'He wants this war. It serves his purpose. He has built an image of Raavan as the perfect villain, like a butcher feeding a sacrificial goat. And now that man wants the ritual sacrifice of Raavan. He wants the war. The Malayaputras will not help Hanuman on this mission. Trust me. I know.'

Ram didn't say anything, shocked at this public display of anger by his *guru*. He had never heard him raise his voice in this manner. Or lose his poise.

Hanuman spoke quietly. 'Guruji, not all the Malayaputras want war. I know some who don't. You too were a Malayaputra once. You know that they can be as divided internally as we Vayuputras are. Some of them will help me, I'm sure. Shouldn't we at least try to avoid a war and save countless lives?'

'I want you to steer clear of Vishwamitra and Arishtanemi,' said Vashishtha sternly. 'You will not take any help from them. You will ensure that they are not even aware of your plans.'

'Yes, Guruji. I will take care,' said Hanuman.

Hanuman thought that Vashishtha was insisting on this because of his enmity with Vishwamitra, the chief of the

Malayaputras. But Hanuman was wrong. Vashishtha had a deeper reason.

Tacticians focus on tomorrow, intent on winning the immediate battle. Strategists obsess about the day after tomorrow. They must win the war. The *rajguru* of Ayodhya, Vashishtha, was thinking about the day after.

Vashishtha looked unconvinced and troubled. And then surrendered. He might disagree with Ram and Hanuman, but he had faith in Sita.

Ram doesn't understand. But Sita will. She will not come back with Hanuman. She will not. She knows she cannot. Even if that means risking her life.

But Vashishtha too was in the dark. He did not know what Vishwamitra knew. He did not know what Sita meant to Raavan.

— JF J5D —

The next day, early in the morning, Raavan ambled into the Ashok Vatika. A regal sixty-year-old with a commanding presence. A hint of a stoop suggested the backbone's reduced ability to bear the load of the massive body. Stretch lines on the shoulders and arms, that had once been mighty and infused with vigour, indicated reduced muscle mass. His forehead was furrowed with deep lines and crow's feet had formed around the corners of his eyes. His cheeks were marked by faded pockmarks, the legacy of a bout of smallpox when he was a baby. The once-thick crop of black hair was now a sparse patch of grey with a receding hairline. The beard remained thick, although white had replaced the virile black of youth.

An ageing, partly enfeebled tiger. But a tiger with renewed purpose. A tiger who had been gifted a second chance.

Beside him walked his brother, Kumbhakarna. He dwarfed even the tall Raavan. His hirsute body made him look more like a giant bear than a human being. The strange outgrowths from his ears and shoulders marked him out as a Naga.

A trail of palace maids and attendants followed the two brothers, carrying trays full of food.

Sita was seated on the veranda outside her cottage, her comfortable cane chair starkly contrasting with her obvious unease. Kumbhakarna's revelations the previous day had robbed her of sleep. She knew she couldn't kill herself now. Not until she knew more about her birth-mother. Also, truth be told, her mother's relationship with Raavan. So Sita had eaten the previous night. Her first meal in Lanka.

She turned her head towards the commotion. Raavan and Kumbhakarna had stepped into the open courtyard and left the treeline behind. The sun arose behind them.

Sita straightened up. And shivered.

Maids ran ahead of the Lankan royals and quickly brought out a cane table from Sita's cottage. They placed it in front of her. Others pulled two cane chairs which were placed around the table. Just in time for Raavan and Kumbhakarna to seat themselves in one fluid motion.

Raavan stared at Sita, a sense of wonder on his face. He had not imagined he would ever behold that face in the flesh again. His heart was racing.

Kumbhakarna spoke. 'May we join you for breakfast, princess?'

Sita remained quiet. Unmoving and silent. But her eyes spoke aloud. *It's your kingdom. It's your city. It's your garden. Who's going to stop you?*

'Thank you,' Kumbhakarna replied politely to that challenging look.

The brothers relaxed in their seats. Enthusiastic maids quickly brought the food to the table. Three silver plates were placed in front of them. A delectable aroma rose up from a large silver bowl and wafted through the air as the chief maid took away its lid. It made even the disinterested Sita look at the food. Processed, softened and flattened rice had been lightly sautéed with mustard, cumin seeds, curry leaves, onion and green chillies. Roasted peanuts added a rich source of plant-based protein to the dish. It was a delicacy from the land of Godavari, called *poha*. The royal chef had assumed that Sita would like it, having spent many years in Panchavati. A maid poured buttermilk into three silver glasses and placed them beside the plates.

Raavan smiled and rubbed his hands together in anticipation. 'Mmm … Smells delicious.'

He was trying really hard. Awkwardly friendly. He did not mention that the rice had been especially imported from Gokarna for this meal. Practically everyone in Sigiriya ate wheat and almost no one ate rice. This was an expensive meal.

Kumbhakarna looked at his brother and smiled softly. He thought about the life they could have lived. If only …

Two maids circled them with a pitcher of water and a large bowl each, enabling the three seated royals to wash their hands.

A third was about to serve the *poha* when Raavan halted her with a raised hand.

'That's all right,' said Raavan. 'We'll serve ourselves.'

The maid was shocked. But she had learnt, like almost everyone in Lanka, that they must never question Raavan. Ever.

She placed the bowl on the table and the assemblage retreated, walking backwards deferentially. They did not dare turn their backs to their king.

Raavan looked at them distractedly and smiled. 'Thank you.'

Kumbhakarna raised his eyebrows, pleasantly surprised by this display of uncharacteristic courtesy. The maids, though, were taken aback. They halted mid-step in confusion, then quickly recovered and disappeared post-haste.

Raavan turned towards Sita. 'Please ... eat.'

Sita did not respond. She was staring intently at the floor.

Raavan stood up, reached over and picked up Sita's plate, served some *poha* onto it, and gently placed it in front of her.

Sita did not raise her eyes.

Raavan frowned.

Perhaps she suspects that the food is poisoned.

He briskly served himself and then picked up a small amount with the tips of his fingers. Good manners. He placed the *poha* in his mouth.

'Mmm ... wow. It's delicious,' cooed Raavan.

Kumbhakarna too began to eat.

But Sita just sat there. Silent. Unmoving.

Staring at her veins. In disgust.

They carried her blood. She could almost feel her appalled heart rejecting the blood it was receiving from her veins.

My blood ...

His blood ...

Lord Rudra ... No ... Have mercy ...

How can you test me like this?

Not this demon ... Not this monster ...

Kumbhakarna suddenly understood what was going on in her mind. His gaze flew towards his brother.

The king of Lanka was staring at Sita and frowning. 'Why aren't you eati—'

Then Raavan got it too. His eyes flashed with anger as he reached for the finger-bone pendant hanging from a chain on his neck. He held Vedavati's hand.

Kumbhakarna almost sprang to his feet and then sat down again as he saw his brother's expression transform.

A rueful smile spread across Raavan's face. She had calmed him down. She had focused him. His Goddess … helping him from the beyond.

Some people say that focus requires a mind with a fearsome intellect. They are wrong. What it needs most, in fact, is a calmly breathing heart. For a fearsome intellect without the curb of a calm heart is like an unguided missile. It can blow up and destroy anyone, even itself.

'Sita …' whispered Raavan.

Sita did not stir.

'Queen Sita!' said Raavan, louder this time.

Sita looked up. And pierced him with her unblinking eyes.

'Your mother's name was Vedavati. She was a Goddess. I loved and worshipped her. I still love and worship her.' Raavan paused before he continued pointedly. 'And your *father's* name was Prithvi.' Raavan laid particular emphasis on the word 'father'. 'Your father was a good man. Weak, but a good man.'

Sita's eyes widened with surprise. Her shoulders sagged with relief as a sigh escaped her lips. Raavan almost heard her thoughts.

Oh, thank God! I don't have his blood!

Sita suddenly realised how rude she had been. 'I … I didn't mean to …'

Raavan began to laugh. 'It's all right. You are Vedavati's daughter. I cannot be angry with you.'

Kumbhakarna stared at his brother with surprise. And regret. Regret for the man Raavan could have been. For the life they could have had. If only …

Raavan smiled as he pointed at Sita's plate. 'There will be time to talk. For now, let's eat.'

Chapter 4

'What does Dada say?' asked Shatrughan.

Bharat and Shatrughan sat in the family room of the Ayodhya royal palace. They had just received a bird courier from their eldest brother, Ram.

'He's asking us to not mobilise the army,' answered Bharat. 'They are trying to find a way to rescue Sita *bhabhi* from Lanka without triggering a war. Something about using a delicate surgical scalpel rather than a mighty war sword.'

Shatrughan frowned. 'I hope it works. But I wouldn't count on it.'

'Ram dada is trying to save the lives of soldiers.'

'Which is the right thing to do … But what if he fails? And we take too long to mobilise? What do you think our subordinate kingdoms will make of it? Some demon kidnaps the queen of Ayodhya and we don't even mobilise our army? We may end up encouraging rebellions all over the land.'

Bharat stared at Shatrughan. 'Is that the strategic mind of the prince of Ayodhya speaking? Or is it the righteous anger of a brother-in-law?'

'Aren't you angry, Dada? She is our *bhabhi*,' said Shatrughan, his fists clenched tight. 'How dare that demon of Lanka do this? Fight as warriors, that is fair. But this … this is *adharma*.'

Bharat nodded.

'Both the *dharma* of the empire and the *dharma* of the family dictate that we mobilise our army and navy,' continued Shatrughan. 'We'll need a few weeks in any case. Let's hope Ram dada succeeds at whatever he's planning. If he fails, we should leave for Lanka within the day.'

'Yes,' said Bharat. 'Issue the orders.'

— JF J5D —

'So good to see you, my friend,' said Naarad as he embraced Hanuman.

Ram, Lakshman, Vashishtha, Hanuman and the Vayuputras had reached Lothal, an important port city of the Sapt Sindhu. Leaving the bulk of the party in the guest house, Vashishtha, Ram and Hanuman had left immediately to meet Naarad, a friend of Hanuman.

Naarad was a brilliant trader, but also a lover of art, poetry and the latest gossip. Hanuman had informed them that he was a better source of information than the intelligence services of the most powerful kingdoms in the Sapt Sindhu.

'It's been too long!' said Hanuman.

'Yeah,' Naarad said with a smile. 'I thought you were avoiding me!'

Naarad turned to the two men who had accompanied his friend.

Hanuman indicated Vashishtha. 'This is …'

'Of course, I know Guru Vashishtha,' said Naarad, bending to touch the sage's feet.

'*Ayushman bhav*,' said Vashishtha, placing his right hand on Naarad's head and *blessing him with a long life*.

'Aah, Guruji …' said Naarad. 'I think a life that burns bright with passion, even for a short while, is better than one that flickers and struggles for a long time.'

Vashishtha did not know what to make of the strange response to what was, after all, a standard blessing. He remained silent.

With a naughty twinkle in his eye, Naarad continued, 'So, speaking of burning bright, why do Guru Vishwamitra and you hate each other so much? And speaking of passion, who's Nandini?'

Vashishtha had been warned by Hanuman that Naarad had a bizarre sense of humour. Despite this, he was taken aback. He hadn't expected the trader from Lothal to be so forward. In a flash, though, he understood what Naarad was doing. He was using humour to gaslight and then gather information. This was the secret behind his talent!

Vashishtha smiled and turned to Hanuman. 'You are right.' Pointing at Naarad, Vashishtha continued, 'This gentleman is a very useful ally.' He smiled at Naarad and said, 'An irritating but useful ally.'

Naarad laughed, appreciating the way Vashishtha had smoothly avoided answering his questions. 'I'm impressed, Guruji.' Turning to Ram, Naarad said, 'So you are the Vishnu, eh?'

Ram was direct, honest to a fault, and transparent like the pure waters of a freshly formed river. Not for him the verbal jousting of men focused on their agendas; he was focused only on the truth and law, even if the truth and law worked against him. His answer was straight. 'My wife Sita has been recognised as a Vishnu by the only ones with the authority to recognise the Vishnu – the Malayaputras. We need to save her, not just because she is my life, but because she is important to Mother India. Are you going to help us or not?'

Naarad did a double-take. Innocence and truthfulness were so rare among adults. Life had a way of torturing those characteristics out of people, leaving resentment or cynicism in their place. Some adults gave their bitterness another word – maturity. A gracious word to hide their selfishness and cowardice. It was a delight to see this rare combination of fierce courage, quiet truthfulness and pure innocence … and in one who had suffered so much. *This man, this king of Ayodhya, is special.*

Naarad smiled. 'It will be my honour to help.'

Hanuman spoke up. 'Will you come with us, my friend?'

'Yes, I will,' answered Naarad. 'But you will also have to tolerate someone else. A former Malayaputra. She has visited Lanka often and is the only one I know who can get us into Sigiriya.'

Hanuman frowned.

Naarad turned to the door and shouted, 'Sursa!'

Hanuman froze. Sursa was an employee of Naarad. Wilful, beautiful and aggressive, she was passionately in love with Hanuman – much to the dismay of the Naga Vayuputra, who had taken a vow of lifelong celibacy.

'Hans!' squealed Sursa, sashaying into the room.

Hanuman winced. He did not fancy that name at all.

Early the next morning, Raavan and Kumbhakarna visited Sita's cottage in the Ashok Vatika.

They had broken the ice the previous day, ably assisted by what Indians are most passionate about – food. Yesterday it was *poha*. Today, the royal cooks had rustled up something different. Rice and *udad* dal had been fermented and ground into a thick batter. Small portions of this batter were wrapped in banana leaves and steamed into cylindrical roundels. They were served wrapped in the banana leaf, accompanied by coconut chutney and a stew made with lentils, tamarind and a unique blend of spices. Dunked in it were well-known immunity-boosters – moringa sticks. They called the food *idli-sambar*.

Rice had been imported from Gokarna once again for this meal.

Raavan ate his breakfast messily, not feeling the need to impress Sita any longer with put-on manners as he had done the previous day. The genuinely refined Kumbhakarna however, continued to eat slowly, delicately.

Sita looked at Raavan and said, 'Tell me about my mother …'

Raavan paused and glanced at her. He picked up a napkin and wiped his hand clean. A wistful smile spread across his face. 'Where do I begin? How do I describe a Goddess?'

'Start at the beginning. A good place, always.'

'I met her when I was four years old.'

'And how old was she?'

'Probably eight or nine years old, I think … I've been in love with her ever since.'

'How can you fall in love at four?'

'You can, if the object of your affection is the *Kanyakumari*.'

'My mother was a *Kanyakumari*?' asked Sita, surprised.

'Yes,' answered Raavan.

An ancient tradition of worshipping the *Kanyakumari, the Virgin Goddess,* prevailed in many parts of India. The *Kanyakumari* was believed to be an incarnation of the Mother Goddess Herself. It was held that She resided temporarily in the bodies of carefully chosen young girls. These girls were then worshipped as living Goddesses. People approached them for advice and prophecies – even kings and queens often became their devotees. When they reached puberty, the Goddess moved into the body of another pre-pubescent girl. India was dotted with temples dedicated to Kanyakumaris.

'Which temple was she the *Kanyakumari* of?'

'Vaidyanath temple in eastern India. But she was beyond comparison. No *Kanyakumari*, who has ever existed or ever will, can match her. She was peerless. Noble. Kind. Generous. Righteous. She did not ever stop being a Goddess. To me she wasn't a Goddess because the Mother Goddess chose her. It was her character that made her divine. Perfect in every way. Perfect ...'

Sita had caught on to something. 'She was from Vaidyanath? How old would she have been when I was born?'

'Perhaps twenty-six or twenty-seven years of age ...' answered Raavan.

Many former Kanyakumaris returned to their temple to live out their remaining years.

'I was found close to Trikut Hills by my adoptive parents. Not far from Vaidyanath.'

Raavan and Kumbhakarna could guess what was coming next. The obvious question. The most obvious question from any adopted child.

'Why did my parents abandon me?' asked Sita. 'Why did they not come back for me? Where are they now? Here in *Lanka?*

Raavan looked down. His eyes had clouded with tears. It had been so many years, and yet the memory of that horrible day made his heart crumble into a million pieces.

Sita turned to Kumbhakarna. 'Why did they abandon me, Kumbhakarnaji? And why did they continue to reject me? Did my mother not want to see her child even once in thirty-eight long years? Is this expected from a noble Goddess and her husband? You say you know them. You must know why ...'

'Brave Vishnu ...' whispered Kumbhakarna, his voice shaking in misery. 'They did not ... The *Kanyakumari* ... She ...'

'Where is she now? Is she here?'

Raavan looked up at Sita, his hand tightly clutching the finger-bone pendant. 'She is here.'

Sita's eyes fell on the pendant hanging around Raavan's neck. Two human finger bones – the phalanges carefully fastened with gold links. Tears clouded her eyes as she understood.

Raavan murmured, as if from a distant land, 'Shortly after you were born, Vedavati and Prithvi died while ...' Raavan stopped. He drew a deep breath and corrected himself. 'Vedavati and Prithvi were *killed* ...'

Sita's hand shot up and covered her mouth as tears flowed down her cheeks.

Raavan wanted to stop. But the words tumbled from his mouth of their own volition. He knew he had to go on. Vedavati's daughter deserved the truth. 'Some ... I ...' He was shivering in misery now. 'I had given her some money as charity. The *basta* ... the *son of the local landlord* ... He came with his gang ... He threatened ... He ... they ... knives ...'

Sita was crying helplessly now.

Raavan couldn't go on any more.

His devoted brother, Kumbhakarna, had to step in. 'Vedavatiji was convinced that she had redeemed Raavan dada. That she had put him on the right path. And she had. He … Both he and I … had done some terrible things. The noble Vedavatiji reformed us … Gave us direction … And the money … It was Dada's first step towards redemption … His first act of charity … It would have been used to build a hospital … When those criminals demanded the money, she refused to hand it over … She offered her own meagre savings instead … All of it… But she would not part with Dada's money … his charity … That was holy, she apparently said … she would not surrender Raavan dada's chance to discover the God within himself …'

An agonised moan escaped Sita's lips. She wept for the virtuous mother she had never met. For the magnificent woman whose blood flowed in her veins.

'They killed Prithvi … They killed her … And stole …'

Sita suddenly felt rage course through her veins. Blinding rage. 'What did you do to those men? What did …'

'We tortured them. We made them beg for death …'

'Every single scoundrel,' said Raavan. Despite the passage of so many years, he still seethed with fury. 'We cut them alive, bit by bit. We burnt them even as they breathed. We cooked them to the bone …'

Sita's body eased with satisfaction.

'And then we massacred the entire village. Coward rascals who stood by while their living Goddess was brutally murdered for a few measly coins! We killed them all! And left them there to be eaten by wild animals.'

Sita stared at the king of Lanka, the same frenzied anger reflecting in her eyes.

Raavan closed his eyes and breathed in deeply. Trying to slow his heart down.

Sita too closed her eyes. She wiped away her tears. But more took their place, moistening her face again. She opened her eyes as she heard Raavan speak.

'Even from the beyond, she reached out to help me,' said Raavan.

Sita looked at Raavan. *How?*

Raavan looked at his right hand, remembering what had been – what would always be – the high point of his tormented life. 'I had touched the Ka ... Ka ... *Kanyakumari* just once in my life ... She had held this hand for a moment ... for a lifetime ... for a moment ... Touched me just that one time.'

Kumbhakarna's tears flowed as he reached out and gently touched his brother's arm.

'Do you know what survives a cremation pyre conducted according to full Vedic rituals?' asked Raavan, before he answered the question himself. 'Almost nothing ... A few pieces of the skull ... Maybe parts of the spine ... Nothing else ... But the *Kanyakumari* ... Vedavati ... she ... left me her hand. The hand with which she had touched me once ... Two fingers ... So that whenever I am lost and alone, I can hold her hand ...'

Sita stared at the pendant hanging around Raavan's neck.

'I always wondered ...' cried Raavan, 'Why ... why did she leave me two fingers? Why two? Now I know ...'

He unclipped the chain and pulled out the pendant. He kept one finger for himself. 'I am not the only one who needs her ... I'm not the only one who craves her hand ...'

Raavan leaned across and handed Vedavati's finger-relic to Sita.

Sita felt an electric current pass through her body as she felt her mother's caress. She brought the finger to her forehead in reverence. It was a profoundly holy icon. She kissed it softly and then held it in a tight grip. She looked up at Raavan.

They were both crying.

For what they had lost. And what they had found again.

Their Goddess.

The *Kanyakumari*.

Vedavati.

Chapter 5

'I had ordered him not to mobilise the army,' said Ram, an unhappy expression spreading across his face.

Ram, Vashishtha, Lakshman, Hanuman and Naarad were on a mid-sized seafaring ship sailing down the Western Sea. They had gathered on the upper deck. Sursa was asleep in her cabin. They had left the Konkan coast behind and were now cruising along the Malabar coast – the lower half of the western Indian peninsular coastline. They were accompanied by forty soldiers, thirty among them being Parihan Vayuputras.

'Hmmm … I heard that's what you expressly ordered,' said Naarad, in a droll voice. 'But your younger brother has disregarded you. He is going ahead and mobilising his army.'

'Perhaps he believes that your mission to Lanka will not be a success, Hanuman,' said Vashishtha, looking at the Naga Vayuputra.

'But that is not for Bharat to decide,' said Ram, cutting in.

'A good brother will not just blindly follow his elder brother's orders,' said Naarad. 'He will do what he thinks is in the best interest of his brother, even if it means disobeying him.'

'If you expect our mission to fail, why have you asked Sursa to take me to Lanka?' asked Hanuman.

'We cannot be certain of anything, Hanuman,' said Naarad, 'least of all this delicate operation. We must try, of course. If there's the slightest chance of saving innocent lives, then we must at least try. But I think the odds are long. Bharat is right. If your mission fails, we will need to move in an army quickly. We don't want to waste months mobilising at that time.'

Naarad looked at Ram as he said this. Ram had a strange expression on his face, a mix of disquiet that his brother had disobeyed the legal order of the king-in-exile of Ayodhya, but also affection for a brother who loved him dearly and would do all that was possible to fight for him and Sita.

'Anyway,' said Hanuman. 'You all can wait at Shabarimalaji temple while Sursa and I steal into Sigiriya with a few soldiers and rescue Sita. The ship will dock at Alappuzha. You can disembark and my Vayuputra soldiers will guide you to the temple hamlet. The Lady of the Forest will give you refuge. Sursa and I will head onwards from Alappuzha with our soldiers.'

The famous Shabarimala temple was dedicated to Lord Ayyappa, son of the previous Mahadev, Lord Rudra, and the Vishnu, Lady Mohini. Devotees from across India visited it during the pilgrimage season after taking the temporary vow of *sanyas, renunciation*. The temple was maintained by a small forest-dwelling community from the region, led by Shabari, the Lady of the Forest. They also managed the affairs of the community that lived around the temple.

'I would love to pay my respects at the Shabarimalaji temple, but I can't,' said Ram. 'I am coming to Lanka.'

Hanuman shot a look at Ram and then Vashishtha.

It was Vashishtha who spoke first. 'You cannot go, Ram.'

Ram's answer was simple and direct. 'Sita is my wife. She is mine to protect.'

'That's noble of you, Ram. But we cannot allow you to put yourself at risk.'

'With respect, Guruji, that is not your choice to make.'

'With respect, King Ram,' said Hanuman. 'It's not your choice to make either.'

Ram was steadily getting upset. But his face and his voice were, characteristically, very calm. 'It's my life. She is my wife. I don't see—'

Hanuman cut in. 'You are not just a husband, King Ram. You are not just an Ayodhya royal either. You have been recognised as a Vishnu by the Vayuputras. We cannot—'

It was Ram's turn to interrupt Hanuman. 'Please accept my gratitude towards the Vayuputras for thinking so highly of me. But the only ones who have the authority to recognise the Vishnu are the Malayaputras. And they have recognised Sita as a Vishnu. So even if your goal is to protect the Vishnu, you should go along with my idea. It is a wise choice.'

'King Ram,' said Hanuman, 'this cannot be argued any further. You too have been recognised as a Vishnu.'

'You might think that this is a wise decision, but it's not,' said Vashishtha to Ram.

Long ago, in the *gurukul*, Vashishtha had taught Ram the three drivers of decision-making: Desire, Emotions and Intelligence. They arrange themselves in a hierarchy, with Desire at the bottom and Intelligence at the top. Desire and Emotions can be allowed to drive decisions at times. But Desire must never be allowed to override Emotions in decision-making. And Emotions must never overpower Intelligence. When we allow our behaviour and decisions to be primarily driven by Intelligence, then we have the opportunity to live wisely. 'You are being driven by your emotions, Ram. Think calmly, with your intelligence, factoring in all the knowledge at our disposal. And then decide.'

'Also,' said Hanuman, 'this may be Raavan's precise plan. If he kills both the Vishnus, or worse, makes both the Vishnus his prisoners, then Mother India is doomed. Not only will he have destroyed our motherland's past, he will also destroy her future. Don't you have a duty to Mother India as well? You said to me once that Mother and Motherland are greater than heaven!'

Ram was quiet. He had no answer for Hanuman.

Vashishtha gently touched his shoulder. 'Ram, it's not in Raavan's interest to kill Sita for as long as you are alive. Raavan is a cold and calculating trader. I know he needs medicines from the Malayaputras. He will blackmail them for it. It is actually Vishwamitra who wants to trigger a war. We want to get Sita out of Lanka quietly to avoid that war. But if you rush into Lanka now, and both Sita and you are captured and thrown into Raavan's dungeons, a war would be inevitable. Think rationally. Decide wisely. Let Hanuman and Sursa go.'

Ram slowly looked down. A shadow pulled over his eyes.

He surrendered.

— JF J5D —

The sun came up over Ashok Vatika. It was a beautiful morning. The air was warm. The wind was soft. Purple, pink, orange and white flowers swayed in unison, as if to shake the dew off their beaming faces. Squirrels skittered about, chasing each other in frenzy. Raavan, Kumbhakarna and Sita were seated at breakfast.

It was slowly becoming a daily ritual now. Anticipated by them all.

They had almost finished eating. And what was most important had begun.

Conversation.

'It was ...' Raavan leaned back and stopped speaking. He looked up at the sky and took a deep breath. As if to compose himself. 'Yesterday was cathartic, Sita ... Speaking of Vedavati ... Grief that had been buried so deep inside me ... For so long ... Speaking of it ... Crying ... Letting it out ... It helped. I feel ... I feel lighter.'

Raavan looked at Sita. 'Thank you.'

Sita smiled and held his gaze, her eyes moist.

Kumbhakarna exhaled deeply and patted his brother's knee. 'Dada, it helped. It helped me as well. I can't say that I have felt anything remotely like your grief ... But I've carried the scars too from that terrible day.' Kumbhakarna turned to Sita. 'I have tried to speak to Dada often about it. To pull him out of his misery. But what I couldn't do in decades, you have accomplished in a few days, Queen Sita.'

Sita smiled. 'I haven't done anything. It's my face. My mother's face.'

'No,' said Kumbhakarna. 'You carry her within your soul. She had a magical ability to make things better just by her presence. You have that ability too ... The Malayaputras have chosen well.'

Sita laughed softly, but didn't say anything.

'I can see the greatness in you, Queen Sita,' continued Kumbhakarna. 'You will make an excellent Vishnu. You have strength, courage, wisdom and empathy. You have the grit and determination.'

Raavan looked at Kumbhakarna and smiled, then turned to Sita. 'And most importantly, you have known grief ... The most powerful emotion. The source of true greatness.'

Sita frowned. *What?*

'I read this in a book once,' continued Raavan, 'that grief and suffering can serve as engines that move life forward. Happiness is overrated. Hatred, of course, is destructive.'

'What sense does that make?' asked Sita. 'Though I agree that hatred is destructive. But grief? Really?'

'Yes, really. It makes sense. Think of the great people you know today.' Raavan widened his chest and almost preened, throwing his head back in challenge.

Sita narrowed her eyes and stared at Raavan. None of the politeness of her birth-mother in her. No hesitation in being brutally honest. She was communicating her thoughts clearly with her eyes. *Great? You think you are great? Really?*

Raavan answered her look. 'Great does not mean good, Sita. Great only means the person makes a real impact on the world. Ordinary people do not impact the world, they are only impacted by it. Now, with great people, the impact can be good or bad. But know this: Happy people can never be great.'

Sita did not agree. 'Come on, Raavanji. Do you actually believe that? My adoptive mother Sunaina was a great woman. She reformed Mithila. Brought peace and prosperity to it, as much as she could. She helped so many. Brought me up. Gave me direction. Gave me strength and motivation.'

'But was she happy?'

'She was always smiling. She was—'

Raavan interrupted Sita. 'That's not an answer to my question. People assume that depressed people *look like* they are in depression. That they cry all the time. Or mope. No. Most people who are depressed, smile. In fact, they smile more than necessary. Because they hide their grief from the world.'

Sita didn't respond.

'What were your last moments with Queen Sunaina like? I know she died a long time back, when you were very young. Yes?'

Sita nodded. 'Yes.'

'So, what did she say to you on her deathbed?' asked Raavan. 'Did she tell you to be happy? Peaceful? Calm? Joyful?'

Sita remembered her mother's words only too well. *You will not waste your life mourning me. You will live wisely and make me proud.*

'She told me that she wanted me to make her proud,' said Sita.

Raavan pointed his index finger at her. 'Aha! That's the difference between great people and happy people. Great people always keep striving, keep achieving, as if they have a monster living inside them that will not let them rest. It is so strong, this monster, that it makes them want to keep growing and achieving even after they die. So, they want others around them, especially the ones they love, to also be great. Happiness as an accidental by-product is acceptable, but it is not the purpose of their lives. Happy people, on the other hand, are satisfied people. Satisfied with what they have. Their smiles are genuine, the kind of smile that reaches the eyes. Their hearts are light. They are warm to everyone around them. And they want others, especially the ones they love, to be joyful, to accept what life has blessed or cursed them with, and be satisfied with it. Basically, their *mantra* is: Be happy by managing your mind rather than changing the world. Great people, on the other hand, want to change the world. Happy people just want to make their minds accept whatever the world throws at them, so that, in their little cocoon, they can be joyful. Like people who are drugged.'

'Oh, come on!'

'No, I mean it,' said Raavan. 'Happiness is like a drug. The ultimate drug. It makes you accept life as it is. Just inject the drug into your mind, be blissed out and don't achieve anything, don't change anything. Just be a joyful idiot.'

'Listen—'

Raavan interrupted Sita. 'But grief, on the other hand, drives you insane. You are not satisfied with anything. Anything. How do you banish that grief from your life? How? By changing the world, or so you think … For no matter how much you change the world, you will not find happiness. Why? Because the only way to be happy is by being drugged; by managing your own mind, rather than changing the world. That is why the only people who bring about change are the ones who are *not* happy, the ones who are grief-stricken.'

Sita narrowed her eyes. 'I have been joyful for the last thirteen years with Ram. These years in banishment have been the happiest of my life. Ram tells me exactly the same thing.'

'And what exactly have both of you achieved in these thirteen years?'

Sita didn't say anything. But the answer was obvious. *Not much.*

Raavan continued. 'There's nothing wrong with wanting to be happy. Many people make that choice. But you must realise what you are giving up – you are giving up any chance of becoming great.'

Sita had a slight smile on her face. She was thinking of her friend Radhika, who had chosen happiness.

'Think of the sun,' said Raavan. 'It is, after all, a gigantic, radioactive ball of fire. No life is possible close to it. And within it is only death. But a mere eight minutes of light-speed away is Mother Earth, teeming with life made possible by the sun. The sun is like a grievously hurting man, burning himself up with his suffering. But his suffering makes life possible some distance away. That is greatness.'

'Yes, but like you say, some distance away. Not alongside the sun.'

'True. The sun can never find happiness. But he is great. It is said that the fate of truly great people is to suffer, but they confuse correlation with causality. It is actually the other way around. Because they suffer, they become great.'

Sita shielded her eyes as she looked up at the brilliant radiance of the sun. She smiled as a thought reinforced her understanding of her husband. *Ram ...*

'Do you agree with me?' asked Raavan.

Sita turned to Raavan. 'Maybe. There is something to it, I admit. But the thing is, it's only if the sun keeps its grief to itself that it can make good happen. When it cannot, it will erupt in solar flares, which will damage and hurt life, even from a distance. Grief can provide the fuel for greatness, but it can also be the trigger for evil.'

Raavan nodded. 'Yes. I have damaged the world a lot.'

Kumbhakarna cut in. 'No no, Dada. You have done some good too. It's not that—'

'Kumbha!' boomed Raavan, admonishing his brother. His eyes, though, twinkled with good humour. 'Love me, but don't lie so much that it is a sin to even listen to you!'

Kumbhakarna laughed, as did Sita.

'I have been a terrible person,' said Raavan. 'I have suffered all my life, and I have, in turn, inflicted that suffering on the whole world. But you,' continued Raavan, pointing at Sita. 'You are different. You are good and perfect.'

Sita shook her head. 'You are once again projecting my mother on to me. Maybe you inflicted ALL your suffering on the world. But it's not that I never did. Often, I absorbed my grief, but sometimes, when it became too much, I lashed out. And those with power in their hands do not have the luxury of lashing out. If I am a Vishnu, I will have that power.'

Raavan looked at Kumbhakarna and then back at Sita.

'Yesterday, when you told me what happened to my mother, and what you did to the people who killed her, for a moment I felt the rage you felt. I thought what you did, torturing those murderers, was justified. But I know a man who would not have felt this way; who, even at such a moment of intense grief, would have been lawful. I know a man who never loses his focus, no matter how much suffering he undergoes. The greater the grief, the more righteous his response. I always thought that he would make a better Vishnu than I would. Now I know for sure.'

Raavan smiled slightly.

Sita looked away for a moment, remembering something. 'You know,' she said, 'I once read that winning wars is different from winning peace. You need anger to win a war. Anger in the moment. And that is why the Mahadevs have always been those with immense anger. But to win peace... that requires something different. You and I can win wars. But war can only take away an injustice. It cannot create justice. War can only take away Evil. It cannot create Good. To create Justice and Good, you need peace. And to win peace, you need a leader who will stay the course, no matter what comes along – grief, suffering – to sway him from his path.'

'True.'

'Ram is that leader,' said Sita.

Chapter 6

The ship docked at Alappuzha in the region of Kerala, the land of Lord Parshu Ram. The party was going to ride over eighty kilometres to the holy land of Shabarimala, which cradled the great Ayyappa temple deep in the forests.

Kerala was blessed by the Gods. It had an excess of everything: deep-water lakes, backwaters and rivers bisected almost every path; dense forests made the road ahead almost unmappable; tall and craggy mountains tested the spirit of even the most devout devotee; and wild animals sometimes brought an unwelcome and sudden end to travel. It made the journey to Shabarimala not an easy one.

But the ancestors had designed pilgrimages to be difficult. The journey must be a penance. It must prepare you for the destination.

The old Sanskrit word for a place of pilgrimage was *teerth sthan*. The root of this word was '*the point of crossing over*'. So, a pilgrimage place was where one's soul could cross over and touch the divine. Which is why, often, pilgrimage temples were built in inhospitable terrain, arduous and difficult to reach; the journey would serve as a preparation, purging the body to prepare the soul.

But Ram was occupied with another journey. The one that Hanuman was about to undertake.

Hanuman and Sursa, along with ten soldiers, were setting out on a cutter boat. They intended to sail farther down to the southern tip of mainland India, and then on to the island of Lanka, where they would beach on the relatively uninhabited western coast. Then they would march towards the centre of the island, towards Sigiriya.

'Please give her this letter, Lord Hanuman,' said Ram, as he handed a rolled and sealed parchment to the Naga Vayuputra. He removed one of his rings. 'And please give her this as well.'

Hanuman looked at the letter and then at Ram, a wan smile on his face. 'You think so too?'

Ram nodded. 'Yes. She will resist coming back.'

Hanuman took a deep breath. 'I will try my best to convince her.'

'Yes, I know. But I am the reason she will not want to escape. I think she will want me to battle Raavan and rescue her. So that my name is indisputably cemented as the Vishnu. But she is wrong. I am not the Vishnu, she is. She has to return.'

Hanuman held Ram's forearms tightly. 'I will bring her back, Great One.'

— JF J5D —

'Where in Lord Parshu Ram's name is Hanuman?' asked an angry Vishwamitra.

A message had been sent by the Malayaputras to Hanuman a few days ago. To Lothal, where it was believed he was to arrive. But they had not received any reply.

'Guruji,' said Arishtanemi, 'it's unlike Hanuman to not respond to us. Perhaps he didn't receive the message.'

'I have heard that... that infernal man was also seen in the area.'

Arishtanemi knew Vishwamitra was referring to Vashishtha. He had heard the news as well. But he didn't want to speculate about what may have happened.

'You go,' said Vishwamitra suddenly.

Arishtanemi was surprised. 'To Lanka, Guruji?'

'Yes.'

'But... but I am not sure that Sita will listen to me, Guruji.'

'Make her listen!'

Arishtanemi remained silent.

Vishwamitra continued. 'We have made so many sacrifices for Mother India. She cannot be stupid now. We are mobilising our own army. We will get them across to Lanka. The Vayuputras will also have to join us ... they will have no choice. Armed with our *daivi astras*, Sita can lead us all into battle and easily kill Raavan. But first, she must arrange a dramatic escape. It will build her image across India. The entire chessboard is set, everything is ready, she just needs to move in for the kill.'

'But Guruji ...'

'She has to listen. She has nothing in her hands now, no cards left. She must be imagining that Raavan will kill her. She doesn't know where Ram is. She has no support. We are her only hope. The Malayaputras have used a *daivi astra* to save her, during the Battle of Mithila. She knows we are loyal to her. We are her only hope. She has to take on her role as the Vishnu.'

'But she is stubborn, Guruji. She doesn't—'

Vishwamitra leaned forward and interrupted Arishtanemi. 'Go to Lanka and make her understand. Do not disappoint me.'

— J⊦ ⌡⊃D —

Raavan shielded his eyes and looked up at the sun. And smiled.

'What's so funny?' asked Kumbhakarna.

Raavan and Kumbhakarna were standing on the veranda of Sita's cottage, waiting for her to emerge. They had just finished breakfast. Sita had gone back into the cottage for her after-breakfast *puja*.

'Just ... the grief-stricken sun,' answered Raavan.

Kumbhakarna grinned mischievously. 'I don't know which version of you tortures me more, Dada. The older version who never listened to me, or this new philosophical version who talks in circles!'

Raavan boxed Kumbhakarna on his stomach. 'Bloody dog!'

Kumbhakarna laughed even more loudly, enclosing his brother in a bear hug. They held each other tightly, laughing till the tears rolled down their cheeks. And then they shed some more tears. This time, tears of sadness. Sadness at the years wasted.

They disengaged when they heard the sound of someone clearing their throat. Sita stood a short distance away, an amused grin on her face.

The brothers wiped their eyes and sat down. Sita sat down as well.

'Are you both all right?' asked Sita.

Kumbhakarna answered for the brothers. 'Never been better.'

Raavan laughed and punched his gargantuan brother on his shoulder.

'So, what are we going to talk about today?'

Raavan leaned forward. 'No more philosophical discussions!'

'By the great Lord Rudra, yes! Enough philosophical discussions!' said Kumbhakarna, laughing.

'Hey!' said Raavan, chortling.

Kumbhakarna leaned back and laughed. Even Sita joined in the inane laughter.

It took a few moments for everyone to settle down, and then Raavan spoke. 'We must decide our next step.'

'Yes,' said Sita.

Raavan continued. 'Guru Vishwamitra will send someone to rescue you.'

'He probably will.'

'And your husband is alive. He will come too.'

'Yes, he will.'

'And what will you do? Will you escape with them?'

Sita knew she couldn't tell them what she really wanted to do. 'Umm…'

'Speak honestly. You are Vedavati's daughter.'

'Well … I mean …'

'All right,' said Raavan, interrupting Sita. 'Let me answer for you then.'

An embarrassed smile played on Sita's face. For she could guess what was to follow.

'Somewhere in the back of my mind I knew what Guru Vishwamitra was thinking,' said Raavan. 'He needed to build someone up into a villain, who could then be destroyed by the Vishnu, so that the rebellious and uncontrollable people of India would follow that Vishnu.'

'Umm …'

'Let me continue,' said Raavan, raising his hand. 'Indians are the most difficult people to manage in the world. Constantly rebelling. They love breaking the law, even if there is nothing to be gained by it. We don't like following orders from any leader. Unless it is that rare leader whom we look up to like a God. We would follow that leader to the ends of the Earth, and beyond. But how do you transform a human being into a God? Even a perfect human being is not enough. People have to want to follow him. He has to earn their admiration and loyalty. And nothing quite like delivering the head of the villain that people hate, right?'

'Raavanji … I don't know what to say … But what Guru Vishwamitra … His plans …'

Raavan smiled. 'No, it's all right… I understand. My life has not amounted to much. Maybe my death can mean something.'

Sita was silent. So was Kumbhakarna.

'But your husband Ram coming here and rescuing you will not set the Indian imagination alight. There must be a great war.'

'But…'

'Hear me out. You and your husband will be making a lot of changes to India. You will be asking people to make a lot of sacrifices. All for the motherland. So that Mother India's future is secure. They will not follow you and make those sacrifices unless they worship you. And to worship you both, they need a spectacle.'

Raavan paused before continuing.

'What will actually help India,' said Raavan, 'is what you two will do later. The reforms that you will make. I suggest you study Lankan administration. There is a lot you can learn from what we've done in Lanka. Roads, infrastructure …' Raavan looked at Kumbhakarna before continuing. 'Though our health facilities could do with some improving… We still haven't been able to figure out how to stop the plague ravaging Sigiriya. But do you think that my Lankans sing songs in praise of the roads

I've built for them? Or the water pipes I've constructed? Or the parks? The schools? Oh no… They celebrate stories of my military victory at Karachapa! It will be the same for the both of you. If you succeed, maybe they will call the perfect Vishnu-created times Ram Rajya or Sita Rajya. And it will be a time of order, comfort, peace and convenience; roads, canal irrigation, hospitals, schools. Most importantly, institutional systems. But trust me, when Ram and Sita's story is written – maybe they will call it the Ramayana or Sitayana, who knows – there will be scant mention of this Ram Rajya we are talking about. No storyteller's imagination is fired by the prospect of writing twenty pages on how a great canal was constructed. Which reader would be interested in that story? What will get the storytellers excited is your adventures. Your love story, your struggles, your time in the jungle, and crucially, your war against me in Lanka. Because that is all that the common folk will want to hear. That's what you will be remembered for. That's what people will follow you for. Because most people are stupid …'

Kumbhakarna stirred uncomfortably.

'Okay, okay, Kumbhakarna, stop frowning,' Raavan said. 'People don't consciously register the things that truly make their life better. Like schools and hospitals. They take these things for granted once they have them. Instead, they focus on the magic of the stories that beguile them, like great battles between a hero and a villain. The common people are, fundamentally, idiots.'

'Come on, Raavanji,' said Sita. 'You can't say that …'

Raavan interrupted Sita. 'You can say whatever politically correct thing you want to say to make yourself feel morally superior. But you know that I am speaking the truth.'

Sita remained silent.

'So, if we have to give them a war, let's give them one. And a good one.'

'Um ...'

'That would serve another purpose too. It would destroy my army.'

'What?'

'The Lankan army must be destroyed. For the good of India.'

Kumbhakarna nodded, in agreement with his elder brother this time.

'Why?' asked Sita. 'Why would you want your own loyal soldiers to be massacred? They would only be following your orders.'

'No. You do not know my army. They don't just follow orders. They enjoy the violence. Those are the kind of soldiers I collected; angry people with tortured, damaged souls, who hate the world and want to see it burn. My Lankan people, the ordinary citizens, are good. And we have an efficient police force here to protect them. But my army ... Well, they are a reflection of what I was ... They are ruthless monsters. And without me to restrain them, they can cause chaos. They are barbarians who will burn alive unarmed people, even children, just to collect some loot, as they did in Mumbadevi. Thugs who will rape any non-Lankan woman who falls into their hands. Butchers who will carry out public beheadings because they enjoy the spectacle. Fiends who will sell people into slavery, even though dharma bans it, because it's profitable. Terrific killers with oodles of courage, no doubt. But without the restraint of *dharma*. I collected such soldiers. I was a connoisseur of such men and women. You know one of them. Samichi. You thought you knew her intimately, but you did not know her at all. Why did I recruit her? Because she is damaged in the core of her being. She has her reasons. Horrific childhood suffering. Her rage against her cruel father deflected into an unfocused anger against the entire world; an unquenchable fury. It makes every living moment a miserable torture for her; and the same fury makes her a killer beyond compare. A killer completely under my control. I have two hundred thousand such soldiers, Sita. They are a threat to any society. Not just to India, but also to my Lanka. They are a threat to *dharma*, since they are an army of *adharma*. They are not strong enough to conquer India right now, because of the plague afflicting us. But they will create decades of chaos in India and Lanka. How will you build a better India then? The Lankan army must be destroyed. And the best way to do that is a war. A war to the very end.'

Sita didn't say anything. What Raavan had said sounded cold, ruthless, but logical.

'Will your husband fight to the very end?' asked Raavan.

'Oh yes, he will… But only if he believes that you are fighting to the end as well. If he suspects that you are not fighting to win, he will stop the battle. Because it's *adharma* to fight an enemy who is holding back. That is the way he thinks.'

Raavan frowned. 'How will he know? Who will tell him?'

He looked at Kumbhakarna and Sita. Neither would speak about this with anyone else.

'But I will genuinely not hold myself back,' said Raavan. 'I will battle hard. Will your husband win?'

Sita smiled. A smile of supreme confidence. 'The only one who can defeat Ram is Ram himself. He will defeat you, Raavanji.'

Raavan grinned. 'It will be a glorious war then.'

'But …' Sita fell silent, hesitating to voice her question.

Raavan understood. But he waited for her to ask.

'But why do this to yourself?'

Raavan smiled. 'Have you heard that statement, "They buried us, but they did not know that we were seeds"?'

Sita nodded. 'Yes, I have. Beautiful. Evocative and rebellious. Who said that?'

'Someone from the Greek islands to our west. I think his name was Konstantinos. But, in my honest opinion, it covers only half the journey towards wisdom.'

'How so?'

'It assumes that the seed itself rises. But we know that is not what happens. The seed will remain dead like a stone if it is not buried in fertile ground. The seed *has* to be buried. And allow itself to be destroyed. So that a glorious tree emerges from its shattered chest. That is the *purpose*, the *swadharma*, of the seed. For as long as the tree lives, songs will be sung of the seed that experienced death – even though it was already dead – to allow the tree to emerge. The seed is either lifeless above ground, or wrecked below ground. But when it rips open to allow a tree to emerge, it becomes immortal. Through the only way any living thing can become immortal: in the memory of others who live on after them. Its sacrifice makes the seed immortal.'

Sita remained silent.

'I died the day Vedavati died. I have been dragging my carcass around all this time. It is time to let my corpse itself die. The right time. I can allow myself to be destroyed so that the legend of Ram and Sita may rise. And as long as the world remembers the two of you, it will remember me. I will be immortal too.'

Sita looked down, her eyes moist with sentiment.

Raavan looked at Kumbhakarna, whose eyes glistened with unshed tears. He looked back at Sita. 'There are three good men in my army. My only request is that they be kept out of this. Kumbhakarna, my uncle Mareech, and my son, Indrajit.'

Kumbhakarna's response was instantaneous. 'No. I am staying. I am fighting.'

'Kumbha … you should …'

'No.'

'Listen to me ... Escape with Mareech uncle and Indrajeet and then—'

'No, Dada.'

'Kumbha ... please.'

'NO, DADA!'

Raavan fell silent. Kumbhakarna stared at his brother. His eyes conveyed a mixture of love, anger and pride. Then Raavan got up and embraced his younger brother.

Chapter 7

Nations that do not have a coastline can be forgiven for thinking that reaching an island is a challenge: they imagine the island as a fortress and the sea as a moat. Which is not true. With good ships and fast boats, the sea can be a highway rather than an obstacle. The real challenge lies in marching inland, especially if the terrain is densely forested and marked by deep rivers and lofty mountains. So, while Ram and his band marched towards Shabarimala, Hanuman, Sursa and ten Vayuputra soldiers had already sailed into the north-western coast of Lanka on a quick cutter boat.

This region of Lanka did not have good harbours. In fact, these were treacherous waters for large sea-faring ships to sail on, due to the massive sandbanks, many of which rose above water level during low tide. It was why Hanuman had decided to use a much smaller cutter boat.

But the sandbanks, and the resultant absence of good harbours, gave this coast an immeasurable advantage for

Hanuman's secret mission: this part of Lanka was largely deserted.

Late in the night, the cutter boat passed the long and not-too-broad Mannar island. It lay south-east to north-west, stretching like a yearning lover towards the Pamban island off the mainland Indian coast a mere twenty-five kilometres away. They sailed farther southwards from the island, deep into the sea. They needed to do this because of the celebrated Ketheeswaram temple on the Lankan mainland, to the east of Mannar. It was the only place in this region that would have some crowds, which they wanted to avoid. For obvious reasons.

As they passed, Hanuman turned towards the Lankan mainland with folded hands in the direction of the lights, and bowed to the Mahadev, Lord Rudra, whose idol was consecrated at the Ketheeswaram temple.

'*Jai Shri Rudra,*' he whispered.

Glory to Lord Rudra.

'*Jai Shri Rudra,*' repeated everyone on the boat.

Around twenty kilometres farther south, the Aruvi Aru River flowed into the sea. The headwaters of the second longest river in Lanka were close to the Lankan capital city of Sigiriya. This should have made the river an important waterway for travelling into the Lankan interior. Theoretically, ships could easily come in from the sea and sail up the river towards Sigiriya. But this had been made impossible due to the insidious sandbanks in the sea around this region. Seafaring ships normally avoided this route for fear of being grounded. As a result, ship traffic towards the hinterland of Sigiriya was captured by the Mahaweli Ganga, the longest river in Lanka, which joined the sea on the eastern coast, on the other side of the island.

It was perfect for Hanuman's mission.

For this north-western coastline of Lanka was almost completely deserted. They could simply sail up the river in their smaller boat, undetected, to reach very close to Sigiriya. This was crucial, because the biggest risk in marching within Lanka was getting lost in the dense jungle hinterland. The river would serve as a guide. There was another possible route: the road from Ketheeswaram temple leading to the Lankan capital. But it was dotted with military barricades, making it a risky proposition.

'There's just one problem,' whispered Sursa.

'What?' asked Hanuman, leaning closer, keeping his voice low.

'There is a lighthouse close to the river mouth. It serves as a warning to seafaring ships to not sail farther north, due to the sandbanks.'

'And it's manned?'

'Yes, it is. Around ten men.'

Hanuman looked back at the ten Vayuputra soldiers behind them. 'I think we can take them.'

'We must do it quickly.'

'Why?'

'There is a full battalion posted just twenty kilometres from the lighthouse, at the Ketheeswaram temple. It protects the royal road from the temple to Sigiriya. It's a mere thirty-minute ride on horseback. If even one soldier escapes, we'll have an entire battalion upon us in no time at all.'

'Hmm. All right. So, we'll have to kill them all. Quickly.'

'Yes.'

'How frequent is the changeover?'

'This unit is largely self-sufficient. And a completely unimportant post where nothing happens. Relief comes once in four weeks. It will be a while before the battalion even knows that these lighthouse soldiers have been killed. By which time we will have finished our work in Sigiriya and be back in mainland India.'

Hanuman nodded and quickly gave orders to his soldiers. Check weapons and shields. Tighten armour. Stretch muscles.

He then sat tall on the thwart, bringing his ridiculously muscular left arm overhead and dropping the forearm behind his back, resting his left hand between his brawny shoulder blades. With his right hand, Hanuman grabbed his left bent elbow and pulled gently. He sighed as he felt a stretch in his powerful left deltoid and triceps muscles.

Almost immediately, he felt someone's eyes upon him. He turned to see Sursa staring at him with open admiration. Hanuman's cheeks turned bright red with embarrassment and he quickly looked away. Sursa laughed and began stretching her own shoulders.

$$— \mathsf{J}\mathsf{F}\ \mathsf{J},\mathsf{\bar{5}D} —$$

Hanuman and Sursa were hiding in the trees along with the Vayuputra soldiers. They had beached their boat a good distance north and then noiselessly made their way south, racing behind the dense treeline. They stood in the shadows, observing the lighthouse across the broad beach. The tall, five-storey structure had a massive fire lit on its top storey, spreading its light and signalling a warning to ships far into the sea. A simple warning: *Stay away*.

'There are ten of them,' confirmed Hanuman, counting the Lankan soldiers who had gathered at the beach and were looking towards the expanse of water. It may have been late at night, but the light of the full moon made them clearly visible. They were only a short distance away.

'But Hans, we should check for men within the lighthouse too,' said Sursa.

Hanuman ignored the fond but inappropriate mangling of his name. 'I agree. But let's get rid of these soldiers first.'

Sursa nodded.

Hanuman turned to his fellow Vayuputras. 'They have spears. Bear that in mind.'

Hanuman and the Vayuputras were armed with swords and knives. The Lankans had these weapons too, but they also had spears, which dramatically increased their reach.

Hanuman drew his sword, went down on one knee, and dug the tip of the blade into the soft, sandy ground. His band followed.

Hanuman closed his eyes, bowed his head and whispered, 'Everything I do, I do for Rudra.'

The words were softly echoed by the warriors behind him. 'Everything I do, I do for Rudra.'

Hanuman rose, his huge frame crouched low, his sword held away from his body. He began to move forward on light feet.

Fast as a cheetah, nimble as a panther.

Hanuman and his platoon were in the open now. On the beach. Racing towards the Lankans, who sat facing the other way. Towards the sea.

A Lankan soldier turned a few moments before the Vayuputras would have been upon them. An ancient animal instinct, from when humans protected themselves from great predators in the grasslands of Africa; an instinct that warns those who remain attuned to their gut reaction.

'WHO GOES THERE?'

In one fluid motion, the superbly trained soldiers of Raavan were on their feet and had whirled around, their spears thrust forward, shields held together with perfect discipline.

This was one of the most potent defensive tactics in open battles. The soldiers held their shields together, each one overlapping partly with the next, forming an impenetrable wall. And through a curved opening on the right edge of each shield emerged a threatening long spear.

The dreaded shield wall.

It was natural for any attacking force to slow down when confronted with a shield wall. For it was almost impossible to penetrate. The attacker would run into the forest of spear blades if he charged, and run himself through.

But Hanuman was no ordinary attacker.

No defensive hesitation in this mighty son of Vayu Kesari.

Hanuman raised his huge frame to its full height. No need to crouch or be silent any more. He did not slow down. His sword was still held to his side.

His platoon fell slightly behind as he raced ahead.

When he was almost upon the forest of spears, Hanuman roared, '*Kalagni Rudra!*'

Kalagni was the *mythical end-of-time fire*; the conflagration that marked the end of an age. And the beginning of a new one. It was the fire of Lord Rudra that signalled the end of time for those who stood against the mighty Mahadev.

'*Kalagni Rudra!*' bellowed the Vayuputras.

Hanuman ran straight towards the spear in the centre of the shield wall. When it almost seemed like the Naga Vayuputra would run into the blade, Hanuman twisted his torso to one side and raised his left arm. Bypassing the spear's blade, he brought his left arm down with force, trapping the spear shaft between his left arm and the side of his chest. Now the Lankan was locked in position for as long as he held on to the spear. Hanuman had not slowed down. His left shoulder rammed into the shield and the Lankan staggered back. Hanuman raised his sword and brutally thrust it into the man's throat. Yanking his sword out almost immediately, he swung his blade to the side in the same smooth movement, slicing the throat of the Lankan next to him.

Within a few seconds Hanuman had killed two Lankans. And, most crucially, the shield wall had broken.

The shield wall is impenetrable when held together. But a single breach can make the entire structure collapse shockingly quickly. The Vayuputra platoon smashed into the opening provided by Hanuman. They cut down the rest of the Lankans with rapid efficiency.

Except for one Lankan, who had dropped his spear and was scurrying away towards his horse. As Hanuman killed the man confronting him, he noticed the Lankan mounting his horse a short distance away.

'Stop that man!' hollered Hanuman as he raced towards him.

The Lankan spurred his horse viciously. It looked like he would escape. And soon warn the battalion at Ketheeswaram temple.

This mission could fail even before it began.

And then Hanuman saw a most exquisite kill.

Sursa thundered down the sandy ground, from the right of the Lankan on horseback. The unfortunate man did not notice death racing towards him. His eyes were fixed on the fearsome Hanuman, on the opposite side. As she neared the horse, Sursa sprang from her feet and vaulted high into the air, bending her knees, perfectly timed, to get maximum lift.

Hanuman felt like he was seeing it in slow motion.

Splendid.

Sursa flying through the air, her back arched, right hand raised high, knife ready. She crashed into the mounted Lankan and brought her right hand down simultaneously. Ramming her blade into the Lankan's left eye. The metal tip tore through the eye socket and sank into the brain. The Lankan and Sursa rolled off the horse as one. The Lankan was dead before he hit the ground.

The horse kept running for a few seconds and then stopped in confusion.

Hanuman could not take his eyes off Sursa, his expression one of awe.

Sursa rolled over one more time and rose in the same smooth movement. She looked around. A jungle cat on the prowl.

All the Lankans were dead.

Her steely eyes settled on Hanuman. 'Let's check the lighthouse quickly.'

Hanuman nodded. He turned towards his soldiers. 'Pick up the bodies and get them into the lighthouse. Tie up the horses.'

'Yes, Lord Hanuman,' they replied in unison.

Hanuman and Sursa moved quickly towards the lighthouse.

—JƎ ꙾Ɔ—

'Father, I deserve to know what is going on,' said Indrajit, politely but firmly.

Raavan's twenty-seven-year-old son had walked into his private chambers unannounced while the king of Lanka was in discussion with Kumbhakarna. Indrajit had the same intimidating physical presence as his father. Tall and muscular, his baritone voice was naturally commanding. But also beguiling. He had inherited his mother Mandodari's high cheekbones and thick brown hair, a leonine mane which he styled with two side partings and a knot at the crown of his head. An oiled handlebar moustache sat well on his smooth-complexioned face. His clothes were sober, as always. He wore no jewellery but for the ear studs that most warriors in India favoured. A *janau*, the *sacred thread*, hung diagonally from his left shoulder, across his chest.

Raavan stopped speaking and turned towards his pride and joy. 'What are you talking about, Indrajit?'

Indrajit stared at his father. And then turned to his uncle. 'Uncle, are you going to talk?'

Kumbhakarna looked away wordlessly.

'Father,' said Indrajit, turning his gaze back to Raavan, 'the last I heard, the plan was to kidnap the Vishnu and then negotiate with the Malayaputras for the medicines that you both need. It has been days since we kidnapped her. Many days. But nobody has been sent to the Malayaputras, nor has any message gone to them. And I keep seeing the two of you trotting off to Ashok Vatika for long conversations with Queen Sita. What is going on?'

'Indrajit, there are things to be considered.'

Indrajit stood silently, waiting for his father to explain. Since no explanation was offered, he took a deep breath and spoke with steely calm. 'Father, do I still have your trust?'

'Of course, you do, my son.'

'Then why are you not telling me the whole truth?'

'My son, there are bigger issues that your uncle and I need to deliberate upon before taking any step.'

'Bigger issues? Father, Ayodhya is mobilising its army. We thought they wouldn't do that if we didn't harm Queen Sita. We were wrong. And if even *I* know what Ayodhya is doing, there is no way that you don't know. If Ayodhya is able to rally all the armies of the Sapt Sindhu kingdoms, we will lose. We will give them a tough fight, but we will lose. You know that. What can be a bigger issue than that?'

Raavan remained silent.

'Father …'

Raavan picked up a scroll from the side table. 'There is this problem.'

'What problem?'

'I need you to go to Bali.'

Bali was an island far to the east of India, an extremely important entrepot for trade with South-east Asia and China. One that Lanka controlled.

Indrajit was shocked, but managed to keep his expression stoic. 'Bali?'

'Yes.'

'Why in Lord Rudra's name should I go to Bali?'

'There are some major trade disputes that need immediate attention. And it can only be sorted out by one of us. Someone from the royal family.'

Indrajit narrowed his eyes in exasperation. 'Trade disputes?'

'Yes.'

Indrajit's fists were clenched tight, his knuckles white. 'Father, I will come back when you are in a mood to trust me.'

Saying this, Indrajit turned and marched calmly out of the chamber.

Chapter 8

It took more than a week to cover the little less than one-hundred-kilometre distance from the coastal city of Alappuzha to Shabarimala. On the last night, Ram and his companions camped beside the Pampa River in the valley below. Early the next morning, they began their march to the mountain top. The temple was at a height of over one thousand five hundred feet above sea level.

They were still some distance from the main temple when they met Shabari, the Lady of the Forest. She had walked up to meet them at the entrance to the complex.

'Lady Shabari,' said Vashishtha, bringing his palms together in a respectful namaste and bowing his head.

Shabari was not a name but a title for the head of the Shabarimala temple. Her formal title was Tantri Shabari. As is the Indian way, a deep symbolism was woven into it. The word *Tantri* in old Sanskrit was gender-agnostic and could be used for a male or a female. The root of the word was *string* or *cord.* The name Shabarimala translated as the Hill of Shabari in the local language. But in old Sanskrit, *mala* meant *garland.* Thus, the *Shabarimala, garland of Shabari*, was held together by a *tantri*, the string.

The present *tantri* was an old woman, at least one hundred years old. Nobody knew her original birth-name. She herself had forgotten her old identity and had committed her entire being to the service of the great warrior-God, Lord Ayyappa, represented in this particular temple in his celibate form.

The wizened old woman had a fair-skinned face and warm, motherly eyes. She brought her calloused and forest-roughened hands together in a namaste. 'Maharishi Vashishtha. What an honour to have you grace our land. *Swamiye Sharanam Ayyappa.*'

We find refuge at the feet of Lord Ayyappa.

'The honour is all mine, great Shabariji,' answered Vashishtha. '*Swamiye Sharanam Ayyappa.*' Then the *rajguru* of Ayodhya turned to Ram and Lakshman. 'Please allow me to introduce—'

'Who does not know the great Ram,' said Shabari, with a smile that began in her heart and extended unbidden to her eyes. 'Welcome, great Vishnu.'

Ram smiled with embarrassment at being addressed as Vishnu. He whispered '*Swamiye Sharanam Ayyappa*' and bent his lean frame to touch Shabari's feet.

She touched Ram's head and whispered, 'May you have the greatest blessing of all: May you be of service to our motherland, India.'

Vashishtha smiled, for he had given this very blessing to Ram's wife, Sita, many years ago.

Ram arose, his hands folded together in a namaste.

Lakshman stepped forward, said '*Swamiye Sharanam Ayyappa*,' bent his massive frame, and touched Shabari's feet as well. He stepped back as soon as he received her blessing.

'Come with me, King Ram,' said Shabari, taking his hand and leading him along the side of the entrance. Most referred to Ram as king, even though he had not been officially coronated as yet. For Bharat had clearly declared that he ruled in the name of Ram.

Ram looked back. Vashishtha and Lakshman were following. Within a few minutes they arrived at a massive stepwell. It had a surface area of nearly five hundred square metres. Shabarimala received plentiful rain during the monsoon season, but the mountain was steep and there were no lakes. They were inundated with water during the rainy season but ran short the rest of the year, especially during the dry summer months. The stepwell was ingeniously designed in the shape of a horseshoe that descended into seven steep levels, the last of which was almost fifty feet deep. Smaller steps from its narrower ends led into the water. The stepwell's massive capacity ensured that it trapped enough water during the monsoon season to serve the needs of the temple complex all round the year.

Shabari skirted the stepwell, her hand still holding Ram's, and walked towards the mountain side.

Vashishtha smiled. For he knew where she was headed. A test. The test of Shabari. A test that no one had passed.

But Vashishtha was supremely confident of his student.

Shabari led Ram up to an installation at the edge of the mountain, just inside the perimeter wall of the complex. The view from here, of the valley below, was breathtaking. But Ram's attention was occupied elsewhere. He was transfixed by two sculptures.

Shabari turned to Ram. 'Tell me, great prince, what do these two sculptures say to you? What is their message?'

Shabari had posed this question to every important visitor to the temple. And none had got it right.

The two sculptures faced each other, a short distance separating them.

A rampaging bull.

A fearless little girl standing right in front of the beast.

The bull was life-sized, an awe-inspiring symbol of aggressive masculinity. Its head was lowered, its nostrils flared, its teeth bared. Its long, sharp horns curved threateningly. As though about to gore the little girl. The ridiculously muscled body was twisted to the right as it charged forward. Its forefeet dug into the ground. Its tail was raised, curling like a terrifying whip.

A livid, fearsome, dangerous beast.

And then there was the fearless little girl.

Petite. No older than five or six years. Hands on her hips, her shoulders thrown back in defiance. Her feet were spread apart and firmly planted for balance. Eyes rebellious. Chin up. Her hair flying back in disarray. Her clothes whipped against her body, as if a great wind was striking her. Unafraid of the beast that was about to run her down. Strong. Heroic.

Ram stared, unblinking.

Lakshman spoke first. He had the same thought as every other person who had seen these figures. 'What a magnificent girl! Powerful! Brave! Fearless! She tells us it is not the size of the person in the fight but the size of the fight in the person that matters!'

Shabari didn't acknowledge Lakshman or his answer. She didn't even turn to look at him. Her eyes were fixed on Ram.

Ram smiled slightly and murmured. 'What a magnificent beast ...'

Shabari cast a glance at Vashishtha and smiled. And then turned her attention back to Ram.

Ram was staring at the sculptures.

'Explain, great king,' said Shabari.

'The little girl is outmatched,' said Ram. 'She may be brave, but somewhere in the back of her mind she would know that she doesn't stand a chance. Had she been confronting a beast of this size and ferocity who was genuinely ruthless and cruel, she would have been trampled to death in moments. There is no way she cannot know that. The emotion with which she is standing, fearless and strong, means that she knows the truth … Not just knows, she has absolute faith in the truth: that the bull will not harm her. That the bull is reined in by *dharma*. The bull will not do any wrong. To my mind, the beast is the Bull of *Dharma*.'

Vashishtha beamed with pride. Since ancient times, *dharma* – all that is right, balanced and perfectly aligned with the universe – had been represented by a bull. All life must aim to live in consonance with *dharma*. And one of the key principles of a *dharmic* life is that the strong must protect the weak.

'The horns of the bull … look at them,' continued Ram. 'There is a thin string tied to the horns and going through the bull's mouth, like a bit. Like a nearly invisible bridle, with the reins attached to the horns. It may appear that the bull is baring its teeth, but actually the bit of the bridle is pulling its cheeks back. It's symbolic. What we do with *dharma* is in *our* control. It is our choice. Only our choice. The bull was charging, but immediately began reining himself in upon seeing the little girl, who is far weaker than him. Look at the body twisting away, almost like the beast is trying to avoid the child. The forefeet are digging into the ground, trying to slow down. Its tail is raised in

an instinctive attempt to balance itself as it evades the little girl
... *Paripalaya durbalam* ...'

Shabari nodded. An old Sanskrit phrase. *Protect the weak.*

Ram folded his hands together and bowed to the bull.

Shabari looked at Vashishtha in approval, communicating
her thoughts with her eyes. *You've chosen well.*

Then she stepped up to Ram. 'Among the most important
components of a strong society is the spirit of aggressive
masculinity. Without it, society would be weak and vulnerable.
It would be conquered by outsiders. It would fall apart. But
aggressive masculinity without the control of *dharma* transforms
into toxic masculinity. It leads to chaos, even more than that
caused by conquerors from elsewhere. Remember the last days
of the *Asuras* ... the violence, rape, pillage and oppression
they unleashed upon the entire land. Aggressive masculinity is
needed, sorely needed. But it must be restrained by *dharma*. So
that the power and strength of the bull are put to use for the
greater good.'

Ram nodded.

Shabari touched Ram's shoulder. 'There is no sight more
magnificent than a dangerous and powerful man, with
complete control over his own base desires, who also has an
innate yearning for justice and a deep, abiding love for his land
and his people.'

Ram stood silent.

'You will fight,' said Shabari. 'You will fight that man from
Lanka who has committed *adharma*. But you will also remember
that Raavan is only your opponent. Your true enemies, the
enemies of your people, are back home in your own land. That
will be your final battle. You will win it. And then you will work
hard to rebuild Mother India's greatness. Once you have done
all that, you can rest. And I can die in peace.'

— ⊥Ŧ ⊥ǯⅅ —

Having finished her morning *puja* and breakfast, Sita stepped out of her cottage. She had been informed that Raavan and Kumbhakarna would not be visiting today and had decided, therefore, to explore Ashok Vatika. Until now she had spent most of her time in the cottages in the centre of the vast gardens.

As she descended the steps, she saw a young man standing a short distance away. He was tall and muscular. Fair-complexioned. With high cheekbones and a smoothly oiled handlebar moustache. Long hair with two side-partings and a knot tied at the crown of his head. He had a lot of his mother in him, no doubt. But enough of his father as well for Sita to guess who he was.

The son of Raavan.

'Prince Indrajit?' asked Sita.

Indrajit was staring at her face. A face he was seeing for the first time. And yet, the son of Raavan was stunned.

'What can I do for you, prince?'

Indrajit seemed to be at a loss for words.

'What is it, great prince?'

Indrajit didn't speak. Rooted to the spot, as if turned to stone.

Sita pointed to the chairs in the veranda. 'Would you like to sit and talk?'

Indrajit moved. He walked up and past her. He sat on the chair. Not once taking his eyes off her face.

Sita sat across from the prince of Lanka, sympathy writ large on her face. She could guess what Indrajit was thinking. 'I guess you've seen the paintings.'

Indrajit nodded.

'They're of my mother, Vedavati.'

'I know ...' answered Indrajit, finally speaking. 'I know the lady in those paintings ... I know every single thing about my father ... At least I thought I did. But I didn't know about you.'

'Your father did not know about me either.'

'Are you ... I mean ... Do I call you *didi*?' asked Indrajit incredulously, using the respected word for an *elder sister*.

Sita reacted immediately. 'No, I am not your sister. Your father may have loved my mother. But he never more than touched her hand once. I am the daughter of Vedavati and her husband Prithvi.'

Indrajit smiled slightly. 'So, I remain the only child of Raavan.'

Sita smiled. 'Apparently so.'

Indrajit looked down.

'You don't hate me?' asked Sita.

'Why would I hate you? I've just met you.'

'I mean ... I am the daughter of Vedavati ...'

She was the daughter of the woman Indrajit's father had loved all his life. And Indrajit was the son of Mandodari, Raavan's legal wife. His mother must have suffered, for his father's heart was never hers. It had always been with another woman, a long-dead woman.

Indrajit had a complicated relationship with Raavan. He loved and admired his father deeply. But he also despised him. He respected Raavan's intellect, his strength, his warrior spirit, his head for business, his artistic abilities. The Gods had blessed his father with all the talents possible. And then had cursed him with an infantile, insecure heart with no control over his desires. In his younger days, Indrajit had detested his father, his cruelty, his temper. But he had especially hated the way Raavan treated his mother. Even more, the way his father surrounded himself with 'flaky dumb bimbos', as he called the women around Raavan; for how could they even hold a candle to his intelligent, calm and wise mother? And then he found out about Vedavati … the *Kanyakumari* …

Indrajit whispered, almost to himself, 'The *Kanyakumari* changed my relationship with my father …'

Sita frowned slightly, but chose silence as a response.

Indrajit had investigated. He had discovered what a great woman Vedavati was. A woman of rare nobility. A *Kanyakumari*. A Goddess. And perhaps, in some ways, better than his own mother. Strangely, knowing that his father ignored his mother Mandodari, for the *Kanyakumari* brought him peace of mind. His father wasn't just a lecherous philanderer. There was, actually, some depth in his heart. And with that realisation, he started seeing his father more clearly. He still saw Raavan's weaknesses. But he didn't judge him as much. Over time, he drew closer to his father.

'I think I understand what is going on …' whispered Indrajit.

Indrajit didn't let the rest of his thoughts escape his mind. *You have the Kanyakumari's face. And just like the Kanyakumari, you will make my father want to be a better man.*

'I don't understand what you mean, great prince,' said Sita.

'A Greek philosopher once said that "Death may be the greatest of all human blessings".'

Sita's expression changed ever so slightly.

'One should not pray for one's own death. For it should happen when it's meant to happen. But one should contemplate it, plan for it, even design it … to the extent possible. For is there anything more beautiful in this entire benighted earth than a good death?'

Sita remained silent.

'His life may have been meaningless, but his death will have a purpose. Having said that …'

Indrajit didn't say anything more. The conflict was clear in his mind. Should he do that which was in the interest of his father's soul or in the interest of his country? Should he be a good son or a good prince?

Sita read the conflict on Indrajit's face. She spoke up. 'Prince Indrajit—'

Indrajit interrupted her. 'No words are necessary, great Vishnu … Don't say anything more. If we don't speak of it further, there is nothing you need to hide.'

Sita didn't speak any further.

Chapter 9

'No ships?' asked Ram, surprised.

Ram, Vashishtha, Shabari, Lakshman and Naarad were sitting a short distance from the main temple base at Shabarimala. The legendary eighteen steps, built from solid granite rock, were visible in the distance. Ram had not climbed the sacred steps, nor done his darshan of Lord Ayyappa, for he had not performed the forty-one-day *vratham*, the *holy vow*, that a devotee who seeks to pray to Lord Ayyappa at this temple must undertake. And Ram was very clear: the laws applied to everyone, including him. He had sworn to return someday, after completing the ritual, to offer his prayers.

Ram had just finished explaining his plan in the event that Hanuman's mission failed. 'Our army will board ships, navigate to Gokarna, then sail up the Mahaweli Ganga River and its tributary – the Amban Ganga – to the point where it is closest to Sigiriya. And then we will march the rest of the distance over land.'

The Mahaweli Ganga was the longest river in Lanka. It disgorged its waters into the Indian Ocean at the sea port of Gokarna on the eastern coast of the island. This river was, in effect, the highway into the heartland of Lanka.

But the Mahaweli Ganga had a choke point at Onguiaahra, where the great river crashed through a narrow opening between some hills before embracing its main tributary, the Amban Ganga River. In a remarkable feat of engineering, the Lankans had converted the hilly chokepoint into a gigantic fort. They had also built well-designed barricades and dams at this point to release water at will, in order to destroy unauthorised ships that sailed up the river. Never in human history had Onguiaahra been conquered.

Ram had been evaluating the various options to breach this citadel, so they could sail farther up the river towards Sigiriya. For there was no other way to reach the Lankan capital. No other navigable river went anywhere close to the city. And marching a large army through the dense forests of Lanka, without the guidance of a road, was fraught with risk. One could easily get lost; these forests were even more dense than those in the Indian mainland.

When Ram was done, Shabari had made a suggestion, that they refrain from using ships to move their main army to the island of Lanka.

'How is that possible, Lady Shabari?' asked Vashishtha.

'Yes, how can one attack Lanka without ships?' Ram asked.

'Oh, I didn't mean that you should not use ships at all, great Ram,' said Shabhari. 'I know your brothers Bharat and Shatrughan are planning to sail down the east coast of India with the Ayodhyan army. I think you should hold the bulk of the army on the Tamil lands to our east. And make those other, lightly manned ships travel the path you've just described. Make them sail up the Mahaweli Ganga River to Onguiaahra. And give the Lankans a fierce battle over there. But this battle will be a feint. For your main army will march across.'

Lakshman did a double take. 'March across? To an island!'

Shabari glanced at Lakshman and smiled. And then she looked at Ram. 'I'm sure you are aware that, in ancient times, Lanka was a part of mainland India. This was before the end of the last great Ice Age, when the sea levels were a lot lower. The human bonds may have frayed, but the sea and the land remember that relationship.'

Ram frowned.

Shabari pulled a map from the folds of her *angvastram*. She spread it out and continued, indicating the various points on it, 'This is the region of the Tamil lands to the south of Vaigai River. Look at the lay of the land here. Mother India is reaching out to her long-lost kin. And the sibling Lanka, in turn, reaches back to her elder sister.'

Ram, Vashishtha, Lakshman and Naarad leaned over to look at the map closely. The mainland Indian territory extended out in a promontory, jutting into the sea, a mere kilometre and a half of shallow waters separating it from Pamban Island. Pamban Island itself stretched north-west to south-east, pointing towards Lanka. Beyond the south-east coast of Pamban, separated by some twenty-five kilometres of sea water, was the island of Mannar, which too spanned north-west to south-east. It almost touched the mainland of Lanka, separated by a few metres of shallow waters.

Shabari looked at Ram. 'It is possible to build some boat bridges from the Indian mainland to Pamban Island, and also cover the very short distance from Mannar to Lanka very easily. But the key problem ...'

'… is the twenty-five-kilometre distance between Pamban Island and Mannar Island,' said Ram, completing Shabari's sentence. 'It's too long to bridge. And that too, over a treacherous sea with the tides pulling in and out regularly.'

'That twenty-five-kilometre gap between Pamban and Mannar has sandflats, King Ram. They are so high up from the seabed that during low tide they are actually visible.'

Ram leaned forward and looked at the map again. Intrigued. He took a deep breath and sighed. 'But it will still be very difficult.'

'Of course it will be difficult. But let us imagine that you manage to bridge this gap and march across with the bulk of your army. When you cross Mannar and land in Lanka, you will arrive at the Ketheeswaram temple, which is dedicated to Lord Rudra. Being a royal temple, it is connected by a broad road that leads all the way to Sigiriya.'

Naarad drew in a quick, excited breath. 'Just a day's march to Sigiriya!'

'Less than a day,' corrected Shabari. She turned to Ram. 'You would take the Lankans by surprise. Nobody expects an attack from the western side of Lanka. All the defences are built on the eastern side. You can beat them before they even get their act together.'

Ram held his chin thoughtfully. 'The entire plan hinges on building a bridge. And that seems almost impossible.'

'Wars are not won by great warriors only, noble Vishnu,' said Shabari. 'They are also won by brilliant engineers who can forge into reality that which most ordinary people consider impossible.'

Ram looked at Lakshman. Both the brothers had had the same thought. Only one genius could pull off such an incredible feat of engineering. Their youngest brother, Shatrughan.

— ᒍᖴ ᒐ5D —

'Brilliant …' said Lakshman. *But …*

Ram looked at Lakshman and smiled, then turned back to Vashishtha. 'You are right, Guruji. This can work.'

Vashishtha had just suggested a battle strategy to Ram. Elephants had been used by Indian armies for decades; even a small number of well-trained tuskers could be devastating to enemy cavalry. They could also break the enemy infantry lines. Elephants often led the charge. They hammered and broke enemy barricades, creating openings for the cavalry and the infantry to swoop in and complete the task.

Vashishtha nodded. 'Lanka has wild elephants too, but they have not been trained for war. The Lankans have never bothered to tame and harness the power of elephants.'

'And why would they?' asked Ram. 'Lanka is an island. They don't need to defend against land attacks. Naval threats are their main worry. And nobody has thought of building ships that can carry elephants across the seas.'

'And nobody has ever marched an army across to Lanka either,' said Vashishtha, smiling slightly. 'We will simply make our elephants walk across to Lanka. We can destroy their cavalry with just a hundred, or even fifty, war elephants.'

'Just one minor, tiny, insignificant, little problem,' said Lakshman. 'The Lankans don't have war elephants. Neither do we. Marching elephants all the way from Ayodhya will take too many months. We don't have that much time to rescue Sita *bhabhi.*'

'We don't need our own elephants,' said Vashishtha. 'We'll get them from our allies.'

'Who? The Malayaputras?' asked Ram. 'But why would Guru Vishwamitra help us attack Lanka? He might want to attack Lanka himself!'

Only the Malayaputras had trained war elephants in the region. Or so Ram thought. The Malayaputra capital, Agastyakootam, was a mere hundred kilometres to the south of Shabarimala. But it was obvious that he could expect very little help from the Malayaputras.

'Not them,' answered Vashishtha.

'Then who?' asked Ram.

'The Vaanars.'

The Vaanars were the legendary dynasty that ruled the land of Kishkindha along the Tungabhadra River, around six hundred and fifty kilometres north of Shabarimala. A fabulously wealthy people, they were known to be allies of Lanka. They were ruled by the warrior king Vali.

'They have war elephants?' asked Lakshman.

'Exceptionally well-trained ones,' said Vashishtha.

'But I have been hearing strange reports of King Vali,' said Ram. 'Lakshman, Sita and I met him briefly many years ago. During a Jallikattu tournament. He was brave but foolhardy. Almost like he *wanted* to die. I have heard he was, and still is, very noble. A good ruler. But for the last decade or so, he has been exceptionally aggressive. He has attacked many kingdoms around his domain and then, inexplicably, not annexed the lands of his defeated enemies. It's almost like he craves the bloodlust of battle.'

'Hmm,' said Vashishtha. 'I don't know what the reason for that is. I'll find out.'

'But these repeated wars would have made his army battle-tested,' said Lakshman. 'An army that has been blooded is an army that knows how to make the enemy bleed. The Lankan army – and let's be honest, the Ayodhya army too – has not fought a real battle in a long time. The Vaanar army would be a formidable partner for us to have.'

'So how do we ally with him, Guruji?' asked Ram.

'Lanka has been taking away a significant part of the trade earnings of Kishkindha for a long time. King Vali has honoured that treaty. He isn't strong enough to take on Lanka, even in its present weakened state. But the combined armies of Ayodhya and Kishkindha can certainly defeat Lanka. He can then renegotiate the treaty and have more money to spare for his own people.'

'We will have the army of Kekaya as well,' said Ram.

Kekaya was ruled by Bharat's grandfather, Ashwapati. It was well-known that King Ashwapati, who had been a loyal ally of Ayodhya while Emperor Dashrath was alive, had tried to increase his influence when Bharat became the surrogate ruler. The king of Kekaya must have assumed that his grandson, the son of his daughter Kaikeyi, could be easily boxed into a subordinate role. But Bharat, loyal to his elder brother Ram, had pushed back. Ashwapati and his allied clan of the Anunnaki had not taken this well.

'Kekaya will not come, Dada,' said Lakshman. 'Not according to the information Naaradji has collected from his extensive spy network.'

Ram suffered from a shortcoming found in many honourable people. They assume that others – or at least, most people – are also honourable. 'King Ashwapati will come, I am sure. Whatever be his differences with us, he will support a *dharmic* war against one who has hurt India.'

'Dada,' said Lakshman, sighing, 'I hate to tell you this, but you are wrong about Kekaya.'

'Anyway,' interrupted Vashishtha, 'let's save this conversation for later. We'll know soon enough if Kekaya and the Anunnaki are coming or not. Let's focus on the Vaanars. King Vali is a devotee of Lord Ayyappa. He'll be arriving in Shabarimala in a few days. Let's ask him then.'

'All right,' said Ram.

Chapter 10

'No killings,' whispered Hanuman.

Hanuman, Sursa and the Vayuputra soldiers had reached Sigiriya without incident. Late in the night, they made their way quietly to the gates of *Ashok Vatika*. Sursa had found out, from her spies within Sigiriya, that Sita had been imprisoned in the *Garden of No Grief*. Leaving the soldiers behind, Hanuman and Sursa scoped out the security at the fabled garden complex. They were now contemplating how to enter the citadel, which was protected by an alert and well-trained platoon of women soldiers.

'You didn't hesitate to kill the soldiers at the lighthouse,' hissed Sursa. 'Are you trying to be "sensitive" because the guards here are women?'

'No, that's not what—'

Sursa interrupted Hanuman, anger bubbling within her like molten lava. 'I thought you were better than that, Hans

… Bloody patriarchy! Women are never given the respect of equality, even when they are warriors!'

Hanuman kept his irritation at bay. 'There's nothing patriarchal about this. A soldier is a soldier. It doesn't matter if they are male or female. I don't want any killing here for a different reason. Nobody will notice for some time that the soldiers at the lighthouse have been killed. Out here, people will.'

'What difference does that make? By the time they realise it, we would have escaped with Queen Sita.'

Hanuman did not respond.

Sursa took a moment to understand. 'Goddamit! You expect Sita to refuse to come with us?'

Hanuman nodded. *Yes.*

'What the hell is wrong with her? Why would she want to remain in this hellhole?' Sursa was clearly exasperated.

'Because she doesn't just think about tomorrow. Queen Sita also tends to think about the day after tomorrow.'

Sursa rolled her eyes. 'I haven't put my life at risk and come all the way here for philosophical lessons. Either we are saving her or we are not.'

'For now, I have to get in without killing or hurting these guards. Let's concentrate on the task at hand.'

'I suppose you wouldn't want the guards to even know that someone has entered Ashok Vatika.'

'Correct,' said Hanuman. He knew that Sursa had spent time in Lanka negotiating Naarad's trade deals. Maybe she could come up with a scheme. 'Do you have any ideas?'

Sursa took a deep breath. She looked up, towards the high walls of the garden, and said softly, 'I may have one. But there will be a cost.'

'What cost?'

She turned towards Hanuman. A wicked smile played on her face. 'You will have to kiss me.'

Hanuman stared back at her, his face deadpan. 'Madam, I have told you so many times, please desist from such talk.'

'Why do you have to suddenly get so formal?'

'I ... Madam, please, can we focus on the task at hand? I mean no insult to you and your beauty, but ...'

'My beauty? You noticed?'

Hanuman hissed softly in anger, conscious that they were in enemy territory and should remain undetected. 'Madam, please understand what I'm trying—'

Sursa waved her hand to get him to stop. 'All right, all right. You could have just said no, Hans.'

Hanuman kept quiet.

'I'll figure something out,' said Sursa. 'Let's rejoin the rest of the group.'

—Jᚠ ᚂᚄD—

'Something is not right,' whispered Sursa.

She had just returned from a recce of Ashok Vatika, having crept close to the main gates and all the secret entrances she knew of already. Hanuman and the Vayuputra soldiers had waited deep in the forest. They were surprised at how quickly she had returned. She couldn't have done a thorough job so quickly.

'What happened?' asked Hanuman.

'All the guards are asleep,' said Sursa.

'Maybe they are tired, Lady Sursa,' suggested a Vayuputra soldier, the youngest of the lot.

Sursa sneered. 'These are Lankan soldiers. Their training is better than what the Vayuputras receive.' She turned to Hanuman. 'What do you think?'

Hanuman observed her thoughtfully. 'I know it would have been very difficult, but did you manage—'

'Yes, I did,' interrupted Sursa. 'I actually tiptoed up to one of the sleeping guards and held a finger under her nose. Deep asleep. Very fast breathing. Abnormally fast. Shallow and irregular. Her nose was slightly blueish. I noticed the slight discolouration of a few other noses too.'

'They've been drugged,' said Hanuman.

'Yes.'

Hanuman frowned. And then it struck him. 'The Malayaputras have arrived.'

'Precisely what I was thinking,' Sursa said.

'Guru Vishwamitra would only trust one man with this job.'

Sursa nodded. 'Arishtanemi.'

Hanuman smiled.

Sursa frowned. 'So, Arishtanemi likes you, does he?'

'Of course he does.' And then, seeing Sursa's expression, Hanuman asked the obvious question. 'Are you telling me he doesn't like you?'

'He hates me.'

'Why?'

Sursa smiled. 'I can be … difficult.'

Hanuman laughed softly.

'It's best that I stay out of the way,' said Sursa. 'I'll go inside Ashok Vatika with you. I'll guide you to the cottages in the centre, which is the only place where Queen Sita could be held prisoner. But I'll ensure that Arishtanemi does not see me. He too must be here to convince Queen Sita to leave with him. How you persuade her to leave with you instead is up to you.'

Hanuman nodded.

'But I am not going to wait very long,' continued Sursa. 'Finish this quickly. We must leave Ashok Vatika before first light.'

'All right.'

—— ꓘ† ꓘꓸꓸ ——

Guided by Sursa, Hanuman slipped into the clearing in the centre of the legendary garden, in sight of the cottages. Sursa and the Vayuputra soldiers remained behind the treeline. The night was faintly illuminated by a crescent moon; it was *Chaturthi* in *Shukla paksh*, the fourth day of the waxing moon cycle of the month.

Hanuman could hear some voices.

'Queen Sita, you cannot be so stubborn,' he heard an obviously exasperated Arishtanemi say.

'I've made my decision already, Arishtanemiji,' said Sita, with utmost politeness. 'My sincere apologies, but nothing you say can change my mind. Please—'

'I have something that may change your mind,' interrupted Hanuman, speaking from where he stood in the darkness.

Arishtanemi instinctively reached for his sword. Upon seeing Hanuman, he relaxed.

'Hanu *bhaiya*!' cried Sita, her face lighting up. She arose and embraced her brother warmly.

'How are you doing, Sita?' asked Hanuman.

Sita smiled as she stepped back and looked at Arishtanemi. 'Not very well right now. Struggling to explain to Arishtanemiji that I cannot come with him.'

'While I, on the other hand, am struggling for another explanation,' said Arishtanemi, bemused. 'How in Lord Parshu Ram's name did you come this far without my soldiers stopping you? They're just behind the treeline. I need to fire them all.'

'Don't blame them,' said Hanuman, laughing softly. 'They know me. They are chatting with my Vayuputras even as we speak.'

Arishtanemi looked at the treeline in the darkness beyond. Imagining wistfully the bonhomie between his Malayaputra soldiers – the followers of the sixth Vishnu, Lord Parshu Ram – and their friends from the Vayuputra tribe – the followers of the Mahadev, Lord Rudra. The companionable banter.

'If only we could work together,' said Arishtanemi to Hanuman. 'We could solve all these problems so easily.'

Hanuman smiled. 'True. But that's not possible unless Guru Vashishtha and Guru Vishwamitra sort out their problems.'

Arishtanemi shook his head and sighed. 'Anyway, since you are here, Hanuman, please try to convince your sister to come with us.'

'There is no argument that can convince me,' said Sita.

'You are not safe here, my sister,' said Hanuman.

'I am.'

'But Raavan is a mercurial monster,' said Arishtanemi. 'He could turn on you any instant.'

'No, he won't,' said Sita. She hid her astonishment as she watched Arishtanemi's expression change ever so slightly. *Does he know who my birth-mother was? Does he know why Raavan will never hurt me?*

Hanuman, on the other hand, knew nothing about Vedavati. 'Sita, Arishtanemi is correct. We cannot trust Raavan. You are not safe here. We have to leave now.'

'No. I know I am safe here.'

'What makes you so sure?' Hanuman asked, exasperated.

Sita had a simple answer. 'Kumbhakarnaji.'

Sita was aware that both Arishtanemi and Hanuman thought highly of Raavan's younger brother.

'But Kumbhakarna cannot control Raavan all the time,' said Hanuman.

Sita answered immediately. 'He has till now, Hanu *bhaiya*.'

'What are their demands?' asked Arishtanemi. His mind raced to consider what it might mean if Sita knew about Raavan's love for her birth-mother, Vedavati.

'You know that already, Arishtanemiji,' answered Sita. 'And their demands are legitimate.'

'I don't know what they want – we haven't received any letter.'

'I am sure you will receive one soon, then,' said Sita. She had already suggested to Raavan and Kumbhakarna that a letter be sent to the Malayaputras. 'They want the medicines that keep Raavan and Kumbhakarna alive.'

'Why are you so interested in keeping them alive?'

'Because the Vishnu has to come and defeat them in battle,' said Sita. 'A great battle. That's when the common folk in India will learn to trust and follow the Vishnu.'

Arishtanemi's heart flickered with hope. 'So you do agree with Guru Vishwamitra's plans?'

'Oh, yes, I do,' answered Sita. 'Except that the Vishnu who will defeat Raavan will not be me. It will be Ram.'

Arishtanemi drew in a sharp breath, irritated. 'You are the Vishnu.'

Hanuman cut in. 'And Sita, you should know that Ram himself does not believe he should be a Vishnu. I'm carrying a letter from him,' he said, holding it out.

Sita smiled as she grabbed the letter from Hanuman. She could guess what was written in it. But she wasn't interested in the words. She needed to touch it because her Ram had touched it.

Sita smelled the letter, her eyes moistening. She caressed the paper lovingly, as if it were Ram's hand. A faint, wistful smile played on her lips.

Hanuman also smiled as he continued, 'I have something else from him as well.'

Sita looked up.

Hanuman reached into the pouch tied to his cummerbund and fished out Ram's ring. Sita reached for it with a longing that was indescribable. She kissed the jewelled ring made from the finest gold. She slid it onto her index finger and gazed at it lovingly. She let out a long breath and then reached for her earrings. She took them off and gave them to Hanuman. 'Give these to my Ram.'

'Why don't you give them yourself? Come with me,' said Hanuman.

'No,' said Sita firmly.

Arishtanemi spoke. 'Queen Sita, even a blind man can see the love you feel for your husband. Return to him. Allow us to take you to your husband.'

'No.'

'In the name of all that is good and holy, why?'

'Because he is not only my husband. He is also the Vishnu.'

Arishtanemi turned to Hanuman and shook his head with annoyance. His hand went to his forehead, rubbing it slightly to control his rising anger.

Sita ignored the duo and turned her attention to Ram's letter. She broke the seal and unrolled the papyrus. The message from her husband was clear.

'Come back with Lord Hanuman. You are the Vishnu. The Vishnu has no right to unnecessarily put her own person at risk. We will return to Lanka with an army later. We will teach Raavan a lesson in dharma.*'*

Sita smiled and kissed the letter, leaving traces of her fragrance on it. Then she picked up a writing stylus fashioned from graphite and wrote her reply on the same papyrus.

'No. I will not return. You will come here. You are my Vishnu. I am your wife. It is your dharma *to fight for me. So, fight for me.'*

'Give this to him, Hanu *bhaiya*,' said Sita, handing the letter to Hanuman. Then she turned to Arishtanemi. 'Arishtanemiji, regardless of what Guru Vishwamitra may say, I expect you, and those loyal to the Vishnu, to join the battle on the rightful side. You will stand behind Ram when he fights Raavan. This is a *dharmayudh*, a *war for dharma*. There are no bystanders in a *dharmayudh*.'

Arishtanemi remained silent.

Sita continued, 'Please go back now. Go with Lord Rudra and Lord Parshu Ram.'

— Jᖴ ꝉᕽD —

'Goddammit,' whispered Arishtanemi.

Hanuman and Arishtanemi were walking back towards the gates of Ashok Vatika, having left Sita behind at her cottage.

Hanuman looked at his friend and smiled. 'What are you going to say to Guru Vishwamitra?'

'What can I say? I failed. It's as simple as that.'

'Guruji doesn't react well to bad news. Or failure.'

'I know. Hence the "Goddammit"!'

Hanuman laughed softly. 'And what are you going to do?'

Arishtanemi stopped in his tracks and looked back towards the trees and into the darkness. Beyond lay the many cottages, with the main one in the centre. In which she sat, the one he respected as the Vishnu. Arishtanemi turned towards Hanuman. 'She would make such a fantastic Vishnu.'

Hanuman nodded and smiled. 'Yes, she would.'

'Ram would make a wonderful Vishnu as well.'

'Yes, that's also true.'

Arishtanemi laughed. 'This is not going according to plan.'

'When has the story arc of any Vishnu or Mahadev in the past gone according to plan?'

Arishtanemi smiled and nodded. 'True.'

Hanuman started walking again towards the gates. 'So, what will you do?'

Arishtanemi walked alongside his friend. 'What else can I do? I have orders from my Vishnu. I will fight in King Ram's army.'

'And Guruji?'

Arishtanemi shrugged his shoulders and sighed. 'That … That will be a difficult conversation. But it's not for today. Let's—'

Arishtanemi's words were interrupted by a loud feminine voice.

'So, two great champions couldn't convince a young queen to accompany them!'

Arishtanemi stopped in his tracks. His eyes closed, his shoulders drooped. He released a long sigh. *Sursa.*

'How much worse will this day get?' he mumbled.

Sursa burst into laughter as she punched Arishtanemi on his shoulder. 'Arishtanemi, you useless wastrel, it will get much, much worse. We are travelling back together.'

Arishtanemi looked at Hanuman, his expression blank.

'It makes sense to travel back together, Arishtanemi,' said Hanuman. 'There is strength in numbers. We will be able to leave Lanka safely.'

Sursa sniggered. 'And Arishtanemi could certainly use some strength. He once lost a duel with me.'

'That was because …' Arishtanemi stopped himself in time. He composed himself and said in a low voice, 'Let's get moving. The sun will be rising soon.'

Chapter 11

'Hmm,' said Vali, thoughtfully rubbing his chin.

The king of Kishkindha had arrived in Shabarimala the previous day, after completing the forty-one-day *vratham*. He had performed his *darshan* and worshipped at the temple. Since the *puja* was completed, he was not dressed in black now. He was also free of the vow of non-violence, a very strict part of the *vratham*.

'What do you say, King Vali?' asked Ram. 'Will you support us in this battle against *adharma*?'

Ram, accompanied by his *guru* Vashishtha and brother Lakshman, had come to the guest house that King Vali was staying in. Vali had readily agreed to meet Ram, for he was, after all, the king-in-absentia of Ayodhya and, technically, the overlord of the Sapt Sindhu. Ram had informed Vali about the kidnapping of Sita by the king of Lanka. He had requested the use of the Kishkindha elephant corps in the imminent battle against Raavan.

'But how will you take my elephants to Lanka?' asked Vali, intrigued.

'We have a plan,' said Vashishtha. He was still not sure if he could trust Vali, despite all the assurances he had received from Shabari. She had said unequivocally that the king of Kishkindha was an honourable man. But Vashishtha did not want to take even the smallest chance of their battle plans reaching the ubiquitous spies of Lanka.

'Hmm,' said Vali again, apparently non-committal.

Vashishtha felt that this was the time to offer the carrot to convince Vali. 'Once we defeat Lanka, the Sapt Sindhu will be happy to revise the trade agreements and double Kishkindha's share in the business with Lanka. The share of the wealth that Lanka corners from the land trade will thereafter go to the rightful owner, the noble kingdom of Kishkindha.'

'Hmm,' repeated Vali.

Vashishtha looked at Ram, not sure what more could be said.

Vali looked at Lakshman. 'I do remember you.'

'And I remember you, Your Highness,' said Lakshman, bringing his hands together in a respectful *namaste*.

Lakshman was usually a tactless man. So, it was surprising that he did not immediately mention that he had saved Vali's life once. This was during a Jallikattu tournament many years ago in a small town called Indrapur. A gargantuan bull would have gored the king of Kishkindha to death had the massive Lakshman not jumped into the fray and waylaid the bull temporarily. Vali had survived. The massive scar running along his left arm was a reminder of that incident. It was a remnant from the many surgeries that had been carried out to repair his shattered left arm. It would have been rude to remind the great king of that day, though. You never reminded a true Kshatriya that you had saved his life. Instead, a true Kshatriya's duty was to remember that he had been saved. And Vali was one of the finest Kshatriyas ever.

Vali turned to Ram. 'But why do you want *only* my elephant corps? Why not take my entire army?'

Ram was surprised. Pleasantly surprised. 'Umm, thank you so much, great king.'

'But there is one condition,' added Vali.

And here we go, thought Vashishtha, expecting some further haggling on the trade deal. But even he couldn't have guessed what came next.

'I demand a duel.'

'What?' asked Ram, stunned.

'You heard me,' said Vali. 'I want a duel. With you.'

'Why?'

'Why not?' asked Vali. 'My terms are very simple. If I win, you don't get my elephant corps. If you win, you not only get my elephant corps, but also my entire army.' Then Vali turned to Vashishtha. 'And I don't want that silly trade deal, Guruji. I am happy with the terms of trade as they are. If Ayodhya defeats Lanka, you can keep all the extra gold from the Lanka overland business. All I want is my duel with the king of Ayodhya.'

Ram and Vashishtha were stunned.

'I hear that Sugreev is here – that indolent cretin of a brother I have been cursed with. Ask that halfwit to come and watch how two real men fight.'

Lakshman was aghast. 'But ...'

Vali turned to Lakshman. 'I understand your shock, mighty Lakshman. For you must be thinking that I am ungrateful. You imagine that you saved my life that day.'

Lakshman glared with thinly concealed anger. Vali was breaking the unwritten code of the Kshatriyas: The debt owed to the one who saves your life is the greatest debt of all. It must be repaid.

'A tiger always fights alone, Prince Lakshman,' said Vali. 'It doesn't matter if he wins or loses, lives or dies. That is the tiger's fate. But receiving help from one weaker than him? A tiger would rather die.'

Ram finally cut in. 'King Vali, I am not sure that this is the best—'

'This is the only deal on the table, king of Ayodhya,' said Vali. 'Take it or leave it. It's up to you. I am here for a week. And I am ready whenever you are.'

Vali stood up, signifying that the meeting was over.

—JF J͵5D—

Rivers are the best passageways in the world. A quick and efficient path to get from the coast to the hinterland, or vice versa. A cutter boat on a river can accommodate many more travellers than a horse on a road. You don't need to stop during mealtimes; you can eat on the boat itself. Most importantly, if you are sailing downriver, a river is a road that moves; it carries you to your destination much quicker.

A few hours later, two cutter boats were navigating the river waters of the Aruvi Aru, having rowed from near Sigiriya to almost the edge of the north-western coast of the island.

One of the boats carried Hanuman, Arishtanemi and Sursa, accompanied by seven soldiers. Ten others were in the boat to the left of it. The Malayaputras and Vayuputras were travelling as a team.

'In a few minutes we will reach the mouth of the river,' whispered Sursa. It was the fifth hour of the first *prahar* of the day, just before dawn. At this time of the year, the sun's rays would break through in an hour and a half at the most. They would be out at sea well before that. 'We have made good time.'

'Yes, we have,' agreed Arishtanemi.

Hanuman was quiet. He was listening intently. His instincts had picked up a warning.

'What's the matter, Hanuman?' asked Arishtanemi softly.

Hanuman looked at him and said, keeping his voice low, 'It's too quiet.'

Good warriors pick up signals from the slightest of sounds. Exceptional ones pick up cues even from silence.

'The brown fish owls are silent,' whispered Hanuman.

Owls are nocturnal creatures. And most owls are silent as they go about their nightly business: flying, hunting, eating. But the brown fish owls, especially common in these parts, were not the quiet type. They made loud hooting sounds: the typical *tu-whoo-hu*, but also the deep hollow *boom-boom* of the exhibitionist male of the species. The most distinctive sound indicating a brown fish owl's presence was its loud, singing wingbeat.

Tonight, there was no sound of wingbeats. Which meant the birds were stationary. Not hunting for food on the seashore, as would be usual at this time of night.

Odd.

Unless they were scared by the presence of another predator.

Perhaps the greatest predator of them all.

Man.

'Do you think we have been detected?' asked Sursa.

'Only one way to find out,' whispered Arishtanemi. 'Let's bank on the right. I'll send two guards out to do a quick reconnaissance.'

Hanuman nodded.

—JF ⟊ЗD—

'Almost half a battalion, Lord Arishtanemi,' said the Malayaputra soldier.

The two guards had just returned from their reconnaissance. They reported that around one hundred and fifty Lankans, armed to the teeth, were lying in ambush at the mouth of the Aruvi Aru River. The place where the sweet waters of the second longest river on the island of Lanka merged into the salty sea waters of the Gulf of Mannar.

They had also seen burning cremation pyres, perhaps of the soldiers killed by Hanuman and the Malayaputras.

'How did they discover the bodies? And our presence?' asked Sursa.

'I don't know,' said Arishtanemi. 'But no point dwelling on that now. If they have sent so many soldiers, they must suspect a big enemy contingent is sailing downriver.'

'Chances are they have sent this information to Sigiriya already,' said Hanuman. 'The Lankans may send more soldiers downriver.'

'We will be stuck in a pincer attack,' said Sursa. 'Lankans behind us, and more Lankans blocking our way at the mouth of the river.'

'There are one hundred and fifty of them, my lady,' said the Malayaputra guard who had returned with the information. 'We are only twenty. We cannot fight our way out of this.'

Hanuman, Arishtanemi and Sursa did not respond. They knew they had very little time. They had to move fast. And there was only one way out of their predicament.

A diversion.

'I'll do it,' said Hanuman. 'I'll take two soldiers with me. Maybe three. You guys wait for my signal and then rush through to the sea at top oar-speed. Pick me up farther north, at the beach. But don't be late. Or else I will be Lankan toast on the Lankan coast.'

Humour among warriors, in the face of death, is a sure sign of courage. And manhood.

Arishtanemi laughed softly. 'The plan is perfect. But it will be *me* creating the diversion. You two make sure that—'

Sursa interrupted Arishtanemi. 'Enough of this testosterone match-up. I'll cause the diversion.'

Hanuman and Arishtanemi looked at her as if she had said something incredibly stupid.

'Really?!' Sursa snapped in response. 'You're going to pull some patriarchal nonsense on me?'

Hanuman showed his irritation. 'Sursa, please stop getting hysterical. This has nothing to do with patriarchy. But it's better if—'

'Why is it better if you two do it? You are big. You move slower than I do. You do not have the skills to create a diversion. I do.'

Arishtanemi made an attempt. 'Sursa …'

'I have spoken, Arishtanemi. You know I will be better at this than either you or Hanuman. If I was a man, you wouldn't be wasting time arguing with me.'

'Sursa …' pleaded Hanuman.

'What does a woman have to do to get respect around here?' asked Sursa.

'It's not about that …'

'It is! You both want to protect me. Protect me? *Me*? I'm one of the finest warriors in the land! You wouldn't think this way if I wasn't a woman. Your job as a warrior is to protect those who are not warriors, be they men or women. And your duty is to take the help of other warriors when you need it, be they men or women.'

Hanuman and Arishtanemi remained silent.

Sursa turned to look at the three guards who had gone on the reconnaissance. They were short. Slim. Lithe.

Perfect. They'll be fast and soundless.

'You three are coming with me,' said Sursa. 'Arm yourselves. Carry as many blades as you can. Bow and arrows too. Short bow. Make sure your leather armour is tight, both front and back. Keep the thighs clear. We will be running fast and hard.'

The guards nodded and rushed to obey.

Sursa turned to Hanuman and Arishtanemi. 'When you hear loud noises from up north, that will be your cue to sail out. Row fast. Get to the sea quickly. Then turn north.'

'Yes,' said Arishtanemi. He held Sursa's arms, just below the elbow. 'Go with Lord Parshu Ram, brave Sursa.'

Sursa nodded, and then looked at Hanuman.

Hanuman drew his knife from his side scabbard. He slid the blade across his thumb, drawing blood. He smeared the blood on Sursa's forehead in a firm stroke. In the tradition of the great brother-warriors of yore, it sealed the pact that his blood would protect her.

'Go with Lord Rudra, noble Sursa,' whispered Hanuman.

Sursa smiled. 'One day I will force you do that with something other than blood. And maybe not my brow but a little higher, on the parting of my hair.'

Hanuman laughed softly.

Humour among warriors, in the face of death, was a sure sign of warriorhood.

'Pick me up north of the lighthouse,' said Sursa. 'The spot where we beached our boat while coming in.'

Hanuman nodded. *Yes.*

'And we'll be coming with the Lankans in hot pursuit. Be ready.'

'We will,' answered Hanuman. 'You make sure you get there alive.'

'That I will,' said Sursa.

— ⅃⸕ ⅃⸗ⅅ —

Sursa had read the Lankans right. She knew their standard tactics.

Lankans never trusted animals completely. Or more accurately, they didn't trust the trainers who trained their war animals. Therefore, unless it was absolutely necessary, they kept their war animals at a distance when setting up an ambush. An ambush required stealth. They didn't trust their animals to be stealthy and quiet.

Sursa and the three soldiers moved through the jungles, quick-footed and silent. They raced along a long arc, avoiding any unnecessary encounters with the enemy soldiers. Soon they were up north, far beyond the point where the Lankan soldiers lay in ambush.

Sursa held up her right hand. Fists closed. The men came to a halt.

They were behind the enemy lines now. Every unnecessary word must be avoided. Quietude was their best shield.

In the dark skies, the moonlight was faint.

Sursa whispered, pointing, 'There.'

About a hundred metres ahead of them, over one hundred and fifty horses were confined. Some were, unwisely, tied to thin trees that they had wound themselves around, so that the beasts had become entangled in their ropes. Others were, wisely, tied to stakes hammered into the ground and had swivel room. But none had wind breaks. The animals were restive.

A thick line of trees obfuscated the path to the animals.

Four Lankan soldiers guarded the horses.

Just four.

'Here's the plan,' said Sursa softly, turning to the soldiers. 'We'll get the four Lankans with arrows. Aim for their throats. All at the same time. Into their throats. No screams. No warning to the others. Then we rush forward and release as many horses as we can. As silently as possible. Once that is done, we mount four horses and ride up north, making a lot of noise as we do so. That will be the signal for our comrades in the river to start rowing towards the sea. Hearing the noise we make, the Lankans will rush back to the beach. They will give us chase. But most of them will be on foot. They will be slow. We must stay ahead. Ride hard. Our friends will meet us farther north. We will ride into the sea. Into the sea, boys. As far as the horses will carry us. And then we jump off and swim to the boats. And from there, we row our way out. Clear?'

The soldiers nodded. *Clear.*

'Remember, they must see as many horses as possible, racing around on the beach. In this dim light they will assume that most of them are mounted. And that all of us are here—their foes. If they see just four, they'll guess that it's a diversion.'

'Yes, Lady Sursa.'

Sursa nodded. She brought her short bow forward and tightened the string on it. Then, like any good archer, she pulled the string and released it close to her ear. To check the cord tension.

Perfect.

Standard warrior rules. Always check the equipment before *battle*.

Her soldiers did the same.

Bows ready. Arrows nocked.

'Let's go,' whispered Sursa.

They moved forward stealthily. And came to a halt some forty metres from the four Lankans. They were clearly not the best, these Lankans that had been left behind to guard the horses. Clustered together, they were engaged in banter.

The first two rules on guard duty. Do not cluster. Do not gossip. You make yourself an easy target. And you are distracted.

Sloppy.

'One arrow, one kill,' whispered Sursa. 'Mark your target. We'll shoot together on my count. That's the plan.'

It's a cliché that most battle plans don't survive the first contact with the enemy. And most clichés have some measure of truth to them.

Sursa began to count down.

'Three ... two ... one!'

Four arrows were released simultaneously. Three of them found their mark, slamming into the throats of three Lankans. They collapsed almost immediately. Soundless. But one arrow missed by just a bit. It sank into the mid clavicle of the unfortunate Lankan. Between the shoulder and the neck. Painful. Very painful. But not fatal.

The Lankan screamed in agony. It was not loud enough to alert his Lankan comrades at the Aruvi Aru River mouth. But it frightened the horses. And the dumb beasts began to neigh and whinny in alarm.

Sursa cursed. She drew another arrow and fired quickly. Straight at the man's throat. Severing his life, and all sound, immediately.

But the horses were panic-stricken by now. They were straining against the ropes that held them, neighing and bucking.

'Follow me!' roared Sursa. 'Quick!'

She raced ahead, throwing her bow aside. It was of no use now. She drew her short sword. Her soldiers followed. Sprinting hard.

'Release as many horses as you can. Quickly! And drive them towards the beach!'

The soldiers rushed to obey. Unhobbled some of the horses. Cut the reins of those tied to stakes and trees. They had to move fast while avoiding the panicky beasts stomping around.

Some twenty-five to thirty horses had been freed when Sursa ordered, 'Enough! Mount a horse! Ride north! We don't have much time!'

Sursa could hear the Lankan battalion running north. Making loud noises. War cries.

'Ride!' ordered Sursa.

Along with her soldiers, Sursa rode out. Onto the beach. They left the treeline behind.

Too many horses had been left back. Sursa knew that. Horses that would be used by their Lankan enemies. She knew that too.

They had little time.

'Fast!'

She looked back. She could see the flame-torches in the distance. The Lankans were far behind. But not far enough. And they would soon mount their horses.

'Ride hard!' shouted Sursa.

They had to optimise this temporary advantage of being on horseback while the Lankans were still on foot. They had to build as much distance as possible.

It was too dark to see far out to sea. To check if Hanuman and Arishtanemi had managed to row out from the mouth of the river into the sea.

She had to trust that they had done so. She had to.

The alternative was terrifying. For ahead of them, a mere thirty-minute ride on horseback, was the rest of the battalion stationed at the Ketheeswaram temple. There was no other way to escape, except into the sea.

'Ride!' Sursa roared.

Her soldiers kept pace with her.

She looked back. The first Lankans on horseback were in sight. The chase had begun.

Some were riding out from behind the treeline on to the beach. Some had begun shooting arrows. From too far though. They were out of range. For now.

'Here!'

Sursa recognised the place where they had tied their cutter boat earlier.

'Ride into the sea.'

Galloping into the choppy waters would slow down their horses, reducing the distance between the Lankans and Sursa. While the Lankans could never catch up with them, they would come within range of the Lankan arrows soon.

'Ride hard! Push your horses!'

The horses panicked at being led into the sea. Their pace slowed, but, admirably, the magnificent animals did not stop.

'Keep going!' screamed Sursa.

The Lankan arrows were close.

In Lord Rudra's name, be there, Hanuman.

Sursa heard a shout from the distance. She recognised that voice. She loved that voice.

'Sursaaaa ...'

'They're here! Ride on!'

Sursa and her brave soldiers pushed their horses farther into the sea. The ground sloped gently here, so they could ride farther in than they would have been able to in most other parts along the shore. But they knew it was a matter of time before the horses turned back in panic. When their feet could not touch the ground any more. And Sursa could sense that the moment was close.

'Push!'

The horses were neighing loudly now, in protest. But they still kept moving ahead. The Lankan arrows were coming thick and fast, but still falling short. Just out of range.

'Sursaaa!' It was Arishtanemi this time. 'We are coming! Swim out!'

Sursa sensed that the time had come. The horses were about to surrender.

She slid her feet out of the stirrups. And shouted over the din of the waves and the Lankan war cries behind. 'Feet out of stirrups! Prepare to jump!'

Her soldiers obeyed.

'Now! Jump!'

They dived into the sea. And began to swim. Tearing valiantly through the waves which were aggressively pushing them back.

Through the dim moonlight, Sursa saw the two cutter boats rushing towards them.

They swam hard.

Towards their rendezvous.

Towards the boats.

The Lankans pushed their horses into the sea, continuing to fire their arrows.

They were now in range.

The arrows fell all around Sursa and her soldiers. They continued to swim. Hard.

The Lankans were shooting blind in the dim moonlight. They were hoping for sheer numbers to make up for the lack of accuracy.

And make up it did.

One of her soldiers screamed in agony as an arrow pierced his thigh. But he kept swimming.

Sursa looked back. He was falling behind.

The two others had already reached the cutter boats and were clambering on.

'Sursa!' screamed Hanuman, stretching his hand out.

But Sursa turned around and swam towards the injured soldier. Arrows were falling all around them like torrid rain. She reached him and began to pull him towards the boats. One more arrow hit the poor soldier. This time on the shoulder. Sursa pushed him towards the boat and he was speedily pulled in.

An arrow sailed in and slammed into Sursa's shoulder. She roared in agony. Arishtanemi jumped into the water, picked her up, and almost threw her into the boat. He climbed back up.

All the Malayaputras and Vayuputras were safely on board. 'Row back!'

Arrows were raining all around them.

The Malayaputras and the Vayuputras began to row.

'Row back! Hard!'

Hanuman looked at Sursa, his brow creased with concern. He tried to break the shaft of the arrow buried in her shoulder. But, in pulling the soldier along, Sursa's leather armour had come loose. It was making it difficult to break the shaft of the arrow.

'Let it … be …' whispered Sursa, still out of breath.

'Sursa …' Hanuman moaned. He recognised the arrow. It was one of the specially created ones. Expensive. The serrated reversed-edges made it difficult for them to be pulled out. And they were, usually, poisoned.

Sursa smiled. 'I'm okay … Just a scratch …'

Humour among warriors, in the face of death, was a sure sign of true warriorhood.

Hanuman smiled. It was a serious injury, but not too serious. The poisoned arrow was worrisome, but it had only embedded itself in the shoulder, not a major organ. She had not lost consciousness. They would reach the Indian coast in an hour or two. They would rush to the closest village from the landing point and pull the arrow out. And stitch up and medicate the wound.

The wound was bad, but not too bad.

As the soldiers continued rowing hard, the boats began to move rapidly, out of range of the arrows. Or so it seemed.

The ancients say that even the best foreteller cannot beat female intuition. Sursa suddenly had a sense of foreboding. Without a thought, she thrust Hanuman aside and turned around, covering him with her own body.

The arrow came in hard. With demonic precision. And timing. It pounded into Sursa's abdomen. If only her leather armour had not come undone earlier. If only.

The cruel arrow rammed deep inside her, slicing through her major organs. The kidney, the liver, even the intestines.

Sursa collapsed backwards onto Hanuman as Arishtanemi rushed towards her.

Hanuman held Sursa in his arms. 'SURSAAA ...'

The soldiers did not stop. They kept rowing. Moving the boats deep into the sea. Away from the Lankan arrows.

Sursa struggled to breathe as she looked down at the arrow buried deep in her abdomen. She recognised the arrow now. She knew her time had come.

Hanuman turned towards the rowers. 'Faster! Get us to the mainland! Quick!'

Sursa held Hanuman's hand. 'It's okay ... It's okay ...'

Arishtanemi was crying inconsolably. 'Sursa ...'

Sursa didn't look at him. Her eyes were pinned on Hanuman.

Hanuman was sobbing. 'It should have been me … It should have been me …'

'It's all right … It's all right …' said Sursa, struggling against the darkness. Refusing to fall into the deep sleep. Not yet. Not yet. She had things to say. 'I had three dreams, Hans …'

Hanuman could not meet her eyes. He looked at the arrow. The flood of blood bursting forth. It was over. No hope.

He finally looked at Sursa's face. His eyes were clouded with tears.

'One dream …' said Sursa softly, 'was to win your love … Another, to die in your arms … And the third … to see you cry when I die …'

'Sursa …' Hanuman whispered.

Sursa smiled. The darkness was closing in. 'Two out of three is not bad … Two out of three … not bad …'

Hanuman closed his eyes, tears streaming down his face.

'Look at … me,' whispered Sursa.

Hanuman opened his eyes.

'I love you, Hans …' murmured Sursa. She looked into the eyes she loved, and then allowed herself to slip into unconsciousness. Into the darkness.

Arishtanemi reached out and held Sursa's hand. He sobbed like a child. He knew this was the last time he was hearing Sursa's voice.

Chapter 12

'This is truly bizarre,' said Vashishtha.

Vashishtha was sitting on a mat in Shabari's simply appointed hut. He had visited the wise woman right after the strange meeting with the king of Kishkindha. He needed her sage advice. The meeting hadn't panned out the way Vashishtha had imagined. Not by a long shot.

Shabari raised her chin and looked out of the window. Towards the temple of Lord Ayyappa in the distance. She held back her words.

'What kind of an outlandish demand is this?' asked Vashishtha. 'A duel with the emperor of Sapt Sindhu as a condition to support him with the Kishkindha army! And only doing so if he loses. Bizarre.'

Shabari said softly, 'Perhaps the rumours are true ...'

Vashishtha narrowed his eyes. 'Rumours? What rumours?'

'I have been hearing them for some time,' said Shabari. 'But I did not give them much credence.'

'What rumours, Shabariji?' repeated Vashishtha.

Shabari looked at Vashishtha. 'Guruji, it seems that Angad was conceived through *niyoga*.'

'What?' asked a stunned Vashishtha.

Niyoga was an ancient tradition in India that stretched back to the hoary past. According to its tenets, a woman married to a man who was incapable of fathering a child could request another man to impregnate her. Usually, she would turn to a *rishi*. For one, the intellectual prowess of the *rishi* could pass on, genetically, to the offspring. More importantly, *rishis* were wandering mendicants and would not lay claim to the child. A child born of a union sanctioned by *niyoga* would, for all practical and societal purposes, be the legitimate child of the woman and her legal husband; the biological father would ideally remain anonymous.

'I have heard that Vali was once grievously injured while saving the cowardly Sugreev. It happened a long time ago during a hunt. As a result of the injuries, and the medicines administered at the time, Vali can't father children.'

'Sugreev has always been a burden on the royal family of Kishkindha,' said Vashishtha. 'But what does this have to do with Vali challenging Ram to a duel?'

'His anger.'

'But why is Vali angry? I don't understand. Our traditions allow *niyoga*. Nothing wrong with it. His wife Tara's child is his child. I understand his anger with his idiot brother, Sugreev. But I don't see the connection. And why is this unfocused anger directed at everyone? Towards Ram? That makes no sense. Not for one as noble as Vali.'

'It's a lot more complex …' said Shabari. 'I have heard that Queen Mother Aruni decided to …'

Shabari hesitated.

'Decided to ... what?' asked Vashishtha.

'You know what Aruni was like.'

'Yes ... She was ... headstrong and stubborn. So, what did she do?'

'Well, apparently she wanted to ensure that it was her bloodline on the throne. So, she ...'

Vashishtha understood. 'Lord Rudra have mercy!'

Queen Mother Aruni's other son. Sugreev.

Vashishtha held his head with both hands. He was dumbstruck. The *niyoga* ritual had been performed by Sugreev. Angad was the biological son of Sugreev.

'This is beyond belief!'

'I know,' agreed Shabari.

Vashishtha now understood Vali's anger and pain. And then something else struck him. 'But this would have been a secret. The *niyoga* would have happened in the Himalayas, according to tradition. How did King Vali discover the truth?'

'There are rumours that Queen Mother Aruni told him herself. On her deathbed.'

Vashishtha's mouth fell open in shock. 'Why did she do that? Why didn't she just keep quiet? Why inflict the truth on someone if it does him no good and only causes pain?'

'Guilt, perhaps? She had wronged Vali. Perhaps she thought that speaking the truth would ease her conscience. Cleanse her soul of the sin.'

'No. You cannot cleanse your soul with selfishness. By telling Vali the truth, she condemned him to a lifetime of torment. And all this just to alleviate her own feeling of guilt before dying. It was a most selfish act.'

Shabari nodded in agreement.

'But Vali loves his son, Angad. That is so obvious.'

'He does love him,' agreed Shabari.

'Angad doesn't know, I hope.'

'I don't think so,' answered Shabari. 'And I don't think the lay public does either. Or even the royals in the Sapt Sindhu. It's only our *rishi* and *rishika* circles that seem to have some inkling of it.'

'Why didn't you tell me about this?'

'I don't indulge in unsubstantiated rumour-mongering, Vashishthaji. But Vali's conduct makes me suspect it's true. I thought his frequent military expeditions were a quest for glory. Now, I understand… he was swinging between his innately noble character and furious rage at what life has done to him.'

Vashishtha let out a long breath. 'Oh, Lord Agni …'

Shabari stared ahead, unblinking.

Vashishtha, single-mindedly committed to what he thought was good for India, saw the situation clearly. Beyond the human emotions at play.

'We cannot defeat Raavan without the elephant corps,' said Vashishtha. 'We need it.'

'True.'

'Perhaps I should advise Ram to go ahead with the duel.'

'Perhaps you should,' agreed Shabari.

Neither of them verbalised the obvious truth. *Vali's unchecked emotions and rage would make him easier to defeat.*

— JF J5D —

'A longsword?' muttered Lakshman, surprised.

Naarad frowned and shrugged.

It was Ram who had been challenged, making it his right to select the type of weapon for the duel. The gallant Ram, though, had offered the choice of weapon to Vali. And Vali had, inexplicably, chosen the longsword. It was odd. Very odd. Vali was muscular and strong, but of medium height. Ram was leaner but much taller, touching six feet in height. A sword master would have advised Vali to pick a short sword. And keep close during the duel, giving Ram as little room as possible, reducing his advantage of a longer reach. By choosing a longsword that was normally held with both hands while fighting, Vali had handed Ram an obvious edge.

'What is King Vali thinking?' asked Lakshman.

Almost all the denizens of the temple complex had gathered to watch the duel. It could obviously not be staged within the temple complex. That would be *adharma*. So, they had gathered at an open training ground, with amphitheatre-style stands built around it, at the base of the hill. The temple was clearly visible in the distance.

Two thousand people stood in the stands. To watch a duel the likes of which they knew they would probably not see again in their lives. Shabari and Vashishtha stood together, their eyes grimly pinned to the centre. The duellists were stretching their bodies on one side of the ground. They had chosen to duel without any seconds to help them.

Vali walked to the centre of the ground. Fair and hirsute, he strode with his chest out and shoulders back. He began to swing his arms, making wide arcs with his sword. Imperious and cocky. Exhilarated. Ram, dark-skinned, tall and sinewy, walked alongside. Head raised. Measured footsteps. Swinging his arms and loosening his limbs in a controlled manner. Focused and deliberate.

Vali thrust his sword into the soft ground, went down on his knees, and faced the great Shabarimala temple in the distance. Ram gently placed his sword on the ground, touched it and brought his hands to his brow in reverence. Offering respect to his weapon. Then he too went down on his knees and faced the temple.

Both the warriors folded their hands in unison and prayed to Lord Ayyappa – among the greatest warriors who had ever walked the holy land of India.

They ended their prayer with a chant familiar to all who are loyal to the Lord.

'Swamiye Sharanam Ayyappa.'

We find refuge at the feet of Lord Ayyappa.

The entire assemblage echoed the prayer. *'Swamiye Sharanam Ayyappa.'*

Ram picked up his sword, rose and held it out. Vali tapped Ram's blade with his own. Tradition before the duel.

The swords are supposed to tap each other and whisper before the murderous argument begins.

Ram looked at Vali and smiled. Vali responded with a curt nod. And they walked to their respective starting lines. Vali looked at his son, Angad. He stood at the edge of the combat circle, a short distance from Shabari and Vashishtha.

Angad. A little less than twenty years of age, he was the spitting image of Vali, his legal father. Fair-skinned. Hirsute. Ridiculously muscled. Gladdening the hearts of all those who looked upon the likeness between father and son. But Vali knew better. For his brother, Sugreev, was also his exact replica.

Vali breathed in deeply and shook his head. Then glanced at Ram. The contestants turned to Shabari and bowed low.

Shabari announced, 'May Lord Ayyappa grant victory to the most worthy.'

And with that the duel began.

Ram, ever the orthodox swordsman, abided strictly by his training. He held the longsword with both hands and angled his body sidewards, offering less target room to his opponent. His sword pointed straight ahead.

Vali held the sword in his right hand, pointing to one side. His body fully exposed. Reckless. As if with a death wish.

Suddenly, the king of Kishkindha roared and charged. As he came close, he pirouetted with abandon, swinging his right arm viciously as he turned. But with no control. Ram bent backwards and effortlessly blocked the blow.

This was rash beyond measure. Pivoting and swinging from a distance while charging in can be a wildly riveting sight in theatrical plays. It always drew applause and loud gasps from audiences who knew no better. But it was unwise. It meant that you turned your back to your opponent for an instant. Ridiculously stupid against a skilled adversary in an actual sword fight. He could simply stab you in the back with ease.

But Ram's integrity was above reproach. He would never stab in the back. He blocked Vali and pushed him away.

Vali turned in the same movement and thrust his longsword forward. Ram had expected this expert manoeuvre. He blocked and pushed Vali's blade aside and swivelled his body. Moving his abdomen out of the way.

And then Vali did something completely unexpected.

He flicked his sword up rapidly, using Ram's sword that was held against his own, as a slide. Vali's strong wrist made the movement so quick that it was difficult to see. Instinctively, Ram threw his head back, avoiding the glancing cut by a microsecond.

Ram stepped back immediately and smiled. Nodding at Vali.

Good one.

Vali, a cocky grin on his face, nodded back slightly.

Ram raised his sword again. Ready.

Vali charged in, dancing on his feet, swinging the sword from the right and then from the left with machine-like precision. Ram took a step back with each defensive stroke, both hands firmly on the grip. The pommel below and cross-guard above kept the sword in place, not allowing Vali to deflect it with his repeated strikes. Ram moved back slowly. Completely orthodox. Or so it seemed.

Vali held the aggressive charge, yelling wildly as he swung his blade hard. It didn't strike him until almost too late. He was walking into a trap.

Ram moved backwards, each step measured and slow. Towards the combat-circle perimeter. Intending to move to the side at the boundary. Vali was now committed to his aggressive forward charge. He would not be able to avoid the deep cut on the elbow that would incapacitate his sword arm.

But Vali pulled back just in time, whirled around, extending his elbows up, with both hands behind his shoulders and holding the sword downwards vertically behind his back. Protecting his back from a blow as he retreated.

As Vali turned around, he found Ram staring at him with narrowed eyes. Forehead furrowed. A severe expression on his face.

Vali understood. Ram's honour had been injured. How could he entertain the thought that Ram would strike him from the back? That would be *adharma*.

Ram was the scion of Ikshvaku. The noble descendant of Raghu. He would rather die than win with *adharma*.

Vali held Ram's glare for an instant. A strange expression crossed his face. As if he was now certain.

Shabari saw that look from the distance. And she recognised it instantly. She had seen that look on a man she had loved, many many decades ago. An honourable warrior with a noble Kshatriya desire: death at the hands of a worthy enemy.

Shabari's mouth fell open in shock. She finally understood what Vali wanted. What he was hankering for.

Vali yelled loudly and charged again.

This time, Ram did not just defend. He pushed back hard. Brutally countering each strike of Vali with one of his own. Their blades clashed repeatedly. Vicious swinging strikes. Sparks flew from the steel. He would not just push back now. He began to use Vali's blows as a spring for his own. This was poetry in motion. A warrior's poem, written by the sword, with the ink of courage.

And then ... the masterstroke.

As Vali struck Ram's blade down, Ram flicked his sword up.

An expert strike. An unreal combination of fierce brutality and exquisite precision.

The return swing converted into a jab, splitting the skin above the right brow.

Vali pulled back, roaring in frustration.

Ram spoke loudly. 'Yield!'

'Never!' was the booming answer.

If one did not understand sword fighting, one would be forgiven for wondering why Ram had demanded surrender after a tiny wound on his opponent's forehead. But a bleeding brow would blind one eye with dripping blood. A serious impediment in a sword fight.

Ram only had to wait it out now. Vali would be severely impaired in a few minutes.

The duellists circled each other. Each waiting for the other to strike.

Vali grinned. He roared as he charged again.

He held his sword with both hands this time. Swinging hard repeatedly. The sound of clashing steel echoed all over the ground. The people knew. They felt it in their bones. In their blood. They were watching history in the making. Poets would write verses in homage to this encounter. Singers would sing paeans. Years from now. Millenia from now. This story would defeat time.

Vali swung hard from a low angle, seeking to disembowel Ram. The king of Ayodhya danced back, letting the blow strike the air. He did not block it. Using Vali's momentum, Ram stabbed forward. A low, brutal strike.

He had expected Vali to bring his sword back in time to deflect the weapon and swivel out of the way. What Vali did, instead, was perform a half action. With precision.

He swung his sword down, but not fast enough. Nor did he swivel. His body remained upright.

It was time.

Ram's blade entered the Kishkindha king's abdomen. Unhindered.

It happened so fast that, for a moment, even the audience did not realise what had occurred. Vali did not cry out. Not in agony. Not in anger. Not in shock. He just let out a long-held breath. His sword dropped from his hand. His body slumped. Shabari could see his eyes. They didn't show the shock of pain, but the peace of release.

Ram stood rooted to the spot. Stunned. *Why didn't Vali swivel out of the way?*

Ram released his hold on his sword.

It was lodged too deep inside; it had pierced the vital organs.

Stillness in the air.

A kill wound. It was over for the valiant Vali.

The king of Kishkindha fell back, his strength ebbing. Ram reached forward and held him, gently easing him to the ground.

'Father!' screamed Angad, running towards Vali.

Ram looked at Angad, and then at Vali. Shocked. Helpless. *Why did he not move out of the way?*

Vali's eyes rested on Angad. Finding the strength to pull his reginal ring from his finger, he slid the bloodied symbol on to Angad's forefinger.

His son. His heir.

Vali was publicly acknowledging him as the next rightful ruler of his people. 'You will be king now... Angad...'

Angad was crying inconsolably. For a father he loved and admired. A father whose approval he had always sought. A father who had strangely, since his grandmother's demise, swung between extremes, sometimes full of deep affection, and at other times, aloof and cold.

Vali held Angad's arm and then pointed to Ram. 'I have promised the king of Ayodhya that our army ... You will ... join him ... Treat him as you would treat me ... Stay with him ... Till the time that Raavan is defeated... Then you will be your own man ...'

Angad wept. 'Father ...'

Ram looked at Vali. At this noble man he had pushed into the arms of death.

'Angad!' said Vali, raising his voice. 'Promise me ... Promise me that you will honour my word ...'

'I will, father ...' whispered Angad through his tears. 'I promise ...'

Vali let out a long sigh. He knew that Angad would never break his promise. Never.

He looked at the Suryavanshi sword buried deep in his abdomen. And then at Ram, kneeling on one knee beside him.

Silent. Respectful. The honourable man who had gifted him death.

He looked around. At his people. Many of them crying. Everyone looking at him with reverence.

Then he turned his eyes towards the temple in the distance. His Lord, his God, Ayyappa.

He finally looked at his son. Angad. Holding his hand in his own.

Perfect.

A worthy death.

Just one thing missing.

The truth.

He understood his mother now. As it prepares to leave the body it is caged in, the soul craves to speak the most important truth. To the most important one in this life.

His mother had to tell him the truth.

He understood her now.

He looked at his son. His boy. He had to tell him the truth. He understood now.

The truth ... The only truth that mattered.

'Angad ...'

Angad was crying.

'Listen ... to me ...'

Angad looked at his father, holding his hand tight.

The truth. The only truth that mattered. It must be spoken.

'I love you, my boy ...' whispered Vali.

'I love you, Father,' cried Angad, pressing his father's hand to his heart.

The blood from the wounded brow was clouding Vali's eyes. And through his blood, he saw his own blood. His son. A man does not become a father merely through his body. A man earns the privilege of fatherhood with his protection, his care, his ability to provide. A man earns fatherhood by being worthy of emulation. A man earns fatherhood through love.

The truth must be spoken. And the only truth that matters is love.

'I love you … my son …'

And, having spoken the truth that mattered, Vali's soul left his mortal body. Ready for its next life.

Chapter 13

'I had told you to stay put in Ayodhya,' said Ram, gently admonishing his brother Bharat. With a smile.

Two weeks after the duel with Vali, Ram had received word that Bharat and Shatrughan had sailed into the Vaigai River which cut across the Tamil lands to the east of Shabarimala. They brought with them a four-hundred-ship-strong navy, each a large vessel that could carry almost two hundred and fifty soldiers. One hundred thousand soldiers had left Ayodhya on these four hundred ships. They had sailed down the Sarayu River till it joined the Ganga, and the great Mother river had safely deposited them in the Eastern Sea. The orderly fleet had then sailed down the east coast of India, right to the mouth of the Vaigai River. At any other time of the year, the Vaigai would not have been able to accommodate such a large fleet. But the south-west monsoon had been particularly bountiful this year. And the Ashwin month had brought the north-east winds, which usually also brought more rain to the Tamil and

Andhra lands. The Vaigai was swollen with floodwaters. It was ready for the task at hand.

Angad had returned to the Kishkindha capital to mobilise his army, as his father had commanded. Ram, Lakshman and Vashishtha had sailed down the Vaigai River with their entourage, to meet Bharat and the Ayodhya navy at the river mouth. They were now on the deck of Bharat's ship. Vashishtha and Naarad had followed Ram and Lakshman aboard.

'I am your younger brother, Dada.' Bharat laughed. 'My job is to do what is in your best interests, not what you order me to do.'

Ram laughed softly and embraced Bharat. Emotions ran high in the two men of strong will. It had been too long. Too long.

'And in any case, Dada,' said Shatrughan, grinning, 'we haven't come for you. We have come for Sita *bhabhi*.'

Ram laughed and extended his left arm. Shatrughan joined the brothers in a bear hug.

'Hey! What about me?' asked Lakshman, raising his hands in the air in mock protest.

'Nobody is interested in you, bro!' Shatrughan laughed.

And Lakshman, with a heart as big as his gigantic body, found tears springing to his eyes. He rushed into the group hug.

Some men don't express love in words but in their actions. And the more love they so express, the more the cutting banter they indulge in.

The four brothers held each other. In a huddle.

Brothers in arms. A fort. Nobody could break them. Nobody.

Vashishtha stood at a distance and smiled.

Naarad turned to Vashishtha and also smiled. 'The brothers truly love each other. That's rare in a royal family. You have done a good job, Guruji.'

'No, no,' said Vashishtha. 'Parents have a greater influence than a mere teacher.'

Naarad looked at Vashishtha with a sly smile on his face. 'If you say so.'

Vashishtha was not a man for unnecessary rejoinders. He smiled.

'They will need this togetherness,' said Naarad. 'Defeating Lanka will be easy. Raavan is merely an opponent. Their actual enemies are in their own land, among their own people. That is when their unity will be truly tested.'

Vashishtha looked at the brothers and spoke with confidence. 'They will never lose this unity.'

— J⊦ �J⊃D —

'Elephants?' asked Bharat, startled. 'Dada, our ships are big … But no ship can carry elephants, to the best of my knowledge.'

The four brothers were supping in the captain's cabin on the royal ship. Vashishtha had wisely left them alone. Allowing them time to reconnect.

Ram smiled. 'Not on the ships. We will march across.'

'March? Walk on water?' asked Bharat.

'Yes,' answered Ram, turning to Shatrughan, who seemed to have cottoned on to the plan already.

Lakshman and Bharat too followed Ram's gaze. Three pairs of eyes rested on the youngest brother. The most intelligent and well-read of them all. The genius.

Shatrughan leaned back and smiled.

'Brilliant …' he whispered. Almost like he was talking to himself.

'Will someone tell me what the hell is going on?' growled Bharat, irritated at being the only one who didn't seem to have a clue.

Shatrughan looked at Ram. 'The sand flats of Dhanushkodi …'

'Bingo!' said Ram, pointing his index finger at Shatrughan.

Shatrughan laughed softly. 'Brilliant … Brilliant … The Lankans will not expect this at all … We'll catch them by surprise.'

'Precisely,' said Lakshman.

Bharat seemed to have also caught on by now. He knew the topography of this part of India. He had occasionally paid attention to the geography lessons conducted by their *guru* Vashishtha all those years ago in the *gurukul*.

South of the Vaigai River mouth, the peninsular part of mainland India extended out into a promontory, jutting into the sea. A mere kilometre and a half of shallow waters separated it from an island called Pamban. Pamban island itself stretched north-west to south-east in the direction of Lanka. Beyond the south-east coast of Pamban island lay Mannar island, separated by around twenty-five kilometres of sea. It also spanned north-west to south-east, almost touching the mother island of Lanka, from which it was separated by a few stray metres of shallow waters.

Bharat had the same thought as Ram had had when Shabari suggested the idea to him. 'I have sailed in these parts before. It might be possible to build some pontoon bridges from the Indian mainland to Pamban Island. The elephants could even swim the short distance. Yes. We can also simply wade across the very tiny distance from Mannar Island to Lanka. Easy. But what about the twenty-five kilometres separating the Pamban and Mannar islands? Fording it is impossible. The waters are too high. And pontoon bridges will not survive the strong high tides. There is no way we can march an army across.'

'We can, if we build a bridge,' said Shatrughan.

'A *bridge* bridge?' asked Bharat. 'As in, a proper bridge?'

'Why would anyone build an improper bridge?'

Bharat burst out laughing and slapped Shatrughan on his shoulder.

'But no, seriously,' said Lakshman, 'do you really think it's possible to build a proper bridge?'

Bharat added with a flourish, 'Yeah... Tell us. For this will be the longest bridge in human history. And it will have to be built even as treacherous tides pull the sea water out and then back in with clockwork precision. We will have a window of no more than six hours from low tide to the next high tide, and then another six hours in reverse. And we have to build this entire bridge in two months flat, for you, Dada, intend to attack just as the north-east monsoon ends.'

Shatrughan nodded. 'It's a bit of a challenge, I admit.'

Ram smiled and patted Shatrughan on the back.

Bharat was not convinced. 'A bit of a challenge? This is impossible! No engineer can pull this off!'

'Correct, no engineer in the world can pull this off,' said Shatrughan, before pointing at himself. 'Except this one!'

Bharat sighed. 'Shatrughan, you know I love you. But this is—'

'Dada,' said Shatrughan, interrupting Bharat. 'You didn't bring me here for my warrior skills, did you?'

Everyone laughed. As far as fighting skills were concerned, Shatrughan had lost the gene pool to the invincible Lakshman. As for intellect, however ...

'Are you sure you can do it, Shatrughan?' asked Ram.

'Do we have a choice, Dada?' Shatrughan countered. 'It's about Bhabhi. I have to get this done.'

Ram, Bharat and Lakshman smiled at their youngest brother.

'Dhanushkodi Setu, the world will call it,' said Lakshman. In the local language, *dhanush* was the *bow*, and *kodi* was the *string of the bow*. 'A bridge across the string of the bow. The greatest bridge ever. The greatest architectural wonder. The greatest monument to what man can do.'

Shatrughan shook his head. 'No. It will be called *Ram Setu*, the *bridge of Ram*. The greatest monument to what man can do, *for love*. And as Lord Rudra is my witness, we will build that bridge.'

— JƎ ꭒ⸝5D —

'We don't have a choice, Guruji,' said Arishtanemi, his head bowed politely. But his voice was firm.

Arishtanemi was with Vishwamitra in the Malayaputra capital of Agastyakootam. Earlier in the day, Hanuman and Arishtanemi had performed the funeral ceremony of Sursa with full Vedic honours. Hanuman had then left, along the Vaigai, to rendezvous with the Ayodhya royals, while Arishtanemi had returned to Agastyakootam.

Vishwamitra nodded in response to Arishtanemi, but did not utter a word.

Vishwamitra knew that Arishtanemi was right. Despite his frustration with Sita for refusing to take up the mantle of the Vishnu, he could not allow for the slightest possibility of Raavan defeating Ram in a battle. That would make it impossible to get Sita to follow his plans. He had only one move left in the game for now: lend support to Ram in this conflict. Which, with the support of the Malayaputras and the Vayuputras, would end in the death of Raavan. Once that was done, he fully intended to bring his plan back on track.

'So, what are our orders, Guruji?'

Vishwamitra smiled wanly. 'The Malayaputras are being forced to support that Vashishtha's candidate. Just because of Sita's obstinacy.'

'True, Guruji. What would you have us do?'

Vishwamitra shook his head and sighed. 'However much I may hate that … that treacherous man, I will always love Mother India more …' Then, almost as if the words were being prised out of him, he announced his decision: 'Take our soldiers. Take our elephant corps. Go join the war.'

'As you say, Guruji,' said Arishtanemi, bowing low with his hands joined in a *namaste*.

As he turned to leave, Vishwamitra raised his hand. 'And Arishtanemi … I am …' Vishwamitra seemed to hesitate. 'I am sorry for your loss.'

Arishtanemi did not utter a sound. He understood. His *guru* was talking about her. The woman he loved. The woman he had always loved. Who had died in the arms of the man she loved. Saving him. Protecting him … His pain was deeper than that of unrequited love. For with unrequited love, there is always hope that the man may someday be able to win the woman's affection. Hope keeps the heart alive. But Arishtanemi's heart had died with his beloved.

He stood rooted to the spot. No crying.

'You will want vengeance. Against the faceless warriors of that battalion at Ketheeswaram,' said Vishwamitra. 'It's fair.'

The general of the Malayaputras gazed back at him.

'You have my permission, Arishtanemi,' said the chief of the Malayaputras. 'When you cross over with our Malayputra soldiers, you may wreak your vengeance upon them. Hand out justice.'

Arishtanemi bowed low with gratitude towards his *guru*. He did not utter a word, afraid that the tears would escape. Saluting his chief, he walked out of the chamber.

Suddenly, an idea struck Vishwamitra. He held his breath.

There is a way. Ram. His obsession with rules. Another daivi astra. *And the punishment would be ...*

Vishwamitra allowed himself a slight smile. Maybe he could still make Sita the Vishnu.

There is a way.

Chapter 14

'The next wave ...' said Bharat.

The four brothers, accompanied by their *guru* Vashishtha, stood next to their cutter boat on the beach of Dhanushkodi on the south-eastern tip of Pamban Island. They, or more specifically Shatrughan, intended to survey the area to begin designing a bridge across the sea. Something that had never been attempted in the history of humanity. They were dressed in simple clothes, like the fishermen of the area, and unaccompanied by soldiers or guards. For that would have attracted the attention of the lookouts at Ketheeswaram, in Lanka, on the other side of the straits. No news of their plans must travel to Sigiriya.

The brothers held the gunwale of the beached cutter boat. Vashishtha was seated on the central thwart. They would not have their *guru* help them push the boat into the sea.

'This is a good one, Dada,' said Lakshman, standing at the rear end where maximum thrust was required. He was the strongest of the four brothers.

The wave crested high and then broke in a fierce curve, washing the Ayodhya princes with its embrace.

'Now!' ordered Ram.

The brothers began to push hard, helped along by the backwash of the wave. The boat lifted off the wet sand and careened gently into the waters, helped along forcefully by the princes.

'Push through!' screamed Shatrughan, bringing his limited muscular strength into play.

Another wave crested over and crashed into the boat. The brothers kept running with the vessel. Into the sea. Their feet dug into the sand as they raced forward, propelling the craft.

'Shatrughan, jump on board!' shouted Bharat over the roar of the waves.

Shatrughan was the shortest among them. He would soon run out of ground to run on. One cannot float and push a boat at the same time. Shatrughan did as ordered. On board, he immediately rushed to the centre thwart, picked up an oar and began pulling hard against the waters. Vashishtha was working the oar as hard as his aged body permitted on the other side.

'Another wave!' yelled Ram.

The three brothers kept pushing. Shatrughan and Vashishtha, within the boat, continued to row. They tore past this wave as well.

They were through.

'Come on board!' ordered Vashishtha.

Ram, Bharat and Lakshman jumped into the boat as it headed deeper into the sea, farther south from Pamban Island, towards Mannar Island.

Lakshman laughed as he shook the water from his long leonine mane. 'What a rush! I love the sea!'

Ram and Bharat laughed as well. They relieved Shatrughan and Vashishtha of the oars, and began rowing.

As the boat settled into a steady rhythm, Ram and Bharat turned towards their youngest brother. Shatrughan had already moved to the forward thwart, his sight pinned beyond the bow of the vessel, looking at Mannar in the distance. There was no time to stop and stare at the power and beauty of the sea. No time to allow his soul to enjoy the pleasure of the moment. He had already begun to analyse and survey.

'How long will you need, Shatrughan?' asked Bharat.

Shatrughan did not answer. He was looking down into the water, at the sandy seabed, six to seven feet below.

'It will probably take the entire day, Bharat,' said Vashishtha, answering on Shatrughan's behalf.

Lakshman sighed and leaned against the stern thwart. *The entire day?!*

The rush was forgotten. Boredom was already setting in. Lakshman looked at Bharat, his shoulders stooped and face deadpan. Bharat smiled at his brother and gestured with his hand. *Patience.*

— JᖴꝆ Ꝇꓱꓷ —

'What do you think, Shatrughan?' asked Ram.

Shatrughan turned to his elder brother, a confident look in his eyes. 'It can be done, Dada. It will take a week to ten days.'

The four brothers and their *guru* had spent the entire day at sea, between the Pamban and Mannar islands, surveying the area in detail. Dressed as fishermen, they did not attract too much attention. It also helped that much of the land around here was thinly populated. At times Shatrughan had asked his brothers to stop rowing and had dived into the sea to check some features underwater. He touched the corals and dug his hands into the sand flats to understand the nature of the material. The grains of sand were finer than gravel, but coarser than silt. Perfect. He had thoroughly scoped out the northern part of Mannar Island and decided where the bridge would end. The sun had almost set and they were now back on Pamban beach. It had begun to drizzle; the God of Rain and Thunder, Indra, had kindly held back the rain all day.

Vashishtha had discussed the finer points of the topography and oceanography with Shatrughan through the day. But even he, who had taught Shatrughan almost all he knew, was amazed at his former student's confidence. 'A week to ten days, Shatrughan? That's it?! We are talking about a bridge across the sea. The longest bridge built in human history.'

Shatrughan's face was calm, focused and self-assured. 'Can be done, Guruji.'

'How?' asked Bharat, incredulous.

'We will need to ensure a few things first.'

'Anything you say, Shatrughan,' said Ram.

Shatrughan turned to Bharat. 'Dada, I understand the overall battle strategy you have in mind. You would lead a feinting naval attack up the Mahaweli Ganga River. The attack will be brutal. It will need a lot of soldiers. We only have one hundred and thirty thousand men. The hundred thousand Ayodhyans and thirty thousand Vaanars of Prince Angad. But—'

Ram interrupted Shatrughan. 'We will have more men, Shatrughan. Rest assured. We will not be launching any attack for another three months, till the end of the north-east monsoons. Angad and his thirty-thousand-strong Vaanar army will of course be here soon … But by the end of the north-east monsoons, the Anunnaki of Kekaya will also be here with their allies from the lands of the sacred River Indus. They will have another fifty to sixty thousand men, at the least.'

Shatrughan looked at Lakshman and Bharat.

Bharat spoke up. 'They are not coming, Dada. I am close to Yudhaajit uncle, not so much to *Nanaji*.' He was referring to the king of Kekaya, Ashwapati. Also, his *maternal grandfather*. 'I'm aware that uncle Yudhaajit is trying his best to help us, but *Nanaji* has decided to stay out of this battle.'

Ram remained still. But his body had tensed in anger. A noble person expects nobility from his close relations and friends. All of them. Such a person is frequently disappointed.

'But there is some good news as well,' cut in Vashishtha. 'From most unexpected quarters.'

The brothers turned to their *guru*.

'The Malayaputras are joining us.'

'What?' Ram was shocked.

'I just received word from Arishtanemi,' said Vashishtha. 'Fifteen thousand Malayaputras will be joining us in battle, including, most crucially, their elephant corps. Combine that with the fifteen thousand Vayuputras who should reach soon, and our army will be at least one hundred and sixty thousand strong – the Ayodhya troops and Vaanar military, coupled with the Malayaputra and Vayuputra soldiers. I was hoping the Vayuputras would give us permission to threaten Lanka with *daivi astras*, so that the war would be over quickly. But they have refused. Their soldiers are coming, but no *daivi astras* will be allowed.'

Ram was not concerned with the *daivi astras*. He couldn't use them in any case, as the punishment for a second unauthorised use of divine weapons was death. But his transparent eyes held a question. For his *guru*. *The Malayaputras are joining us? Why?*

'It's not about you,' clarified Vashishtha. 'And, honestly, it's not about Sita either. I know my ... my friend ... Vishwamitra. I know his faults. But I also know his strengths. His anger is uncontrollable and he has a mighty ego. But I also know this – however much he may hate me, he loves Mother India more.'

Ram looked at Bharat, smiled slightly and shook his head. A noble man is frequently surprised. Sometimes by the lack of nobility in those he expects it from. At other times, by a display of nobility in those he did not expect it from.

'When all is said and done, he is a good man, this friend of yours, Guruji,' said Bharat.

Vashishtha let out a long breath, his expression stoic. Even remote. Just a trace of moisture danced within his eyes. It did not slip out.

Ram looked at the sky and folded his hands together in gratitude. 'Praise be to Lord Indra for this blessing.'

'Praise be to Lord Indra,' everyone repeated.

Bharat turned to Shatrughan. 'So, I can guess what you want, Shatrughan. You want to keep a majority of the men here.'

'Yes,' answered Shatrughan.

'How many?'

'Around one hundred and twenty-five thousand.'

'One hundred and twenty-five thousand?!'

'Yes, Dada. I will need that many to build the bridge. This will not be an easy task.'

'You want me to conduct a combined naval and land assault on the main Lankan defensive formations of the Mahaweli Ganga River with only thirty-five thousand soldiers?'

'You don't need to win that battle, Dada,' said Shatrughan with a hint of a smile. 'Just keep them busy till we cross over from here. Our main attack will come from here.'

Bharat laughed softly.

'And if I come along with you to the Mahaweli Ganga, Bharat Dada,' said Lakshman, 'we might just win the battle. Even with only thirty-five thousand soldiers.'

'That we will, brother!' said Bharat. 'We will win.'

Lakshman looked at Ram for confirmation. Ram nodded his assent. Lakshman would go with Bharat.

'Anything else?' Bharat asked Shatrughan.

'Yes,' said Shatrughan. 'We can gather the material for the bridge in secret. But once we move it to Pamban Island and start preparing for construction, there is no way that it can be kept quiet.'

'True.'

'And therefore, the Lankan battalion at Ketheeswaram ...'

Shatrughan didn't complete his statement. But it was obvious what he was saying. The Lankan soldiers stationed in and around the Ketheeswaram temple had to be neutralised. Either imprisoned or killed. Not a single one of them could escape to warn the Lankans in Sigiriya of the goings-on in this part of the island.

Bharat looked at Ram and nodded.

'It will be done,' said Ram.

'Now, enough already!' said Bharat. 'Tell us how you will build the bridge.'

'All right, all right.' Shatrughan laughed. 'But first you need to understand something about the Eastern Sea. Something that makes it different not just from the Western Sea, but all the other seas in the world.'

'What?' asked Lakshman.

'Do you know the difference between sea water and river water?' asked Shatrughan with a gleam in his eyes. He was clearly enjoying this. This was his domain. His realm. Knowledge.

Vashishtha leaned back and smiled. He thought he understood where Shatrughan was going with this. *Genius.*

'Sea water is salty, while river water is fresh and sweet,' answered Ram.

'That is true of every sea in the world,' said Shatrughan. 'But only partially true of the Eastern Sea. Most of the Eastern Sea has a thin layer of fresh water on top of the sea water. The depth of this fresh water varies, at different times of the year, from a few inches to substantially more. It is also not uniform across the entire stretch of the Eastern Sea.'

'No way!'

'Yes way!'

'How? Why?' asked Lakshman, who had paid very little attention in school. He threw an apologetic glance at his teacher Vashishtha and then looked back at his twin brother.

'Mother India has been abundantly blessed with rivers. More than any other land. Egypt is called the Gift of the Nile River System. Mesopotamia exists because of the Tigris–Euphrates river system. They are lucky lands since they have a large river system. That's what makes civilisation possible. Some really, really fortunate lands have two, or maybe even three large river systems. Our Mother India has seven!' Shatrughan began to name the great river systems, counting them off on his fingertips. 'The Indus river system, the Saraswati river system, the Ganga–Brahmaputra river system, the Narmada river system, the Mahanadi river system, the Godavari–Krishna river system, the Kaveri river system. And then there are many smaller ones, like the Tapti and Penna, which we don't even count among the seven, but they each carry as much water as the Euphrates River! Even the Mahanadi, which is the smallest of the seven major river systems, often carries as much water as the Nile River!'

'Woah!' said Lakshman.

'No wonder our ancestors insisted that India is the land most blessed by the Gods.'

'*Jai Maa Bhaarati*,' said Vashishtha. *Glory to Mother India.*

The brothers repeated his words. '*Jai Maa Bhaarati.*'

'So, we have these mighty river systems in India. And a majority of them empty gigantic quantities of fresh water into the Eastern Sea. Even the massive Irrawaddy and Salween from the foreign lands to the east – Myanmar and Thailand – pour into the Eastern Sea. And not just this, the south-west monsoon releases huge quantities of rain into the Eastern Sea as well. But by far the biggest infusion of fresh water into the Eastern Sea is from the Ganga–Brahmaputra river system. All this creates the layer of fresh water on the Eastern Sea. And this layer is deepest in the northern parts close to the mouth of the Ganga–Brahmaputra river system.'

Bharat nodded his understanding.

'And we are in the Bhadra month.'

'So?'

'So, this is the time when the East Indian coastal current starts flowing down south, bringing even more fresh water from the northern parts of the Eastern Sea, close to the Ganga–Brahmaputra river system, to the south Indian coast.'

'How in Lord Indra's name does that help us?' asked Ram.

'It helps us with wood.'

'What?'

Shatrughan explained. 'To build this bridge, we need wood that sinks in water and stone that floats on water. Lots and lots of such wood and stone.'

Shatrughan had now left everyone even more befuddled. Including Vashishtha.

'Let me explain,' said Shatrughan.

'Please do!' said Bharat, grinning delightedly.

'We cannot build a traditional bridge, with piers and a roadway on top. We don't have time to plant pillars in the sea.'

'Correct.'

'So,' said Shatrughan, 'we will build a causeway across the Dhanushkodi straits. In effect, blocking the flow of water …'

Vashishtha spoke up immediately. 'But that will—'

Shatrughan interrupted his *guru*. 'No, Guruji. It will not weaken the bridge. We need the piers in traditional bridges because they allow the flowing water to pass under them. That is not a problem here. This is the sea. Water doesn't constantly flow here.'

'But there is the tide,' said Vashishtha. 'Coming in and out, changing direction every six hours and a bit. The tidal currents may not be as strong as flowing river water. But—'

'Guruji, look at the sea here,' said Shatrughan, interrupting his teacher again. 'We can call it Palk Bay and Gulf of Mannar if we want. But it's essentially the waters of the Eastern Sea in Palk Bay and the Indian Ocean waters in Gulf of Mannar. Both the waters crash into each other here – at Dhanushkodi – and dissipate each other's energy. Therefore, the sea is relatively calm here. If there is any place in this entire region which is perfect to build a bridge across the sea, it is this.'

'But no matter how relatively calm the waters, it is still the sea. It has tides and waves that are strong enough to weaken a bridge.'

'Not my bridge.'

'Why not your bridge?'

'It's in the design, Guruji. And the material.'

'The wood that sinks and the stones that float?' whispered Bharat.

Shatrughan nodded, grinning. 'Yeeesss, Dada! I know what you are thinking. But this is not a fantasy.'

'I believe you, brother. Now, what is this magical wood that sinks?'

'The wood of the *ebony* tree,' said Shatrughan. 'It's called *kupilu* in old Sanskrit.'

Vashishtha rocked back, holding his head, his mouth open with awe at the sheer audacity of innovation. He understood it now. Ebony wood. Fresh water. The tidal current. The sandbanks. The season. It all came together finally. He had not heard, seen or read about such brilliance since the *greatest scientist of them all, who lived many millennia ago*. 'By the great *Lord Brahma* himself, you are a genius, Shatrughan! But I still don't understand the thing about the floating stones.'

'Guruji,' said Lakshman, folding his hands together in an apologetic *namaste*. 'I am still stuck at trying to understand the sinking wood. So are my *dadas*. Can you please wait for your turn?'

Vashishtha laughed and gestured for Shatrughan to continue. 'Carry on, wise Nalatardak,' he said, calling him by his *gurukul* name.

Shatrughan resumed, 'So, ebony is one of the hardest woods in the world. It is native to this region of south India and Lanka. The strangest thing about it is that it is stronger when it is wet.'

'But I thought,' said Ram, 'that wood swells and weakens when wet. Isn't that true?'

'That's right, Dada,' said Shatrughan, smiling, 'but only up to a point. The wood fibres expand with a little moisture, and contract when the moisture disappears. And the wood weakens due to this. But when the moisture content goes above a certain limit – I think for ebony it should be around thirty to forty per cent – wood fibres actually become more stable. The wood becomes harder.'

'So let me get this,' said Bharat. 'If we subject wood to some moisture, it swells, but when you subject it to excessive moisture, it hardens.'

'And we will not just be "subjecting it to moisture". We'll be drowning the damn thing!'

'Woah …' said Lakshman. 'This is next level, brother.'

'But what about the fresh water?' asked Ram. 'Why did you tell us that long story about the fresh water layer in the Eastern Sea?'

'That is the true genius of the man!' said Vashishtha, looking at Shatrughan with fatherly pride. 'Go on, explain it.'

'What do you think happens when you leave something in salt water, as compared to fresh water?' asked Shatrughan.

'It erodes,' answered Bharat.

'Precisely. The wooden logs will be the foundation of the bridge. If they erode, the bridge will not last for very long. But since the sea floor is not more than six to seven feet deep in this region, most of the water here is fresh water. The logs will not erode and the bridge will stand strong for a long time.'

'But,' said Lakshman to Shatrughan, 'we don't need this bridge to last very long. We need just two or three days to march the army across. So long as it holds for those many days, we are set.'

'And what about our return?' asked Shatrughan. 'How will we bring the elephants back? We do have to return them to Kishkindha and to the Malayaputras. And we don't know how long the campaign will last. It could be a month. It could even be a year. An engineer must prepare for the worst-case scenario.'

'So, what are you saying?' asked Lakshman. 'That this bridge will last for a year?'

Shatrughan leaned forward. 'It's my bridge, Lakshman. It will last for at least one thousand years. If not more.'

'No bridge can last that long, Shatrughan!' said Bharat. 'You know I love you and respect your intelligence, but this is stretching it.'

'It's not,' said Vashishtha. 'That is his genius. The way he is designing it, or at least the way I think he is designing it, it will become almost like a natural feature. It will last a really, really long time.'

'But why use wood as the foundation?' asked Lakshman. 'Why not big boulders and rocks? Won't that be harder and better?'

'Many reasons,' answered Shatrughan. 'First, not every soldier in our army is as massive as you are, Lakshman. Quarrying, carrying and placing large boulders in the sea will be very difficult for average-sized men. But logs of ebony wood can be easily carried. They are lighter. And once placed in the sea they will slowly harden and become heavy, as water works its magic on the wood. This will make them sink gently, so the wet sand underneath is not displaced. Not too much at least. A heavy boulder, with its sharp edges, might shift the sand too much. That would be disastrous. We need the foundation to settle gently into the wet sand, with the grains surrounding it. That will hold the logs in place, a little like how our gums hold our teeth in place. We will also pour more sand in between the logs, filling up the open spaces, thus giving solidity to the foundation. And remember, the sand we pour in will moisten from the sea water here, thus becoming harder and more adhesive.'

'And that's what makes his design superlative,' said Vashishtha. 'There is a lot of sand in the area. So much that both high tide and low tide move it in from the sandbanks. Since this bridge, with its log foundation, will be the strongest structure in the vicinity, wet sand will naturally collect around it with the tidal movements. It will make the foundations stronger and stronger.'

'Brilliant!' said Ram. 'You intend to use the forces of nature to reinforce the bridge.'

'Thanks, Dada. There's more, though. We will place small stones atop the wooden foundation, which will serve as a secondary base and help keep the logs below in place.'

'I have a question,' said Vashishtha.

'I'm coming to the floating stones, Guruji.'

'No, no. You explain that later. I have one more question on the matter of the tides. I have no doubt you have thought about this, but if the bridge is built in a straight line from Pamban to Mannar, the tidal current could wear out the centre. The bridge will still hold for a year, I think. But there is a risk that, over time, it may crack in the middle. How do we mitigate that?'

'I've thought of that, Guruji. Have you studied aerodynamics?'

Vashishtha let out a loud laugh. 'I know you are very smart, Shatrughan, but I am your teacher. Do not forget that. Yes, I understand aerodynamics.'

Aerodynamics had been studied by ancient Indians in the fields of defence technology and ship-building. Essentially, they studied the motion of air and its interaction with solid bodies that moved either with or against it. Less wind resistance aids the trajectory of an arrow or a spear, for instance. It moves faster and farther.

'Sorry, Guruji,' said Shatrughan, smiling and folding his hands together into a *namaste*. 'It struck me that aerodynamics is the study of the movement of air. But even water is a bit like air in its movements. Fluid movements. It's just a lot denser. So, I thought, why not apply aerodynamic principles to the bridge?'

'Oh, brilliant!' said Vashishtha.

'Oh, what?' asked Bharat. 'I don't understand.'

'Basically, Dada,' said Shatrughan, 'we will not build a straight causeway across Pamban and Mannar. Guruji is right. The force of the tides will be stronger on a straight wall. But if we curve the bridge in a great arc, this force will get distributed. Simple principles of aerodynamics. There will be less erosion. The bridge causeway will curve like a bow. That will make it longer, yes. But it will make it more stable.'

'So how long will the bridge be?' asked Ram. 'The straight-line distance between Pamban and Mannar is around twenty-five kilometres.'

'By my calculations, it should be around thirty-five kilometres in length,' said Shatrughan. 'And I'm thinking we will make it around three and a half kilometres broad.'

'That broad?' asked Ram. 'That will require a lot of material and men.'

'We have enough men. And we have three months to gather the material. We can begin construction only after the north-east monsoons. Remember, Dada, the broader the bridge, the more stable it will be. The principles of this particular bridge are very different from those that work in the case of a normal bridge.'

The three brothers nodded. Understanding ... somewhat.

'My main question has still not been answered, though,' said Vashishtha.

'The floating stones,' said Shatrughan, smiling.

'Yes, the floating stones. Why? Why not just use normal rocks?'

Lakshman cut in. 'And even more importantly, where will we find these floating stones?'

'We'll find them right here,' answered Shatrughan. 'The floating rocks are Platygyra coral stone.'

'What?' asked Bharat. 'Corals aren't stone. They are plants … or maybe animals … or …'

'Corals look like plants, Dada. But they are actually animals.'

'Whatever … They are beautiful things that live in the sea. They're certainly not stone.'

'They are not stone when they are alive, Dada. But once they die, they turn into stone.' Shatrughan pointed at a huge rock next to them. 'Can you lift that rock, Dada?'

'Are you crazy, Shatrughan?' asked Bharat. 'Even Lakshman will find it difficult to pick that up without risking a slipped disc.'

The diminutive Shatrughan took a few quick steps and picked up the rock. With one hand.

Lakshman was dumbfounded. 'What the …'

'Coral stones are very light. Very easy to carve and flatten. And yet, they have tremendous load-bearing strength. We can even construct small buildings with them. They are perfect architectural material. And they abound in this region. We will use Platygyra coral stone for the top layer, and bind it with wet sand. On which our army will march.'

'So, we will not be actually walking on floating stones?' asked Lakshman, disappointed.

'Of course not,' answered Shatrughan. 'But all the stones we use for the bridge, the small ones in the foundation and the flat ones on top, will be coral stones.'

'What is the advantage? Why not use harder rocks as a top layer?' asked Vashishtha. 'Won't hard rocks give the bridge stability?'

'They will be more difficult to carve into flat stones. It will take too much time. And I fear that the top surface may not be completely flat otherwise.'

'Our soldiers are tough.' Bharat laughed. 'They can survive a few pricks on the foot if the surface isn't completely flat.'

'Yes, they will be all right, but it is the elephants I'm thinking about,' said Shatrughan. 'Panicky elephants will be a disaster on the march.'

'Fair enough.'

'More importantly, no matter how well we stack and bond the top surface bricks, some of them will get displaced during the march. After all, elephants will be walking on it. And many of those stones will fall into the sea.'

'So?'

'Heavier stones will sink,' said Shatrughan. 'And then they will be moved around by the tidal currents. They will bang against the bridge foundations. Hard stones hitting the bridge repeatedly with incoming and outgoing tides … Not good for the bridge.'

Vashishtha nodded. 'Hence the floating stones … Even if some of the stones get displaced, they will float on the sea surface and not damage the bridge foundation. And being very light, their impact on the top level will be minimal.'

'Precisely.'

Vashishtha's face broke into a massive smile. 'You've thought of everything!'

Shatrughan preened with mock pride. 'I am Nalatardak!'

He had used his *gurukul* name from when the brothers studied, many years ago, in Vashishtha's *school*.

'Our genius brother!' said Bharat fondly.

'Forget the earlier name!' said Ram. 'This bridge will be called Nala Setu, after the one who will build it!'

Chapter 15

'*Namaste*, Raavanji and Kumbhakarnaji,' said Sita. 'Where have you been all these days? It's been a long time.'

It had been two weeks since Raavan and Kumbhakarna had last visited the Ashok Vatika. However, they were aware of Hanuman and Arishtanemi's rendezvous with Sita. They also were aware of the attack on the Ketheeswaram battalion by a small band of foreigners who escaped down the Aruvi Aru River that night. There were a few casualties, but the skirmish was not too serious. Clearly, whatever message Hanuman and Arishtanemi had for Sita had been delivered, and they had gone back. Raavan and Kumbhakarna were considering leaving a skeletal staff of soldiers at Ketheeswaram and recalling the rest. For the main attack would come from the east. They knew that the Ayodhyan navy had sailed down to south India and was waiting in the Vaigai River. Once the north-east monsoon ended, it would sail out and then move up the Mahaweli Ganga River into the hinterland of Lanka. The first battle would be fought at the great river fort of Onguiaahra that protected the waterway of Amban Ganga to Sigiriya, the Lankan capital.

'The battle will begin soon, queen,' said Raavan. 'Any time after the north-east monsoon. Just a few more weeks. A few weeks left to enjoy all there is to life, before war destroys us. So, I have been busy with that which is most important.'

'The battle plans?' asked Sita.

'Oh, that too!' said Kumbhakarna. 'Dada and I have been strategising on how to make it difficult for the Ayodhyan navy. But Dada has also been busy with things he considers more important!'

'What can be more important than battle preparations before a battle?' asked Sita.

'Art,' answered Raavan.

'Art?'

'Yes. I will never again be able to paint or sculpt or play instruments or sing. So, I have been enjoying as much of that as I can. But mostly painting and sculpting.'

Sita smiled and shook her head. 'You never fail to surprise me.'

'Yes ... I either surprise or disappoint. I never seem to meet expectations!'

'What paintings and sculptures have you created? What will you do with it?'

'Well, there's some for my brother, some for my son, some for my wife and even some for that useless mother of mine.'

Sita frowned with disapproval.

'Yeah, yeah. I know you don't like my speaking about my mother like this,' said Raavan. 'But not every mother is like your mother. Some mothers are a burden that children carry.'

'No mother is a burden.'

'Only someone who has had not one but two perfect mothers can say something so breathtakingly broad-brush and erroneous.'

'Big words!' laughed Sita, raising her eyebrows. 'You have been reading!'

'I always read. I read a lot. But lately I have been reading the works of those who think big words replace deep thoughts. There is a comforting pleasure in reading their supercilious nonsense.'

Sita looked at Kumbhakarna. 'Is he always like this?'

'Usually worse,' said Kumbhakarna, laughing softly.

'Aaaanywaaay,' said Raavan, laughing, 'I have made some stuff for you as well.'

Sita smiled. 'More paintings of my birth-mother?'

Raavan shook his head. 'No. Of you and your husband.'

Sita was surprised. This, she hadn't expected.

'And I'll have you know, my art is bewitching,' said Raavan. 'History will remember Ram and Sita the way *I* painted and sculpted them.'

Sita smiled, used by now to Raavan's bombastic words and almighty ego.

Raavan clapped his hands and a retinue of attendants apparated in a flurry, carrying large packages. Raavan got up with a flourish and summoned one over.

Sita's heart began to thud in anticipation. She had seen Raavan's work. His talent. But her mind pulled back in judgement. She said to herself that she would politely appreciate the painting to an appropriate measure. Not less. Not more. *This is the way history will remember the seventh Vishnu, Ram? I don't think so...*

Raavan theatrically removed the cloth covering and revealed the painting like a magician. Sita gasped. It was her. And yet she could never have imagined that she looked like this. This ... divine.

This was she, not her mother. The body was lean, more muscular. The face and arms carried faded battle scars. She was seated alone in the Ashok Vatika. Everything looked exquisite. The sky radiated the beauty of the early morning sun. The trees painted so realistically that they created an optical illusion of swaying in the breeze, watching the wondrous Goddess seated amidst them. Deer and peacocks danced in devotion, craving her attention. At the heart, in the centre, was Sita. Dressed in a *dhoti*, a blouse and an *angvastram* that fell from her right shoulder. Virginal white. A pendant made from the bones of a single finger—a relic of her mother Vedavati's body—with the phalanges carefully fastened with gold links, hung from a black string tied around her neck.

Sita was depicted sitting on a large rock. In the Ashok Vatika. Her legs rested on the ground, crossed at the feet. Her hands clasped together, with fingers interlocked, resting on her thighs. Her back was slightly slouched. She gazed into the distance. A picture of contemplation and repose.

What was passing through her mind? Was she thinking of Ram? Pining for him? Longing for a reunion? Or was she just melancholic? Lonely?

Distant. Divine. Like a Goddess.

Sita was both fascinated and dispirited by the painting, if that was possible. 'Where is Ram?'

Raavan smiled. 'I'm sorry I took you away from him. But it won't be too long now. You will meet him again soon.'

Sita smiled slightly and gazed again at the painting. She couldn't have imagined that a painting could conquer time. A copy of it would hang in a secret temple, in a city that was yet to be built, a city that would be named after the five banyan trees in that area. In future, Sita would expressly order that her image not be recorded anywhere. But some would still keep copies of this painting. They would worship her in this form. They would call her Bhoomidevi, the Goddess of the Earth.

'Thank you,' said Sita. And then she added, without knowing why she said it, 'I will try and be worthy of this painting.'

'You already are, princess,' said Kumbhakarna gently.

'And now,' said Raavan, 'the next one …'

Another painting was brought to them by the attendants. Raavan removed the cloth covering with some more drama. Always the showman. He made the staff hold the painting aloft. Sita blushed and broke into a delighted smile. For it was her, along with the object of her deepest affection. Ram.

Ram and Sita were dressed simply, with no royal ornaments or crowns. They wore plain hand-spun cotton, the clothes of the poorest of the poor. Their eyes rested on each other. Oblivious to the world. It was a look of love, trust and, most importantly, respect. A man and woman made for each other. Sita held Ram's right hand from below, as if supporting him.

Again, Sita could not have known the future. How could she? But this image would serve as model for the main gargantuan *murti* in a great temple dedicated to the Vishnu himself, in the noble city of Ujjain. Many, many centuries later, a rough-hewn saviour from Tibet would look up and behold the idol in that great temple. In a meeting with a tribe that was yet to be created – the Vasudevs. In the effort to fulfil his mission – removing Evil.

'Ram will become the Vishnu,' said Raavan, 'because of you. And he will be a great Vishnu.'

Sita shook her head. 'He will become the Vishnu on his own. The best one. My task is to assist him.'

Raavan smiled and did not contradict her. He signalled for the next piece of art. This was not a painting but a sculpture. A small work of exquisite art. He removed the cloth covering to reveal a bust. Sita's eyes welled up with emotion. A soft smile played on her lips.

She looked at Raavan, smiled broadly and applauded. 'Your talent is unique.'

'I know.'

Sita laughed and shifted her attention back to the sculpture. It was Ram. Ram, the way he would be decades later. For Raavan's special ability was to age a person in his mind's eye and capture it in a work of art.

'This is Ram,' said Raavan, 'after he has achieved all that he will as a Vishnu. When he has established a new empire. When people are happy and prosperous. When there will be order and beauty. When our beloved Mother India will lead the world once again. This is how he will look after fulfilling his role. This is how he will be remembered.'

Sita murmured, 'We will call the empire *Meluha*.'

Raavan smiled. '*The Land of Pure Life* ... A nice name.'

'He has the look of a *rajrishi*,' said Sita.

Raavan nodded. 'This is the way he came to me. A *priest-king*.'

Rajrishi, an old Sanskrit word, was a conjoint of *raja* and *rishi*. *King* and *sage*. It was sometimes used for kings who walked away from kingship and became sages. But more often, it referred to kings who ruled like sages. Who dedicated their energy, emotions, mind and their very soul to one purpose alone: the good of their people.

Sita was hypnotised by the sculpture. Flawless in its beauty and form, it was the head and upper torso of Ram. He was bare-chested and wore a simple patterned *angvastram* that was wrapped around his right armpit and his left shoulder, covering his left arm completely but leaving the right sword-arm and right shoulder bare. The *angvastram* was delicately decorated with trefoil embroidery: overlapping ring patterns filled with red pigment. Simple and elegant. He wore no jewellery save for modest gold-stud earrings. Raavan had drilled holes in the exquisitely sculpted ears and adorned them with gold studs. Ram wore a fillet or ribbon headband, etched with astounding detail. The headband held an inlay ornament in the centre that dangled high on his forehead. It was the Sun, with its rays streaming out. The symbol of a *Suryavanshi*, the *Solar Dynasty*. The simplest of crowns for one who was, after all, a *rajrishi*. A similar, smaller amulet was tied to his right upper arm with a silky gold thread.

Sita looked closer. 'What are those symbols on the amulet?'

'Random symbols for now,' said Raavan. 'But you had once told me that Ram is obsessed with merit. I remember your exact words: that people's status and regard in society should be defined by their *karma* and not their birth. I thought he would like a system in which people display that acquired status ... Perhaps a chosen-tribe instead of a birth-tribe ... that they have earned with their merit ... And wear with pride on their arm bands.'

Sita smiled. *That would be so Ram ...*

Raavan smiled with rare embarrassment. 'Just a thought ...'

She walked around the sculpture. She looked at the back. The two ends of the fillet-crown were neatly tied behind the head. His hair was punctiliously combed and gathered into a large neat bun at the crown of his head. The moustache and beard were neatly trimmed. Everything about the figure was immaculate, sober and modest.

So very Ram ...

But what captivated her were the eyes. Deep and incisive. Half-closed. Like a monk in meditation. Calm. Gentle.

'Wow …' whispered Sita. Mesmerised. 'This is how people will remember Ram.'

'This is how people will remember Ram,' repeated Raavan.

Raavan was right. The people would remember this image. For millennia.

They would remember their *rajrishi*.

They would remember their *priest-king*.

They would remember their Vishnu, Ram.

For as long as the land of India breathed, it would sing the name of Ram.

— J干 Ɉ𝟛D —

'All preparations over?' asked Ram.

Bharat nodded. 'Yes, Dada.'

The north-east monsoon had been extremely intense in the first month this year, but had inexplicably died down almost completely after that. Ram and his brothers had decided to bring forward their planned attack on Lanka. They were ready. Shatrughan and his assigned soldiers had worked double quick in gathering the material needed for the construction of the bridge. In just one month. The Malayaputras had arrived with their fifteen thousand troops and their elephant corps. So had the Vayuputras, with another fifteen thousand warriors. And Angad too had marched in, with his Vaanar soldiers and elephants. Provisioning this massive army for another two months would prove unnecessarily expensive when the opportunity to launch the war had already presented itself. Furthermore, as all good generals know, a bored army is a dangerous thing. Testosterone-laden men, held back from battle with the enemy, can instead turn on each other.

It made perfect sense to launch the attack without delay.

The invasion of Raavan's Lanka would begin the following day. The first day of the month of Ashwin.

Ram boxed his younger brother's shoulder. 'I missed you, you stupid oaf!'

Ram and Bharat were alone together. A rare occurrence in the hectic frenzy of war preparation. They sat on the beach next to the mouth of the great Vaigai River. Their armies visible in the distance.

'Who told you to banish yourself?' said Bharat gruffly, laughing also, as he put his arm around his brother's shoulder.

Ram smiled quietly. He stared into the distance. At the point where the night sky touched the calm waters of the Eastern Sea at the horizon.

The brothers sat in silence. Bharat knew that Ram was troubled. He also knew that however close Ram was to Lakshman, he could not express his apprehensions to their hot-headed brother.

So, he waited for Ram to speak.

'Bharat ...'

'Yes, Dada ...'

Ram sighed.

Bharat waited again. In silence.

'I don't even ...'

Bharat held Ram's shoulder. 'Raavan wouldn't kill her, Dada. He needs Bhabhi alive. We know that.'

Ram looked at the sea, averting his eyes from his brother. Kshatriyas hide their tears, even from their own.

'He won't kill her,' repeated Bharat. 'You know that.'

'Yes. But he could hurt her. He's a monster.'

'If he has dared to do that, Dada, then I swear we will make him suffer. We will be more monstrous than that monster.'

Ram continued to look into the distance. Soft tears fell in a steady flow now. And then it slipped out. The thought in his head. That had not escaped his lips. For who could he speak to besides Bharat?

'I failed,' Ram whispered in an agonised voice.

'No! No, you didn't, Dada ...'

'She's my wife. It is my duty to protect her from harm. It is my duty to die for her. I was not there ... And she was kidnapped ... I failed in my duty ...'

Bharat allowed his elder brother to speak.

'She's the love of my life. She's my woman. And I let some monster ... to my ...'

Bharat held Ram's hand. No words.

'I shouldn't have gone after that deer ... I could have run faster ... I could have ...' Ram halted as the tears overwhelmed him.

Bharat reached over and embraced his brother. Ram held him tight. He allowed the tears to flow. He let the agony of the months of separation from her seep out.

Bharat silently held his brother. He straightened when he felt Ram relax.

'You know, Dada,' said Bharat, 'most women can do everything that a man can, except fight physically with men. The average man is bigger and stronger than the average woman.'

Ram looked at Bharat quizzically. For this had nothing to do with what he was troubled by.

'But,' continued Bharat, 'Sita *bhabhi* is not an average woman. She can fight. She can hold her own in battle.'

Ram smiled.

'If you ask me, honestly,' said Bharat, 'I am not worried about what harm Raavan could do to Sita *bhabhi*. I would worry more about what harm she can do to him!'

Ram smiled fully.

Bharat held Ram's hand. 'Dada, you haven't failed. Fate is testing Sita *bhabhi* and you. But even if you do believe that you have failed, remember that it isn't as if great men never fall. Everyone falls some time or the other. Great are those who rise after they fall, dust themselves off and get right back into the battle of life.'

Ram nodded.

'And you are not just a great man. You are the Vishnu.'

Ram rolled his eyes. 'It's Sita who is the Vishnu.'

Bharat sighed. 'You settle that between the two of you. All I know is that you are a tough, powerful man. And you have your brothers and your people standing right behind you. Raavan has stirred up a hornets' nest by taking us on. We will teach him a lesson that the world will remember forever.'

Chapter 16

Bharat, Lakshman and the Ayodhyan navy sailed out from the Vaigai in the morning. The sun was setting behind them as the lead ship sailed into the Gokarna Bay. By the time the last ship anchored it was well past sundown. The Ayodhyan navy was massive.

Gokarna – literally, the cow's ear – was the main port of Lanka. Located in the north-east of the island, its natural harbour was endowed with a deep bay. The land extended into the sea, serving as a natural breakwater. It received and safely anchored the seafaring Ayodhyan navy ships. A majority of Bharat's ships remained outside the bay, safe from any surprise attacks.

The *Mahaweli* Ganga flowed into the Gokarna Bay at its southern end. Named the *Great Sandy* Ganga, it was the longest river in Lanka and had a navigable channel with a deep watercourse, which allowed ships to sail into the heart of the island. Much farther upriver, ships sailed into the Amban

Ganga – a tributary of the Mahaweli Ganga –which allowed a craft to reach very close to the Lankan capital, Sigiriya. The capital lay around one hundred kilometres to the south-west of Gokarna, and the journey to it was mostly navigated through water.

One would have predicted some military resistance to the expected attack from the Ayodhyans at Gokarna. But one would have been wrong to do so.

Lanka focused all its energies on two fronts: trade, and warfare which supported that trade. Not much else. Most Lankans were either warriors or businessmen, or those who served these two groups. There were almost no farmers, Lanka producing very little of its own food requirements. This made sense for an island that thrived on free trade. Food was expensive to grow in Lanka and they had the Sapt Sindhu next door – the territory with the largest proportion of arable land in the world. Lanka could import cheap and high-quality agricultural produce from the Sapt Sindhu, and devote all its energy towards trade and warfare to abet that trade.

While this state of affairs made sense from a free trade perspective, it was disastrous militarily. An enemy could easily blockade the Gokarna port and starve people there into surrendering in a short time. Gokarna was the import hub for Sigiriya, which made the Lankan capital itself vulnerable to such a siege.

Kumbhakarna had understood the military disadvantage of importing all their food and had, over the years, encouraged farming in and around Sigiriya. But Gokarna had remained stubbornly addicted to imported food. Few Gokarnans wanted to shift from profitable trade to low-income farming. And how does one farm without farmers?!

So Raavan had made his soldiers retreat from Gokarna and set vigil in Sigiriya when he received news of the Ayodhyan navy preparing to set sail from Vaigai. It made sense to prepare for the siege in Sigiriya and not waste precious resources in defending a city like Gokarna that was so vulnerable to a blockade.

True to its mercantile spirit, senior officials from the Gokarna trading guilds had gathered at the main port quay to welcome the Ayodhyan navy. Businessmen in this Lankan port city were determined to remain pragmatic. To business-focused minds, everything is negotiable. They chose to surrender to the invaders instead of putting up resistance bound to be ineffective. They would allow the soldiers free passage to Sigiriya in return for their safety and security. Whoever won the battle in Sigiriya would later become their administrators and overlords, they had calculated.

Logical.

Bharat and Lakshman looked on bemused as their ship captain expertly navigated into the quay.

Musicians, singers, priests with *puja* thalis, top businessmen dressed in their finery …

'They have lined up a welcoming party!' exclaimed Lakshman. 'You were right about them, Dada.'

Bharat nodded. 'Hmm … Let's hope I am right about what they will do later on as well.'

Bharat's ship docked at the quay and the gangway plank was quickly fixed. The Ayodhya sailors began to lower the sails and pack them in as Bharat and Lakshman disembarked, preceded and followed by fierce bodyguards.

As they stepped on land, they were besieged by smiling businessmen rushing in with garlands and *laddoos*. Musicians injected renewed energy into their sonorous musical *ragas*, welcoming the brothers to Lanka. The city's artistic elite lined the road, gently showering rose petals on the brothers.

'Lord Bharat,' said an obviously eminent citizen, having confidently walked up to the prince of Ayodhya. 'Has Emperor Ram not accompanied you?'

Bharat cast a quick glance towards their grandest ship, farther back in the middle of the bay. And then he turned his attention to the businessman. 'Why don't we speak first?'

The businessman bowed low with his hands folded in a namaste. 'Of course, of course, Prince Bharat. Greetings to you as well, Prince Lakshman. Please do follow me.'

Bharat was pleased to note that Lakshman was following instructions. He was keeping his mouth shut. He had faithfully followed his brother's gaze and also glanced at the grand ship that had not come up to the quay.

Bharat was not sure of the businessmen's motives. They might also be spying on them for Raavan. He had warned Lakshman that under no circumstances were they to give the impression that Ram and Shatrughan were not with them. That would make the Lankans suspect that this naval assault up the Mahaweli Ganga River was a ruse, and that the actual attack would come from elsewhere.

The Lankan merchants were now convinced that Ram and Shatrughan were in the grand ship that had stayed back.

Bharat nodded to Lakshman and they both began to walk alongside the merchant. The brothers' bodyguards moved with them in a discreet semi-circle of protection.

—— JF JSD ——

'Remember our orders, Arishtanemi,' said Hanuman.

It was late in the night. A thin sliver of moon was struggling to illuminate the dark. Hanuman and Arishtanemi pushed their cutter boat out to sea, accompanied by twenty able soldiers. They moved past the second wave, jumped into their boat and swiftly rowed deep into the Dhanushkodi straits. A few hours would bring them to the Lankan mainland.

Arishtanemi was as silent as a meditating monk. After some time, he looked to the right. Cutter boats sailed behind, faintly visible in the distance, almost noiseless. It was dark, but streaks of white foam in the inky black sea brought them occasionally into view. The small boats were valiantly battling the sea as they moved towards their target. He could not hear his deathly silent comrades. But the rhythmic sounds of the rowing made it known to him that they accompanied him.

A hundred cutter boats. Two thousand Vayuputras and Malayaputras. More than enough.

The enemy was outnumbered. Arishtanemi and Hanuman knew that the bulk of the Ketheeswaram battalion had been recalled to Sigiriya a few weeks ago. The few that remained would not number more than a hundred. They had rarely been sighted in the last few weeks by the Ayodhya scouts. Perhaps they remained confined to their quarters, fearful of attacks from the Ayodhyans just a few hours away by boat. They would also be under the impression that most of Ram's army was on its way to engage in battle from the eastern front of Lanka. No, they would not be expecting soldiers rowing silently towards them.

Two thousand soldiers. Against one hundred enemy ones. More than enough.

Hanuman's orders from his commander Lord Ram were clear. They should try and arrest the Lankans at Ketheeswaram. Only kill if necessary. None would be allowed to escape. News of the bridge-building at Dhanushkodi could not reach Sigiriya before the Ayodhyans did. That would be an unmitigated disaster.

So, Hanuman had been given two thousand soldiers for this mission. One needs more soldiers to capture the enemy alive, much fewer to simply kill them.

'Arishtanemi?' Hanuman said again.

Hanuman knew that they must arrest the Lankans. Not kill. But he also knew what Arishtanemi would want to do. Kill.

Arishtanemi did not answer. He held the gunwale tight and stared straight ahead.

Hanuman fell silent.

—— J⨍ ⫛⸺D ——

An hour before dawn, the waves swept the Ayodhyans on to the beach, two kilometres south of the Ketheeswaram battalion quarters. The soldiers quickly jumped off and pushed their boats high above the waterline.

They had timed their arrival well. It was peak high tide. The boats had landed high on the beach, pushed by the natural thrust of the waves. The waters would slowly recede now and rise to these levels again after twelve-and-a-half hours. They did not need the usual animal-powered pulleys to pull their boats to higher ground, for fear that they could be dragged out to sea.

Twelve hours. Ample time. To overwhelm the Lankans at Ketheeswaram and get back. Shatrughan's bridge construction could then begin.

'Landing report,' Hanuman addressed a soldier.

The soldier saluted Hanuman and rushed to tally the boats that had beached.

Hanuman pulled Arishtanemi to the side.

'Arishtanemi, let's avoid the killing if we can,' whispered Hanuman.

Arishtanemi looked blankly at Hanuman.

'Listen to me …'

'You did not love her,' said Arishtanemi. 'I did.'

'Brother …'

'You did not love her,' repeated Arishtanemi. 'I did.'

'Those Lankan soldiers were only doing their duty.'

'And I will do mine.'

'Sursa would not have wanted you to do this.'

'You know that's not true. Had you been killed, Sursa would have roasted them alive.'

Hanuman remained silent.

'One who doesn't feel love cannot know how love feels. One who doesn't know love will feel no need for vengeance.'

'Arishtanemi, listen to me …' pleaded Hanuman.

'Do not come between my vengeance and me,' said Arishtanemi. He walked away from Hanuman.

— Jᖴ⅃⌗D —

'This is strange …' whispered Hanuman.

Hanuman and Arishtanemi were hiding behind the treeline, two hundred metres from the Lankan battalion quarters. The light of dawn had begun to dispel the darkness. Vague shadows could be discerned. With effort.

The battalion quarters were a mess. Scattered leaves. Animal droppings. Stale puddles of water. Two horses had escaped from the stables, their restraints having come loose. They were aimlessly roaming around the elaborate flowerbeds and trees at the entrance. Chomping at the leaves.

Arishtanemi looked at Hanuman. 'I know Lankan traditions. Their army is brutal but very well-trained. Their quarters are always well ordered. Spick and span. Those trees are not just for show, their leaves are medicinal. Why are the horses eating them? What's going on?'

Hanuman considered sending in a small team to investigate. He turned back to his men.

'Don't send in anyone just yet,' said Arishtanemi in a soft voice, almost as if he had read Hanuman's mind.

'What do you suggest?'

Arishtanemi, the besotted lover seeking vengeance, was gone. Arishtanemi, the feared warrior with legendary tactical brilliance, had come to the fore.

'Give me a minute,' he whispered as he stealthily crept forward.

—JF J5D—

Arishtanemi rushed back to Hanuman fifteen minutes later. Alarm writ large upon his face.

'What's the matter?'

'The plague ...'

'Plague?'

'Sigiriya has been afflicted by a plague for many years. For some reason it hadn't spread to Gokarna. Nor to Ketheeswaram. It appears that it has now.'

Hanuman instinctively stepped back.

'I didn't go too close. It was clear from a distance ...' said Arishtanemi. 'Typical symptoms are severe pain, sluggishness, fatigue, etc. But there is a new addition recently ... of relentless spells of coughing and loss of breath. Don't worry – the Malayaputras have the medicine for this disease and we are carrying enough, even for our army.'

'All right then. We will arrest these men and take them back with us. They can be taken care of in our field hospitals. The Malayaputra medicines can be used to ...'

Hanuman stopped speaking as Arishtanemi turned towards his Malayaputra lieutenant at the back, giving quick hand-signal commands.

Hanuman instantly understood. 'Arishtanemi ... no ...'

Arishtanemi looked at Hanuman. A silent rage flashed in his eyes.

'They are incapacitated ... They cannot fight back ... This is *adharma*.'

Arishtanemi loosened the scabbard-hold on his sword and checked the assorted knives tied all over his body in different sheaths.

Hanuman held his friend's arm. 'You are better than this, Arishtanemi. Don't ... Come on ... Don't force me to ...'

Arishtanemi glared at Hanuman. 'You will do nothing. You will wait here.'

'Don't do this ... You're better than this ...'

In a flash, some two hundred Malayaputras had lined up behind Arishtanemi, whose loyal lieutenants briskly briefed them. Hanuman knew that the Malayaputra soldiers were not merely following orders from their revered leader. Sursa was a former Malayaputra as well. This was personal. For all of them.

'Arishtanemi ...' whispered Hanuman. Beseeching his friend.

'Stay here. Don't get involved.'

Arishtanemi drew his sword and turned to his men. And nodded.

The Malayaputras pulled their blades out and began moving forward.

Sursa would be avenged.

Blood would be answered with blood.

Chapter 17

'Where is your militia?' asked Bharat.

Bharat, Lakshman and their bodyguards had awoken early from a restful night's sleep in their comfortable quarters. A section of Raavan's mansion in Gokarna had been allotted to the Ayodhyan princes. Late into the second *prahar*, senior partners of the trade guilds of Gokarna had trooped in to meet the brothers.

The businessmen had begun their negotiations with a flow of flattery. Bharat and Lakshman were the rays of sunshine in their bleak horizon, they had said. The brothers – the true rulers of the Indian subcontinent – would liberate them, they had said. Bharat speedily brought the pantomime to an end and they had gotten down to work.

Time was of the essence. He would not waste a second.

Manigramaa was the senior managing partner of the Cotton and Silk Guild. It was the richest guild in Gokarna.

She responded cautiously to Bharat's question. 'Militia, great prince?'

Most manufacturers, merchants and traders across the Indian subcontinent were organized into guilds: essentially corporations composed of members pursuing a common craft or trade. Aspiring individuals entered a trade guild as apprentices and climbed the ladder based on the profits they earned for the guild – becoming managers, then ship captains and then partners. Five managing partners were elected by the members on a biannual basis. No managing partner could hold office for more than two consecutive terms.

Each member of the guild received a portion of the annual profits. All accounts were kept open at the guild offices and, manager upwards, members could inspect the accounts at any time of their choosing. Systematically, then, all members could focus on guild profits. For these profits directly determined the profit-shares of the members.

Pirates attacking trading ships in the Indian ocean were bad for profits. It made sense then for the guilds to either maintain their in-house militia to guard their ships, or hire the services of the Lankan army.

'Yes, Manigramaaji,' said Bharat. 'I am certain your guild has an in-house militia. You wouldn't waste money on the expensive Lankan army. Your guild is big enough.' Reverse flattery proves useful sometimes. 'Where are the militia soldiers?'

Manigramaa looked at her co-managing partner, and then at the managing partners of the other guilds. All nodded imperceptibly. Lying to the Ayodhyans would be bad for business.

'Great prince,' said Manigramaa. 'Our militia has been commandeered by emperor ... I mean the ... the evil kidnapper, Raavan. We do not have any soldiers here with us.'

Bharat looked into Manigramaa's eyes. She was not lying. But he did not want to trust her.

'Your boats …' said Bharat.

'Yes, Lord Bharat?'

'I need your boats.'

'But …' said Manigramaa softly. 'Great prince, the Mahaweli Ganga is in flood. Your own seafaring ships can go up the Mahaweli Ganga since there is enough water in the river channel. You do not really need our small riverboats. Your bigger seafaring ships can ram into and destroy the riverboats of the Sigiriya navy.'

Bharat was impressed by the trader's knowledge of warfare. She was right. But only partially so. His seafaring ships could go up river, yes. But they would prove too bulky at the Onguiaahra River fort. The smaller riverboats of the guilds would be useful at that crucial point. Once the fort was breached, his ships could sail through.

There was one other reason why he intended to commandeer the guild ships. He didn't want to leave vessels behind, which could be used to attack his navy from the rear when he sailed onward into the Mahaweli Ganga River. Some of the guilds could be loyal to Raavan. Abundant caution would dictate that he destroy the guild ships he could not use.

In war, one hopes for the best and prepares for the worst.

'Thank you for the wise military advice,' said Bharat. 'All the same, I want those ships. *All* your vessels. The seafaring ones as well as the riverboats.'

'Um …'

Manigramaa looked at her companions, all shifting uncomfortably in their seats. Some were looking at her. Others were staring fixedly at the floor.

Bharat understood. Ayodhya and the Sapt Sindhu held businessmen in great contempt. Unlike Raavan, who was at heart a trader, most Sapt Sindhu kings did not understand the concept of property rights of businessmen. Bharat guessed that the Gokarna guilds suspected they would not be compensated for the loss of their ships.

'I will pay a fair price for all your ships,' he said.

Manigramaa brightened up. She did not need to look at the others in the delegation before responding. 'Then we will be very happy to hand over our ships to you.'

Bharat nodded. 'Thank you.'

'In fact,' continued Manigramaa, sensing an opportunity for further profit, 'if the Ayodhya treasury is short of funds for this purchase, or any other supplies you may need, our Cotton and Silk Guild would be very happy to lend you the money. Our interest rates are quite competitive. Far lower than what is charged in the Sapt Sindhu.'

Bharat smiled ruefully. The Lankan guilds were legendarily profitable, and he knew that many were sitting on huge amounts of excess money that they had now deployed in banking. In effect, they were muscling into the market of the traditional moneylenders. And since they were flush with cash, they happily charged lower interest rates. But Bharat had already raised money in Ayodhya. At high interest rates, yes. The rates would be unnaturally high in a land that resented its traders and business houses, and loans would be difficult to come by. But the task was done. It was too late now.

He politely declined. 'Thank you, Manigramaaji. But no thank you.'

Manigramaa smiled genially. 'All right, then. I guess our business here is done.'

'Yes, I would think so.'

'Thank you, great prince,' said Manigramaa rising. 'You are a fair and just man. I did not expect this from a Sapt Sindhu royal.'

'We are not all bigoted,' Bharat said with a smile, standing too in respect. 'Or foolish. I understand that traders generate wealth for our land.'

Manigramaa held back her emotions with restraint. She was unaccustomed to receiving respect from the royals of the Sapt Sindhu. She smiled and folded her hands into a *namaste*. 'May Goddess Lakshmi bless you with victory and success, great prince.'

'Thank you,' said Bharat, folding his hands into a respectful *namaste*.

She seemed to hesitate a bit before adding, 'You can trust us, Prince Bharat … I don't think Emperor Ram and Prince Shatrughan need to remain in the royal ship. They can be brought on shore.'

Bharat smiled genially. 'It is an Ayodhya royal ship, Manigramaaji. Trust me, it's very comfortable.'

Manigramaa smiled with understanding. Bharat had, in effect, told her he couldn't afford to risk his king's life. It was a pragmatic choice. But he had implied this with grace. Without insulting her honour. *A good man.*

'I will take your leave then,' said Manigramaa, bowing low.

Bharat nodded his head slightly, his hands folded together into a *namaste*.

Manigramaa, followed by the rest of her delegation, walked out of the chamber.

Bharat waited for the Lankans to leave and then looked at Lakshman. 'And now we must meet that traitor.'

'Are you sure, Dada?' asked Lakshman. 'Can we trust a man who is betraying his own elder brother?'

'We certainly cannot trust him,' said Bharat. 'But we can use him. Have you sent our soldiers to man the peaks on the hills surrounding the city?'

'Yes, Dada. Done already. I have also set up a courier system from the heights to warn us of any sneak Lankan land attacks. Our ship is not too far from here. We can make a quick getaway if Raavan tries anything underhand.'

Bharat nodded. He was a careful commander. 'All right, then. Send a messenger and get the Lankan turncoat here.'

— ⨌ ⫝̸⸝⸎ᴅ —

'We have come to take your leave, princess. It is time,' said Raavan.

Raavan and Kumbhakarna had arrived in Ashok Vatika dressed in the uniforms the Lankans wore when they went to war: black *dhotis* and *angvastrams*. The *angvastram* was wrapped around their nose and mouth, like a mask. They stood at a distance from Sita, who had just finished her breakfast.

She frowned. She hadn't heard the news. It was only a day since the disease had been discovered.

Kumbhakarna turned to a lady physician standing behind him. She too had her *angvastram* wrapped around her nose and mouth. She bowed low, holding in place a bag slung over her shoulder.

Sita stepped back instinctively. 'What's going on?'

Raavan looked at the doctor. 'Step back.'

The physician took a few steps backwards.

'Out of earshot,' hissed Raavan.

The doctor turned around and ran back a few more steps.

Raavan looked at Sita. 'It's for your protection, princess.'

'From what?' asked Sita.

'Princess, we have been struck by another flu pandemic,' said Kumbhakarna. 'This one is dangerous. It seems to be hitting the older ones hard.'

'We have enough Malayaputra medicine for now,' said Raavan. 'But we need to prioritise its use for the army. And for you. My army cannot fight if it is difficult for them to even breathe. And I cannot meet Vedavati in the land of the ancestors if I allow you to die before your time.'

Sita stepped back in horror. 'Your primary duty is towards your citizens.'

'We have enough for the first round of medicine for them,' answered Raavan, expecting this objection from Sita. 'The next round for the citizens will be needed two weeks later. I am hoping you will convince Guru Vishwamitra to send some more medicine by then. But to convince him, you need to remain alive.'

'Why does this plague keep hitting Lanka? It doesn't occur in the rest of India so much.'

'Perhaps I will do research on that in my next life. For now, we need to ensure that you are safe. Please take the medicine.'

Sita smiled and nodded.

Kumbhakarna turned towards the physician in the distance. And gestured for her to come forward.

The doctor began to walk towards them.

Raavan snapped. 'Move. Move. Move!' he boomed.

The physician broke into a run. As she came close, Raavan sneered, 'Are we waiting for the next monsoon season?'

'My apologies, Your Highness,' said the doctor.

'Give the medicine to the princess.'

The doctor had made the medicine paste already. She quickly opened her cloth bag, unlocked the container and, using a fresh spoon, offered the medicine to Sita. Sita swallowed the bitter medicine and the doctor quickly locked the container. The medicine could not be exposed to the elements.

'*Jai Rishi Chyawan*,' whispered the doctor.

Glory to Rishi Chyawan.

It was well-known that this Malayaputra medicine had been formulated by the great Rishi Chyawan in ancient times. In his honour, the medicine was sometimes called *Chyawanprash*, the *medicine of Chyawan.*

'*Jai Rishi Chyawan*,' repeated everyone.

'Leave the medicine here please, respected doctor,' said Kumbhakarna.

The doctor immediately placed it on the table and turned towards Sita. 'You have to take this medicine once a—'

Sita bowed low in respect, folded her hands into a *namaste* and said softly, 'I know the dosage, respected physician. Thank you so much for all your help.'

The doctor smiled and stepped back.

Raavan pinned his eyes on the doctor. She immediately twirled around and retreated to a safe distance. Out of earshot.

'Be sure to get a lot more of this medicine for the entire city, princess,' said Kumbhakarna. 'Guru Vishwamitra will not deny you.'

'I will,' promised Sita. 'Your citizens will not die from this disease.'

Kumbhakarna smiled. 'I know you will honour your word.'

'I have another request,' said Raavan.

'Tell me,' said Sita.

'I have packed off my son Indrajit to Bali, along with my uncle Mareech. To sort a trade dispute, they have been told …' Raavan smiled as he said this, impressed that he had managed to fool his son and uncle to save their lives. 'They will return in a few weeks. Everything will be over by then. Please ensure that your husband Ram does not oppose Indrajit's ascension to the throne of Lanka. He will be a good king.'

Sita thought it unlikely that Indrajit had left for Bali. She suspected that he would fight alongside Raavan. And he would not aspire for a noble death, but victory in battle. However, if Indrajit survived the battle, she would ensure that the capable and *dharmic* son of Raavan became king of Lanka.

'I promise, Raavanji,' said Sita.

'Give my son this letter from me,' said Raavan, handing over a sealed scroll to Sita.

'I will,' said Sita, accepting the letter.

Raavan smiled. There was nothing more to be said. Except goodbye. The final goodbye.

'Are you leaving today?' asked Sita.

'Within a few hours, actually,' said Raavan. 'Your husband and his army have reached Gokarna. They should be within sight of Onguiaahra in a few days.'

Sita nodded. In all probability this was her last meeting with Raavan and Kumbhakarna. She had enjoyed her conversations with them, discovering so much about her mother, learning so many things. They had forged a bond of friendship.

She folded her hands together into a *namaste* and bowed low towards Raavan, showing respect to the man he was becoming. Instead of the monster he had been.

Raavan smiled and raised his right hand from a distance. '*Akhand saubhagyavati bhav,*' said Raavan, blessing Sita with the traditional invocation. *May her husband always be alive and by her side.*

A generous blessing, from one who was about to battle her husband.

He may have lived badly. But he will die well.

— ⅃ᚪ ⅃ɔᗮ —

'*Namaste*, great prince,' said Vibhishan, as he sauntered in with cultivated confidence into the chamber. Bharat and Lakshman were waiting for him.

'*Namaste*, noble Vibhishan,' said Bharat with a winsome smile.

Bharat gestured to his soldiers to wait outside. They saluted the prince of Ayodhya and left. Vibhishan was alone with the brothers.

Vibhishan looked at Lakshman with a friendly smile, folding his hands into a *namaste*. 'This meeting is taking place in much more fortuitous circumstances than the earlier one, Prince Lakshman.'

They had last met in Panchavati, where things had speedily devolved into a knife fight. Lakshman was convinced that that particular series of events had in fact triggered this war. He could not have fathomed that the war was inevitable, regardless of what had transpired in Panchavati.

Lakshman grunted and perfunctorily brought his hands together.

Vibhishan let the insult pass. He turned to Bharat. 'Will not the virtuous King Ram join us, Prince Bharat?'

'Why don't you speak with us first?' Bharat spoke in a dulcet voice. 'And then we will decide what to do next.'

'I do not intend to assassinate your commander, Prince Bharat,' said Vibhishan, attempting a feeble joke as he preened with self-delight.

Bharat suppressed an amused grin. This joker actually thought he could kill Ram.

Never confront a fool with his stupidity, though. It only incites a cycle of ego-driven, unproductive counter-reactions. Praising the 'intelligence' and leveraging the self-satisfaction helps further one's cause.

'We trust you completely, Prince Vibhishan,' said Bharat. 'But we also know your fearsome valour. I'm sure you will understand that it's wise for us to err on the side of caution. The king must be protected in a game of chess.'

'I understand, Prince Bharat. Perhaps I would have done the same in your position.'

'Thank you, Prince Vibhishan,' said Bharat. 'Now, you had sent a message that you have some information to share.'

Vibhishan smiled, clearly thrilled by his own brilliance. 'Not just information ... I have come to provide assistance.'

Lakshman could barely suppress his mirth. *This imbecile will help us against his formidable brother, Raavan, is it?!*

But he had been given strict instructions by Bharat to keep quiet. So, he kept quiet.

'Assistance, brave prince?' asked Bharat, feigning intrigue.

'Perhaps the better word would be a trade-off.'

'Yes, yes, a trade-off between equals.'

'Yes, of course,' said Vibhishan, preening some more. 'A fair trade-off. Victory for your brother, Emperor Ram, and the throne of Lanka for me.'

Bharat smiled. 'Sounds fair. Courageous even. But what are you offering? Besides yourself, of course ...'

Vibhishan looked at Lakshman, a proud smile spread across his face. He looked back at Bharat. 'I bring the keys to Onguiaahra.'

Bharat leaned forward. Genuinely interested now. And hence, silent.

'You do know of the great river fort of Onguiaahra,' said Vibhishan.

Bharat nodded. *Yes.*

'It has never been conquered. It is impossible to conquer. And without control over Onguiaahra, your ships cannot sail farther up the Amban Ganga – the tributary of Mahaweli Ganga – and get close to the port of Sigiriya. And your army cannot march through the dense forests of Lanka. They will be hopelessly lost. They will die. The Amban Ganga River is the only path. And Onguiaahra blocks it resolutely.'

'I am aware of this, Prince Vibhishan,' said Bharat. 'What are you offering?'

'Onguiaahra cannot be taken with a direct assault. It is impossible. I will share the maps and designs of the fort with you.'

Bharat had already procured the maps of Onguiaahra through his spies. He knew that a direct assault was pointless. Siege specialists hold that every fort has some flaws, some weaknesses. But try as he might, Bharat could not divine any flaws in Onguiaahra's design. The topography around the citadel, and its skilful use by the fort builders, made it impregnable. No invader had ever breached it.

'Are you saying that your elder brother made a mistake in the fort design?' asked Bharat.

'No,' answered Vibhishan. 'My elder brother made a different mistake. He trusted the wrong person.'

Bharat maintained a deadpan expression. 'Carry on.'

'My brother is an extremely suspicious man. He distrusts even his own army. And he understands the importance of Onguiaahra. As long as Onguiaahra holds, Sigiriya is safe. So, he didn't leave Onguiaahra in the hands of the local commander.'

'And have you brought over the commander?'

Vibhishan shook his head. 'No. The commander – Dhumraksha – is loyal to Lanka. He is a ruthless and fierce warrior. But since Raavan dada didn't trust him completely, he instructed that a secret underground passage be built without the knowledge of Dhumraksha, leading into the fort's rear embankments. In fact, two secret underground passages. One which opens downriver in the direction of Gokarna, and another upriver, towards Sigiriya.'

Bharat kept the excitement off his face. 'I guess he wanted to ensure that if Dhumraksha turned, Raavan could quickly enter the fort in secret and regain control.'

Vibhishan nodded.

'And how do you know about these passages?'

'I built them,' said Vibhishan.

Bharat nodded. 'Take us into Onguiaahra and the throne of Lanka is yours.'

Vibhishan smiled. 'I know you will honour your word, great prince. But can I also hear this from the emperor of Ayodhya, Ram?'

Lakshman burst out in anger, 'Do you doubt the words of a prince of Ayodhya? Don't you know that we Ayodhyans would rather die than break our promise?'

Bharat glanced at his brother. 'Relax, Lakshman. I understand why Prince Vibhishan wants reassurance.' Bharat looked at Vibhishan. 'I will issue a proclamation, sealed by my brother Ram himself, acknowledging you as the rightful king of Lanka. Good enough?'

Vibhishan folded his hands together into a *namaste*. 'More than good enough, Prince Bharat. You are fair and just.'

'And you will stay with us as our honoured guest till we enter Onguiaahra,' continued Bharat.

Bharat did not trust this man.

Vibhishan frowned. 'But I am used to comfort.'

'And you shall be very comfortable, I assure you.'

'All right,' said Vibhishan. 'I shall be your guest till we take Onguiaahra.'

The deal had been sealed.

Vibhishan looked out the window, at the Ayodhyan ships anchored in the Gokarna Bay. He was also aware of the many vessels stationed outside the bay, in the open ocean. He turned to Bharat.

'I hope you have enough soldiers, Prince Bharat,' said Vibhishan.

'The Lankan army may not be what it was, but my brother Raavan will feel no fear. For he knows that two hundred thousand soldiers stand between him and defeat.'

Bharat smiled. 'We have one hundred and sixty thousand soldiers. And they will feel no fear. For they know that Ram stands between them and defeat.'

Chapter 18

'You may need to wait, Lord Hanuman and Lord Arishtanemi,' said Angad.

It was the day after the massacre of the leftover Lankan battalion at Ketheeswaram. Ram had been extremely angry about the attack; they were incapacitated soldiers and this was against the rules of honourable warfare, he had said. But he also knew he could not punish the Malayaputras. Not only was it their right to seek vengeance, he also knew that he needed the fifteen thousand Malayaputra soldiers; more so, their elephant corps. Sometimes, a general must tolerate the excesses of his men for the greater good of the war. Ram had swallowed this bitter pill.

Arishtanemi and Hanuman had settled near a beachhead at the Lankan mainland, planning stockades as protection for Ram's army when it would land. Leaving their men to complete this work, the duo had rowed across the Dhanushkodi straits and returned to the Pamban island, where Shatrughan was supervising final preparations to build the bridge between Mannar and Pamban. The building material was being transported from the Indian mainland by the Ayodhya army. They forded the shallow sea flats on foot. Over three hundred elephants from the Malayaputra and Vaanar corps made the task easier and quicker than had been originally envisaged.

'How much longer will the *puja* take?' asked Arishtanemi.

Hanuman, Arishtanemi, Angad and Naarad stood a short distance from the spot where Ram and Shatrughan had begun a Rudraabhishek *prayer and worship ceremony*, conducted by their *guru* Vashishtha. The *puja*, dedicated to the previous Mahadev Lord Rudra, was usually conducted to ward off negative energy. There was one other reason. Lord Rudra was one of the greatest warriors the world has ever seen, and they sought his blessings before a war. The *puja* was being conducted on a flat promontory-type sandy patch of land that extended in a north-easterly direction on Pamban Island. The bridge would begin from the south-east end of the island, two kilometres from here. Years from now, a great temple to Lord Rudra would be built on this spot. It would be known as the temple of *Ram's God* or *Rameshwaram*.

'This is not the standard Rudraabhishek *puja*, Arishtanemiji,' answered Naarad. 'Guru Vashishtha began it two hours back. It should be ending soon.'

'Hmm,' answered Hanuman.

'Yes, we have had our medicine,' said Vashishtha, in answer to Arishtanemi.

'Good,' said Arishtanemi. 'This disease is dangerous.'

The Malayaputra medicine had been administered to the Ayodhyans, Vayuputras, Malayaputras and Vaanars within the day. The benefit of disciplined armies: soldiers follow orders and do not question.

'Do we have enough medicine for the next few months?' asked Shatrughan. 'This campaign may last a long time. Or should we delay the bridge construction till we have enough medicine?'

Ram shook his head. 'We cannot delay the construction. Bharat is already at Gokarna. He has to start sailing up the Mahaweli Ganga soon, or else he risks making Raavan suspicious. We cannot assume that the king of Lanka is a fool. Raavan's army is already marching towards the Amban Ganga. He is preparing for a traditional naval battle. We need to distract his army at Onguiaahra in the east, so that no Lankan expects our main army to be marching in from the west.'

'I agree,' said Vashishtha, who had also read the coded message from Bharat that had arrived by bird courier. 'Bharat has made an alliance with Vibhishan. Raavan's younger brother will guide Bharat's army through a secret passage into the Onguiaahra citadel. Once Bharat controls Onguiaahra, he can easily inflict severe damage on Raavan's navy. The king of Lanka will be forced to retreat. Then Bharat can move his army up the Amban Ganga River and march to Sigiriya from the east, while we move in from the west. Having said that, Vibhishan could be a double agent. Or he might ultimately help whoever he thinks is winning. If Bharat delays his advance, Vibhishan is likely to think we have run into problems with our invasion, and he may switch sides again.'

'So, net-net, we must start building the bridge tomorrow,' said Shatrughan.

'Precisely,' agreed Hanuman.

Angad spoke up. 'Prince Vibhishan reminds me of that ancient code for a king. Avoid both trustworthy fools and untrustworthy experts. Raavan has trustworthy counsel in Kumbhakarna and Indrajit. But he doesn't listen to them.'

'Vibhishan is neither a trustworthy fool nor an untrustworthy expert,' said Naarad. 'He is the worst combination: an untrustworthy fool. Why Raavan even allowed that imbecile to stay with him in Lanka is a mystery.'

'That's not our problem,' said Shatrughan. 'Our problem is that we will soon need more medicine. This could be a long campaign. Can it be arranged, Arishtanemiji?'

'I'm conscious of this need, Shatrughan,' said Arishtanemi. 'I have already asked a group of Malayaputras to travel to Agastyakootam. They are leaving tomorrow morning. I've asked them to row down south along the coast, and then up the River Thamiravaruni. They should be back in a week, at most.'

'That's good news,' said Vashishtha.

'Can we get a month's supply for the city of Sigiriya as well?' asked Ram. 'Ayodhya will pay for those medicines.'

Arishtanemi's eyes widened in shock. 'You want to help the enemy?!'

'Just the citizens,' answered Ram. 'They have done nothing wrong.'

Ram was upset enough over having been forced to countenance the killing of incapacitated Lankan soldiers at Ketheeswaram. He would not allow ordinary non-combatant citizens to suffer.

'Don't do that, great Vishnu,' said Naarad. 'Know that the ends justify the means. Raavan must be destroyed for the good of India. Let's not lose sight of that goal.'

'The end exists only in our minds,' said Ram. 'Time never stops. So, there is no real end, is there? There is only the path. All of us are stuck with the means, for we will never reach the real end. Therefore, we have to think very carefully about the means. Innocent non-combatants cannot be killed, even if it is by omission and not commission. That is *adharma*.'

'But you just spoke of laying siege to Sigiriya, even stopping their food supply,' said Vashishtha. 'Isn't that against the citizens? Aren't those questionable means?'

'I'm hoping the siege and blockade will encourage the citizens to revolt against King Raavan. We'll go slow. The citizens won't die. They will be given every opportunity to help themselves by rebelling against their ruler. But if we don't give them the medicine for this disease, they will die. And soon. There is a difference between squeezing enemy citizens to incite a rebellion and directly pushing them into the jaws of death. The first is a legitimate means of war. The second is a war crime.'

'But Raavan could divert the medicine to his army. It would sustain his soldiers longer,' countered Hanuman.

'We will catapult messages into Sigiriya, informing the citizens that we have given the Malayaputra medicine for their use. And that Raavan is diverting it to his soldiers. That, too, will encourage disaffection. A siege works well when the citizens of a besieged city rebel against their own lords and army. We must get Sigiriya to rebel.'

Everyone kept quiet. Only Naarad sported a hint of a smile.

'I know what you are thinking,' said Ram. 'That I am naïve. But I am not. We will follow *dharma* by giving medicine to the citizens of Sigiriya. And our generosity towards King Raavan's citizens will raise agitators in his city. This is *dharma* as well as good battle strategy.'

'Do you remember what Raavan's army did in Mumbadevi?' asked Naarad. 'Let me remind you. The peaceful Devendrars were burnt to the last man, woman and child. The commander who led that brutal invasion – Prahast – wasn't punished. Instead, he was promoted. This is what you are facing. This is what your enemy is like. Raavan may just allow his entire citizenry to die. You are rationalising your need to be ethical by convincing yourself that it's also good battle strategy. But your enemy has no ethics. Raavan only wants to win. That is the difference between you and him. Between us and them.'

'Yes. That is the difference,' said Ram. 'And that difference must be maintained. We will win. But we will win the right way. We must set an example for a better India.'

Naarad smiled, keeping his thoughts to himself. *I may just be on the side of Good this time … Let's hope we win …*

'All right,' said Arishtanemi. 'I will tell my soldiers to get more medicine from Agastyakootam. Enough for the citizens of Sigiriya as well.'

—JF J,5D—

The day finally dawned.

Vishwakarma, the God of the Architects and Engineers, was propitiated in a solemn ceremony. Lord Varun, the God of Water and the Seas, was also ritually invoked. The former was to bestow diligence and expertise, the latter to allow their work to flow unhindered through His realm. The material for the first phase of construction had reached the south-eastern part of Pamban Island. The nadir of the low tide would soon be upon them. Perfect timing.

The initial batch of elephants and soldiers had been trained and deployed; the workers would be rotated in short shifts of four hours each, for this was hard work.

Four mahouts on elephants had been tasked with marking the northern and southern boundaries of the bridge that was being built west to east. It was a low-tech, effective method designed by Shatrughan.

Two elephants stood in line in the shallow water while their mahouts held a rope at two ends, which served to represent the northern edge of the starting point of the bridge. Ram and Shatrughan stood some distance away, observing man and animal working in tandem. Another set of two elephants with their mahouts had been placed in an exact mirror formation, three and a half kilometres to the south. The ropes held by the two sets of mahouts represented the northernmost and southernmost edge of the breadth of the bridge. All building activities would be conducted within the rope boundaries which curved gently, creating the aerodynamic – rather, hydrodynamic – bridge that Shatrughan had envisioned.

'Dada,' said Shatrughan, handing a Platygyra coral stone brick to his elder brother. Ram looked at the brick. His name had been carved into it on one side. On the other side was engraved the number '1'. 'Drop this into the water and let the construction begin. This will be our first offering to Lord Varun.'

Ram looked at the brick and then at Shatrughan. He took a few steps, bent and picked up a sharp stone. He began carving a few more words on the Platygyra brick. Shatrughan leaned over to see what his brother had written.

Ram had added the names of his brothers. Bharat, next to his own. And Lakshman and Shatrughan below.

'I don't work alone,' said Ram. 'I am nothing without my brothers.'

Shatrughan smiled and touched his brother's arm.

Ram flipped the stone over. 1 became 4.

'Hold the stone with me,' said Ram.

Shatrughan reached out and held the brick. Then the brothers walked into the sea.

They whispered the chant of ancient Indian mariners.

Sham No Varunah.

May Varun, the God of Water and the Seas, be auspicious unto us.

They bent low and dropped the brick into the water. It floated on the surface, swaying gently with the waves.

The waves did not push the stone back to the beach.

Lord Varun had accepted the offering.

Ram nodded. 'Let's begin.'

'Tell him to wait,' Bharat ordered his attendant.

The attendant saluted and left the room.

The construction of the bridge had begun off the western coast of the island of Lanka two days back. Of course, no Lankan on the eastern part of the island had an inkling of this.

Bharat and Lakshman were at their temporary palace quarters in Gokarna. They had spent the previous night in the Ayodhya royal ship. Gokarna was still convinced that Ram and Shatrughan were on board. The Ayodhya ships had moved in the night from Gokarna Bay and had anchored themselves, along with the rest of their fleet, in the open ocean. Bharat and Lakshman had returned in the morning with a fresh set of orders for their soldiers. And information to gather.

Vibhishan had arrived unannounced. Bharat had decided he could wait.

'Any news, Dada?' asked Lakshman.

Two days back, Bharat had ordered a few soldiers to take a quick cutter boat and row up the Mahaweli Ganga to the Onguiaahra River citadel. They had been told to strictly avoid all confrontation and being seen. Their job was to check if the Lankan army and river-navy were on the other side of the choke point at Onguiaahra.

Bharat looked at Lakshman and nodded. 'Raavan has taken the bait. He has brought almost his entire army to Onguiaahra. They are all aboard ships on the Amban Ganga, at the place before it meets the Mahaweli Ganga.'

Lakshman clenched his right fist and banged it into his open left palm. 'Fantastic. We've pulled them here. Ram dada and Shatrughan have a clear field on their side.'

'Hmm. And we'll have to keep them here.'

'We'll not just keep them here, Dada. We'll destroy them here. Ram dada will not waste his time battling. He can just march triumphant into Sigiriya.'

Bharat smiled fondly. It had been so long. He had almost forgotten what Lakshman was like, having spent close to fourteen years with Shatrughan. Lakshman and Shatrughan were like chalk and cheese despite being twins. Shatrughan was calm, cerebral and pragmatic, while Lakshman was aggressive, impulsive and short-tempered. But both had hearts of gold.

Fierce confidence is highly effective in a warrior but oftentimes, it is counter-productive in a general, who must be realistic. He must think two steps ahead of his enemy, and fight only when he knows he can win.

A good general does not let his soldiers die in vain.

Bharat was a good general.

'Let's see, Lakshman,' said Bharat. 'Our main aim is to hold Raavan here as long as possible. If we can give his army some body-blows, all the better.'

Their attention was suddenly diverted by some loud explosive sounds. Lakshman looked out of the window. 'It's begun, Dada.'

Bharat walked over to the window. From the high perch of their palace, he had a clear view of Gokarna Bay.

'Lakshman, did you deliver the *hundi* to the guilds? To purchase the Gokarna merchant ships?' asked Bharat.

'Yes, Dada, just as you ordered.'

The Gokarna merchant ships now belonged to Ayodhya. And all them were lashed together and anchored at the bay centre. Fire raged through the fleet now, aided by some wax and oil that had been liberally poured onto the decks. Many ships had the secondary square-rigged masts open to half height – cloth with oil would catch fire quicker. Bharat had carefully planned the details. A combination of charcoal and saltpetre – used in fireworks – had been placed in the cargo holds of some of the bigger merchant ships in the knotted fleet. One of those explosive mixes had just erupted.

A spectacle of hellish flames. For the benefit of Raavan's spies.

Bharat could guess at the kind of reports that would travel to the Lankan high command. The Ayodhya commanders were covering their backs. Preventing any likelihood of merchant ships launching a surprise attack on the Ayodhyan navy from the rear. The inference was obvious: the attack via the Mahaweli Ganga River was imminent.

'You don't think it's a little too obvious? The very public burning?' asked Lakshman. 'We could have just sunk the ships. Raavan could become suspicious.'

Bharat opened his eyes wide in amusement. 'Lakshman, my darling brother, are *you* talking about subtlety?'

Lakshman laughed and slapped his elder brother on the back.

'I want Raavan to think that we are angry. Fire of vengeance and all that sort of thing,' continued Bharat. 'I want him to think that we have allowed emotions to cloud our judgement. It's best that the enemy underestimates you in battle.'

'Hmm …'

'So, when Vibhishan comes in this time, let loose a bit. Let him see that you are angry. Hint that so is Ram dada. And I am the only one holding you people back with some dose of realism.'

Lakshman nodded. 'Do you think our conversations with Vibhishan are reaching Raavan?'

'I have no doubt they are. Maybe not through Vibhishan himself. But through others here. Vibhishan just needs to be a little loose-tongued with someone he thinks is a friend in this city. The heart of an efficient government is a good spy network that keeps the ruler one step ahead of everyone else. And Raavan is an efficient ruler. He has built all this from scratch. We may hate the guy, but we must respect his abilities.' Bharat turned towards the door and spoke loudly to the doorman on the other side. 'Let Prince Vibhishan in.'

Vibhishan sauntered in with affected nonchalance. Arms stretched out to accommodate non-existent biceps in a reed-thin body. *'Boils under his armpits, apparently ...'* Bharat remembered Lakshman's laconic remark and smiled.

Vibhishan had raised his game with his clothes, though. He wore a purple silk dhoti and *angvastram*. Purple was the most expensive dye in the world, the colour of royalty. His jewellery, too, was no longer understated; extravagant gold and ruby-encrusted earrings, a delicately fillgreed necklace and a diamond line bracelet encased in gold.

Clearly, he was already seeing himself as a king.

'Welcome, Your Highness,' said Bharat, leaning into Vibhishan's weak character with the term of address.

Vibhishan preened pretentiously. 'What a pleasure to meet you again, Prince Bharat.' Vibhishan turned to Lakshman and executed an elaborately extravagant *namaste*. Lakshman nodded cursorily. Vibhishan, as always, ignored the insult. 'So, when do we sail, Prince Bharat? Now that you have covered your rear flanks by making a bonfire of the merchant ships ... Which is a brilliant move, might I add.'

Bharat's answer was simple and pithy. 'Soon, Your Highness.'

'We should burn this entire city down, Dada,' said Lakshman suddenly, anger blazing in his eyes, 'and not just the ships. Lanka will pay for messing with the Sapt Sindhu royals.'

Vibhishan looked at Lakshman, alarmed. Sigiriya may be the resplendent capital of Lanka, but the port city of Gokarna was the engine that drove Lankan prosperity. Sigiriya may well be destroyed, but a ravaged Gokarna would be the end of Lanka.

Bharat raised his palm as if advocating calm. 'Lakshman ...'

'Ram dada is right, Bharat dada,' said Lakshman, his face red with rage. 'We need to teach them a lesson. I don't know why you—'

'Enough!' said Bharat loudly and firmly.

Lakshman fell silent.

'Leave me alone with Prince Vibhishan,' said Bharat.

'Dada ...'

'Which part of my order did you not understand, Lakshman?' growled Bharat.

Lakshman glared at Bharat for a few seconds and then stormed out of the chamber.

'I'm sorry that you had to see that, Your Highness,' said Bharat to Vibhishan.

Vibhishan was too stunned to say anything. He had witnessed Lakshman's temper once, in Panchavati. But it was shocking to discover that even the serene Ram was enraged; angry enough to want to destroy an innocent city like Gokarna, it would seem. Perhaps it was understandable. Sita was his wife, after all. For a brief moment, Vibhishan wondered if he had made a mistake in seeking Ayodhya's help. But Raavan probably knew about his treachery by now. His boat, too, had burned. There was no going back; not for him. He would either sink or swim with Bharat now.

'We must keep our alliance strong, Prince Bharat,' said Vibhishan, his voice almost a whine. The earlier insouciance had disappeared. 'Otherwise too many innocents will die.'

'I know,' said Bharat. 'I am a practical man. I want to win the war with as few casualties as possible among my soldiers. Our friendship can ensure that.'

'Yes, Prince Bharat, it certainly can.'

Bharat reached over to his table and handed a rolled-up scroll to Vibhishan. 'And as a token of our friendship ...'

Vibhishan guessed what the scroll was, but he still couldn't contain his excitement as he rolled it open. A royal Ayodhyan decree, marked with the seal of the emperor of the Sapt Sindhu, Ram. It formally acknowledged Vibhishan as the king of Lanka and committed Ayodhya through all means, including military, to placing Vibhishan upon the Sigiriya throne.

His heart skipped a beat. *I'll show that ... that monster ... I'm unworthy, he said ... I'll show ...*

Vibhishan's train of thought was interrupted by Bharat. 'Now ... I will need a token of friendship from you in return, Your Highness.'

'Anything,' said a grateful Vibhishan.

'I'd initially thought that you could accompany Lakshman and guide him through the secret tunnel into the Onguiaahra fort.'

Vibhishan visibly recoiled at the thought of being stuck in the thick of battle, not least of all with the hot-tempered Lakshman.

'But,' continued Bharat, 'seeing the emotions that are coursing through my brother's veins – all my brothers, really – I would much rather send Lakshman and his battalion without you.'

'That may be wise, Prince Bharat,' said Vibhishan, his shoulders sinking with visible relief. 'The conquest of Onguiaahra is a job for butchers, not for kings.'

Bharat struggled to keep the contempt off his face. 'Yes, of course, Your Highness.' He pulled up a detailed map of the course of the Mahaweli Ganga and the Amban Ganga on which Sigiriya and Gokarna were clearly marked. Then he picked up some sheaves of papyrus and a graphite pencil. 'I will need you to mark the entire secret passage.'

'Of course,' said Vibhishan. He took the map, the papyrus leaves and the graphite pencil from Bharat.

'Please mark all indicators and cues to identify the entrance to the passage as well. And also put down all the features of the tunnels that Lakshman would need to know to march quickly through it. The length, breadth, height, airflow holes, lighting holes, floor construction and evenness, and so on. I want him to "see" the passage in his mind before he enters it. You can make separate notes on the papyrus sheets.'

Vibhishan was already at work. 'I designed and built the tunnels, Prince Bharat. Mind you, I'm a trained architect and cartographer. I'll make the map and instructions foolproof.'

'I have no doubt you will.' Bharat smiled.

Chapter 19

'You missed your true calling, bro!' Bharat laughed.

'I put up a good show, didn't I?' gloated Lakshman, with a proud half-smile.

After Vibhishan had left the royal chamber, Bharat had sent for Lakshman and ordered that dinner be served.

'Actually, I take back the compliment,' teased Bharat. 'You were not acting. You were just being yourself!'

Lakshman guffawed as he tore a piece of *roti* and used it to gather the vegetable on the plate. 'Has he given you proper maps?' asked Lakshman.

'Hmm,' said Bharat, chewing his food slowly.

'Awesome.'

'But he is a sly one, this Vibhishan.'

'That I've always told you. But what brought on this sudden epiphany?'

Bharat stopped mid-action, leaving his piece of *roti* on the vegetable, his eyes opening wide in mock shock. 'Epiphany?! Where in Lord Indra's name did you learn this word?'

'From Shatrughan, of course?!' Lakshman laughed. 'Why? Did I use the word wrong?'

'No, no ... Epiphany is a sudden and great revelation or realisation. And you used it sarcastically. So, you used it right, my brother ...'

Lakshman smiled beatifically, extended his left arm above his head, bent his elbow and patted himself on the back. 'Well done, Lakshman. Well done.' He laughed uproariously.

Bharat laughed along. 'I've missed your antics, you clown! We've been apart too long.'

'Yes, we've been apart too long ...' Lakshman echoed.

'Getting back to the tunnels,' said Bharat. 'Apparently no one in the Onguiaahra citadel is aware of them. Neither is the Lanka administration nor, of course, the ordinary people. Only Raavan, Kumbhakarna, their maternal uncle Mareech, Raavan's son Indrajit, Vibhishan and the workers who worked on the tunnels.'

'The workers did not talk about it with anyone? Strange.'

'Dead men don't talk. The workers were killed after the construction. To the last man.'

'Woah ... That is ...'

'... ruthless, and paranoid,' Bharat completed Lakshman's words. 'But also efficient. Very Raavan. That's why almost no one knows about these tunnels.'

'But why did Raavan use Vibhishan? That man is shifty, clearly a sneaky weasel.'

'Apparently, Vibhishan has the best architecture and engineering skills in the Lankan royal family. Or so he professes.

He claims to have designed the tunnels and supervised the construction.'

'Then he can give us the best information on the tunnels.'

'It gets better. We have to assume that Raavan knows that Vibhishan has joined us. His spy network in Gokarna is very good. He would logically deduce that Vibhishan has revealed the existence of the tunnels to us. Obviously, then, Raavan will ambush us in those passages or he will collapse the tunnel at the Gokarna side so that we cannot use it.'

Lakshman nodded. It was the most logical line of reasoning.

'But,' continued Bharat, 'we have another route open to us.'

'Which one?'

'Vibhishan must have planned his betrayal over a long time. He built yet another hidden passage into Onguiaahra from downriver, as a back-up to the back-up.'

Lakshman started laughing. 'How many bloody tunnels go into that citadel?! Is it a fort or a waystation?!'

Bharat laughed.

'So, anyway,' said Lakshman, pulling himself together, 'there is one more tunnel leading into Onguiaahra ... which Raavan, Kumbhakarna and Indrajit are not aware of. Only Vibhishan knows of it.'

'Vibhishan and the workers who built the tunnel.'

'The workers that are dead.'

'Yes.'

'We really got lucky when we snared this Lankan traitor.'

'Vibhishan would have gone to any credible enemy of his brother,' said Bharat. 'When he built this tunnel, Ayodhya had no reason to declare war on Lanka. Vibhishan was waiting for anyone who would pick a fight with King Raavan.'

'I guess Raavan sealed his fate the day he decided to trust Vibhishan.'

'Actually, he sealed his fate the day he decided to not trust his battalion in Onguiaahra. And in trying to cover that risk, he opened the possibility for us finding an easy route to defeating him.'

'Hmm.'

'Shatrughan told me something once. Something a writer from the far west, beyond Greece – someone called Fontaine – had said. "A person often meets his fate on the road he took to avoid it".'

Lakshman smiled. 'Yeah … And we'll lead Raavan to the end of his road.'

—JF ᒍᔕD—

Four days had passed since the bridge construction on the north-western side of the island of Lanka had begun. On the north-eastern side of the island, at the southern end of Gokarna Bay, Lakshman and Bharat stood on their lead ship, ready to sail up the Mahaweli Ganga River. They had received a messenger bird informing them that Shatrughan had constructed more than half the bridge. Three days from now the main contingent of the Ayodhyan army would march on to Lankan ground, and rush towards Sigiriya.

'Shouldn't we meet Emperor Ram before we sail out?' asked Vibhishan.

Vibhishan stood alongside the brothers. They were on the bow upper deck, hands on the balustrade, looking at the river extending endlessly ahead. The vessel was poised at the mouth of the Mahaweli Ganga, where the river emptied into the Gokarna Bay. Bharat had organised the fleet in a convoy of two abreast, extending behind them in a long double line. Four hundred ships in two hundred rows of two vessels each, one behind the other. The ships extended way beyond the bay into the Indian Ocean. An onlooker on the banks at the mouth of the river could spend four hours watching the entire convoy of the Ayodhyan navy from the first ship to the last sail by; the fleet formation was that long. It was a show of strength from the Sapt Sindhu military. A shock-and-awe campaign to cow down the Lankans into submission.

'Bharat dada and I met him this morning,' said Lakshman in answer to Vibhishan. 'Why do you want to meet him? What do you want to tell him that you cannot tell us?'

'It's nothing like that, Prince Lakshman,' said Vibhishan. He was smiling, his standard response to the constant hostility from Lakshman. 'I just thought that, since I am an ally, I should meet the leader of our army before we begin our invasion of Lanka.'

Lakshman's face exhibited intense hostility. 'You are not an ally. You are a collaborator. It is a trading relationship between us. We get Onguiaahra. You get the Lanka throne. Don't try to be something you are not.'

'Lakshman ...' said Bharat, pretending exasperation.

'Dada, I am listening to you and following your directions,' said Lakshman. 'So is Ram dada. But tell your friend to know his limits.'

'Lakshman,' growled Bharat. 'Leave me alone with King Vibhishan. Leave.'

'He's not a king yet,' sneered Lakshman.

Bharat stepped towards Lakshman. 'Are you suggesting that we Suryavanshis break our word of honour?'

Lakshman fell silent.

'Leave us alone,' ordered Bharat. 'And that's an order. Go, do your job. Let's start sailing up the Mahaweli Ganga.'

Lakshman saluted like a subordinate following an order from his general and not a loving brother, and left. Bharat made a mental note to compliment Lakshman on his histrionics later. Lakshman was clearly enjoying this.

Bharat turned to Vibhishan. 'I'm sorry, Your Highness. Not all my siblings are happy about taking your help. They would much rather win without subterfuge. They want to win like warriors of the old school. But I understand that war is nasty business. We must win, with all the means at our disposal.'

'But—' began Vibhishan.

He was interrupted by a loud noise. Both turned. The lead ship horn had blasted a long hoot, which was followed by three short bursts. And the flags were raised. The convoy was too massive for orders to be conveyed through verbal commands. And sending row boats with written instructions would take too long. So, Bharat had instituted a system in which commands could be conveyed through blasts of a ship horn, accompanied by various flags atop the mainmast. Each combination of coloured flags broadcast a specific simple instruction in a code understandable only to the ship captains. The instruction being communicated right now was clear: Set sail.

Bharat looked at Vibhishan. He guessed what was transpiring in the mind of Raavan's younger brother.

'King Vibhishan,' said Bharat softly, 'I can understand what you must be thinking … *Can I trust an emperor who hates me? Will he honour his word and make me king?*

Vibhishan remained quiet.

'My brother Ram sticks to the path of honour even if it hurts him personally. Which is why he does not want your help right now. Do you think such a man will refuse to keep his word to establish you as king? Something that he has committed in writing to you?'

Vibhishan let out a long breath. The logic was irrefutable.

'But, yes, he doesn't like you,' continued Bharat. 'He will not meet you.'

The conversation stopped as the ship began to move. The sails had been raised and the rhythmic drumbeats of the ship count-masters could be heard. A drumbeat to which the rowers synchronised their rowing. Six battalions—three each on the western and eastern banks of the Mahaweli Ganga—marched alongside the navy in lines of four abreast on the banks of the river. Their shields raised towards the forest side. Spears and swords ready. In case of surprise attacks by the Lankans.

Bharat was a careful general.

The marching soldiers served one other purpose. They provided a credible excuse for the slow movement of the Ayodhya navy up the Mahaweli Ganga River. A half-day journey would now take two days, since the boats would need to slow down and remain in alignment with the soldiers on the banks. Guarding against possible ambush attacks would not arouse suspicion. The real reason was to delay the battle at Onguiaahra as much as possible, to give Ram and Shatrughan time to build the bridge and march across.

'I'm sure Emperor Ram will like me once he knows how I have helped weaken his enemy's capacity to battle,' said Vibhishan.

'What do you mean?' asked Bharat, intrigued.

'Do you know that Sigiriya has been weakened by a plague?'

'I've heard of the flu pandemic.' Bharat did not reveal that he had received this information from a bird courier sent by Ram. He had also been sent medicines through Arishtanemi's fast cutter boats. 'And we have enough Malayaputra medicines with us. You needn't worry.'

'Oh that—I know you can manage that. There is another plague that they have been suffering from for a long time. Many years, actually. It has weakened Sigiriya and their army.'

'What is it? I don't know about this plague.'

'Most people outside Lanka don't. My brother Raavan has kept it secret for obvious reasons. And the strange thing about the plague is that it has not travelled to Gokarna. Many believe that Sigiriya is cursed. And all who live there will suffer.'

'What is it?' Bharat repeated.

'This plague is not an infection, or a curse of the Gods,' said Vibhishan, laughing softly. 'It is something that Sigiriya brought on itself.'

'What?'

'My brother wanted to supply water to people's homes.'

'So, what's the problem? I have had wells dug across Ayodhya, close to every home so that people have easy access to water.'

'No, no!' laughed Vibhishan. 'He wanted to make it even more convenient for citizens. If you dig wells, people need to maintain them. Which is inconvenient. And Raavan dada didn't want the hardened brick-type pipes you have in some Sapt Sindhu areas for obvious reasons. So, he designed what he thought was a brilliant thing: metal lead pipes. They would be easy to make. Easy to build right into homes. No leakages. Minimal maintenance required. And he could deliver water to his people. They all blessed him for it. Of course, he had me do all the hard work. I designed and built it.'

'I still don't see what the problem is.'

'Well, I discovered later that lead is not good for you.'

'What? We use lead in the Sapt Sindhu too!'

'Yes, but the Sapt Sindhu doesn't use lead in large quantities. You primarily use copper vessels and pipes. Copper is good. You use lead very sparingly. In excessive quantities, lead begins to poison and weaken you. You see, lead dissolves in water, especially the kind of water we have in Sigiriya. And everyone who drinks that water slowly starts showing signs of illness. It seems like the plague. But it is not the plague. The illness spreads gradually, over many years. Net-net, Raavan dada has been slowly poisoning himself and his beloved city.'

Vibhishan sniggered as he said this.

Bharat was shocked. 'Why didn't you save the—'

Vibhishan interrupted Bharat. 'I saved my immediate family and my mother and sister. They live in Gokarna now. But Raavan's army, which is largely based in Sigiriya, has been slowly poisoned over the years. The lead poisoning is also why they suffer more from the flu pandemic than your soldiers will. They are much much weaker than you think.'

'But … but what about the citizens of Sigiriya?'

'Collateral damage, Prince Bharat,' said Vibhishan. 'As you said, war is nasty business. So, as you can see, I have been weakening Lanka for a while. All for Emperor Ram and you. You will win easily. I have been helping you even before I met you! Once I become emperor, I will replace the lead pipes with copper pipes or some other metal. I will save the people and they will thank me for it.'

Bharat turned away and stared at the river. Trying to keep the disgust he felt for Vibhishan off his face.

Chapter 20

'Guruji?' questioned Matikaya, surprised.

Vishwamitra suppressed his irritation. *The idiot believes that his understanding is critical for solving a problem. He thinks he can improve upon a solution that I myself have conceptualised. FOOL!* Vishwamitra preferred Arishtanemi to Matikaya. Arishtanemi was intelligent enough to know when not to ask questions. Matikaya was constantly hungry for more information.

Vishwamitra had been laying out the plan for a few months now. Communicating in secret code. Through bird couriers. But now he had to send something. A large box, almost a trunk. With precious merchandise in it. Very precious. In the trunk was a weapon. A bird could obviously not carry it. And, therefore, he needed this idiot Matikaya. He could not trust anyone else. Matikaya would keep on with his questions, but he knew how to stay silent about the instructions he received from Vishwamitra. This, the formidable *guru* knew.

'Just carry this, Matikaya. And leave it at the Devagiri *ashram*. It will be picked up from there.'

'But … but the Devagiri *ashram* has been abandoned, Guruji. Nobody there. I mean …'

'Do you think it is possible that I don't know something that even you know?'

'My apologies, Guruji,' said Matikaya, folding his hands together into a penitent *namaste*.

The Saraswati was the holiest river in India. Therefore, it was held as neutral ground. It was not under any king's jurisdiction. No forts along its banks. The place was left to the sages, intellectuals, monks and mostly to Mother Nature Herself. Everyone passed these lands without let or hindrance. It was considered *adharmic* by many to even fight alongside the banks of the Saraswati.

And since nobody fought wars along the Saraswati, these lands had not been surveyed from a martial perspective. Therefore, no one understood the military significance of Devagiri. *Almost* no one.

'Just do what I tell you to do,' ordered Vishwamitra.

'Of course, Guruji,' said Matikaya, saluting smartly.

Vishwamitra turned his head. Towards the grand ParshuRamEshwar temple, the heart of the Malayaputra capital, Agastyakootam. The heart of his being.

Lord Parshu Ram, I beg you … Bless that descendant of Yayati and Sharmishtha. His sacrifice will not be in vain. It's all for Mother India.

Of course, the descendant of Yayati and Sharmishtha did not know that he was being readied as a sacrifice.

—Jᚁ ⌡꙳D—

It had been six days since Shatrughan had begun constructing the bridge. They expected to touch Mannar island in a day. Thereafter, a day's march would get them to Sigiriya via the Ketheeswaram road.

The sky was an ethereal mix of a strikingly vibrant red and an unusual, melancholic purple. It was early evening and the sun was sinking into the horizon. The Sun God, Surya, had painted a stunning picture on the canvas of the sky. A parting gift to his devotees who looked up in wonder. Till he would meet them again. Next morn.

Vashishtha, Ram and Shatrughan sat on the edge of the bridge, mesmerised by the gorgeous sky.

'Rarely have I seen a construction project move exactly to plan,' Vashishtha said with a smile, looking at Shatrughan.

'Thank you, Guruji,' said Shatrughan, folding his hands together into a *namaste*.

'Have you measured—'

Shatrughan interrupted Ram. 'Yes, Dada. We have already built a little more than thirty kilometres of the bridge length. Just five kilometres more, which we will finish tomorrow. And then we will be on Mannar island. The army can cross over the day after tomorrow.'

Ram smiled. 'We will be in Sigiriya within three days.'

'Bharat and Lakshman?' asked Vashishtha.

'They are reaching Onguiaahra tonight, Guruji,' said Ram. 'They have to keep the Lankan army busy for only three more days. By then we will reach Sigiriya and the battle will be over.'

'I have been studying the plans of the Sigiriya fort system, Dada,' said Shatrughan. 'Arishtanemiji and Hanumanji shared it with me. A siege will be long and difficult. It truly is a well-designed fort. I can't see any weakness.'

'Every fort has a weakness,' said Ram.

'It appears that this one doesn't.'

'Every fort has a weakness. And do you know what Sigiriya fort's is?'

Shatrughan shook his head. *No.*

'That the defending army will be away in Onguiaahra when we arrive. That is its weakness!'

—— JꟼＦ Ｊ5Ｄ ——

The Lanka countryside was an unending jungle. Denser and thicker than any forest that the Ayodhyans had ever seen, including the famed Dandakaranya of peninsular India.

Lanka was a tear-drop shaped island in the Indian Ocean. Highlands and mountains ran in a north-south direction down its central spine. Placed thus, both the south-west and north-east monsoon winds precipitated plentiful rain on Lanka. Most of the Indian subcontinental mainland had six seasons, one of them being the monsoon. But Lanka had two full-blown monsoon seasons, with two inter-monsoon seasons separating them. And it rained even in the inter-monsoon period due to Lanka's proximity to the equator.

Their yearly climate was simple: Rain. Very heavy rain. Rain. Exceptionally heavy rain. And heat all year round. All dispensed upon an extraordinarily fertile land.

Perfect conditions for dense rain forests.

The forests were so impenetrable that the marching soldiers had no visibility beyond fifteen to twenty feet from the river banks into the jungles. They kept their shields raised at all times. At night, they retired to the ships and the vessels simply anchored mid-river.

Progress was slow.

Finally, they approached the enemy stronghold. They were now about two kilometres downriver from the great citadel of Onguiaahra.

Lakshman had disembarked in the morning and marched alongside the battalions advancing along the eastern banks of the north-flowing Mahaweli Ganga River. Bharat did not want a Lankan spy to see an Ayodhya battalion disembarking from the ships at night. So, he had decided that some soldiers from the eastern banks would simply disappear into the jungles when the sun set. And sneak quickly into the secret tunnel.

Bharat was a careful general. And a careful general does not underestimate the opponent or his spy network.

The sun was close to the horizon. It was twilight. Time for the Ayodhyan ships to anchor mid-river and the marching soldiers to board the ship. Bharat made no attempts to keep the morning disembarking and evening embarking operations quiet. He wanted the Lankans to know that he was being careful, following standard protocols for military movements.

Amidst the noise of the soldiers boarding the ships, no one noticed that some – almost a mid-sized battalion of elite special forces – had melted into the half-light. Lakshman, along with five hundred soldiers, soon assembled two hundred metres inside the jungles. Not visible from the river.

Their shoes were coated with extra leather to smother the sounds of their footsteps. Their blades were wrapped in cotton cloth, muffling the soft din of the steel rubbing against the scabbard. The cotton cloth would tear away when the sword was drawn. Their *dhotis* were tied tight, military style. Their armour was made from leather, instead of metal. Less protection but also less noise. These were Ayodhya special forces. Accomplishing the mission was more important than protecting their lives. No verbal orders were to be given; only hand signals. They quickly fell into double file. A thin rope was tied from the waist of one to the one behind, all down the line. Each soldier had a buddy to the side and was literally tied to the entire group, through the man in front and behind.

Lakshman identified the marker to the covert pathway that would lead them to the secret tunnel. Vibhishan's maps were easy to decipher.

It was a simple marker. A Fiji dwarf coconut tree. A very pretty small coconut palm with long fronds and leaflets, midget coconuts and pronounced bronze-coloured leaf-ring scars on its trunk. The fruit of this tree was not high up, and coconuts could be removed without the need to climb it. Its name was a true descriptor: dwarf coconut tree.

Lakshman smiled.

Smart.

Obviously, Vibhishan couldn't leave a signpost at this place with the legend 'This Way to Secret Tunnel' inscribed on it. But even a blank marker could easily have aroused suspicion, for there was no reason for the presence of a manmade sign in this part of the jungle. It was best to hide the marker in plain sight. This place had a remarkable abundance of trees. So, why not use a tree itself as a marker? But to distinguish the marker, this was a tree that had no natural reason to be here. The Fiji dwarf coconut tree was not native to the region. And this would be missed by most casual observers. Only someone specifically looking for this tree would have found it.

Hidden in plain sight.

Lakshman had already memorised the map. He pulled out his compass to orient his direction, then touched the tree, being careful to hold the south side of the trunk. Then he turned to the right and walked five foot-length steps, then three steps to the left and another step to the right.

He looked down. He felt the pointy end of a stone underneath the thin upper layer of soil, poking into his shoe. The pointy stone. The starting point. The other stones, buried lightly underground, would mark the way.

That Vibhishan may be a sneaky weasel, but he is a smart sneaky weasel.

Lakshman turned to his soldiers and raised his right hand, palm open and at a right angle to his face, fingers together and pointing at the sky. And then he flicked his wrist, the fingers now pointing east.

A clear hand signal: march east.

The signal was quickly relayed down the line. And the battalion began to march. Together. In step. Guided by the rope that tied them into one mass and the buried stones that lay under their feet.

— JF ᒐ5D —

'Do you think your father knows that we did not leave for Bali, grand-nephew?' Mareech asked Indrajit. 'And that we are here in Onguiaahra?'

Onguiaahra was not just a fort, it was also a dam. One with an ingenious design. Originally conceptualised as a barrage, Kubaer, the previous ruler, had begun its construction many decades ago. The obvious place for a barrage was the cataracts between the hills of Onguiaahra. These hills on both sides of the great Mahaweli Ganga naturally constricted the river, thus quickening the water flow. The cataracts made it impossible to sail farther up the Mahaweli Ganga, with boulders and small rocky islets sticking out of the riverbed. Therefore, ships would naturally divert into the calmer Amban Ganga, the tributary which merged into the Mahaweli Ganga downriver from the cataracts. The barrage across the cataracts of Mahaweli Ganga would, then, not impact shipping and its trading profits. The supporters of the project saw many benefits as well. The barrage would divert the floodwaters from the Mahaweli Ganga to the Amban Ganga and increase its flow size. This would ease the passage of even seafaring ships up this tributary. An aqueduct from the river would also provide ample drinking water for the rapidly expanding population of Sigiriya. One barrage, so many benefits.

But what about the costs of construction?

The Mahaweli Ganga was squeezed between the hills of Onguiaahra. So, the barrage would be relatively narrow for the scale of the massive river that was being barricaded. And the rocky cataracts meant that the foundations did not need to extend too deep into the earth. All this significantly lowered the construction costs, a very important factor for the profit-conscious Kubaer.

'I don't think so, grand-uncle,' said Indrajit, to his grandmother's brother. Indrajit wasn't sure how old Mareech was, but he was certainly more than seventy. The man could still pack a warrior punch, though. 'But I am not about to go to Bali for some silly trade dispute. We need to defeat the Ayodhyans and protect Lanka. And this is the best place to beat back Emperor Ram and his army.'

'True,' agreed Mareech. 'I would much rather not face them in Sigiriya. I don't know how much grit our citizens have to live through a long siege. The plague has weakened many.'

Indrajit nodded and looked over the fort wall railings, at the artificial lake behind the dam.

Raavan had realised the military significance of the barrage at Onguiaahra. Around thirty years ago, he deposed Kubaer and took over as the ruler of Lanka. And immediately ordered that the under-construction barrage be redesigned as a dam. The dam reservoir would hold back the waters of the Mahaweli Ganga and create a massive artificial lake. The change in design significantly increased the cost and complexity of the project. But Raavan was not lacking in wealth or boldness.

As compared to a barrage, the benefits of a dam were even greater. The huge artificial lake gave the citadel defenders access to massive quantities of water. They could release it at will, through multiple sluice gates, into the river below. They could release small quantities of water as well, through delicate control of the smaller sluices, and fill up the control-steps downriver. This naturally regulated the number of ships allowed to or prevented from sailing up the Amban Ganga.

Opening all the sluice gates simultaneously and releasing the massive hold of the artificial reservoir would push all the ships downriver. But the floodwaters would travel all the way to Gokarna at the mouth of the Mahaweli Ganga and destroy the city, of course. Therefore, this was a desperate measure, a nuclear option. Not one to be exercised lightly.

The sluice gates were resolutely shut at this moment. As were the floodwater spillway gates far away at the back of the artificial lake, which allowed water from the reservoir to flow, via a canal, into the Amban Ganga upriver. This reduced the flow of water at the control-steps and made it impossible for a ship to sail farther up beyond the steps of Onguiaahra.

All sides are in defensive positions just before the onset of battle. That's natural.

'But, nephew, do you really need so many men stationed at the tunnel entrance? One hundred?'

This was a substantial number for the Onguiaahra defence forces. All in all, it was a small team of only five hundred soldiers. Every soldier was a legend in his own right. Commanding the

Onguiaahra battalion, or even being a part of it, was among the highest honours for a Lankan soldier. For they protected that which was most precious: their capital city. And being small made the Onguiaahra battalion an exclusive club. What is easily available is not often desirable. What was true among lovers is also true among warriors. It requires great wisdom and discernment to differentiate unavailability from desirability. But there is something about love and bloodlust which diminishes the ability to be wise.

Having said that, the size of the Onguiaahra battalion was not dictated by the needs of exclusivity but the limited capacity of the citadel itself. The Onguiaahra fort was originally designed as a barrage and later converted into a dam. By design, the heart of the fort was a strong wall across the breadth of the Mahaweli Ganga River. An engineer cannot make a dam wall too thick. The costs, for one, would escalate prohibitively. But structural issues were more important. The thicker the wall, the farther away the toe of the dam would need to be on the downstream side, to stabilise the wall. This would create space constraints. Also, the sluice way from the upstream to downstream side, for the dammed reservoir water, would need to lengthen. That would create its own instabilities. Onguiaahra was primarily a dam and not a fort: so Raavan had done the next best thing, and created small bastions at both ends of the wall, which dug into the hillsides.

It was at the secret tunnel entrance within the bastion on the eastern side of the wall that Indrajit had placed these one hundred soldiers.

'Yes, we do,' said Indrajit. 'The Ayodhyans will come from there. Trust me. I am absolutely sure that Vibhishan uncle has betrayed us.'

Raavan had designed the Onguiaahra fort in the shape of a dumb-bell. The 'barbel bar' was the dam wall that blocked the Mahaweli Ganga River. The 'handles' and 'weights' at both ends of the dam wall were the bastions built on top of the hills into which the dam wall foundations were extended. The two bastions on the eastern and western ends of the dam wall were round-shaped with double walls, towers and two gates. Within the inner wall boundary were quarters, armouries, a kitchen, a training ground, an exercise hall, a medical bay, toilets and all else required by a healthy and effective battalion. Steps ran down the inner gates of the bastions, leading to the sluice gate controls on the dam wall. The hills near the bastions had been scarped and the slopes were steep, almost perpendicular. An attacking army would encounter cliff-like hillsides. And charging up the dam wall was impossible. Onguiaahra was unconquerable. A limited battalion of five hundred was enough. More than enough, the son of Raavan knew.

Except if the invaders slipped into the bastion through a secret tunnel.

'My child, I am not sure,' said Mareech. 'I know Vibhishan is weak. But I think he has only escaped to Gokarna to the safety of your grandmother and aunt, since the Ayodhyans will not attack non-combatant women and children. I agree with Raavan. Vibhishan is a coward, not a traitor. It's unlikely that he will betray us.'

'He will. Trust me.'

'I do trust you, even if I disagree with you on this. I proved it by allowing you to reveal the secret entrance to Dhumraksha, didn't I?'

'General Dhumraksha was not happy,' said Indrajit.

'Dhumraksha has a right to be angry. He may be an aggressive warmonger but he has been loyal to us for decades, and Raavan did not trust him enough to tell him about the secret tunnel.'

'Hmm.'

'But he remains here. I give him credit for that. He's still willing to battle for Lanka.'

'This will not be a battle, grand-uncle. It will be a massacre. When we pounce upon the Ayodhyans skulking up the tunnel that they think is the secret to destroying us!'

Chapter 21

'Ram is very slow and very careful,' said Raavan, as he and Kumbhakarna headed out on to the deck of their lead ship. They were anchored mid-river on the Amban Ganga River, safely behind the control-steps of Onguiaahra. They knew that the Ayodhyans had arrived downriver on the Amban Ganga. But no attempt had been made to sail closer to the control-steps that loomed just after the Amban Ganga merged into the Mahaweli Ganga. The control-steps were like an inverse amphitheatre; the highest 'step' was on the eastern banks of the Mahaweli Ganga, and each successive step progressively lowered towards the western banks. Each step width was massive, large enough to accommodate even sea-faring ships. Low water levels covered just the last step close to the western banks, allowing one ship to sail through. Increasing the water levels covered more steps, allowing more ships to row through. And if the water levels were very low, no ships could pass. The steps were built from granite, the hardest rock known to man, and could destroy ship hulls.

All in all, the Lankans had built an artificial cataract, which was regulated by the reservoir waters held back by the dam-fort of Onguiaahra. A simple idea brought to life by brilliant engineering.

'Right,' said Kumbhakarna. 'King Ram is staying put where the spillway canal merges into the Mahaweli Ganga. Well behind.'

An additional spillway canal moved the waters of the Mahaweli Ganga from the dam-fort of Onguiaahra in a long arc, bypassing the control-steps. The waters merged into the same river farther down. It ensured that flood waters did not overwhelm the control-steps with water. Therefore, despite the present flood in the river, resulting in excess water behind the dam-fort of Onguiaahra and downriver at the merge-point of the spillway canal and the Mahaweli Ganga, the great river had regulated water at the control-steps midway.

'Ram has made a mistake by bringing seafaring ships up the Mahaweli Ganga,' said Raavan. 'He probably thought he would have an advantage over our much smaller riverine ships. My spies tell me that the front bow sections of his ships are reinforced with metal. He can ram our smaller ships to oblivion. The problem for him is, there isn't enough water for his big ships to sail upriver!' Raavan laughed softly as he said this.

'He is not stupid. He wouldn't have brought his seafaring ships all the way here without a plan. Do you think that Vibhishan ...'

'No,' said Raavan, shaking his head. 'Vibhishan is a coward. He doesn't have the guts to be a traitor.'

Kumbhakarna kept quiet.

'Let's see what Ram does now. He can't remain anchored forever.'

— ꓒᖴ ꓤꟓꓓ —

Lakshman and his troops had marched for over an hour, following the zig-zag path marked by the buried stones. They now stood near the tree marking the entrance to the tunnel. The next rung in their expedition.

Lakshman smiled again. He was beginning to like Vibhishan. Just a bit.

Sneaky weasel. But a very smart sneaky weasel.

The map had instructed Lakshman on what to expect; despite this, he was impressed. Sheer genius. The entrance had been made to look completely natural. A small rocky cave was quite organic in these highlands.

The thick tree-cover and fading twilight made for poor visibility, but Lakshman could discern a shallow cave, extending inwards not more than five or ten feet. His eyes fell on a jagged rocky outcrop from among the rock edges. The lever that would open the secret door.

Brilliant. Looks so bloody natural. That Vibhishan fellow is a good architect.

Notwithstanding Vibhishan's engineering skills, though, Lakshman still did not trust the man.

He held up his right hand and raised three fingers, separating each from the other. He paused for a moment and then raised all his fingers, this time sticking together, palm facing outward. He flicked his wrist and the fingers now pointed east. Then he raised the fingers skywards again and closed his fist into a ball. He stuck his thumb out horizontally.

A clear message. Three men. Go east, around and behind the cave entrance. Check and come back and report.

Three men untied the linking rope from their waist, broke away and followed the orders.

Lakshman repeated similar hand signals, this time pointing west. Three more soldiers stepped away from the formation and moved stealthily away.

The soldiers soon returned and silently conveyed their reports. Nothing. No threats. All clear.

Lakshman then pulled his *angvastram* loose, wrapped it around his nose, and secured it behind his head. Vibhishan's notes were clear and detailed.

His five hundred soldiers followed their commander and did the same with their *angvastrams*.

They were ready.

Lakshman took one step into the cave and halted, drawing his sword. The four soldiers who followed him also drew their blades.

Lakshman closed his eyes and allowed his pupils to expand and adapt. The cones within the retina rested, the rods kicked into work mode and his dark vision improved. He blinked a couple of times and took a few quick steps forward. Just a few feet; it was a shallow cave. Seeing clearly in the dark now, he moved unerringly to the stony jagged sprout. Nobody would have divined it was man-made. With his left hand, he gently pushed the sprout backwards. The stone depressed with a hydraulic hiss.

The stony sprout fell into a hollow and the back wall of the cave appeared to loosen.

Lakshman held out his sword. Ready for surprises.

Though warned earlier via Vibhishan's instructions, the shock of the assault was devastating.

An assault on his nose.

As the back wall slid sidewards, a feral stench hurtled out from within the cave, smacking the olfactory nerves of the soldiers standing in the hollows. Lakshman struggled to hold in the vomit. He pressed his *angvastram* against his nose. He did not step back. Admirably, neither did his soldiers.

The back wall had revealed itself as a sliding door. It was surprisingly smooth and silent as it moved slickly aside.

There was no sound. Except for the almost-noiseless attempts of Lakshman and the four men behind him to not gag.

By all that is good and holy! This is beyond tolerance!

Lakshman held out his sword and pointed at the dark passage that had opened up behind the cave back-wall. He stepped back and walked away from the cave mouth. As did his relieved soldiers.

— J∓ ꓳꓛꓷ —

The men sat outside the cave. Not directly in line with the cave opening, but to the side, for the malodour still infected the air. In disciplined lines of two abreast. Quiet. Patient.

This was the key difference between special forces and ordinary soldiers. Of course, the quality of training was better. Physical fitness was superior. The military equipment sanctioned to special forces was high grade. But the key difference was patience. Ordinary soldiers lack patience. Special forces can hold still, without sound and movement, disciplined and focused, for hours on end. And can spring to action at a moment's notice.

Eight soldiers remained at the entrance with drawn swords. In readiness for untoward incidents. Changeover provided relief every fifteen minutes. This was necessary. The horrific odour was unbearable.

Lakshman stared at the cave.

To be fair, Vibhishan had warned him in the notes. The stench collected from fifteen years of the fort's drainage—that was how long the tunnel had remained shut. While the drainage had a separate exit leading directly into the river, one end of the tunnel, at the top of the fort, was close to the barracks toilets. A smart place to end the tunnel. The drainage would not be checked unless clogged. And the sheer incline from the fort to the river ensured that the drainage never blocked. Vibhishan's design was faultless.

Vibhishan had advised that they wait for an hour after opening the cave door. The stench would dissipate, he'd said. He had built hidden ventilation ducts which allowed airflow once the cave door opened.

Lakshman had thought he was being ridiculous at the time, asking them to wait for an hour to clear the air. Now he wondered if an hour would suffice. He decided they would wait for two hours.

He looked up at the sky. It was the fifth day of the fortnight of the waxing moon, and moonlight was faint. They were more than halfway into the fourth and last prahar of the day. Midnight was approximately three hours away. Enough time. They would attack in the morning.

He signalled his lieutenant, Kshiraj. An Ayodhyan. *We'll wait for two hours.*

Kshiraj smiled with relief.

— JF J͞5D —

Shatrughan shook his head. 'Bloody hell!'

'This is sheer bad luck, Shatrughan,' said Ram. 'What can we do.'

The end of the fourth hour of the fourth *prahar* was drawing near. Midnight was two hours away. The Ayodhya war camp, spread over the Mannar island and the Indian mainland, was mostly asleep. Armed guards patrolled the thirty-kilometre length of the under-construction bridge. They had planned to complete the remaining five kilometres of the bridge the following day. But an unexpected problem had presented itself.

'I am sorry. I think it was my black tongue,' said Vashishtha guiltily. A few hours earlier he had commented that he had never seen a construction project go exactly to plan.

'No, Guruji,' said Naarad, always ready with a clever one-liner. 'I'm afraid it wasn't your black tongue, but the black *maansaudan* that did this!'

Vashishtha looked at a grinning Naarad and rolled his eyes.

Maansaudan. Meat rice. Mentioned in the Shatapatha Braahmana, this meal was a particular favourite with the soldiers. Fine rice is first rinsed, soaked and drained. Tender meat of the quail bird, minced to the same size as the grains of rice, is then added. The European quail, being a migratory bird, visited southern India in the winter months like clockwork. Its fresh meat was readily available this time of the year. Freshly made ghee and coconut milk is blended into the rice and meat. Musk and camphor are added for fragrance, for the ancients strongly believed that food must appeal not only to the senses of taste and vision, but also to the olfactory sense. The vessel is closed with a heavy lid and the mixture is cooked on a low flame for hours. The contents are periodically stirred till it becomes a smoothly amalgamated gooey mass. The cooked musk gives this delicacy a distinctively deep red colour.

When the *maansaudan* is ready to serve, it is garnished with petals from the *ketaki* flower. The Parihans, Lord Rudra's people, took this simple gastronomical delight from India to their own land, and named it *biryani*. Sinfully decadent and nourishing, no meal could please the tastebuds of warriors more. Regrettably, stale meat could sometimes cause a stomach upset. The *maansaudan* that evening was almost black instead of deep red, which should have triggered a warning. But, as the Parihans often said, any red-blooded man would merrily die for the taste of *biryani*. What's a tiny stomach upset in comparison? An infinitesimal health problem.

Health problems frequently occur in battle. Too many men, travelling and living in proximity out in the open, absence of civilised drainage facilities and assured, nutritious food. Soldiers fall ill. Animals fall ill. These things happen.

A good general not only divines brilliant war strategies and tactics, but also manages logistics efficiently.

And Ram, ably assisted by Vashishtha, Shatrughan, Hanuman, Arishtanemi, Angad and Naarad, had managed logistics exceedingly well.

Ram had insisted on one thing though: that all units eat together and not just with their own communities. A spirit of comradeship had been subtly built across the entire army. Over the last few months, it had helped forge disparate forces into one united army under the stewardship of King Ram.

The elephant mahouts were either Malayaputras or Vaanars. They had never interacted with each other till they became a part of Ram's army. Now they were eating together on a regular basis. But as luck would have it, it was the food for the mahouts that turned out to be bad that evening. They were stricken with diarrhoea. This is not a serious physical hazard in a battlefield. Diseases and injuries can get much worse. Most mahouts would recover within a day, at most two.

But the elephants were critical to build the last five kilometres of the bridge the following day. And while elephants are docile and obedient animals in the able hands of their mahouts, they are unmanageably fearsome with strangers.

Work on the bridge seemed impossible the next day, or even the day after. Which would delay the army's arrival at Sigiriya.

'What now?' asked Arishtanemi.

'We'll wait till the mahouts are healthy again.'

Shatrughan looked at Ram. 'Bharat dada and Lakshman will need to drag out their battle for three more days at least. We must reach Sigiriya before the Lankan army returns from Onguiaahra if we want this war to end quickly. It may be best if Bharat dada delays his attack.'

'He was planning to attack tonight. He may have launched it already. There's nothing we can do.'

Naarad spoke up. 'You are right, there is nothing we can do now.'

Everyone looked at Naarad. Waiting for him to say something sarcastic or inappropriate.

And Naarad obliged. 'The wise have always said that if you find yourself awake and troubled in the late hours of the night, when there is nothing that you can do about what troubles you, then the best idea is to simply go to sleep. That is what *dharma* dictates.'

Nobody said anything.

'Well, at least I'll follow my own advice. You all can stay up and worry. Goodnight.'

— JF J5D —

It was an hour to midnight.

Lakshman had led his soldiers into the tunnel. As mentioned in Vibhishan's notes, many torches—numbering over two hundred and made from limestone—were fixed into nooks on the wall. Every second soldier carried a piece of cloth doused with sulphur and lime. Over the last hour, they had wrapped the cloth around the top of the torches and lit them. While Vibhishan had said that they needn't close the cave door as the rocky overhang and dense tree cover would prevent the lights from being seen from the hill fort in the distance, Lakshman erred on the side of caution. After the last man stepped into the tunnel, the sliding cave door had been shut. Almost completely. It had been left open just a smidgen to allow for airflow. Faint traces of the malodour remained.

Lakshman and his troops moved silently. The tunnel entrance was a kilometre and half from the hill upon which the east wing of the Onguiaahra citadel stood. Lakshman planned to move slowly and cover the distance in an hour. There was no rush. They could attack in the morning. He did not want to risk his men getting injured in a dimly lit tunnel.

Even as he marched, Lakshman's regard for Vibhishan's prowess increased. The floor was packed earth, and reasonably flat. It was covered with cobblestones, giving it solidity. Easy to march on. Small drainage lines ran on both sides of the path, which would allow water seeping in from the regular heavy rains of Lanka to drain out of the tunnel without causing structural damage. The tunnel was bigger than he had expected. Broad enough for two soldiers to walk abreast, and tall enough for even him to not have to bend his gargantuan frame. In fact, a soldier could walk his horse through the tunnel without any difficulty. Riding would not be possible, of course. Not enough headroom. But even this much was amazing in a secret tunnel. The walls had been reinforced with rock, making them solid and impregnable. They did not come across any cave-ins, which was surprising, given that the tunnel was fifteen years old and had had absolutely no maintenance work in that time. Vibhishan's work had been thorough. A straight excavation with almost no twists and turns. High-quality planimetry while digging underground, along with exceptional structural strength, called for rare design and architectural skill.

Sneaky weasel. But a very, very smart sneaky weasel.

An hour later, Lakshman and his five hundred men reached the end of the tunnel at the base of the hill. Or more specifically, in the innards of the rocky hill, as Lakshman guessed by observing the changes in the floor and sidewall patterns.

And now he was truly in awe.

Vibhishan and his workers had burrowed their way up the inner bowels of the hill. The path rose steeply in a westerly direction for around twenty metres and then took a hairpin bend, turning and rising in an easterly direction. At the next hairpin bend, the tunnel turned again, towards the west. Essentially, a giant staircase excavated *inside* a hill. A spectacular piece of engineering.

A large cavity was dug out at the nose-end of each hairpin bend: an extension of the staircase landing, deep into the hill.

Lakshman mused, *What is this for? Why this cavity?*

Those climbing the staircase would use the landing and turn towards the next set of steps. Why was a cavity needed? Then it struck him. It had been built to collect and store loose stones or cave-in material that rolled down the steps. A back-up that would ensure the staircase landings remained clear.

Wow. This is next level, man.

A complex tunnelled-staircase built inside a hill. Directly from the flat tunnel under the jungle ground. The flat part of the tunnel would have required sound planimetry and the tunnelled-staircase, altimetry of a divine order. And he did all this in secret. Without anyone finding out about the goings-on. While also building two other secret tunnels.

Bloody smart sneaky weasel!

Lakshman turned to his men and signalled, slowly. He raised his hand high, ensuring that everyone received the order in the dim light of the torches.

The message was clear: Start climbing. Quietly. And wait at the top.

Chapter 22

'Go to sleep, prince,' said Dhumraksha. 'It's close to midnight. I'm on guard. As are the hundred soldiers, awake and alert.'

Dhumraksha had appointed a rotating strength of one hundred soldiers in shifts of six hours each. They guarded the opening to the secret tunnel in the eastern wing of the citadel, swords drawn. The entrance to the tunnel was unopened and unlit. The Ayodhyans would not suspect that they were walking into a trap.

Indrajit shook his head in response to Dhumraksha's suggestion. *No.*

Dhumraksha, the name, meant *smoky eyes*. And his eyes did rage with aggressive fire. His parents had named him well. Of massive build and fierce temperament, he was born to be a warrior. As the commander of the Onguiaahra battalion, he headed the Lankan special forces. Being a good warrior, he respected fellow warriors. Indrajit had come all the way to the citadel to face a possible attack from enemy special forces. The royal had put himself in harm's way. It was worthy of respect. And old smoky eyes treated the respect-worthy with very obvious, ostentatious regard.

Dhumraksha looked at Mareech. 'Lord Mareech, one of us must remain awake all the time and be ready for the attack. We must take turns to sleep.' Pointing at the commander's quarters, which were at a height, above where the youngest Lankan soldiers in the battalion lived, Dhumraksha continued, 'You both can sleep for now. In my quarters.'

Indrajit looked to where Dhumraksha was pointing. 'That's too far. I have a strong feeling they will attack tonight. We'll stay here.'

'Prince Indrajit,' said Dhumraksha, 'I will blast the war-horn the moment the enemy arrives. They can only emerge in twos from the tunnel. We will hold them here. And keep enough of them alive for you to kill.'

Indrajit laughed softly.

Mareech spoke up. 'General Dhumraksha is speaking wisely, Indrajit. Let's take his advice. Join the next watch, and get a few hours of sleep at least.'

Indrajit relented and got up, adjusting the scabbard sideways.

Mareech leaned towards Indrajit as he began to walk. 'But first…'

'Yes, grand-uncle?'

— Jf J5D —

Lakshman and his soldiers had reached the top of the staircase and were standing before the exit.

Vibhishan's work quality had been such that Lakshman was assured that the light from the torches would not slip out through the sealed door in front of them. Unless he opened it, of course.

Using hand signals, Lakshman warned his soldiers to stay away from the clearly marked lever at a height on the wall. The lever that would open the door. He did not want it opened by mistake.

Lakshman rested his ear against a specific spot on the rocky door. He had been informed that, from here, he could hear the goings-on outside.

He heard … nothing.

He looked at his troops.

Suddenly a loud bell rang out. His ears reverberated painfully.

Bloody…

Stunned by the clarity of the sound, and despite the aural discomfort, Lakshman did not move from the spot. He had to hear this.

Another bell.

And then silence.

Lakshman turned to his soldiers and made hand signals.

Second hour of the watch has begun.

Lakshman calculated. The standard shift in Onguiaahra was six hours. Four hours from now, the sixth hour of the watch would begin.

That would be the best time for attack. The soldiers on guard would be tired as they approached the end of their shift.

He made hand signals again.

We wait. Four hours more.

The message was relayed down the line.

Lakshman placed his ear against the little patch on the wall. He wondered at the technology Vibhishan must have used to make sound travel with such clarity through a thick rocky wall.

Not for the first time did the same thought run through his mind. *Vibhishan. Genius sneaky weasel.*

He listened for voices. But there were none.

Maybe there is nobody on the other side of this door.

He looked at his soldiers. Stationary. Deathly silent. Patient. Just like soldiers in the special forces should be.

No reason to assume that the Lankan special forces would be less well-trained. They could be right outside. Quiet, as discipline dictated.

We'll know in four hours.

Lakshman assigned a soldier to man the sounding post. He then sat on the floor, rested his back against a wall, and decided to get some sleep.

— J𝖿 J̐5D —

Lakshman opened his eyes as he felt a light touch. The hand signal from his soldier was clear.

The sixth hour of the watch had begun.

Lakshman rose quickly and gave orders through hand signals.

Prepare.

The soldiers stretched their arms, shoulders, back and legs. Loosening them.

They speedily drank from the water carriers. Then reached into their bags and quickly wolfed down dry fruits and gram. Having emptied their food and water containers, they left the bags in the tunnel; they wouldn't need them anymore. Quickly checking their weapons, they loosened the hold covers on their scabbards. They unhooked their shields and held them in position.

Ready.

It had taken them ten minutes. They were special forces soldiers.

Lakshman looked at them. Satisfied. He carefully gave hand signal orders.

Remain quiet outside. We assemble first. Then attack.

The soldiers had been briefed earlier. They knew the tunnel exited into a space hidden from view by a colonnaded passageway with a low ceiling. At least one hundred from among them could assemble before charging. The rest would follow in unceasing waves.

Lakshman drew his sword, as did the others. He nodded at the soldier standing near the lever and edged towards the door. Kshiraj darted ahead, putting himself at risk as the door opened. Lakshman hissed softly in annoyance. Kshiraj looked at Lakshman and smiled. But refused to yield the vanguard position.

Lakshman surrendered to Kshiraj's valour and remained behind in the line. He raised his left hand and closed his fist abruptly. All the torches were put out and the tunnel plunged into darkness. And the lever was pressed.

The feral smell assaulted them again. But it wasn't as intense as when they had opened the tunnel entrance earlier in the night. They were prepared. They expected it. They knew they would exit near the drainage. So, none reacted.

But Lakshman frowned. Something was not right.

No sound. None at all. In a camp full of testosterone-laden soldiers.

Strange. Eerie.

Are the Lankans expecting us?

The faint light of dawn filtered into the tunnel.

Kshiraj crept out of the tunnel and, as had been planned, advanced quickly to the right. Lakshman stepped out and moved to the centre. Very soon a hundred soldiers had manoeuvred into formation outside the tunnel.

There was a sinister silence.

They were in a colonnaded passage which had been carved into the black stone of the hill. It was built such that, while Lakshman and his soldiers were hidden in the dark, the rest of the compound was visible. To the right, the passage led to the common toilets. To the left, it led to the rookies' dormitory, where the youngest Lankan soldiers in the battalion lived. Ahead of them were steps that descended to the common ground in the eastern wing of the fort. To the far right of the common ground was the east-wing gate to the central dam wall. Lakshman remembered this from the map.

Couldn't have exited the tunnel at a better place. Lakshman silently thanked the Lankan traitor Vibhishan again.

Their pupils slowly contracted and they began to see more clearly in the dawn light. Lakshman raised his left hand and flicked his wrist to the left. Fifty soldiers padded in the direction of the rookies' dormitory, knives drawn.

Fifty others stealthily moved out of the tunnel to take their place.

Lakshman wondered where the Lankan guards were.

And then he saw them.

Oh Lord Rudra!

He made hand signals and pointed. The signals were relayed down the line.

A hundred Lankan soldiers stood at the other end of the courtyard, some distance away. They huddled silently against a wall next to the small fort temple. Lakshman saw that they stood with their swords drawn.

He suppressed a soft laugh.

They are expecting an attack from the other tunnel! They have no idea about this tunnel.

Yet again, Lakshman silently thanked Vibhishan.

Lord Indra bless that sneaky weasel!

None of the Lankans looked in their direction. They had some more time.

He gave another order through hand signals. Ten soldiers broke formation. And slunk silently up the railing-protected stairs on the edge of the fort wall. Towards the commander's quarters at the height. If they got lucky and found the commander, the battle would be over before it could begin.

Ten more soldiers emerged from the tunnel and replaced those who had stepped away.

Lakshman looked to the right. In the distance he saw the east wing's gates to the central dam of Onguiaahra. They were open. He had been briefed by Vibhishan to take control of those gates immediately. If the Lankans succeeded in locking the gates from outside, the Ayodhyans would be trapped inside. The Lankans could then destroy the sluice controls, thus compromising Lakshman's ability to release water into the control-steps downriver. That would make the conquest of Onguiaahra pointless. However, Bharat had repeatedly emphasised that Lakshman should gain complete control of the eastern wing first, and only then move towards the central dam. Bharat didn't want unnecessary Ayodhyan casualties while facing attacks from the rear.

In any case, Lakshman couldn't order his soldiers to take the gate. Not yet. For it was clearly visible to the Lankans who were next to the fort temple.

Enough time for that.

He looked to the left. One of his soldiers stepped out of the rookies' quarters. He was wiping his knife on his arm band. He looked towards Lakshman and signalled.

Fifty Lankans. All dead now.

Lakshman ordered them to remain where they were.

Fifty gone. Another hundred at the other tunnel entrance. The rest would be asleep. The main dormitory to the left had a capacity of two hundred, according to Vibhishan. So, there were at most three hundred and fifty Lankans here, fifty of whom were dead. The other one hundred and fifty would be at the western-wing of the Onguiaahra fort, far away at the other end of the central dam. They would play little role in this battle here.

My five hundred versus their three hundred. Good odds. Especially since we have the element of surprise as well.

He looked at the commander's quarters. His soldiers were still inside. He would ideally want that quarter covered as well to prevent any attacks from the rear when he charged.

He raised his hand and gave orders to the soldiers who were still in the tunnel.

Go towards the main dormitory. When I say so. Kill all there.

The command was relayed down the line.

Lakshman looked up at the commander's quarters again. A soldier stepped out and signalled: *Nobody here.*

No problem, Lakshman whispered to himself. The Lankan commander Dhumraksha must be with his soldiers at the other tunnel entrance. *We'll kill him there.*

All he had to do now was silently creep ahead with the men who had already emerged from the tunnel, get as close as possible to the Lankans at the other tunnel entrance, and surprise them before they turned around and made formations again. It would be an easy massacre.

He was about to relay his order when he stopped dead in his tracks.

Goddammit!

Lakshman looked towards the courtyard and groaned soundlessly.

As history had been witness, Lakshman was not an early riser. He was fond of his sleep. Only war or the express command of his elder brothers could awaken him early. And, like most late risers, he despised those who woke up early for no good reason.

Two such specimens walked out of the main dormitory now. Lankan soldiers. Muscled and fit. Bare-chested, wearing only loose lungis. One of them scratched his backside and the other yawned loudly.

Don't come here. Don't come here.

They began to head in Lakshman's direction. Holding mugs. Indians, like most civilised people, washed rather than wiped.

Lakshman looked to his right. His soldiers stood exactly in front of the toilets.

Dammit. There goes the surprise element.

If that advantage was gone, Lakshman thought, he may as well use his favourite weapon. He pushed his sword back into its scabbard, carefully.

The blade made a soft noise as it slipped back into its sheath. Most would have missed it. But it was a sound that a good soldier would recognise anywhere, especially in the quiet of an early daybreak. The two Lankans froze. They could not see anything, as the Ayodhyans were hidden in the colonnaded passageway. The dim light of the dawn did not reach that corner. They glanced at each other briefly, confirming that they had both heard it. They strained their eyes to get a better look.

Lakshman reached behind and unhooked his favourite weapon. The war mace.

A typical mace is a type of club with a heavy head on one end, which can deliver powerful strikes. But Lakshman's weapon had been specially engineered for him. It had a strong, heavy metal shaft, and a head made of metal as well. The head and handle were forged from one piece, giving the mace a fearsome solidity. Moreover, the head contained sharp metallic flanges from top to bottom and along the left and right axes. They helped penetrate leather armour. There was more. The head was covered with sharp metallic spikes all around. Forget leather, even metallic armour would give way with a strong blow from this head. Normally a mace measures two to three feet in length, about the same as a sword. But this weapon had been stretched and lengthened for Lakshman. It was a little over three and a half feet; longer than a longsword.

This formidable and heavy weapon would be difficult for most ordinary warriors to hold, let alone wield. But Lakshman was six feet ten inches tall and built like a bull. In his hands, this mace was terrifying beyond measure.

Lakshman untied the thick leather cover from the mace head and cast it aside. He would retrieve it in good time.

No point in remaining silent now.

'Kshiraj,' he whispered, 'cover the gates.'

And then Lakshman stepped out of the passageway onto the landing. In the open. One hundred soldiers followed him.

The two Lankans immediately dropped their mugs, which clattered noisily, breaking the silence all around. They ran back to their quarters for their weapons, screaming at the top of their lungs. 'ENEMY AT PASSAGEWAY! ENEMY AT PASSAGEWAY!'

The Lankans at the other tunnel whirled around and stood rooted to the spot. Shocked into momentary paralysis. Meanwhile, Kshiraj and his ten soldiers were sprinting towards the gates.

'Charge!' roared Lakshman. *'Ayodhyatah Vijetaarah!'*

The conquerors from the unconquerable city!

'*Ayodhyatah Vijetaarah!*' shouted Lakshman's men.

Lakshman and his first line of soldiers stormed towards the Lankans at the other tunnel entrance. The rest of the Ayodhyans began pouring out of the secret tunnel. Some ran behind Lakshman, but most rushed to the main dormitory. As they had been ordered to.

To his credit, the stunned Dhumraksha immediately rallied. His loud commanding voice instilled instantaneous purpose into his soldiers.

'Upon me!' thundered Dhumraksha. 'Charge! *Bhaarat Bhartri Lanka!*'

Lanka, owner of India!

'*Bhaarat Bhartri Lanka!*' the Lankans bellowed loudly as they charged towards the Ayodhyans.

One Lankan ran towards the Ayodhya prince; he was tall, and yet dwarfed by the gargantuan Lakshman. It was a brave and smart tactic. Take down the opposing commander; his soldiers would surrender. Unfortunately for the Lankan, the opposing commander was Lakshman.

The Lankan held his shield high, intending to block the standard downward strike from Lakshman's mace. After which he would aim to draw close with the same move and turn the long reach of the mace into a disadvantage. Then, with an upward movement of his shorter sword, he would stab Lakshman's abdomen. That was the plan.

Bad plan.

Disposed of at first contact with the enemy.

The mace is a fearsome weapon on its own. When wielded by Lakshman, with his unbeatable combination of colossal size, bull-like strength and swashbuckling skill, it is invincible. The club ripped through the leather and wooden shield. It struck the Lankan's left arm. Lakshman's mace didn't just break bones, it shattered them to powder. The Lankan's elbow joint, parts of the humerus bone above, and the radius and ulna bones below almost instantaneously crumbled into fragmented bits of calcium and collagen. The Lankan looked down, stunned. His mangled left arm was hanging limp by his side, connected by stray strands of sinew at what had been the elbow. His brain had blocked the pain, which was beyond endurance. The sword dropped from his other hand. Soon thereafter he was put out of his misery as Lakshman swung brutally from his left and his mace crushed the right half of the Lankan's head so that it sunk into the other half.

Lakshman continued the same swing onwards, and the spikes in the head of the mace buried themselves in another Lankan's head. The unfortunate soul was fighting an Ayodhyan. A Suryavanshi blade had ripped into his heart as Lakshman had smashed his mace in. It was difficult to tell what killed the Lankan – his crushed head or the steel through his heart.

Even as Lakshman was swinging at the next Lankan charging towards him, his soldiers in the main dormitory were massacring the enemy. Lakshman had given his soldiers clear orders: No mercy. Kill all Lankans who resist. And all of them were resisting.

The situation wasn't any better for the defenders of Onguiaahra in the courtyard. Lakshman's soldiers were scything through most of the battalion, killing all who stood in their path.

To Lakshman's admiration, not a single Lankan surrendered. With the odds clearly stacked against them, they kept on fighting.

Worthy enemies.

The bloodletting continued. Mostly with the blood of the Lankans.

'Wait!' roared Lakshman.

Almost all the Lankans were dead. The rest were injured so badly that survival was difficult.

One Lankan was still standing. Injured. Bloodied. But proud and unbowed.

General Dhumraksha.

'Hold,' ordered Lakshman. 'And disarm the Lankans.'

The Ayodhyans immediately began to follow Lakshman's orders. But none approached Dhumraksha. Those who had been fighting him a moment ago stepped back.

Lakshman stared at the Lankan commander.

Dhumraksha was a physically intimidating man, but not as big as Lakshman was. The Lankan general was six and a half feet in height. Muscular. Fair-skinned. He sported a long handle-bar moustache and was clad in sleeveless leather armour. He wore black arm bands and a black *dhoti*, tied in military style. His body was covered in blood, most of it his own.

He breathed heavily, trying to regain his strength and composure. He stared back at Lakshman with unblinking eyes. Defiant.

Lakshman noticed the weapon in Dhumraksha's hand. A war mace.

Lakshman recognised it immediately. 'Kodumanal?'

Dhumraksha smiled and nodded his head slowly. 'The best will only use the best.'

Lakshman smiled.

A worthy enemy.

Kodumanal was the great city of the Cheras on the Kanchinadi, a tributary of the sacred Kaveri River. It was widely acknowledged to be the best place in the world for manufacturing swords and maces. Dhumraksha's war mace was crafted by the hands of the finest metallurgists and blacksmiths of Kodumanal. As was Lakshman's.

Dhumraksha raised his mace. One last duel.

Lakshman raised his mace as well. Challenge accepted.

Lakshman gave due respect to a soldier of Dhumraksha's calibre by holding his mace with both hands. No imprudent swinging with one hand against a skilled warrior. The prince of Ayodhya held his position. No careless charging against the Lankan general either.

The two warriors began to circle one another. Gauging each other.

Dhumraksha moved first. He took a quick step forward and swung his mace hard. Lakshman stayed rooted but leaned backwards, easily avoiding the blow like a deft boxer. His back sprung forward with the same velocity and he swung his mace from the left. Aiming at Dhumraksha's shoulder. But the Lankan flicked his wrist and his mace deflected the blow.

Lakshman stepped back, smiling and nodding.

As did Dhumraksha.

They had crucial information about each other now. Most bulky, muscular men possess strength and power, but not speed and agility. However, these apparently contradictory qualities mingled comfortably in both these men.

This will be interesting, thought Lakshman.

Dhumraksha charged again and Lakshman parried the blow.

A voice boomed from behind Lakshman. 'My Lord, finish this! We have a lot to do!'

Lakshman ignored it.

Dhumraksha charged again. Lakshman sidestepped and jabbed his mace forward with force. The sharp point at the top edge of the mace head poked Dhumraksha's chest. Not deep enough. It had sliced through the leather armour though.

Lakshman had drawn first blood. Dhumraksha stepped back and darted suddenly to his right. Lakshman had expected that. He swung in quickly from the left. Dhumraksha's mace hit first. It collided with Lakshman's shoulder. A micro second later Lakshman's mace head struck Dhumraksha's left shoulder, but it was a weak blow. Lakshman had just been hit.

A direct hit from a large Kodumanal mace head would have shattered, or at least broken a bone, in most warriors. But when the bone is protected by layers of bull-like muscle, as in the case of Lakshman and Dhumraksha, it would not be so. Blood burst steadily from wounds on both the warriors. But they still had use of their shoulders.

The voice was heard again, from behind Lakshman, this time laced with impatience. 'My Lord!'

Dhumraksha charged, swinging his mace from left to right and right to left, as if it was a sword. Lakshman parried each blow, stepping back slowly. As if retreating. But he was drawing Dhumraksha into a trap.

As Dhumraksha swung hard from the right, Lakshman's parry became more rigid. He held the mace in place as Dhumraksha pushed forward. The Lankan realised only too late what he had done. Moving quick like lightning, Lakshman pressed a lever on his mace handle with his right thumb. His left hand slipped down, just as a knife, hidden within the mace handle, ejected quickly. Lakshman grabbed the knife and stabbed. Before Dhumraksha could disengage, the knife had sunk into the heart.

It all happened within the blink of an eye.

Lakshman had done what Dhumraksha had intended in the very next strike.

The prince of Ayodhya pushed the knife in deeper, and felt a thump. A reverberation. Dhumraksha had dropped his mace.

Lakshman held the knife and felt another thump on the blade. It was Dhumraksha's mighty heart, still beating, transmitting its muscular vibration onto the metal, which carried the pulse into the handle of the blade that Lakshman held.

Dhumraksha collapsed backwards. Lakshman dropped his mace and eased him to the ground.

The Lankan commander was smiling with satisfaction. As if he was thanking his enemy. He had been accorded an honourable death. No warrior wishes to be killed by inferior hands, like hyenas surrounding a lion. If he must die, then it must be in a duel with a worthy adversary. Another lion.

Lakshman gently touched Dhumraksha's forehead. 'May Lord Yama guide you across the sacred Vaitarni, brave Dhumraksha.' The next world, the land of the ancestors, lay beyond the mythical river, Vaitarni. Yama, the Lord of Death, guided souls into that stopover land. After some time, the souls either returned to this earth reincarnated, or moved onwards towards moksha, liberation from the cycle of rebirths.

Dhumraksha raised his weakened hand and touched Lakshman's forehead. 'I will … see you … on the other side …'

'I will see you on the other side, brother.'

Dhumraksha's hand fell to the ground and his soul slipped away.

Lakshman took a deep breath and bowed his head low. Having paid his respects, he rose and looked at his men. 'Well done, boys.'

'Thank you, Lord.'

Lakshman then glanced at the gates in the distance.

And cursed loudly.

Chapter 23

As luck would have it, Indrajit and Mareech had been awake when Lakshman and his troops emerged from the secret tunnel. They had woken up an hour earlier and had gone down to the guards' room next to the east-wing gate. They were with the guards, making small talk, when Lakshman had ordered his soldiers to charge.

Indrajit, Mareech and the fifteen Lankan soldiers in the guards' cabin were completely out of sight for Lakshman and his Ayodhyans.

Kshiraj and his Ayodhyan soldiers had not seen the Lankans emerge from behind as they had raced to the gates. Many Ayodhyans were killed before they had even turned around to face the enemy.

Mareech had bellowed an order as his guards had rushed towards Kshiraj. 'Don't kill him! Drag him out! I want him alive!'

Indrajit had wanted to move farther into the courtyard and attack the Ayodhyans as they charged into Dhumraksha and his men close to the fort temple. But Mareech had pulled his nephew back. 'This is not the time to be a hero. This is the time to be a leader!' Mareech had implored Indrajit.

Sometimes the hero and the leader can fuse in the same individual. But often this does not happen. A hero does not need followers, a leader cannot be imagined without those he leads. A hero sacrifices himself, while a leader may not succumb to this magnificent impulse. A hero must be courageous, a leader does what must be done, even risk being perceived as cowardly sometimes. A hero inspires the storytellers, a leader lives on in the hearts of his followers. A hero is concerned with what the gods will think of him, a leader is concerned with protecting and nurturing his people and his land. A hero will not leave the moral high ground, even if it hurts his people, while a leader will step down from the moral high ground if need be, and even sacrifice his own soul for the good of the people he leads.

A hero will fight the enemy against insurmountable odds and embrace death with a flourish.

A leader will respond calmly and deny the enemy a key strategic advantage in a battle.

Indrajit had listened to Mareech, and behaved like a leader.

They had retreated from the gate to the central dam area along with fifteen soldiers. The fighting continued to rage at the other end of the courtyard of the east-wing. They had found some hammers in the guards' cabin, to be used for repairs. Now they would be used for destruction.

Kshiraj had tried to warn his fellow Ayodhyans who were battling Dhumraksha and his men at the other end of the courtyard. But a soldier from Indrajit's tight band had knocked him on the head and carried the unconscious Ayodhyan out. The gate had been quickly barred from the outside and barricaded.

They had then set to work.

The levers of the sluice gates were destroyed. The loss of even a few major sluice gate controls would have hampered Ayodhya's ability to manage water-outflow. Nevertheless, Indrajit had insisted that every sluice control, even the minor ones, be smashed. The spillways were already closed. It would take the Ayodhyans at least a week to repair the controls. Their ships would be stuck downriver on the Mahaweli Ganga till then.

The Lankans had bought a week for themselves. To evaluate and formulate new strategies to take on the Ayodhyans.

As Lakshman had killed Dhumraksha, the last of the sluice controls had been destroyed by Indrajit's men. This was when the Ayodhyan prince had noticed the barricaded gates of the eastern-wing.

He immediately ordered that they be broken. But that would take some time. It was a high-quality Lankan construction, designed by Vibhishan.

Indrajit looked back. He could hear the battering ram pounding at the gates. He looked at Mareech and smiled. 'That will take them half an hour, almost forty-five minutes, in fact. Unless they burn the gate.' Indrajit turned to two soldiers. 'Race to the western-wing.. Gather our soldiers and horses in the courtyard there. Move!'

The Ayodhyan attack on the eastern wing of the Onguiaahra citadel had begun just fifteen minutes ago. Those fifteen minutes had changed the war dynamic drastically.

As the two soldiers sprinted across the central dam wall, Indrajit and Mareech walked briskly towards the western-wing. The rest of the soldiers followed.

'What do you plan to do?' asked Mareech. 'Will you defend the western-wing?'

Indrajit shook his head. 'No. That's pointless. We will lock the western-wing gate from the inside; that will make it difficult for the Ayodhyans to enter from the dam side. Then we will salvage what we can and burn the rest of the stores; we will not make it easy for them to survive here. Then we will ride out and warn our ships below.'

Mareech smiled. 'There is no dishonour in retreating when it is the best course available. Now you are thinking like a leader, not a hero.'

Indrajit smiled slightly. 'I am sorry. I became emotional earlier.'

Mareech patted Indrajit's shoulder as he walked beside his grand-nephew. 'You are young. And young people like to be heroes. It takes wisdom to do adulting.'

Indrajit raised his eyebrows. 'Are you learning our words, grand-uncle?'

Mareech laughed softly. 'I must learn at least a bit if I want to get through to you people.'

They passed the gates at the western-wing. Indrajit turned around and gave precise orders. 'Bar the dam-side gates from the inside. Lock and barricade them thoroughly. Then gather our horses and the provisions that you can carry. We ride out from the main hillside gate.'

His lieutenant saluted.

'And one more thing,' continued Indrajit. 'Burn all the provisions that we cannot carry with us.'

'Lord?' asked the lieutenant, hesitating.

'You heard me.'

'Yes, My Lord.'

The lieutenant and the soldiers saluted, and rushed to obey.

'And what do we do when we ride out?' asked Mareech.

'Grand-uncle, you should go to father and update him on all that has happened. Tell him that I will come within a day, and then we can decide on our subsequent battle strategy.'

'What do I say when Raavan asks me why you are here and not in Bali?'

Indrajit laughed. 'Tell him that I am the son of Raavan. Breaking rules and disobeying orders are a part of my genetic makeup!'

Mareech laughed and patted Indrajit on the back. 'But where are you headed? Where are you planning to go for a day?'

'I'm taking these men to the flood-water spillway gates far away at the back of the reservoir,' said Indrajit. 'The one that allows water from the reservoir to flow via a canal into the Amban Ganga upriver. I will block that spillway and break the controls.'

Mareech frowned. 'How will that help?'

'Jiujitsu.'

'What?!'

Indrajit didn't answer immediately, as his attention was diverted by the sound of the western-wing gate being shut and the wooden barricade being laid. He turned back to Mareech. 'Jiujitsu is a form of martial art from the Far East, grand-uncle. In it, we use our opponent's strength against him.'

Mareech frowned, confused. 'What does that have to do with the flood-water spillway, Indrajit?

'Think about it. What is the Ayodhyan navy's main strength over our own?' asked Indrajit.

Mareech curled his lips in a snarl, exposing his upper teeth. 'Their ships are bigger than ours. Much bigger.'

'Precisely. They have used the floods on the Mahaweli Ganga and sailed their larger seafaring ships upriver. They assumed, logically, that our seafaring ships would be in Gokarna, and only the river navy would be here in Onguiaahra. My spies told me that their larger ships have metal-reinforced bow sections. They planned to ram our riverine ships with their seafaring ones and sink them. And with uncle Vibhishan—that traitor—in their camp, they expected to take control of Onguiaahra, flood the chokehold control-steps, and sail their bigger ships upriver. A smart strategy.'

'So what's your point?' asked Mareech, confused. 'Their seafaring ships are here. They will soon have control over Onguiaahra. It will take them a week at most to repair the sluice controls. They still have Vibhishan, and he is a brilliant engineer. Once the sluice controls are repaired, they can sail their seafaring ships here and ram us into oblivion.'

Indrajit smiled. 'What do seafaring ships need, grand-uncle, that riverine ships don't?'

And then it hit Mareech. 'Greater draught ... water displacement ...'

'Precisely. Much, much greater.'

Mareech smiled. *Brilliant!*

A ship displaces some amount of water in a river or sea, to take its place. The ship floats if the weight of the displaced water is more than the weight of the ship. Being bigger and heavier, a seafaring ship needs to displace more water. Obviously. Draught is the depth of the bottom-most part of the ship below the water line. Usually, the greater the water displacement, the greater the draught. The riverine Lankan ships had a draught of about one metre. If the Amban Ganga River retained a depth of more than one metre, they would float.

'So, what's the draught of the Ayodhyan ships?' asked Mareech.

'Skilful ship designers inscribe the draught across the ship hull. It's good product design. My spies tell me that seafaring Ayodhyan ships have a draught of five metres.'

Mareech could tell that Indrajit had some greater insight. 'And?'

'See, grand-uncle, the thing is that ship designers calculate the draught for seafaring ships only with sea water. Obviously. Not with river water …'

Mareech smiled. 'River water is less dense.'

'Precisely. A ship that floats on the sea at a particular draught needs much greater draught in river water. Simple science.'

Mareech laughed.

'Like I said, the seafaring ships of Ayodhya have a draught of five metres in the sea. But they would need five and a half metres in river water. Which is good enough for the flooded Mahaweli Ganga. It would be fine in the Amban Ganga as well, if the flood-control spillway gates remained open and more water flowed into that river. However, if they were closed, then the Ayodhya ships would cross the control-steps but not be able to enter the Amban Ganga and confront the Lanka ships. They would get grounded.'

'Had they been conservative, they would have brought riverine ships and been able to sail up the Amban Ganga,' said Mareech.

'Exactly. But it's too late for that now.'

'Brilliant. Their strength – the bigger ships – has turned into a weakness. Jiujitsu.'

Indrajit nodded. 'They will eventually understand the reason behind the water shortfall and attack us on the reservoir as well. That's open ground, difficult to defend. And the extension walls from the Onguiaahra citadel cover the reservoir too, almost completely. They will ultimately take the flood-water spillway as well. But we will delay them by another week, maybe more.'

'That will frustrate them and bog them down. And they are far away from their supply chain. We are not. We may not defeat them, but we can drag this on and tire them in a battle of attrition.'

'Exactly.'

'Go do it, my boy. I'll handle Raavan.' Mareech looked at the unconscious Kshiraj. 'And what do you want to do with him?'

'I want to ask him some questions. I have a gut feeling that we are missing something. Something big. Maybe he can throw some light on what that is.'

'Do you want me to …' Mareech didn't go too deep into the indelicate manner in which Kshiraj could be made to talk.

'No, grand-uncle. Let me handle this. You go to father.'

'All right, my boy.'

—— J⨍ ⊥⁵ᗡ ——

'He's taken the eastern wing,' said Vibhishan, looking through his telescope.

As the early morning sun shone through, Bharat and Vibhishan stood at the poop deck of the lead ship of the Ayodhyan navy. The elevated deck was ideal for observation. Bharat could see the standard flag of Ayodhya on the eastern wing of the Onguiaahra citadel through his telescope. The regulation mark of the Ayodhyans was a white cloth with a red circular sun in the centre, its rays streaming out in all directions. At the bottom half of the standard, suffused by the bright rays of the sun, was a magnificent leaping tiger. Bharat saw their flag had been raised. But not on the western-wing. The Lankan flag continued to flutter in the air on that side. It was a black flag in which the head of a roaring lion emerged from a profusion of fiery flames. Bharat couldn't see the details in the flags, but the white and the black stood out in stark contrast.

'The western-wing is still under Lankan control,' said Bharat.

'Are those flames?' asked Vibhishan.

'Looks like it.'

'Dammit. They are burning up the stores. I hope Prince Lakshman isn't boxed in within the eastern wing. If the Lankans destroy the sluice controls on the dam, it will delay us by many days.'

Bharat remained silent.

Vibhishan turned to Bharat. 'Do you know, Prince Bharat, that the nerve fibre length in the human brain, when stretched end-to-end, is over eight hundred and fifty thousand kilometres long? That is more than twice the distance between our earth and the moon.'

Bharat tried not to reveal his perplexed irritation as he looked at Vibhishan. *What in Lord Indra's name is this fool talking about now? What does this have to do with Onguiaahra?*

Vibhishan spoke again. 'There is no instrument as powerful as the human brain. And it is time to use my brain over your brother's brawn.'

Bharat kept quiet.

'The sluice controls have most probably been destroyed,' continued Vibhishan. 'That's what I would do if I was Dhumraksha. That is why I had asked your brother to make quick work of it. I will need to go and start repairing the sluice controls. Conquering Onguiaahra is useless unless we control the dam waters.'

'You are right,' Bharat was constrained to admit. 'If Lakshman doesn't control the dam, that is.'

'I fear I might be right. For I don't see our flag fluttering over the central dam.'

Bharat continued to stare at Onguiaahra in the distance.

'Let me go,' continued Vibhishan. 'I can ride quickly up the main road to the eastern wing now. It's in our control. Send one hundred men with me. I will have the sluice controls ready for you in a few days.'

'I'll send three hundred men with you.'

Vibhishan bowed low, theatrically. 'Thank you, good prince.'

'But I want you to first bring the western-wing fires under control, make sure the tunnel to the western-wing is destroyed, and the main gate is effectively barricaded.'

'You are being too conservative, Prince Bharat. Doing all you ask will take a day or two. It will delay the repair of the sluices. I know the Lankans. They will not return. We need to be aggressive and move fast so that—'

'No,' said Bharat firmly. 'I will not risk unnecessary casualties.'

'But—'

Bharat moved close to Vibhishan and dropped his voice menacingly low. 'You will do as I tell you. Is that clear?'

Vibhishan surrendered. 'Yes of course, Prince Bharat.'

— J╬ ╜⁊D —

'They now control Onguiaahra,' said Vashishtha. 'But it's a half-victory, says Lakshman.'

A messenger bird had arrived from the battlefront at the Mahaweli Ganga River. Bharat and Lakshman had taken some Indian peregrine falcons along with them; these fast-flying birds delivered messages across the island of Lanka in just a few hours. Well before lunch then, Vashishtha, Ram and members on the war council discussed the contents of the message.

'Half-victory?' asked Hanuman.

'They conquered the eastern wing in fifteen minutes, early this morning.'

'And the west wing?' asked Arishtanemi.

'They had control over it three hours later. The Lankans retreated to that wing and held off Lakshman's soldiers behind barricaded gates. They then set fire to their own stores. Lakshman had to get his soldiers to scale the wall and put out the fires. There were no Lankans around to offer any resistance by that time. They had all escaped through the open main gates of the fort.'

'So, we have control over both the wings of the citadel,' said Arishtanemi. 'We control all Onguiaahra. How is that a half-victory?'

'Did the Lankans destroy the sluice gate controls?' asked Shatrughan, immediately guessing what it meant.

'Yes,' said Vashishtha. 'So, we have won the prize basket. But the prize itself has been stolen.'

'Not stolen, just broken, Guruji,' said Shatrughan. 'A good engineering team can repair those sluice gates within a week, maybe even sooner.'

'True,' said Vashishtha. 'But we will not be able to flood the control-steps for one more week. Bharat's ships are stuck till then.'

'But this is perfect,' said Ram. 'I wouldn't call it a half-victory. I would call it a two-fold victory!'

Everyone turned to Ram.

Ram continued. 'Lakshman sees it as a half-victory because he is driven by bravery, not strategy. Bharat's daily message usually arrives by nightfall. I'm sure he will see it the way I do.'

'And how do you see it?'

'It is the perfect outcome. Had Bharat made no attempt to attack the Lankans, they would have gotten suspicious. Bharat knows that he is desperately undermanned, with only thirty-five thousand soldiers. Yesterday, his report stated that the Lankans have brought almost their entire army to Mahaweli Ganga. That is around one hundred and eighty thousand soldiers. The Lankans have the advantage of numbers and the additional advantage of being upriver. This is the reason why Bharat took the big seafaring ships with him. It isn't about attacking better, but defending better.'

'Fair point,' said Naarad.

'Attacking the Lankans against these odds is unwise. And not attacking them will make them suspect that our entire army is not there as yet. This is perfect. See this from the Lankan perspective. Bharat launched an audacious attack on Onguiaahra, with the help of the traitor Vibhishan, simply because Bharat is eager to cross over with his larger ships. But the brave Onguiaahra battalion has delayed him by smartly destroying the sluice controls. The Lankans will wait patiently at the river till Bharat's engineers repair the Onguiaahra sluice controls. And by the time it is repaired, we will move in from the west and be in Sigiriya.'

'Hmm,' said Hanuman. 'If Bharat's numbers are correct, then only twenty thousand soldiers are left in Sigiriya. We can simply march in. The battle will be over even before it begins.'

'Precisely,' said Ram. 'This is perfect.'

Chapter 24

Indrajit stared in frustration at Kshiraj, the captured Ayodhyan soldier.

It was late evening and Indrajit and his soldiers had blocked the flood-control spillways at the back of the reservoir to prevent deluge water from flowing into the Amban Ganga. After this they had destroyed the spillway sluice controls. Then they had retreated to the positions held by the Lankan navy on the western banks of the Amban Ganga. Deeper into the forest.

He looked at his soldiers, annoyance writ large on his face. 'Where the hell is she?'

Kshiraj bent forward, limp. His arms were stretched back and tied around a tree with a strong hemp rope. His legs were similarly stretched and tied. The rope was rough and hard, precisely as intended by the Lankans. It had made vicious cuts into his wrists and ankles as he had struggled. Of course, these were the least of the injuries on the unfortunate Ayodhyan.

Blood dripped from the open wounds where his finger nails had been pulled out. His eyelids had been pulled back and snipped off. Some toes were missing. His knees had been smashed with a hammer. A nail had been hammered into the crook of his right arm. It had dug into the anconeus muscle and cut the ulnar nerve. That had been particularly painful.

Kshiraj had screamed in pain, pleaded for mercy, cried out for his mother.

But he had not talked. He did not divulge any secret of the Ayodhyan army.

Indrajit was beginning to suspect that maybe what they knew was all there was to Ram's strategy: an overwhelming attack from the Mahaweli Ganga River and using the captured Onguiaahra citadel to open the floodgates. Maybe there was no secret to unearth. But a deep instinct continued to nag him that there was more. Like an itch he couldn't reach. And so, he was reluctant to give up on Kshiraj.

But he also understood that this method was not delivering results. He needed to tweak the torment. He needed a better torturer. And he had sent for one.

'Where is Brigadier Samichi, dammit? It's been two hours since I sent for her!'

Samichi, in an earlier life, had been the police and protocol chief of Mithila, working under the direct supervision of Princess Sita, the prime minister of the kingdom. Unknown to Sita, however, Samichi was a Raavan loyalist. When she was a child, the king of Lanka had saved her from her abusive father. It was this loyalty that had driven Samichi to betray her princess. Indrajit was aware that Samichi, along with her lover Khara, had extracted critical information from a Malayaputra soldier; an extremely tough warrior to break. The information was on the whereabouts of Sita, her husband Ram, his brother

Lakshman, and sixteen Malayaputra soldiers who were hiding in the forests of Dandak, close to the Godavari River. It was why Raavan had been able to kidnap Sita so easily, and with minimal loss of life.

Maybe Samichi would succeed with this obdurate man.

'My Lord!' said a relieved soldier. 'Brigadier Samichi has arrived.'

Indrajit turned around.

Samichi immediately went down on one knee and brought her clenched right fist up to her chest. 'My prince, I'm honoured to be called to your service.'

Samichi had been removed from her post by Raavan when she had tried to injure Sita in the Pushpak Vimaan, immediately after the princess had been kidnapped. Samichi's attempted assault was a natural reaction – Sita had killed Samichi's lover, Khara. Raavan had granted Samichi pardon in recognition of past services. However, to be discarded by her liege was a punishment worse than death for a warrior. She was, therefore, delighted to be called back to service by the Lankan royal family. Even if it was by the prince and not the king.

'Brigadier Samichi,' said Indrajit. She had been briefed already. But he wanted her to hear it from him directly. 'I fear that this Ayodhyan soldier has very little life left in him. I also have a suspicion that we are missing something – there is some part of King Ram's strategy that we are not aware of. I need this man to talk. And to live till he does so. Can you strike that fine balance?'

'Of course, My Lord!' exclaimed Samichi, smiling, eager to please. She turned to a Lankan soldier and said, her tenor radically different with a subordinate, 'You! Don't stand around staring like an idiot. I want you to tie the Ayodhyan scum's forehead to the tree. Keep it tight. He shouldn't be able to move his head.' Then she turned to some other Lankans standing to the side. 'You five, come with me! On the double!'

And Samichi raced into the forests, followed by the five Lankans she had picked.

Within less than half an hour, Samichi was back.

Each of the five soldiers carried large banana leaves, with nests perched on them. They weren't traditional nests made of sticks, grass and leaves. These nests were made from the bodies of the animals that they were carrying.

Indrajit looked bewildered. *Ants?*

Human beings labour under the delusion that they are the most successful species on earth. It is a highly questionable assumption.

Ants have been on earth for nearly one hundred million years, well before human beings made their appearance. They were around when dinosaurs walked the earth, and survived whatever it was that destroyed those massive beasts. And then their population exploded a few million years later. The ant population is large, some estimates placing it in many thousands of trillions. They constitute between fifteen to twenty per cent of the terrestrial animal biomass; more than all humans and mammals combined!

They build large, complex colonies and organise themselves efficiently along job specialisation: some are worker ants, others are soldiers, and most importantly there is the queen who founds a colony of ants and dedicates herself to laying eggs and producing the next generation. Ants, like human beings, conduct wars and exhibit complicated battle strategies. Enmities last generations. Their main competitive advantage is that an entire colony, comprising perhaps a million to twenty million ants, has a hive mind. Millions in one colony can self-organise and work together, like an eerily coordinated superorganism.

When moving together, this 'superorganism' stretches many hundreds of metres.

These details about ants did not interest Samichi. What did interest her was their immense strength relative to their small size. It allowed them to deliver pain to the most unusual places.

'Place the nests over there,' said Samichi to the five soldiers, pointing to a spot in the distance but in full view. 'And make a small moat of water around the banana leaves, so that the ants cannot escape.'

'Yes, Brigadier,' said one of the soldiers, saluting.

Indrajit couldn't contain himself anymore. He wondered if he had made a mistake in summoning Samichi. 'Ants? Really?'

'They are not ordinary ants, great prince,' said Samichi. 'These are driver ants. More specifically, the soldiers of a driver ant colony.'

Driver ants are carnivorous; they feed on the flesh of other insects. When they attack in swarms, led by their soldier ants, they have been known to dismember and carry away far bigger creatures, such as chickens and goats. Even pigs, if they are injured or are unable to escape the marauding ants.

'Build a fire quickly,' Samichi brusquely ordered a soldier. And turned to Indrajit with an ingratiating smile. 'They are females ants, noble prince. Much more vicious.'

Indrajit wanted to ask how Samichi knew that the ants were female, but thought better of it. If he had asked, she would have told him: practically, the entire driver ant colonies are female; the males live for only a week and they either die or are killed after procreation.

Indrajit walked over to see the soldier ants. They were smaller than the queen ant but bigger than worker ants. The queen only delivers babies; she does little else. The worker ants only, well, work. The soldier ants are the warriors in the colony.

Fiercely protective of their own and aggressively combative with foreigners. They carry vicious weapons built into their body in the form of serrated claws and mandibles.

Samichi picked up a twig from the fire, brought it close to one of the nests on a banana leaf and blew smoke on to it. The temporary 'nests' of the soldiers among driver ants are not like those of other ants; they are made of the ants themselves. They cluster together to form walls and fasten onto each other using their mandibles and the claws on their legs, assembling what is in effect a living bivouac. As the smoke disturbed them, the bivouac began to dissolve and the ants scattered themselves across and beyond the banana leaf. A few of them drowned in the tiny watery moat around the leaf.

Samichi turned to a soldier and barked, 'Make a few hollow straws from the river reeds. Keep them ready.'

She then carefully picked up an ant with a pair of pincers. Watchful not to injure the tiny beast. The ant was a little less than one centimetre long; a good size for a driver ant. It had massive jaws; in fact, the jaws of soldier ants are so big that they are unable to feed and must rely on worker ants to give them all the nourishment they need. The soldier ant had a pale orange head, dark orange legs, and large, dark mandibles that were sharp and poisonous. It had fearsome claws on its legs. Its antennae jut out aggressively as Samichi carried it. Its serrated, poison-tipped mandibles clawing the air.

Indrajit watched. Captivated.

Samichi stared coldly at Kshiraj and said in a low, cruel whisper, 'Look at this soldier ant, Kshiraj.'

Kshiraj returned her stare, grim determination writ upon his face. He had survived everything they had done to him. What could an ant do? What could be worse?

But torture was a fine art for Samichi. Constant, gnawing pain can break the spirit. But only if it is carefully calibrated to a level of tolerance that the brain does not shut out.

Samichi gestured to one of the soldiers, who rushed forward and pushed a soft bit between Kshiraj's teeth. Samichi turned to Indrajit with an eerie smile. 'We don't want him biting off his tongue in pain. Otherwise, how will he talk?'

Indrajit stared at Samichi, a smidgen of cold fear gripping his heart. *She actually enjoys this…*

'I know what you are thinking, Kshiraj,' said Samichi to her prey, her tone soft and creepy. 'What can an ant do, right?'

Kshiraj did not respond.

Samichi continued. 'But an ant can do a lot. The venom of its sting will make even the true king of the jungle, the mighty elephant, holler for mercy.'

Samichi turned to another soldier, who ran up with a hollow reed straw that he had fashioned. Samichi took the straw from him.

'But it is crucial to ensure that the ant is in the right place.' Samichi laughed softly as she said this. 'It can do little on an elephant's back, which it will simply not penetrate. But deep inside an elephant's trunk … aah, well.'

Samichi came close to Kshiraj's ear and whispered, 'I wonder if you know that your ear canal extends nearly three centimetres into your head.'

Kshiraj shrank with terror, not fearful of the ant but the freakishly monstrous aura that this woman exuded. But he could not move. His head had been tied tight.

Samichi continued to murmur, her face hideously excited with the prospect of inflicting pain. 'Do you know that we have very sensitive nerves on the other side of the eardrum? I have often wondered how to get deep enough inside the ear canal with something small and deadly.'

Samichi carefully pushed one end of the hollow reed deep inside Kshiraj's ear. As far as it would go. 'The obstacle, as I am sure you understand, is the structure of the ear canal. It's just too small. And not straight. But if we can get something sharp and deadly, deep enough in there ... Mmmm.' Samichi stepped back to admire her handiwork. 'Do you know that the nerves on the other side of your eardrum take all sensations from the ear directly to the brain? No filtration at the spinal cord. You will know soon enough. It took me some time to perfect this technique ... Some interesting experiments. You will find it ... memorable.'

Kshiraj's agitated eyes swivelled and stared at the wriggling insect. A drop of venom dribbled out of the soldier ant's serrated mandibles.

Samichi brought the soldier ant up to the hollow reed. And dropped it in. Then she covered the open end of the reed with some clay. And stepped back.

'Listen to it coming towards you.'

Kshiraj writhed in fear as he heard the footsteps of the ant, amplified by the hollow reed pushed almost up to his eardrum. It sounded like the distant thumping of elephant feet.

'Feel it coming ... hear it coming ...' Samichi whispered.

He made desperate attempts to drive the ant out. He tried to shake his head, his eyes rolling with possessed madness. But his entire body, including his head, had been tied securely to the tree, restricting his movements. And the hollow reed was lodged too deep inside.

He could feel it now. The ant had stepped out of the reed hollow and was in his ear canal. Scurrying around in anger, its body had released a piercing chemical stench, a natural reaction to perceived threat. The odour drove the ant into greater frenzy. It turned back into the hollow reed and rushed forward. It hit the soft clay covering the opening, turned around in a furious rage and charged.

Kshiraj was screaming inaudibly now, the sounds muffled by the bit in his mouth.

The soldier ant reached Kshiraj's eardrum, tested the tissue with its antenna, threw its head back, spread its poison-tipped mandibles and bit hard.

Kshiraj shrieked in agony. The bit could not hold back the sound. His eyes rolled into his head, the whites of his eyeballs staring blindly at the sky. His rigid and tense body strained against the unforgiving ropes that bound him in a vice-like grip. Desperate tears streamed out like a tiny river in spate. He was bathed in sweat. He lost control of his bowels. The contents of his intestines burst through and ran down his legs.

He screamed repeatedly. Howling for his God. Screeching for his *guru*. Wailing for the most powerful benefactor of all, his mother. His mouth cramped with the bit, it all emerged as a mash of indistinguishable blubber.

Indrajit looked at Samichi with horrified awe. 'Just an ant ...?'

'It's all about putting it in the right place, great prince. The vestibular and cochlear nerves are very close to the eardrum. But wait ... The real fun will begin if the ant manages to tear the eardrum. But that's up to the ant, of course. I cannot control that.'

Indrajit looked at Kshiraj.

The Ayodhyan was twisted with spasms of unbearable pain. The ant had caused a minor tear in the eardrum and the man was bawling with agonised desperation. He lost control of his bladder. Thick yellow urine dribbled down his legs to mix with his excreta. He was straining miserably against the ropes. The veins in his neck threatened to burst with his repeated attempts to shake his head.

'He'll break his neck,' said a worried Indrajit.

'No, he won't, My Lord,' insisted Samichi.

'He is no good to me if he dies.'

Samichi sighed inaudibly and walked up to Kshiraj. She took a swig of water from her bottle, removed the clay cover from one end of the hollow reed and spat the liquid through the reed into Kshiraj's ear. The water drowned the ant and its carcass emerged from the ear, flowing out and then sticking to Kshiraj's neck.

The Ayodhyan hung limp against the tree, his eyes swivelling wildly, his head and body shivering violently within the constraints of the tight ropes.

Indrajit flicked his fingers. A Lankan soldier rushed up to Kshiraj and removed the bit from his mouth. He loosened the bonds around the Ayodhyan's arms. He did not move. A thin dribble of vomit fell like droplets from the side of his mouth.

Indrajit walked up to Kshiraj, holding his angvastram against his nose to block the stench of the Ayodhyan's faeces and urine. 'Talk. And you shall have mercy.'

'You will have to wait for a bit, noble prince,' said Samichi. 'The inner ear is also the centre of the sense of balance. He is deeply disoriented right now.'

Indrajit waited for a few seconds and then spoke again. 'Talk … What is King Ram's secret strategy?'

Kshiraj's head moved infinitesimally, indicating response. A faint will to talk.

'Was that a nod, Prince Indrajit?' asked Samichi.

Indrajit looked at Samichi. 'Loosen the restraints around his head. But only a little.'

Samichi did as ordered. Kshiraj moved his head. He was shivering, his eyes wild and disoriented.

Indrajit stepped up close. 'Talk.'

Kshiraj's plea was frantic. 'Please ... please ... kill me ...' His voice broke.

'Talk.'

'Please ...'

'TALK!'

Kshiraj was silent for a few seconds, and then he spoke the words. Almost like they were prised out of him. 'Main army ... not here ...'

Indrajit glanced at Samichi and then back at Kshiraj.

'Main army ... coming ... from west ...'

'From the west?' asked Samichi. 'That's not possible. There are no ports there. He's lying!'

Indrajit looked into Kshiraj's eyes. 'No, he is not.'

'But—'

Indrajit raised his hand and Samichi fell silent. What Kshiraj was saying sounded ludicrous, but some instinct in Indrajit made him believe it.

Indrajit asked Kshiraj again. 'From where in the west?'

Kshiraj remained silent.

'Do you want another ant?'

'Please ... no ...'

'From where in the west?'

'Dhanushkodi ...'

'Dhanushkodi?! The sand flats are too high. Their ships will get grounded. They will not reach Lanka.'

'Crossing ... to Lanka ... on bridge ...'

Indrajit's mouth fell open in shock. *A bridge? Across the sea?*

Dhanushkodi is right next to the Ketheeswaram temple. If they did manage to build a bridge and arrive in Lanka in that region, they would get to Sigiriya within a day via the royal road. He turned his head and looked at the river, towards the Lankan ships. *While we are stuck here, we will lose our capital.*

He looked at Kshiraj. *There's more. I know it …*

'What else?' asked Indrajit.

Kshiraj shook his head.

'Talk, Goddammit,' growled Indrajit.

Kshiraj refused to open his mouth.

Indrajit turned to Samichi. 'Another ant.'

Samichi carefully picked up another specimen from the banana leaf with her pincers. But before she could take her first step towards the Ayodhyan, he jerked his head forward and pushed his body against the ropes with sudden violence. The ropes held his head, legs and feet in an iron grip. But the binds around his arms had been loosened, allowing his torso some movement. Enough for his neck to snap as he jerked forward.

'Son of a …' Indrajit cursed in frustration, his hands flying to his head.

Samichi rushed forward and pulled Kshiraj's limp head up. He was dead. She looked at the ant she was holding, a deeply disappointed expression on her face.

Indrajit turned to a soldier. 'Get a rowboat. Quick. I must meet my father immediately.' As the soldiers rushed to obey, the Prince of Lanka turned to Samichi. 'You have done well, Brigadier. Thank you.'

Samichi had a half-smile on her face. She looked again at the ant and then crushed it between her fingers.

Chapter 25

'Go back to Sigiriya?!' asked Raavan, flabbergasted. 'Are you crazy?'

Raavan, Kumbhakarna, Mareech and Indrajit had gathered in the Lankan Emperor's sumptuous private cabin in the navy's main ship. Indrajit had reached the vessel late in the night. He had interrupted his father's dinner, insisting on meeting him immediately.

'Yes, father,' said Indrajit, his voice calm and confident. 'They have only sent a small diversionary force here.'

'Small diversionary force? Have you counted the number of ships?'

'Yes, I have! Perhaps they want to give us the impression that they have many soldiers. These ships are probably manned by skeletal staff. We cannot know for sure till we actually enter their ships, isn't it?'

'Perhaps? Probably? You want me to change my entire battle strategy on your "perhaps" and "probably"?'

'Father, I feel it in my guts – the information is correct. Their main army will come in from the west. They will conquer Sigiriya easily if we all remain here.'

'And what if you are wrong? What if we leave this river post and give the Ayodhyans an easy victory? And then they march all the way up to Sigiriya?'

'Even if that happens, we will be safely ensconced in our fort. Well-stocked and defended. They will be stranded outside with stretched supply lines. Trust me, it will be far worse if the Ayodhyans actually come from the west and take our capital. Then they will be inside our fort, well-stocked and defended, while we will be stuck outside. They will wear us down.'

Kumbhakarna spoke up. 'And how will they come from the west? What is your information on that?'

Indrajit looked at Mareech. He knew his father and uncle would find it difficult to believe what he had to say. Mareech nodded. *Tell them.*

Indrajit turned to Kumbhakarna. 'They are crossing over at Dhanushkodi, uncle. And then they will march up the Ketheeswaram temple road. It's less than a day's march to Sigiriya.'

'And how exactly will they cross over from the Indian mainland to Lanka?' asked Raavan, an incredulous look on his face. 'You know that area. Many sandflats are actually above the water level during low tide. No ship can safely anchor there.'

Indrajit took a deep breath. 'I believe they are building a bridge.'

Raavan and Kumbhakarna burst out laughing.

'Father ...' growled Indrajit, upset and angry.

Mareech cut in. 'Raavan, Kumbhakarna. Listen to Indrajit. I believe the information he has is true.'

Raavan turned to Mareech. 'Uncle, do you believe this nonsense? A bridge across the sea?! Really?!'

Mareech kept quiet.

'I think that the youngest among the brothers—Prince Shatrughan—could do it,' said Indrajit. 'He is brilliant.'

'Shatrughan may be brilliant, my boy,' said Raavan. 'But he's not a wizard. Nobody can build a bridge across the sea.'

'Father, trust me. I can feel it in my bones. The information I have is right.'

'Indrajit, don't be childish. You want me to retreat from here, based on something you extracted from a person you tortured. Do you realise how this will appear to our soldiers? They will see me as a coward! I'd much rather die here. Fighting.'

Mareech cut in once again. 'How about sending a few quick riders to Ketheeswaram to check this out? If it's nothing, then it's nothing. But if the Ayodhyans are actually crossing, then we can …'

'All right,' surrendered Raavan. He turned to Kumbhakarna. 'Send some riders tomorrow morning.'

'No, father,' said Indrajit. 'If you send them tomorrow morning, they will only return the day after. It may already be too late by then. Send them right away.'

Raavan was clearly irritated. 'My boy …'

'Father! Please! Just trust me!'

Raavan closed his eyes and shook his head. 'Fine! Send them now, Kumbha.'

—J⊦ ⅃ɜD—

'Overproduction of elites? That's your big theory?' asked Vashishtha.

Vishwamitra, Vashishtha and Nandini were sitting on a large rock outside their gurukul, on the banks of the Kaveri River. The three friends were teachers at the gurukul of Maharishi Kashyap, the celebrated Saptrishi Uttradhikari, successor to the seven legendary seers. The three were in their early forties. Vishwamitra and Vashishtha had been students of the gurukul in their early years. Upon graduation, they had gone their separate ways. Vashishtha had shone as a celebrated teacher while Vishwamitra became a distinguished and feared Kshatriya royal. Two decades later, they had joined the prestigious institution again, this time as teachers. They had instantly rekindled their childhood friendship. In private, they still referred to each other by the gurukul names of their student days: Kaushik for Vishwamitra and Divodas for Vashishtha. There had been another student at the gurukul: Nandini. A brilliant girl from the land of Branga, the lush, rich, fertile delta that the confluence of the Brahmaputra and Ganga rivers watered. She was now a stunningly beautiful woman. Nandini had been just an acquaintance during their childhood, but had now become a good friend. She had not just converted the duo to a trio, but had dramatically improved the quality of the group. For not only was she as intellectually luminous as the formidable Vishwamitra and Vashishtha, she was more attractive than the two men could ever have hoped to be!

'Not just overproduction of elites, Divodas,' said Vishwamitra to Vashishtha. 'That is only one half of the theory. The other half is the immiseration of the masses.'

'Immise-what?' asked Nandini.

'It means economic impoverishment. Making someone poorer.'

'So why not just say "impoverishment of the masses" then?' Nandini joked. 'Using big words doesn't make you sound more intelligent, Vishwamitra.'

Vishwamitra narrowed his eyes and mock-glared at Nandini. The love he felt for her made him control the irritation that yearned to express itself on his face.

'You are intelligent enough as it is, Vishwa,' said Nandini. *'All of us know that.'*

Vishwamitra smiled. He loved it when Nandini called him by that nickname.

'So,' continued Vashishtha. *'The immiseration of the masses and overproduction of elites ...'*

'Yes,' continued Vishwamitra, looking pointedly at Nandini with a smile, *'the* impoverishment *of the masses and overproduction of elites. This theory only applies to large, complex civilisations, obviously. Not to small groups. The key ingredient that makes large and complex civilisations possible is cooperation among massive numbers of people. At the biggest scale, even millions of people can cooperate and live together, like in our India. And this entire societal structure among humans works on a social contract between an elite which leads, and the masses that follow.'*

'But some New Age people say that this entire concept of elite and masses is a social construct,' said Nandini. *'It's artificial and should be broken. We should go back to the natural way.'*

'The "natural way" means an average lifespan of thirty years, many women and infants dying in childbirth, even a small cut on a finger probably leading to death, violence and hunger every few days. Because in the brilliant "natural way", we would be living like animals. Of course, the concept of an elite and the masses living together in large societies is artificial. The entire idea of millions of individuals cooperating is artificial. But just because it's not "natural" doesn't mean that it's not good.'

'But I think the point they make is about the difference between the elite and the masses. It is not inclusive.'

'I agree that too much power concentrated in the hands of the elite is not good. We must have balance. But swinging to the other extreme is also not good. Also, this thing about being inclusive ... Look, by its very nature, excellence is not inclusive. It cannot be

inclusive. It has to be exclusive. You can either have inclusiveness, where everyone feels involved, or you can have excellence, where those who are good at a certain thing are given the freedom and encouragement to achieve, with the hope that society at large will also benefit. But you have to pick one, either inclusivity or excellence. You cannot have both. And without excellence, civilised life is not possible. But I'll say it again, we need balance. The elite should not be too powerful.'

'And, hence, the social contract. Which is a balance between the elite and the masses. Neither side becoming too powerful.'

'Precisely. If the social contract works, then both the elite and the masses are happy, and the society is successful. If the social contract breaks down, the society collapses into political violence and chaos.'

'So, why do the social contracts within societies break down?' asked Nandini. 'And what does your theory say about how it can be prevented?'

'I should clarify,' said Vishwamitra, 'it's not my theory. At least not originally. I have built on it, but I heard the basics of this theory from a man I met in the Yamnaya steppelands, a man called Turchin.'

'The Yamnaya?!' Vashishtha was shocked. The Yamnaya were one of the tribes that lived on the vast steppes that stretched over eight thousand kilometres from Europe through Central Asia to Eastern Asia. These fertile, undulating grasslands were perfect for breeding the best horses in the world, far superior to the smaller equus found in India. They also produced hardy, tough, nomadic humans, among whom the males were usually raised from childhood for one profession alone: the fine art of killing and plundering. And among the most brutal and genocidal of these steppe tribes were the Yamnaya. 'They are just brutal killers. There cannot be any intellectuals among those barbarians.'

'Well, Lord Turchin is the exception that proves the rule.'

'*Actually, it makes sense,*' said Nandini. '*The entire way of life of the people of the steppes is to attack and plunder the settled civilisations. Those civilisations that exist along the Mediterranean Sea, the Middle East, the Indian subcontinent and China. If they want to attack and plunder us, they need to understand us. They need to know when and where to attack so that they get the maximum loot for every person they kill.*'

'*Correct,*' said Vishwamitra. '*The hunter must understand the prey.*'

'*We are hardly the prey!*' exclaimed Vashishtha.

'*Well, we are not the prey when we are strong. But when we are weak, yes, we do become the prey to the killers of the steppes. The best defence against external enemies is our own strength and unity.*'

'*Hmm ...*'

'*So, the theory ...*' said Nandini. '*Why do civilisations weaken and collapse?*'

'*The theory states that this is a natural corollary to success. Some call it catastrophic success. The seeds of failure of some complex societies are sown in their journey towards success.*'

'*How so?*'

Vishwamitra continued, '*When a society is on the path of success, it gets richer steadily. And if the elite is efficient and just, as it would be in a successful society, they would share the rewards fairly with the masses. So, the masses also get richer and healthier steadily. But resultantly, the masses multiply. They grow in numbers. And as their numbers increase, the labour supply also grows. This is not a problem if the elite continuously finds new ways to grow the economy and absorb the increased labour into jobs. But if they fail to do that, and the supply of labour keeps growing, then the price of labour—wages—will steadily fall. And as wages for the masses fall, they get poorer and angrier, creating the conditions for rebellion, even revolution.*'

'But wages can fall for other reasons, right?' asked Nandini. 'Like the elite allowing in a massive number of immigrants, without creating enough jobs to absorb those immigrants. Or the elite importing goods from other lands where the masses earn less.'

'True,' said Vashishtha. 'And I guess we can call that elite selfish. But they write their own long-term doom. The main point is that, if the masses become poorer or unhealthier as compared to before, they are unhappy and this creates the conditions for a revolution. A smart elite, with basic survival instincts, should want to control this and ensure that the masses don't become too unhappy.'

'Absolutely,' said Vishwamitra. 'Every member of the elite should realise that he or she needs to help the poor masses constantly. It is in their own selfish interest. If they don't do that, they will need to spend more and more money on a bigger security and military set-up to keep the masses suppressed and under control. And even that has limits. At some point or another the military will get overwhelmed. But a revolution won't be triggered just by the masses getting impoverished. The masses, by definition, don't lead. They follow. Their unhappiness creates a necessary condition for rebellion, political violence and social breakdown. But it is not sufficient. This discontentment must be accompanied by another phenomenon.'

'What phenomenon is that?' asked Vashishtha.

'The rise of a counter-elite,' said Vishwamitra.

'Those who will lead the rebellion and revolution?' asked Nandini.

'Exactly,' said Vishwamitra. 'And the conditions for the emergence of a counter-elite are created by the impoverishment of the masses. As the masses become poorer, their wages fall, and those who consume the labour of the masses – the elite – become wealthier. As the gap between the two increases, the aspirations of the masses become focused and acute. The talented among them are *desperate to enter the elite ranks. In fact, more and more people from the masses try ever harder to join the elite, because the rewards appear so attractive. This is especially true if the elite is ostentatious, showing off their wealth rather than being conservative and understated.*

'Some among the masses gradually become a part of the elite. They work hard, educate themselves and rise. But the problem is that the elite cannot keep expanding. There are only so many elite positions. There can only be one king. There can only be one chief general of the army. There can only be one chief priest of a religion. A big lie told to children today in civilised societies is that all of them are special, all of them can aspire to reach the top. This is nonsense. The top does not have endless space. The nature of a complex society makes the elite a small class. And if there are more and more aspirants for the elite class, logically more and more people will be denied their ambitions and psychological space under the sun. And these aspirants then get frustrated and become the counter-elite.'

'Since, usually, the counter-elite has risen from the masses by the dint of their hard work, are they more capable than the children of the old elite?' asked Vashishtha.

'Precisely,' agreed Vishwamitra. 'The elite aspirants who have risen from the masses have fire in their belly. This is why they have risen. And the children of the old elite are born with a silver spoon in the mouth. Most of them have very little appetite for hard work and the sacrifices necessary for success. They think they are entitled to be the elite and that mommy and daddy will ensure it for them.'

'True,' said Nandini, smiling wickedly. She and Vashishtha were both self-made.

'Hey!' said Vishwamitra, laughing softly. For he was the son of a king, clearly a progeny of the old elite. 'Not every kid born with a silver spoon is fat and lazy.'

'I agree with you on lazy,' said Vashishtha, sniggering. 'But fat? I don't know ...'

Vishwamitra looked at his massive belly and laughed aloud. He playfully punched his friend Vashishtha on the shoulder. Vashishtha leaned over and hugged his friend, both laughing in unison now.

Nandini also laughed. 'All right, all right. Settle down, you two.'

'Yeah, okay,' said Vishwamitra, patting Vashishtha and leaning back.

'So ... these changes in society, they take place over long periods of time, right?' asked Nandini.

'Yeah, of course. These changes take place over decades. So those who are in charge of the long-term health of a society should keep a check on some parameters, so they have enough advance warning of oncoming societal chaos. What should those parameters be? Like these... How much inequality exists between the masses and the elite? What should its limit be, beyond which some intervention must be made? Is there an overproduction of elites? How many aspirants compete for each elite position? Is a counter-elite rising?'

'One clarification, please. When you say elite, you don't only mean Brahmins, Kshatriyas and Vaishyas, right?'

'Of course not,' said Vishwamitra. 'There are many Brahmins, Kshatriyas and Vaishyas who are not part of the elite. For example, teachers in small schools, or soldiers, or sub-traders in a trading guild. And many Shudras are a part of the elite: for example, Shudra artistes, like storytellers and painters with big followings, are part of the ideological elite. So, this is not about the varna that people belong to. It is about power; those who have it and those who don't. The elite class is defined by one thing alone: power. Those who exercise power over others in their society are members of the elite.'

'Okay,' said Nandini.

'So, how do we control this process?' asked Vashishtha. 'A smart elite should be able to anticipate these problems and avoid or control them, before they blow their society up.'

'Right,' said Vishwamitra. 'The first and foremost way is ensuring that the material life of the masses steadily improves. Whatever varna the masses belong to, their life must continuously improve, even if in small measures. Remember, the masses don't evaluate their state in comparison to people from other countries. They compare it to their own past. India is the richest country on earth. So, the Indian masses are far richer than the Greek masses, for instance. If the Indian masses become worse off, they will move towards dissatisfaction, protests and rebellions, even if, in their poorer state, they remain economically better off than the Greeks.'

'Yeah,' said Vashishtha. 'That's true.'

'So, it is in the interest of the elite to help the poor. Be mindful of them. When in doubt, help the poor. When you have nothing else to occupy yourself with, help the poor. The default position of a smart elite must always be: help the poor.'

'And the problem of overproduction of elites?'

'It's different for the elite. I don't think their material life should be on an ever-improving spiral. In fact, I do think that for the sake of stability in a society, there must be a periodic culling of the elite. So that the old elite, which has become fat and lazy, is replaced by a new rising elite, with more energy and drive.'

'Culling?' asked Nandini. 'Isn't that cruel? Really, Vishwa, I wish you would measure your words. Words have energy, my friend!'

'Look, I speak my mind, using the most descriptive and not necessarily appropriate words. In any case, that's what happens with political civil violence, doesn't it? Many elite members are killed, and then there is less internal competition in that class. In fact, often, elite overproduction leads to some of the old elite or even the counter-elite, inviting foreign intervention. Garnering additional *support and validation. This is the point that Turchin from the Yamnaya tribe was making to me. He said that Yamnaya warriors are on the lookout for countries with too many people in the elite class. Some among them are open to inviting these warriors of the steppes to assist them in their internal battles with the other elite in their own nation. Like a flock of sheep inviting wolves to kill the sheep they don't like. This normally doesn't end well for the sheep that sends out the invitation as well. Intra-elite civil war is disastrous for a society.'*

'So, competition between different elite groups must be reduced before it reaches this stage, I suppose.'

'Precisely. There are many ways to achieve this, if we want to avoid intra-elite civil wars and the incumbent chaos. The simplest is to expel specific elite groups from the country. Subtly, of course, by creating conditions for their departure. Let them compete in some foreign land, not in India. Then there will be less intra-elite competition within India. But there is one other way.'

'Your Maika system …' said Vashishtha.

'Maika system?' asked Nandini. 'What is that?'

'Kaushik had expanded upon this once,' Vashishtha took over, using Vishwamitra's gurukul name. 'Quite a radical idea. He suggested that children must be compulsorily adopted by the State at the time of birth. The birth parents would surrender their children to the kingdom. The State would feed, educate and nurture the innate talents and capabilities of these children. At fifteen years of age, they would be tested on their physical, psychological and mental abilities in a rigorous examination. Based on the results, appropriate castes would be allocated to them. Subsequent training would further polish their natural skills. Eventually, they would be adopted by citizens of the same caste as the one assigned to the adolescents through the examination process. The children would

not know their birth parents, only their adoptive caste-parents. The birth parents, too, would not know the fate of their birth children.'

Nandini raised her eyebrows. 'Only someone who has not had children will think that parents will willingly hand over their child to the State.'

'But this system will be perfect for society, Nandini,' said Vishwamitra. 'Think about it with an open mind. In a sense, we are reducing the status of those who are incapable among the old elite's descendants every generation. They will become a part of the masses. And those from the masses, who are capable, will join the elite. In an open and fair way. Even those descendants of the old elite who are capable can rejoin the elite club, but without any special boosts that a doting mummy and daddy may give them. The elite will remain efficient and capable for much longer. It will keep the society stable. It will also keep it competitive.'

'But you're envisioning a society built exclusively around duty and efficiency. What about love? What are we human beings without love?'

'Love is the greatest illusion, Kaushik believes,' said Vashishtha, smiling. 'Or at least, that's what he believed many years ago.'

'Really?' asked Nandini, looking at Vishwamitra, eyes twinkling.

Vishwamitra didn't say anything.

Nandini turned to Vashishtha. 'Maybe love is an illusion, maybe it isn't. But even so, there is no reason we should not enjoy it while we feel it. Illusion or not. Only those who have not suffered the dreary desert of grief will deny the ethereal, even if temporary, comfort of love.'

Vashishtha seemed uncomfortable. He went back to the subject at hand. 'Well, I don't know if such a society is even possible. Where can the Maika system be implemented? I admit, though — it would be a very interesting experiment.'

Nandini smiled and looked away from Vashishtha, almost imperceptibly shaking her head.

'I am sure I can convince the next Vishnu to implement this system,' said Vishwamitra.

Nandini laughed softly. 'You have to become the chief of the Malayaputras first.'

'That will happen ...'

'That certainly will,' said Vashishtha. 'My friend will make it.'

Vishwamitra looked at Vashishtha, smiled, and patted his friend's hand.

Nandini looked at both of them as a shadow of pain briefly crossed her face. And then it lifted. 'I have one more question.'

'Shoot,' said Vishwamitra.

'Many Kshatriya royals attack Vaishya businessmen these days. I think there may come a time when they will start appropriating Vaishya wealth. Would you call that a culling of a segment of the elite, in a manner of speaking?'

'No, I would call it bigotry and stupidity.'

'Why? You just said that there must not be too many elite members.'

'It's like this. There are four kinds of power: military, economic, political and ideological. Military power is based on the ability to use violence. This could be the army or police or any other such agency. Economic power is not about just wealth, but the ability to use that wealth. For example, a wealthy businessman may have more personal wealth than the managing partner of a large trade guild, but the managing partner can wield power derived from the guild's money. So, this hypothetical managing partner of ours may have less money than the businessman, but she is more powerful. Therefore, she is elite. Political power is exercised by politicians and administrators; basically, the king, top bureaucrats, the judges, et al., who use the administrative machinery of the State to enforce

their will upon the people. Lastly, ideological power is the ability to make the masses buy into ideas and memes that are supportive of the elite group's grip on power. The ideological elite could include storytellers, academics, reporters, artistes and such others. Now, a coherent elite group will have ALL four power sources. They must have intra sub-groups with the ability to deploy all these four sources of power. Therefore, one sub-group attacking another sub-group in its own elite group is stupidity and, frankly, long-term suicide.'

'Interesting ...' said Vashishtha. 'So, which are the elite groups in India today, you think?'

'I think the groups aren't as obvious as you might imagine. I believe there are three elite groups in India. The holy Saraswati River divides ...'

Vashishtha suddenly awakened from the dream. A dream that recalled a memory that was more than a century old. 'Oh Lord Brahma!'

It was late in the morning. Vashishtha knew that Shatrughan was planning to restart construction a day earlier than planned. Half the mahouts had recovered. The pace of work would be slower, but it was better than nothing. Vashishtha had dozed off again after breakfast. A short nap on the beachside of Pamban island. And this dream had come to him. For a reason.

I know what he will do ...

Vashishtha looked at the sky. Remembering his friend turned foe.

Kaushik ... I know what you will do ... the Anunnaki ...

Chapter 26

The Lankan lay on the ground, struggling with surprising strength given the knife buried deep in his abdomen. The Ayodhyan sat astride him, beating his face repeatedly with his right fist. He had covered the Lankan's mouth with his left hand and was straining to get to his throat. Strangulate and finish the scuffle. The Lankan kept shifting, not giving the Ayodhyan clear punches. He boxed the Ayodhyan's chest, slapped his head. But each successive Lankan blow was weaker. He was losing too much blood from the wound in his abdomen.

The Ayodhyan held his grip on the Lankan's mouth. He had to. If the Lankan screamed, they would be discovered. There could be others.

The Lankan had locked his chin into his chest. Protecting his neck. At last, the Ayodhyan managed to prise his head away, while continuing to keep his mouth covered. He quickly gripped the Lankan's neck with his right hand. A vice-like grip. The Lankan was bucking desperately. Trying to push the

Ayodhyan off. The Ayodhyan's thumb found the bony cartilage of his larynx. And he pressed. Hard. Now he could safely release his left hand from the Lankan's mouth. No sound was possible anymore. He quickly brought both his hands into play and squeezed brutally. The Lankan's hands and legs thrashed the soft muddy ground. His eyes bulged from the vicious pressure on his throat.

'Just die, dammit,' whispered the Ayodhyan.

The Lankan was twitching weakly now. The Ayodhyan increased the pressure mercilessly. Harder and harder, he squeezed. Finally, the Lankan lay still, his limp tongue protruding from his mouth. The Ayodhyan picked a stone from the ground and banged it repeatedly on the Lankan's head, breaking it. Just in case.

He got up. Exhausted. And looked around.

Five Lankans lay dead around him. And four Ayodhyans; his comrades.

The Ayodhyan was a member of a small squad, a hunter-gatherer band that had spread out into the Lankan heartland to rummage for food. To provision the massive Ayodhyan army that was on the verge of crossing over. This particular band were early-morning scouts who hunted nocturnal animals just as they prepared to turn in. None of the Ayodhyan bands had run into Lankans until now. They believed that the Lankans had retreated to Sigiriya.

Hence, they had been momentarily stunned when they ran into the small band of Lankans. The Lankans were clearly shocked too. The clash had been swift and brutal.

The Ayodhyan slowly got his breathing back to normal. He had to rush back and report. To the commander of the landing brigades, Arishtanemi.

The Lankans are here!

As his breathing returned to normal and the adrenaline eased up, he looked at the scene around him with fresh eyes. He knew that Arishtanemi would ask him probing questions.

What the hell were these Lankans doing here by themselves? So far from their base?

He looked at the Lankan horses that they had ridden on. They had probably come from far. The Ayodhyans had no horses, for they foraged on foot.

The Lankan horses were tied to stumps. *These men were waiting here. Why? Lying in ambush for us? But our path was not pre-determined. They were waiting here for some other reason.*

And then he noticed something he should have seen earlier. There were six horses. And only five dead Lankans.

Oh Lord Ru—

The Ayodhyan didn't have the time to complete his thought. A knife flew in and pierced his throat. He fell back on the ground. Right next to the Lankan he had just killed. Through blurring eyes, he saw a man descending from the tree branches. The man came up close, pulled out another knife, and savagely stabbed the Ayodhyan in the heart.

Having silenced the enemy, the man, a Lankan, rose to his feet and rushed to his horse.

He had seen all he needed to see. He had climbed up the tree earlier to get a better look. From his vantage point at the top of the tree on the dense forested hill, he had seen a lot. Far into the distance, towards the beach of Ketheeswaram. It was early morning but there was enough light. He saw at least two thousand Ayodhyans at work; cutting trees, building stockades and generally preparing for the arrival of an army.

By the size of the stockade, it would be a formidable army.

He could also see the Ketheeswaram battalion quarters, the local base for Lankan soldiers. Or what was supposed to have been the base. For the building was burned down.

The Ketheeswaram temple remained untouched. Of course. No civilised man would damage a temple to the Gods. He had, in fact, seen some Ayodhyans enter the temple with garlands made from flowers. Perhaps for the morning prayers.

He couldn't see beyond the south-east coast of Mannar island, so he couldn't be sure whether a bridge was being built or not. When he had been specifically tasked with checking that, he had been incredulous.

A bridge across the sea? Ridiculous!

But one thing was certain. Whatever method the Ayodhyans were using to cross over to Lanka, clearly they were preparing for it.

I must rush back. To warn the king.

— JF J5D —

'I will not go back to the land of the Indus, Guruji,' said Naarad firmly. 'The battle is here.'

Vashishtha was speaking with Naarad in one corner of Pamban island. They were alone. And yet, Vashishtha was whispering. He knew that Arishtanemi's Malayaputras were all around.

'Listen to me, Naarad,' Vashishtha said softly. 'This is critical. Please. You needn't go yourself. But you must send a message to your best spy. I need this information.'

'But the other day you said that the Anu were not coming. That they will not support King Ram.'

'I am not talking about this battle, Naarad. I am talking about the battle that will follow this one.'

Naarad remained silent.

'I am not thinking about tomorrow,' whispered Vashishtha. 'It is the day after tomorrow that I worry about. You have one of the best intelligence-gathering networks in the land. Do this for me. Do this for the good of Mother India. Please.'

Naarad nodded. 'All right, Guruji.'

—— JF J͞5D ——

'My son ...'

Raavan was clearly moved. A rare display of emotion. He held Indrajit's head, bent over, and touched his forehead to that of his son. His eyes closed. His breathing was ragged.

Late in the evening, the Lankan royal council had received word that the Ayodhyan army had gathered on the north-west coast of Lanka, close to the Ketheeswaram temple. After the initial shock, the decision to be taken was obvious to all. The bulk of the Lankan army would disembark from their ships and be taken on a forced march to Sigiriya to reach their capital before the Ayodhyans did. And prepare for siege.

A small contingent of the Lankan forces would remain on the ships at Onguiaahra. And hold these Ayodhyans here as long as possible. If the Lankans abandoned this area completely, the Ayodhyans would lower their cutter boats from the massive seafaring ships, quickly row to the landing point for Sigiriya, march up the road and attack the Lankan army from the rear. But if a part of the Lankan river navy remained, the Ayodhyans would be wary of taking them on in their tiny cutter boats.

Net-net, the Lankan army needed a rear-guard to protect its retreat from the Ayodhyan navy at the Mahaweli Ganga. And Indrajit had offered to lead that rear-guard.

'Father,' grinned Indrajit. 'Don't worry. I'm not going to die. I'll see you in Sigiriya.'

Raavan laughed softly. 'You remind me of me sometimes.'

'I am better than you, dad. I can defeat you in a one-on-one.'

Raavan laughed loudly now. 'You are the only one who can say that and remain alive!'

'A man never gets defeated by his son,' Mareech said. 'He just sees a better version of himself.'

Raavan and Indrajit smiled and hugged each other.

Kumbhakarna stepped forward and patted Indrajit on his back. 'I'll see you in Sigiriya, my boy.'

Indrajit hugged Kumbhakarna. 'I'll see you soon, uncle. Prepare for the siege.'

'Yes, we will.'

'Are you sure about this, uncle?' Raavan asked Mareech.

Mareech had offered to stay back with Indrajit. To fight the Ayodhyans at Onguiaahra.

Mareech smiled. 'Well, there has to be some adult supervision!'

All four burst out laughing.

— JℲ ↓ƆD —

Seafaring ships have many strategic advantages in battles. They have many sails, so they can catch even the slightest wind and harness it to power the ship. They have many decks, one above the other, to allow for offensive attacks from many levels. Some well-designed vessels have reinforced bows, to ram other ships. But it is the massive mainmast that provides the key edge in a riverine naval battle.

If the sails are big, the mainmast must be very tall. And on Bharat's lead ship, it soared to almost a hundred and fifty feet. This was very useful for gathering information.

High-quality information is as valuable as tonnes of gold in a war.

All seafaring ships have a lookout point at the top of the mainmast. It is essentially a barrel with a reinforced bottom and railing, rigged up high on the mainmast. The barrel-man is usually one of the youngest in the crew and with the best eyesight. He mans the lookout points and reports his findings below.

Bharat was speaking with the barrel-man.

'What do you see?' asked Bharat, speaking loudly into the speaking-trumpet.

Through out the night, the Ayodhyans had heard distant sounds of trees being hacked with axes from beyond the control-steps of Onguiaahra. Bharat had wanted this checked at first light of dawn. The answer was not a surprise to the crew.

'They are cutting trees, My Lord,' the barrel-man hollered into the speaking-trumpet. 'Some of the tree trunks have been dropped into the river.'

Bharat looked at Lakshman. The latter had returned to Bharat's lead ship after securing both wings of the Onguiaahra citadel. The sluice-gate controls were being repaired by Vibhishan and his engineers.

'Dada,' said Lakshman. 'It's a simple idea ... They will clog up the Mahaweli Ganga with wooden logs. Making it difficult for us to sail up the river, even after we repair the Onguiaahra dam sluice controls. These are delaying tactics. It can slow us down but it will not stop us.'

Bharat frowned. Something didn't feel right. *This is too defensive. Not like Raavan at all, whose aggressive proclivities are well known. As it is, we are delayed due to the repair work at Onguiaahra. How much will the wooden logs help them? They will be useless against seafaring ships. We can just break through. Such logs are effective only against small riverine ships and cutter boats … How will this move help the Lankans?*

And then it struck him.

Dammit!

He looked at the barrel-man and thundered into the speaking-trumpet. 'Come down! Now!'

'Yes, My Lord,' replied the barrel-man.

Bharat fixed the speaking-trumpet back on its mainmast hold. He removed his angvastram from his shoulder and handed it to Lakshman.

'Dada?'

Bharat looked at Lakshman.

'Dada …' said Lakshman. 'You are thirty-three years old. Not as young as you used to be. Are you sure that you—?'

Lakshman stopped mid-sentence as Bharat glared at him. He immediately raised both his hands in surrender and grabbed the angvastram.

Bharat bent and gathered the mid-pleats of his dhoti. He tucked them into his waistband, both front and back. The ends were well above the knees now and tightened around his thighs.

Meanwhile, the barrel-man had descended onto the deck.

Bharat grabbed the climbing rope with both hands, swung his knees and ankles around it, grinned at Lakshman, and began climbing. Smooth, fluid motions. Just like he had learnt in the *gurukul*. Using the hands to haul himself up, and the ankles and knees for support and stabilisation. He used the rigging to rest briefly when necessary, for Lakshman was right; Bharat was getting on in age. But he made it above the windless sails in almost the same time as the much-younger barrel-man had.

Bharat dropped into the barrel of the lookout point. Or crow's nest, as it was called in naval lingo. He was a little short of breath.

Lakshman is right. I am getting old.

He took a moment to catch his breath and allow his heart to slow down. He was well above the treeline. Well above the stale odour of the perpetually moist sail canvas. Well above the dank, constant smell of human refuse and sweat of sailors who lived, slept, ate and abluted on the ship. Well above the tangy fragrance of soggy Lankan soil. Well above the dense tropical trees and vegetation.

Fresh clean open air.

Bharat breathed it in deeply. It calmed his heart and at the same time energised him.

He looked upriver. Into the distance.

Along the curve of the Mahaweli Ganga, beyond the Onguiaahra control-steps, he saw the trees being cut. Some logs were already floating in the river. Others were piling up at the control-steps that were above water. The clogging would spread.

Some lead Lankan ships had pulled back. Logical. To create space in the water for the logs of wood.

Where is Raavan's ship?

The chief admiral led from the front in Indian naval battles. It was a tradition. He wouldn't hide behind the cover of lead ships. That would be pusillanimous. More importantly, his pennant flapped proudly from the top of the mainmast. It was a challenge to his enemies: here I am. Come and get me.

That is how real men fought.

So ... where is Raavan's ship?

It had been spotted earlier. It had definitely been there. True to tradition and valour, right at the head of the Lankan command. Bharat had a sinking feeling in the pit of his stomach that his suspicion was right.

He looked upriver.

Legends hold that the term 'crow's nest' was coined by the Asura navigators. They were the first to travel deep into the oceans. Most seafarers preceding them always kept land in sight while sailing, their shipping lanes hugging the coast lines. This imposed longer routes and, hence, prolonged travel times. The Asura ships travelled straight, as 'the crow flies'. They were able to do this due to better navigation equipment that helped them venture far into the oceans. There were rumours about a peculiar element: that they always travelled with a cage filled with crows, secured to the lookout point on the mast. In poor visibility, a crow was released and the navigator plotted a course corresponding to the bird's flight path. As the crow would invariably head towards the nearest land mass.

The Asura Divine, it was believed, had imposed one strict diktat: that the crow's nest must *not* be placed at the absolute top-point of the mainmast. For the top of the ship was the seat of their God, who guided the sailors of the ship. And, it was believed, their God did not like crows. Not beside him.

Was it true, this legend? Only the Asura God knew.

But the tradition passed down with fidelity. The lookout point barrel was always fixed a little below the mainmast's top point. There was, therefore, a point at least seven to eight feet higher than the crow's nest.

A better view. If Bharat could climb it.

And he made the choice. He began to climb.

'Dada …' whispered a worried Lakshman from the deck, over one hundred and fifty feet below.

The climb was fraught with risk. The top of the mainmast wasn't designed for climbing. It was slippery wood. There were no safety nets below. A fall from that height to hard wood below would not lead to serious injury—it would mean death.

Bharat made quick work of it.

And looked deep upriver into the Lankan naval positions.

Lord Rudra, have mercy!

Chapter 27

It was late in the morning, the second hour of the second prahar. The Lankans were relentlessly cutting trees – more and more and more – and pushing them into the river, ahead of their positions. Between them and the Ayodhya navy. The cutting and chucking had begun the previous night, almost immediately after Raavan, Kumbhakarna and most of the Lankan navy had retreated. Indrajit had stayed behind with a skeletal convoy of twenty riverine ships. Arrayed against a massive naval armada of four hundred Ayodhyan ships.

The son of Raavan intended to conduct a rear-guard defensive action for as long as possible, to allow the rest of the Lankans to retreat behind the fort walls of Sigiriya, safe and sound. After which he would retreat as well, along with his remaining soldiers.

'King Ram – or whoever is in charge, if King Ram is on the western front – would have been informed by his lookouts at first light that the bulk of the Lankan navy was retreating,' said Indrajit. 'The Ayodhyans would know that they cannot get their seafaring ships past the control-steps and up the Amban Ganga River. But their seafaring ships would be loaded with multiple cutter boats. Hundreds of these boats could set sail, each loaded with soldiers. These smaller cutter boats could easily get past the control-steps, and then attack and overwhelm us with their sheer numbers. We have only twenty ships now. They could then give chase to our Lankan comrades who are on their way back to Sigiriya. These logs are good enough to stop their cutter boats.'

Both Indrajit and Mareech were on the top deck, in the bow section of the lead riverine ship of the Lankan convoy. They saw the logs of wood slowly clogging up the entire breadth of the river. Right ahead of them.

Mareech smiled. 'This is such a brilliant idea. Brilliant in its sheer simplicity. Sometimes, not offering battle is the best way to win that battle.'

Indrajit laughed softly. He raised his head. And looked far ahead. To the Onguiaahra control-steps. And whispered softly to the Ayodhyan ships he couldn't directly see, which were far downriver. To the Ayodhyan commander of that navy, whose identity he did not know, he said, 'Your move.'

—— JᴲF Jᴣᴅ ——

Arishtanemi quickly scanned the concise letter, turning increasingly aghast as he read each word. 'Goddammit!'

He handed the letter to Hanuman, who read it almost as rapidly as Arishtanemi. 'Lord Rudra, have mercy!'

Naarad grabbed the letter from Hanuman. He raced through the words. 'By the cursed balls of a diseased dog! This destroys our battle plans!'

Naarad finally handed the letter to Vashishtha. The great *rajguru* of Ayodhya read the contents. Even he was constrained to admit it, though only within the quiet confines of his mind: *this is a disaster.*

The Lankans were retreating from Onguiaahra. It could be safely assumed that they had somehow found out about the impending Ayodhyan invasion from the west. And would be secure behind the walls of Sigiriya by the time Ram and his army arrived. The Ayodhyan military council had suspected as much when the corpses of a few Ayodhyan hunter-gatherer scouts were found deep in the forests that morning. Along with the bodies of some Lankan soldiers. This letter confirmed their worst fears.

Vashishtha looked at Ram. The only one in the assemblage whose face was calm and eyes still. But Vashishtha knew Ram; the angrier or more troubled he was, the calmer he appeared. He would force the stillness upon himself. To allow himself to focus and solve the problem at hand.

A troubled mind cannot solve a problem. It only makes it worse.

'What now, Ram?' asked Vashishtha. 'Do we tell Shatrughan to speed up?'

'Don't trouble Shatrughan at this moment, Guruji,' said Ram. 'The mahouts are back in action. The elephants are at work. He will finish the bridge by evening. Telling him now will only make him nervous. He is brilliant, but is easily shaken.'

'So then?' asked Hanuman.

'We prepare to cross over this evening itself. Along with our special forces. As soon as the bridge is ready.'

The original plan had been to prepare for the march over the next few days, with a conservative marching speed. This way, the troops would be fresh when they approached Sigiriya.

They had intended to rush into Sigiriya when they reached within viewing distance of the Lankan scouts. And overwhelm the defenders with speed. But that plan would be abandoned now. Obviously.

'So, we march to Sigiriya tonight?' asked Arishtanemi.

'No,' answered Ram. 'I cannot predict King Raavan's actions. He may choose to be conservative and secure himself behind the walls of Sigiriya. Or he may aggressively send out a few brigades to attack us here, even as we cross over. He may decide to not give us the opportunity to get entrenched with a strong beachhead in Lanka.'

'What are your orders?' asked Hanuman.

'A few. Firstly, I'd like you and Lord Arishtanemi to cross over with as many soldiers as will fit on our boats. Begin expanding our stockade along the landing point at Ketheeswaram immediately. This will provide cover for Lankan attacks. Secondly, I want our elephants kept back. Hidden. The secret of the bridge may have been revealed. No reason to believe that they also know about the presence of our elephants. That can be an element of surprise at Sigiriya. Thirdly, we leave for Sigiriya tomorrow morning in a standard secure formation, with flank protection. It'll be slow, but will protect against any Lankan attacks. Fourthly, I will write to Bharat to cross over the Onguiaahra control-steps as quickly as he can, and meet us outside Sigiriya. But he should leave around five thousand men manning his seafaring ships at the Amban Ganga wharf, and also patrolling downriver. We want control of the river, all the way to Gokarna.'

'So, we lay siege on Sigiriya?' asked Naarad.

'We have no other choice,' answered Ram.

'Ram, you understand war tactics better than I do,' said Vashishtha, 'but a siege is a war of attrition. Raavan will be comfortable in his well-stocked city. We will be outside, deep in the hinterland of Lanka, with no major villages or cities close by. How will we supply our massive army?'

An army marches on its stomach, it is said. A competent general focuses on good battle tactics alone. A great general has his eye on supply lines as well.

'Hence the control of the river route, Guruji,' said Ram. 'There are no resource installations outside Sigiriya. But we can easily keep ourselves supplied from Gokarna, if we control the river route. Which Bharat can readily ensure with the men he leaves on his ships. It's a good thing that Bharat was kind and accommodating with the traders at Gokarna. They will continue to supply us with provisions. Raavan will be holed in, while we will have an open supply line. We will outlast him.'

'This will not be a short battle then,' Naarad said, sighing.

'What's the rush?' asked Arishtanemi, laughing. 'Do you have a party to attend?'

Everyone laughed.

— JF ⫣ЭD —

It had been a week since the Lankans had retreated from Onguiaahra.

Ram had marched his army into the large plateau that nestled the capital of the Lankans: Sigiriya. They were at the outskirts of a city that was protected by sturdy fort walls and moats all around.

Ram had set up camp and besieged all the four gates of the Sigiriya fort: the Bull Gate, Elephant Gate, Boar Gate and the Outer Lion Gate. They were marked by huge petroglyphs of the animals they were named after, chiselled into the rocky stone surfaces of the central archways. The Outer Lion Gate at the northern end was prefixed with 'Outer', as the road it protected stretched seven kilometres in, winding through the city into the heart of the Lankan capital. At the other end of the road was an archway called the Lion Gate.

The Lion Gate was the entrance to a much smaller path that was a steep climb up a massive monolith, called Lion's Rock. It rose, sharp, edgy and sheer, to a height of two hundred metres from the surrounding flatland and towered over the city, spreading over two square kilometres at its summit. In fact, the city was named after this rock, Sigiriya being a local-dialect adaptation of the Sanskrit *Sinhagiri* or *Lion's Hill*. At the top of the monolith was the enormous palace complex belonging to Raavan. It had multiple pools, verdant gardens, luxurious private chambers, courts, offices, and a parking bay for his Pushpak Vimaan. No gainsaying, it contained the best luxuries the world offered, for the richest man in the world.

Two fort walls encompassed the entire city in concentric circles, with no man's land between the outer and inner walls. Beyond the outer fort wall lay open land that was lined with multiple boulder-strewn hills. The flat tops of these towering boulders served as secure foundations for small structures that housed soldiers who provided protection from an unassailable height. These buildings lay abandoned as the Lankans had retreated rapidly into the fort, en masse. Ram had moved quickly and stationed his soldiers on these heights. They could now track any Lankan attempt to escape the siege, even in small numbers. And arrest it.

A siege is effective only when it is utterly absolute.

'Nobody can escape, right?' asked Ram.

'Not a chance,' said Bharat. 'Nobody will escape or enter Sigiriya.'

Vibhishan had surprised Bharat by speedily repairing the sluice gates of Onguiaahra. It had taken him three days. He had also opened up some of the sluice gates at the back of the reservoir, thus allowing the excess flood waters to flow into the Amban Ganga. Both the Onguiaahra control-steps and the Amban Ganga now had enough water to allow Bharat's seafaring ships to sail upriver. He had ordered thirty thousand soldiers to disembark as soon as the Ayodhya navy ported on the Amban Ganga wharf. Five thousand soldiers remained on the four hundred ships. These five thousand, under the command of a rear admiral, were tasked with protecting the Amban Ganga wharf and patrolling the river route, all the way to Gokarna at the mouth of the Mahaweli Ganga. They would secure the Ayodhyan supply lines. Meanwhile, Bharat, Lakshman and the thirty thousand men who had disembarked had marched on in standard secure formations. They had converged with Ram and his troops outside Sigiriya.

Bharat and Ram sat on top of a boulder rock and looked at the fort walls of Sigiriya in the distance.

'Good,' said Ram.

'The siege will be long and hard, Dada,' said Bharat. 'Sigiriya is too well-stocked. There is a massive lake within the city itself. And the twice-a-year monsoon in this island ensures that that wretched lake is perpetually full. They will never run out of water. They are well-stocked with food as well. These people grow their own crops on the open land between the inner and outer fort walls. They have almost everything that their citizens would need to handle a long siege. Even medicines. Except for that one …'

'Bharat,' said Ram, interrupting his younger brother, for he knew where he was going with this. 'We will give them the Malayaputra medicines.'

'Dada ...'

'We are *Suryavanshis*, brother. We are the descendants of the finest among men, the greatest among the greats. We have the blood of Ikshvaku and Raghu running in our veins. We will not bring dishonour to the name of our clan. We will fight hard. But we will fight fair. With *dharma*. Not *adharma*.'

Bharat sighed and kept quiet.

Everyone in the Ayodhyan army knew that Sigiriya was suffering from a flu pandemic. It had affected the Ayodhyan army too, but stocked as they were with enough Malayaputra medicines – the only known cure for the illness – they had remained unfazed. Many among the Ayodhyans believed that to deny the medicines to the Sigiriyans was a legitimate war tactic. It would force them to surrender.

But Ram had been clear from the beginning. Siege tactics – even slowly squeezing food supplies – were legitimate in war. The enemy could respond without hurting civilians. But a pandemic which spread and killed rapidly in the absence of medicine, and to which the elderly were particularly vulnerable, could not be used as a tool of war. That was *adharma*. Ram's decision was unambiguous and inviolable. The Ayodhyans would give the Malayaputra medicine to the Lankans.

'I believe many among our men think that I am naïve about this,' said Ram.

Bharat didn't respond.

'Bharat, I am thinking about the period after we win the war,' Ram continued. 'I am thinking about winning the peace. There may be two hundred thousand Lankan soldiers. But there are over eight hundred thousand citizens here. They could become unmanageable if they believe that we could have saved their elders but did not. If, on the other hand, they perceive us as honourable, they will be easier to handle when we win.'

Bharat did not say anything. At least not out loud. *But first we have to win.*

'You handled the businesspersons of Gokarna with even-handedness and grace. They were not combatants. Did it not stand us in good stead? Our supply lines are open and secure.'

Bharat nodded. He was constrained to agree. 'Yes, you are right.'

'Will you go tomorrow?' asked Ram.

Bharat looked at his brother. 'I will oppose you when I disagree with you, Dada. That is my right. But I will only do it in private. Once a decision has been made, I will always support it in public. That is my duty.'

Bharat left another thing unsaid. He was widely seen as Ram's second-in-command in the Ayodhyan army. And many common soldiers had misgivings about giving the medicine to the Lankans. Fate had handed them an easy path to victory. The enemy was on the ropes. Why let them escape? Bharat, and all other commanders in the army, had to unequivocally support the decision to ensure that everyone fell in line. And the most effective way to establish that was for Bharat to lead the delegation that handed the medicine to the Lankans. The following day.

Ram smiled, reached over, and held Bharat's hand. 'Brotherrrrr ...'

Bharat grinned and squeezed Ram's hand hard. 'Brotherrrrr ...'

They both sat silently. Looking at Sigiriya in the distance.

'She's in there ...' whispered Ram.

Bharat patted Ram on the back. 'She'll be back with you soon.'

Ram looked at Bharat. 'We have to get her out of there for Mother India. She has to be the Vishnu.'

Bharat smiled. Ram was almost trying to justify the war. Convincing himself that it wasn't just about the love of a husband. There was a larger purpose.

'That is also true. But there is nothing wrong with you wanting her back as a husband. Great leaders are also human beings.'

Ram laughed softly. 'It's difficult for me to pretend to keep secrets from you.'

'So don't even try.'

The brothers laughed.

'Wars are usually a messy business,' said Bharat. 'But here we have a war that will be good for Mother India and for you. So, it has my full endorsement!'

Ram smiled.

'But you *are* lucky that you have someone like her,' said Bharat. 'She truly is a remarkable woman.'

Ram smiled dreamily. '*Mritaih praapyah svargo yadiha kathayati etad anritam.*

Paraksho na svargo bahugunamihaiva phalati.'

Ram had recited a couplet from an ancient Sanskrit play: *They say that only the dead are allowed to reach heaven. But that is false. True heaven is not beyond us in this life. It is right here on earth. With the one you love.*

Bharat cast a surprised look at his elder brother, eyebrows raised. 'Wow … Quoting Bhasa himself?'

Bhasa was acknowledged across India as the greatest Sanskrit playwright ever. But Ram was not known to be interested in poetry. Or plays.

'Impressed?'

'Not by you. Impressed with love, actually. It can make even someone like you a lover of poetry!'

Ram laughed. 'She is the morning to my night. She is the destination to my travels. She is the rain to my cloud. Whatever be the questions of my life, she is the answer.'

Bharat laughed softly. 'You have really enjoyed the last fourteen years, haven't you?'

'This exile has been the best time in my life. Who would have imagined that? I only missed Shatrughan and you. If you both had also been there, my world would have been complete. My wife, my brothers. I don't need anything else.'

Bharat laughed. 'Who would have imagined this? I was the romantic one in the *gurukul*. You were the straight and sober one.'

'Hey, I am still straight and sober!' said Ram, laughing.

Bharat laughed too.

'But Bharat,' said Ram. 'It has been so long. Over sixteen years. You have to move on.'

Bharat took a deep breath. 'Dada … I can't … I can't forget her …'

'Bharat …'

'Let it be, Dada … Let it be. Let's talk about the war.'

'No, let's not.'

Bharat looked at his brother.

'I wish I could help you, Bharat. You have a good heart. You deserve to experience the indescribable beauty of loving a woman who loves you back.'

'Life is long, Dada. There are still many years left. You've travelled a long way. Maybe I will travel back too.'

Ram smiled and put his arm around Bharat's shoulders.

Bharat grinned and said, 'Of course, that is assuming we survive this war! Life is simultaneously long and short!'

Ram laughed. 'We will live. And we will win.'

Chapter 28

More than half way into the second prahar the next day, Bharat, Hanuman and Naarad marched in through the Elephant Gate of the outer wall of Sigiriya. They were accompanied by twenty soldiers.

Kumbhakarna, Indrajit and Akampana waited for them in the open ground between the inner and outer wall. Twenty Lankan soldiers stood behind them.

One Lankan soldier carried a white flag. Emblazoned on it was the image of Shantidevi, the Goddess of Peace. She was seated on a lotus, wearing a serene and compassionate expression on her face. One of her four hands held a *kamandalu*, while another held a water pot. The third held a *rudraksh mala*, and the fourth stretched gently in the *varada* posture. It was a mirror image of the flag carried by the Ayodhyans.

As the Ayodhyans approached, Kumbhakarna held out his hands and received a small water pot from a soldier. He stretched his right hand in the *varada* posture and poured water on it, allowing it to fall to the ground. He ensured that the Ayodhyans saw the ritual.

'*Om Shanti*,' said Kumbhakarna.

Let there be peace. For now.

Bharat repeated the exact ritual. With this ancient custom, both the parties committed themselves to a peaceful conversation by sacred oath.

The Goddess watched. No one in this gathering would draw their weapons. The karmic consequences on the soul would be dire.

Kumbhakarna spoke first, folding his hands together in a namaste. 'Prince Bharat, Lord Hanuman and I'm afraid I don't know who you are ...'

'No need to be afraid. I am Naarad,' said Naarad.

Kumbhakarna raised his eyebrows and laughed softly.

'Prince Kumbhakarna, Prince Indrajit and Lord Akampana,' said Bharat, folding his hands into a *namaste*. 'It's a pleasure indeed.'

Akampana was surprised that Bharat knew his name. *Perhaps that traitor Vibhishan has told them.*

'To what do we owe the honour of your presence?' asked Kumbhakarna.

The Ayodhyans had asked for the meeting.

Hanuman spoke up. 'Kumbhakarna, old friend, the crop fields outside the city have been burnt, the wells have been poisoned with the carcasses of dead animals, storehouses at the Amban Ganga wharf have been destroyed.'

Hanuman the Vayuputra had saved the life of the Lankan prince once. Since then, they had been friends.

'Scorched earth policy, Lord Hanuman,' said Kumbhakarna courteously, referring to the tradition of destroying all means of sustenance for the enemy, like food and water sources, in the area that they camped in. 'With utmost respect, you do not expect us to make it easy for you, do you?'

'In any case, you have secured a supply line through the river route all the way from Gokarna,' said Indrajit. 'A more expensive supply route, but one that works.'

'And a supply route that you won with the help of a traitor,' said Akampana, his aged body shaking with fury. 'That … that viper Vibhishan helped you take the Onguiaahra citadel through deceit.'

'Are you simply repeating old news?' asked Naarad, grinning at Akampana. 'Or offering your services as well?'

'Enough,' said Bharat firmly, raising his hand.

All fell silent.

'Prince Kumbhakarna,' said Bharat, 'many tactics are fair in battle. We don't hold a grudge against you. But one tactic is never fair; knowingly hurting innocent civilians. That is *adharma*.'

Kumbhakarna frowned. The Lankans had done nothing of the sort in this war. At least as far as he knew.

'We know that your city is suffering from a flu epidemic,' continued Bharat. 'We have the Malayaputras with us. And, hence, we have their medicine.'

Kumbhakarna was even more confused now.

'Bring it,' ordered Bharat.

The twenty Ayodhyan soldiers immediately marched up, carrying large sacks. Indrajit reached for his sword.

'Prince Indrajit,' said Bharat, a disapproving tone in his voice, 'we have taken the Shantidevi oath.'

Indrajit moved his hand away from his sword.

'Bring one sack here,' ordered Bharat.

An Ayodhyan soldier marched up to Bharat with a sack. He placed it on the ground, between Kumbhakarna and the

Ayodhyan prince. Bharat opened the sack, revealing a dark brown powder. He picked up a pinch with his thumb and index finger, and placed it on his tongue. And then looked at Kumbhakarna. Kumbhakarna nodded, acknowledging the safety of the powder.

'You know how to convert this powder into the medicine that can be distributed, right?' asked Bharat.

'Yes,' said Kumbhakarna. 'Our doctors can do it.'

'This should be enough for a week for all your citizens. We'll speak again after that.'

Kumbhakarna nodded at his soldiers. They briskly walked up and took custody of the sacks. Kumbhakarna looked at Bharat, a puzzled look on his face. 'Why? Why help our citizens?'

Bharat's chest swelled and his eyes narrowed with pride. 'Because our commander is a man called Ram.'

Kumbhakarna smiled slightly. *Queen Sita was right. Her husband is special.*

'I will see you on the battlefield, Prince Kumbhakarna,' said Bharat. 'We will not be so kind to your soldiers.'

Kumbhakarna bowed his head with respect. 'I look forward to it, noble prince.'

Bharat turned around. As did the others accompanying him. Hanuman looked at the fields of crop as they walked out. An idea had just struck him.

—— JF J5D ——

The Ayodhyan war council had gathered in Ram's tent. They sat around a round table, placed on which was a scale model of the city of Sigiriya: its fort walls, moats and the surrounding plateau. The talented model builders had worked fast, aided by the detailed information provided by Vibhishan.

Ram looked at the others. 'I am open to ideas.'

Vashishtha, Bharat, Hanuman and Lakshman sat to the left of Ram, while Shatrughan, Arishtanemi, Angad and Naarad sat to his right. All remained silent. None verbalised what appeared to be abundantly clear.

It had been a truism among soldiers for millennia: every fort had a weakness. Every single fort. Well, Sigiriya proved it a fallacy. It was without a chink. None could divine a way for Ayodhyan soldiers to slip into the fort. And the problem was compounded by the fact that the Ayodhyans did not have a numerical advantage over the Lankans. Numerical superiority can help an attacking force against an enemy safely ensconced behind impregnable walls. There was another stumbling block: the Sigiriyans were comfortably stocked with provisions that would last for months, if not a couple of years.

'There are no weaknesses,' Vibhishan said with a sigh. 'The fort walls of Sigiriya are impregnable. We should have defeated them on the river, or got here early enough to secure ourselves inside the fort. We lost both chances.'

Bharat was finding Vibhishan increasingly irritating. This defeatist attitude could cast a pall of gloom over the soldiers.

'Prince Vibhishan,' said Lakshman, 'have you not built any astutely-designed tunnels here as well? Like the ones you built at Onguiaahra?'

Always susceptible to flattery, Vibhishan smiled happily. 'I didn't get the opportunity, Prince Lakshman.'

'More's the pity.'

'I could have built something glorious. For most agree that I am the best engineer in the world.' Vibhishan pointedly glanced at Shatrughan as he said this.

Shatrughan raised his eyebrows in disdain and smiled. But did not rise to the bait. There were more important tasks at hand. A silly royal dolt's insecurities deserved a hard pass.

Ram repeated himself. 'Any ideas? I am open to anything. Even if unconventional.'

'I have an idea,' said Hanuman.

Everyone turned to the great Vayuputra.

'If the mountain will not come to Verulam, then the Verulam must go the mountain,' said Hanuman.

'What?' asked Arishtanemi.

'I heard this idiom during my travels in the West. Basically, if we can't enter the fort, then we must force the Lankan army to come out.'

'Hmm,' said Naarad. 'Good idea. I think they might well do it too, if we ask them nicely enough.'

'Naaradji,' said Angad, 'let's hear him out. Lord Hanuman is one of the finest battle strategists ever.'

'Lord Hanuman,' said Bharat, 'why will the Lankans leave the walls of Sigiriya?'

'Food,' answered Hanuman.

'But they have enough food for months,' protested Vibhishan. 'Their crops are ready for harvest.'

'Which crops?' asked Hanuman.

'What difference does that make?' asked Vibhishan. 'It will be edible grain, I assure you. My brother Raavan learnt this tactic from Mithila, actually; the idea of two concentric walls. He got the outer wall built to enclose the inner wall, a few years after the Battle of Mithila. And used the land in between the walls to grow crops. That stretch of land is at least one kilometre wide and runs a circumference of fifty kilometres all around the city. It is a massive area. Lush with food crops. The city cannot go hungry. It is impossible.'

'Woah ...' whispered Bharat. He had zoned out the harangue from Vibhishan and had just realised what Hanuman was thinking of. For he had seen the land. *Awesome.*

'What?' asked Ram.

'I think Lord Hanuman should have the honour of explaining it,' said Bharat. 'It's his terrific idea.'

Ram, and everyone else in the war council, turned to Hanuman.

'What is the most popular grain across the Indian subcontinent?' asked Hanuman. 'What do most of us eat?'

The answer was obvious. 'Rice.'

'Yes, most of us eat rice. Many eat wheat too. But we mostly eat rice.'

'And?' asked Ram.

'Which is the only region of India that doesn't eat rice? But only eats wheat.'

'Only the north-west,' answered Vashishtha. 'From Indraprastha westwards, including Punjab.'

'Especially the land of the Anu,' said Naarad. 'They only eat rotis made from wheat. No rice.'

Naarad glanced at Vashishtha with a slight grin as he said this. But Vashishtha did not look at Naarad.

'Again, so what?' asked Vibhishan. 'To answer your question, yes, Raavan and my family mostly eat rotis. We rarely eat rice. We are from the land close to Indraprastha. And the Sigiriyans, in their slavish devotion to my brother, also shifted to wheat en masse. We're perhaps the only city outside the north-western region of the Indian subcontinent that exclusively eats wheat. Almost no rice.'

'Hang on, hang on,' said Shatrughan. 'Are you telling me that wheat crop has been planted between the inner and outer walls of Sigiriya? And only wheat? And nothing else but wheat?'

Vibhishan turned to Shatrughan with an expression of utter scorn. 'Yes, obviously!'

'Woah …' said Shatrughan, holding his head. He looked at Hanuman and smiled. And nodded his head in agreement. 'Brilliant. Brilliant. This will certainly work.'

'What will work?' asked Naarad.

This war council had the finest warriors, but they were warriors from urban lands. They weren't farmers. Agricultural affairs did not strike them immediately. Unless they had experienced it, like Bharat. Or had read about it, like Shatrughan.

'Rice crop needs a lot of water,' said Hanuman. 'From its initial planting phase until its transplantation. The soil remains wet even during harvest. But wheat … wheat is different. It requires much less water. It requires much less care.' Hanuman leaned forward and whispered, 'And during harvest time, wheat is dry as bone.'

'Woah,' whispered Ram, understanding Hanuman's plan now.

'What?' asked Angad. 'I don't understand.'

'We burn their fields?' asked Lakshman.

'Precisely,' answered Hanuman. 'We don't need oil. We don't need paraffin. We don't need anything inflammable. The entire field of about-to-be-harvested wheat is highly combustible right now. All we need to do is to light a fire …'

Everyone leaned over the table and peered at the model of Sigiriya city, the fort walls and the surrounding land. And, the no man's land between the outer and inner fort walls that surrounded the entire city. It would be a massive wall of flames, over one kilometre thick and fifty kilometres long, all around the city.

'Not only will it drastically reduce their food supplies,' said Vashishtha, 'the sheer heat and smoke from the flames wafting in will severely hit the morale of their citizenry.'

'They used a scorched earth policy to reduce our food supplies,' said Bharat, looking at Ram. 'We are only paying back in kind. This is not *adharma*. This is legitimate siege tactics.'

Ram nodded.

The decision was obvious. There was no need for debate. Just one thing was left to be decided.

'When?' asked Hanuman.

'Is it absolutely ready to be harvested?' asked Ram.

'I am surprised they haven't harvested it yet,' said Hanuman. 'They will probably do it any day now.'

'Then we need to attack right away,' answered Ram briskly. 'Tonight.'

Chapter 29

'Halt,' whispered Hanuman, raising his right hand. It was balled into a fist.

The eleven Vayuputra men behind him immediately came to a halt.

They were behind the treeline and at least two kilometres of open space stretched ahead of them. At the other end loomed the outer fort wall of Sigiriya – a massive twenty-five metres in height. It was the night of *amavasya*, the *new moon*. The darkness hid the Ayodhyans deftly. The distinct nip in the air helped them as well. For the Lankan guards had lit bonfires atop the broad wall-walks on the fort ramparts to warm themselves. But the fires also gave away their locations to the intruders.

Stupid.

Hanuman turned his head and spoke softly. 'Vibhishan's information seems correct. Most Lankan soldiers are trained for naval warfare. They are not adept at siege tactics for land battles. King Raavan has posted his better soldiers on the inner wall.

And the less-trained ones on the outer wall. Logical. They don't mind a trespasser jumping over the outer wall. They want us to make a dash across the one-kilometre kill zone between the two walls. The expert soldiers atop the inner wall will then shoot us like fish in a barrel.'

The veteran Vayuputra soldiers nodded. That would be the Lankan strategy.

'We don't want to fight the better soldiers on the inner wall tonight,' said Hanuman. 'They are ruthless monsters. And they have a huge strategic advantage over us, high up on their walls. So, we don't want them to notice anything. We must take care of the relatively amateur soldiers on the outer wall. Kill them. Quietly. No noise.'

'Yes, Lord Hanuman,' was the quiet chorus.

'We stick to our plan,' said Hanuman. 'No changes.'

'Yes, Lord Hanuman.'

'Last weapons check.'

The soldiers silently checked their blades. Each had seven knives and one long sword. They loosened the leather-strap holds, freeing the weapons slightly. Each soldier then checked the leather armour strings on his buddy soldier. Each armour, coloured deep black, was fitted well. The dhotis were also black and tied in military style. Their faces, arms and legs were camouflaged with black polish. It made them meld into the black moonless night. Eight soldiers were carrying bows. They strung them and fixed the weapon on the band-hold across the torso. For ease of running. They carefully checked the fletching and the resin-cloth-wrap on the head of each arrow. This was their most crucial weapon. Then, they slipped the arrows back within the separate niches in the quiver. Long black climbing ropes were rolled up, clipped together, and slung over their shoulders.

Two groups of two soldiers each, who did not carry bows, checked two sets of slim wooden logs. They were from the sheesham tree, one of the hardest Indian woods. They too were painted black. The two sets of logs, more than twenty-five metres long, had been innovatively designed and built rapidly by Shatrughan for this operation: a collapsible, easily portable ladder.

All this checking of equipment was done in less time than you took to read the two paragraphs above. These were trained Vayuputra soldiers. Among the finest in the world.

The soldiers turned to Hanuman. Ready. Waiting.

'Half of you, follow me. We move east for four hundred metres,' whispered Hanuman. 'The other half remains here. On the bird call signal, both teams start running towards the moat surrounding the wall. Slow-speed. Don't tire yourselves. Both teams must reach at the same time. You know what we have to do then.'

Ram had put the soldiers through rigorous marching drills as they waited for the monsoon to end. They had been trained to run at the same pace and stick to formation even when out of each other's line of sight. They had been trained to follow three levels of pace: slow, fast and charge-speed.

'Any questions?'

'None, Lord Hanuman.'

Hanuman stretched his arm forward. The soldiers stepped up and one by one, and placed their hands on top of Hanuman's.

'*Kalagni* Rudra.' Hanuman whispered the Vayuputra war cry.

Kalagni is the mythical end-of-time fire; the conflagration that marks the end of an age. And the beginning of a new one. The Vayuputras also believed it to be the fire of Lord Rudra and it signalled end-of-time for those who stood against the mighty Mahadev.

The fire was about to be lit.

'Kalagni Rudra,' repeated the soldiers.

Hanuman nodded, turned east and began to trot. Five soldiers followed in step. Two carried one logs-ladder between them. They moved on light feet. Easy smooth breathing.

Six soldiers stayed behind at the original location. The other ladder with them.

In a few minutes, Hanuman and his soldiers reached their destination. He looked up at the campfire atop the wall-walk on the fort ramparts. An imaginary straight line from the fire would bisect almost exactly halfway between the platoon of soldiers with Hanuman, and the other that was four hundred metres to the west.

Perfect.

The Lankan guards would be attacked from both sides.

Hanuman pursed his lips together and made a near-perfect bird call. Almost instantaneously, they heard an answering bird call.

Hanuman nodded at his men. 'Now.'

The six began running towards the outer fort wall of Sigiriya. At the standard slow-speed. Completely out in the open now. But almost completely invisible in the dark.

In just short of ten minutes, they crossed the two-kilometre distance and drew near the moat that surrounded the outer fort wall. A relatively leisurely pace, to conserve energy. For they would need it now.

The moat was around ten metres wide.

Hanuman looked up. The campfire burned some two hundred metres to the west, on top of the wall. The light was starkly visible in the dark night.

He sniffed softly. No talking from now. Too risky in the silent, dark night, so close to the wall.

He conveyed his instructions in coded bird calls. *Ladder.*

Three soldiers placed the wooden logs on the ground. Then slowly extended them over the entire moat. Keeping it steady. Noiseless.

The ladder had had to be twenty-five metres long. They would use it to scale the twenty-five-metre-high fort wall later. The moat was only ten-metres-wide. The ladder's length was more than enough for the moat.

For the moment, though, the wooden logs had not been prised open into a ladder. They were folded together. Compressed and strong.

The logs soon found purchase on the strip of flat land on the inner side of the moat, close to the fort wall. Then, the biggest soldier in the half-platoon, Obuli, put his entire weight on the end of the logs, anchoring them to the ground. Thereafter, Deepankar, the lightest soldier, got down on all fours and began crawling across the logs.

This was the riskiest part of the operation.

Though not as wide as most, the moat was deep. At some points, the width had been reduced, as the boundary of the outer wall had been extended to increase the land under cultivation within the city walls. The moat was usually populated with crocodiles and alligators – aggressive amphibious creatures with a powerful bite strength. You wouldn't want anyone's body trapped between their jaws. Fortunately for the Vayuputras, many of the animals had been infected by the plague virus and succumbed to it.

But Deepankar wasn't worried about slipping and becoming food for the few surviving crocodiles. Dying was an ever-present risk for the special forces. He was more worried about the noise of the splash if he fell into the water. It would alert the Lankans, thus compromising the entire mission.

He needn't have worried. He was across in quick time.

Deepankar sat on the logs, anchoring them to the ground on the inner side of the moat. And then he whistled a bird call.

The four remaining soldiers, including Hanuman, crossed over to the other side. Once there, Hanuman whistled. Oboli immediately stepped off the logs and began pushing the ladder up. The five on the other side leveraged it from the other end. Soon the logs were leaning against the fort wall, the top end extending beyond the embrasures of the wall ramparts; in fact, reaching the merlons. Hanuman sniffed twice. Two soldiers held one log, while the mighty Naga Vayuputra and two soldiers held the other. They prised the logs apart; the leather treads stretched in between. The ladder had opened. The treads were fabricated from chemically-treated and extremely strong leather, supported by a folding cross metal strut that opened out. It made the ladder lighter to carry, and surprisingly sturdier than those that were traditionally designed.

Good soldiers win wars. But so do good engineers.

Deepankar held the bottom of the ladder steady, ensuring that the base didn't slip back.

Hanuman began to climb and three soldiers from his half-platoon followed. Deepankar remained below.

Hanuman reached the top, climbed through the embrasure and dropped lightly onto the rampart wall-walk. The three others followed, landing silently. Hanuman blew out air from his nose. A soft hiss; a command. The soldiers unclipped the black ropes from their shoulders, slipped the pre-tied large loop across the merlon, checked the slack on the knot to ensure that the rope didn't slip, and then flung the other end of the rope down on the outer side of the wall.

This was a precaution. For a quick getaway if they were discovered by the enemy. They would rappel down the rope instead of using the ladder. Such measures saved lives in emergencies. A special forces soldier was expensive to train. No army would want to lose these lives cheaply.

Deepankar had begun to drop the ladder back over the moat, slowly, for Obuli to catch it on the other side. It would be ready and available, when Hanuman and his soldiers returned.

Hanuman softly blew out some more air from his nose. The four soldiers of Ram's army drew their short knives and moved stealthily westwards. Still hidden by the dark night, they moved towards the small bonfire. Towards the Lankans.

Rapidly drawing close, they saw the enemy clearly in the light of the flames. Six Lankans sat around the fire, lulled by the comforting warmth; three on the eastern side from where Hanuman and his soldiers approached, and three on the western side from where the other Ayodhyan half-platoon were, no doubt, drawing near. Hanuman could hear them gossiping; something about Lankan businessmen that were profiteering from the siege; and some about the illicit relations of a few noble women. One Lankan sighed and asked in a murmur why ordinary soldiers like them should die to protect these corrupt, selfish, supercilious elites.

This was a common complaint among frontline soldiers of all armies. Who were they dying for? Who were they killing for? Was it worth it? Ordinary citizens sometimes value soldiers, who protect them. But warriors make the ultimate sacrifice even for unworthy countrymen, who do not appreciate their valour. Why? Because that is what heroes do.

Hidden by the darkness, Hanuman whistled a perfect Asian koel bird call.

A Lankan soldier immediately turned his head. He stared into the darkness. Hanuman was a few metres away, but the Lankan saw nothing.

'Stop trying to birdwatch in the dark, Jormuyu,' said one of the Lankans. 'Wait until the first light of day.'

Another Lankan laughed. 'Jormuyu is in the wrong line of work! He should have been an ornithologist!'

Jormuyu continued to stare into the darkness. Hanuman almost felt as if the Lankan had seen him. Jormuyu suddenly smiled wistfully, convinced he had seen the Asian koel bird, and then turned away.

A veteran's instinct would have warned him. These guys are truly amateurs.

There was the sound of another Asian koel. This time from the westward side.

It was time.

Hanuman rushed forward, covering the distance in little over a second. His soldiers drew in from both sides.

Sorry, Jormuyu.

Before Jormuyu could react to the sudden appearance of the hulking warrior, Hanuman covered his mouth and slashed his neck with his long knife. Right across. Deep. The knife sliced extensively through the sternomastoid muscles, the jugular vein, and also a part of the deeply embedded carotid arteries, both on the left and right side of the Lankan's neck. Blood squirted out like a child's holi water jet. Hanuman immediately stepped back and melded back into the shadows.

Hanuman's soldiers had done the same to their marked men.

It was all over under four seconds. Vayuputras had emerged from the shadows noiselessly, covered six Lankan mouths, sliced their throats and retreated into the shadows.

The Lankans now lay prone on the wall-walkway. Bleeding to death. Out of the line of sight of Lankans on the inner wall, as their bodies were hidden by the three-foot-high stone parapet.

Jormuyu was dead in ten seconds. Hanuman's cut had been mercifully deep. Some of the other Lankans suffered silently for a while longer. But they were all dead in two minutes. And no Lankan on the inner or outer wall was any the wiser.

Travel safely to the other side of the sacred Vaitarni, gentle Jormuyu. I am sorry I had to do what I had to do.

Having ascertained that the Lankans were dead, Hanuman made a bird call again. He continued to desist from voicing commands.

An Ayodhyan soldier from the westward side quietly moved forward. He was careful not to slip on the floor, slick with fresh Lankan blood. He had drawn his bow and the arrow was nocked. He held the resin-cloth-wrapped arrowhead to the Lankan bonfire. Instantly, the resin was aflame. The Ayodhyan leaned over the parapet and shot the arrow straight down into the gold-coloured wheat fields.

A mistake.

The arrow whizzed down and buried itself into the earth, between the wheat stalks. The flame snuffed out instantly.

The soldier stepped back into the shadows with a chagrined expression on his face. He looked in the direction of his commander.

Hanuman made two short bird calls.

The Vayuputras came to a dead stop.

Hanuman unclipped his bow, held it aloft, carefully pulled out an arrow from the quiver and nocked it on the string.

He stepped forward. As he reached the bonfire, he quickly looked east and west. Towards his soldiers. The message was clear: *Watch and learn. For this is how it's done.*

Hanuman held the arrowhead over the fire. It sprang to life. Aflame. He stepped close to the parapet, and bent forward from his hip. He held the bow horizontally and arched his torso over it. His head bent sideways, his right eye aligned to the line of the arrow. He flexed his mighty shoulders and upper back, and pulled the string, almost to his ear. As he released the arrow, he flicked the fletching. The arrow sailed. Almost horizontally, gliding at a gentle angle towards the wheat fields. Very different from the sharp-angled quick descent of the previous arrow.

The arrow kissed the top of some wheat stalks. And then bounced over successive stalks. Like a flat pebble chucked horizontally over a still pond. The arrow travelled over a long distance, setting fire to several wheat stalks over a fifty-metre distance. It bounced four times before it fell to the ground. Almost all the wheat stalks in its path were ablaze. The fire rapidly spread to the neighbouring stalks.

Hanuman looked at his soldiers and stepped back.

It had seemed beguilingly simple, his shot. A wheat stalk is driest at the top, slowly becoming humid down the kernel. The simple lesson: if you want to burn wheat, start at the top.

Hanuman's soldiers stepped up. One by one. Six arrows were fired. And almost the entire wheat field in the area was soon alight. The fire travelled with the wind. It bounced from stalk to stalk. The flames began to stretch frighteningly high.

It all happened under three minutes.

They heard the panicked cries of the Lankans from the outer wall now, and even some parts of the better-staffed inner wall.

'FIRE!'

'FIRE!'

'GET WATER!'

'FIRE!'

Loud noises everywhere. No need for silent signals now.

'Enough!' ordered Hanuman. 'Retreat!'

The Vayuputra soldiers took flight. Half to the east, half to the west. Back to the climbing point. They grabbed the ropes and rappelled down the outer wall rapidly, and then crossed over the moat to the other side. They abandoned the ladders and sprinted back at charge-speed. Racing back to the safety of the treeline.

Hanuman's platoon was one of six that tore back at almost the same time. The other five were led by Ram, Bharat, Lakshman, Arishtanemi and Angad.

Fifty kilometres of crop land, one-kilometre wide, encircled Sigiriya in a giant arc. It was covered with precious about-to-be-harvested wheat crop. All of it was aflame.

— ⨌ ⫣ —

'My husband is brilliant, no doubt about it,' said Sita, her eyes shining with pride. 'But I suspect the genius in this particular project was Shatrughan's.'

Raavan and Kumbhakarna were visiting Sita in Ashok Vatika. They had walked through a protected path between two extensions of the fort walls. The path was lined by towers for easy defence and led from Sigiriya to the citadel of Ashok Vatika, over eight kilometres away. It was the first night of relative calm. The siege seemed to have settled into a stalemate, Raavan believed. This would last for a few weeks. Having not met Sita in many days, he had decided to dine with her and his brother. Of course, Sita and the brothers had made their goodbyes before the Lankans had marched to Onguiaahra a few weeks earlier, but that battle had been a feint, and the Lankans had rushed back to Sigiriya when they found out about the Ayodhyans marching in from the west.

'All the same,' said Raavan, respectfully, 'the very idea of building a bridge across the sea … Brilliant. I expected Ram to be courageous. I expected him to be a man of integrity; he provided medicine for our citizens. But I did not expect this innovative brilliance … whether it was his own or that of his brother, does not matter. This war will be magnificent.'

'Why do men enjoy battle so much?'

'And you don't?'

'No, I don't.'

'Don't lie so much that it's a sin to even listen to you!' joked Raavan. 'Of course, you enjoy war. That is why you fight so well.'

'I may fight well, but I don't enjoy it. I'd much rather avoid war if I—'

Sita stopped speaking as she noticed a flock of birds flying above them. As if they were fleeing. *Weird …*

But Raavan was continuing the conversation. 'Some men do enjoy it. That is a fact. And, like I told you once, many such men are in my army! But without war we human beings would not have become civilised, I think. It forces societies to organise and learn to work together. An external enemy can make fractious men in a society find common ground. It leads to the birth of new technology, whose products help ordinary non-warriors as well. War has a purpose. War is at the heart of civilisation.'

'I don't know if—'

Sita stopped speaking again. A much larger flock of birds were now flying past above their heads. It seemed as if they were escaping from Sigiriya.

'What's going on?' asked Kumbhakarna, looking up. 'This is bizarre …'

'There's some kind of glow from the direction of Sigiriya,' said Sita.

Raavan and Kumbhakarna stood up and looked into the distance. And detected a faint, flickering glare.

Raavan turned to a lady guard standing near them. 'Go up to the watch tower and report.'

The guard sprinted towards the watch tower built atop a cluster of tall eucalyptus trees. The trees were over three hundred feet tall, but the guard raced up the wooden winding staircase built around the tree, and reached the platform built at the top in less than a minute. She looked in the direction of Sigiriya. And was locked into paralysis.

'What the hell is going on?' shouted Raavan from below, impatient.

The voice of her liege pulled the guard out of her shocked state. She unclipped the speaking-trumpet fixed to the parapet of the platform, and spoke into it, loudly. 'Your Highness, please come up and see this!'

Raavan began climbing the stairs. Kumbhakarna and Sita followed. Raavan was getting on in age, so it took them two minutes to reach the top. On reaching, their eyes turned towards Sigiriya.

'What the hell?!' roared Raavan, aghast.

It looked like Sigiriya, the capital city of Lanka, was on fire.

Sita's mouth was open in awe. *Woah ... How did you pull this off, Ram?*

Chapter 30

'Thank you,' said Ram, bringing his hands together into a namaste and bowing his head. It had been two days since the burning of the wheat crops of Sigiriya.

Gajaraj, the chief of the village, also folded his hands together into a respectful namaste, and bowed his head much lower. He was meeting Ram for the first time. 'Please do not thank me, great king. It is my village's honour to help you.'

Gajaraj's village – twenty-five kilometres north of Sigiriya – was almost completely populated by Naga refugees from the Sapt Sindhu. The Ayodhya war camp had been erected midway between the Lankan capital and Gajaraj's village. Being Nagas, the villagers faced universal discrimination and persecution. Ordinary people had a superstitious dread of them. Raavan and Kumbhakarna were also Nagas, but they were too powerful to face the same prejudice.

Around twenty-five years ago, Kumbhakarna had convinced his brother to allow Naga refugees to live close to Sigiriya. They had been settled in this village. Over the years, as the Lankan royals became busy with their dreams and ambitions, the village administration passed into the hands of local Sigiriyan bureaucracy. And this bureaucracy was as bigoted as the ordinary people. Administration soon turned into exploitation. The Nagas in Gajaraj's village did not complain. They were grateful for a village of their own, close to a rich city like Sigiriya, which offered many opportunities for livelihood. They built their lives. Slowly. They offered impeccable elephant management skills to the citizens of Sigiriya. Elephants were commonly used in Lanka for transportation, construction projects and even for temple rituals. They made reasonable money from renting the elephants they reared. But their entire model of living, built over twenty-five years, had been destroyed in a few hours. Lankan soldiers had burnt their crops, poisoned their wells and demolished their homes.

Scorched earth policy.

To prevent the Ayodhyans from procuring local supplies.

Those who depended on the earth that had been scorched, were collateral damage.

'Please accept my apologies for disturbing you so late at night,' said Ram politely.

'Of course not, Your Highness,' said Gajaraj. 'I understand that you could not have risked exposure by coming here during the day. Lankan spies may recognise you.'

Ram nodded.

'Would you like to see them, Lord Ram?' asked Gajaraj.

'Yes, I would. If it's not too much trouble.'

Gajaraj smiled. 'No trouble at all, Your Highness. It is your right.'

Gajaraj led the way. Ram was accompanied by Bharat, Hanuman, Arishtanemi and Angad. A small bodyguard platoon of ten soldiers followed them discreetly.

'We saw the flames, Your Highness,' said Gajaraj. 'Burning the crops – it was a brilliant war tactic.'

Ram gestured towards Hanuman as he walked. 'All credit is due to Lord Hanuman. He came up with the idea. And planned the entire operation.'

Ram was ever-willing to share glory. He was not a jealous leader who cornered all credit for himself. It's amazing how much can be achieved when one gives people the recognition they deserve.

Hanuman folded his hands together in a namaste and smiled.

Gajaraj continued. 'The granaries will run out of stock in a few weeks. They were counting on the new harvest from within their walls. The price of essentials has shot up in the city. I have heard that the morale of the citizens has collapsed. King Raavan's army cannot remain behind the walls of Sigiriya much longer. They will have to step out and battle you in the open. Which is what you wanted, I guess, Lord Ram. Their numerical superiority will count for less when they are not perched high up on the impregnable fort walls of Sigiriya.'

Ram smiled warmly and kept pace with Gajaraj.

They soon reached their destination.

Ram walked up and smoothly jumped over the low fence. He stepped up confidently to the mighty beast and touched its trunk.

Gajaraj took a deep nervous breath, but didn't say anything. War elephants can only be handled by their mahouts. They are extremely volatile and hostile with anyone other than their mahouts. Usually.

War elephants are usually male. And there are multiple reasons for this. Testosterone gives male elephants robust bone density, substantial muscle mass and strength and, most importantly, fierce aggression. Critical for war. Male elephants have long tusks as well, whose tips can be sharpened and used like spears by adept mahouts in battle. Favourable for war. Also, crucially, male elephants are generally used to being abandoned. In popular imagination, elephant herds are believed to be kind, nurturing and protective of each other. They are. But only the female elephants, led by the matriarch, are a part of this idyllic set-up; the chief of an elephant herd, incidentally, is always female. Male elephants are ordinarily expelled from the herd when they reach adolescence. Thereafter, they either fend for themselves or join nomadic and unstable male herds. The male elephants are allowed into the much larger, more stable female herd only during mating season, and after their job is done, they are kicked out again. Most of the time.

The male of the species, over generations, has made peace with this unfairness and loneliness. But the survival instinct has simultaneously increased their aggression. When in captivity, these abandoned male elephants bond deeply with their human mahouts, who are the only ones who treat them like family. Like good soldiers, they do whatever the mahout orders them to do. Without a second thought.

Very useful for war.

Abandoned and lonely male elephants, just like abandoned and lonely men, can make for efficient killers.

Giriraj was surprised, therefore, when the elephant bobbed its head warmly when it sniffed Ram. It extended its trunk out and embraced the king of Ayodhya. Ram patted the elephant's trunk affectionately.

The biggest challenge for Ram had been to hide his three hundred war elephants till the battle began. They were the main element of surprise in his strategy. Effective use of the elephants at the beginning of the battle could dramatically rebalance the numerical superiority of the Lankan infantry.

But how does one hide three hundred massive elephants from Lankan spies, whose eyes were pinned on the Ayodhyan war camp? In plain sight, it would seem.

Gajaraj's village was forced to abandon their elephants when their lands were ravaged by the Lankan army. Running out of food and water to feed themselves, it was impossible now to look after their elephants. They had driven the animals into the jungles farther north, where they hoped the beasts would be able to fend for themselves. The village sanctuary was empty. And Ram's soldiers had managed to convince Gajaraj to accommodate the Ayodhyan army's elephants there. In return for money and, more critically, supplies of food and water, which the Ayodhyans were getting from Gokarna. A Lankan spy would believe the pachyderms in the village were the in-house beasts.

Ram's main strategic battle weapon – his elephants – were hidden in plain sight. And no Lankan was any the wiser.

'He likes you, my lord,' murmured Gajaraj.

Ram patted the elephant's trunk once more and smiled at Gajaraj.

'I need to explain why I did what I did,' said Gajaraj.

Ram looked at Gajaraj with surprise. He stepped out of the low fencing. Hanuman, Arishtanemi and Angad were checking on the other elephants. Only Bharat remained.

'You don't need to explain anything, my friend,' said Ram.

'I do,' said Gajaraj. 'For I am sure you must be thinking that if I betrayed Lanka, would I not betray you as well?'

'If I thought that, then I wouldn't be keeping my elephants with you.'

'Even so… Please allow me to explain.'

'Go ahead, noble Gajaraj,' said Ram. He saw that this was important to the village chieftain.

'I will always be grateful to King Raavan, and even more to Prince Kumbhakarna, for offering us refuge twenty-five years ago. We built our lives here, away from the non-Nagas, who dislike us. Both of them were good to us, but their bureaucrats, their soldiers ... They are monsters. We tolerated it for so long, only out of loyalty to King Raavan and Prince Kumbhakarna. But when they attacked us ten days back ... They ... they could have ordered us to burn our crops and poison our wells and leave. We would have done it. They know us now. But they wanted to do it themselves. They beat us, killed some of us, assaulted some of our women ...'

Tears sprang in Gajaraj's eyes. Ram drew near and placed his hand on the village chief's shoulder.

'But it isn't desire for vengeance that is making us help you,' continued Gajaraj. 'Your soldiers ... They were different ... They were polite. Calm. They requested us ... didn't order us. They gave us food and water before we had agreed to help them. Your soldiers are as strong, well-armed and powerful as the Lankan soldiers. But they behaved with grace. They conducted themselves with *dharma* ...'

Ram kept silent. Allowing Gajaraj to speak.

'A soldier's conduct is a reflection of the general, King Ram. All soldiers are aggressive. It's the nature of their job. They have a monstrously violent side to them. A leader like King Raavan gives free reign to this side, letting them rape, loot, plunder, till it's almost second nature to them. They behave this way even if a decent option is available. On the other hand, a leader like you, Lord Ram, teaches these soldiers to harness their monstrous side for the greater good, to protect the weak, to use their strength in the service of *dharma*. No soldier of yours would kill non-combatant women or children, because they know, I have heard, that you will punish them severely for that.'

Ram remained quiet.

'You are a better leader, King Ram. You will be good for Mother India. That is why we are helping you.' Gajaraj gestured towards the elephants. 'These wild elephants were lucky to find their mahouts, who, with their kindness and firmness, gave them purpose. You are the mahout of men, King Ram. You are our mahout.'

Gajaraj bent to touch Ram's feet, but Ram stopped him and pulled him into a bear hug.

'I am no mahout of men,' said Ram. 'I am just a devotee of Mother India. As are you. We will fight for our mother. And restore her glory together.'

—JF J5D—

'Yes, I agree with you,' said Ram.

Ram and Bharat had just returned from Gajaraj's village. They were sitting around a small bonfire, outside the royal tent. It was dinner time.

'Hmm …' said Bharat. 'I managed to change your mind, right, Dada?'

'No.' Ram laughed. 'You didn't change my mind. You just read my mind.'

Bharat laughed. He scooped some vegetables with a piece of roti and placed it in his mouth. Bharat had just told Ram that Shatrughan should not be put to active service in the army. Their youngest brother was brilliant and had already contributed immensely to the war effort by building the bridge across the sea. But unlike the other three siblings, Shatrughan was not warlike. It served little purpose to risk his life by making him fight in the battle. Ram had agreed with Bharat's suggestion instantly.

Lakshman and Shatrughan walked in. They had checked on the horses and gone over the preparations for the cavalry. It was in order. They could not know when the Lankans would step out of the city and offer battle. They had to be battle-ready at all times.

'Come, brothers,' said Ram. 'Eat.'

'Yes, Dada,' was the chorus from the twins.

Lakshman and Shatrughan washed their hands and sat around the bonfire. Attendants brought in their food as well, on banana-leaf plates.

'Horses okay, Lakshman?' asked Bharat.

'Yes, Dada,' said Lakshman, even as he began eating. 'No influenza, no diseases. But they are getting skittish. They haven't been taken for a run for a week.'

'The Lankans will give them some cause for action soon, we hope,' said Ram. Then he turned to Shatrughan. 'Shatrughan ...'

'Yes, Dada?' asked Shatrughan, looking up from his plate.

'Listen, Bharat and I were just talking ... and we think ... about you and the battle ...'

'I know,' said Shatrughan. 'Lakshman was thinking the same thing. He spoke to me while we were inspecting the horses. I agree. It makes sense. I am certainly no warrior.'

Ram smiled, relieved that he would not need to have what he thought would be a difficult conversation. 'I had forgotten how practical you were, Shatrughan. You don't let ego get in your way.'

'Why should there be any ego, Dada? I know my strengths. I also know my weaknesses. Every person should know these things. With honesty and without any self-delusions. For that is the only way to be the best you can be.'

'True,' said Ram. 'But while most find it easy to celebrate their strengths, they find it difficult to even acknowledge their weaknesses. Usually, they see only their strengths and in others, only their weaknesses. *I am perfect, everyone else is imperfect!*'

'Freedom comes from understanding that there is no perfection. Nothing in this universe can ever be perfect. Nothing can have all qualities. Gold has no fragrance; sugarcane has no fruit; and sandalwood has no flowers. But that doesn't take away their beauty, does it?'

'Absolutely,' said Bharat.

'And your intellectual strengths are glorious, Shatrughan,' said Lakshman. 'For as long as the story of this war will be told, no one will forget your building a bridge across the sea. And that we actually marched war elephants into Lanka!'

Shatrughan smiled and continued eating.

'Also,' said Bharat, 'only the gods know who among the three of us will survive the war. If we all die, then Shatrughan will carry forward our line.'

'Dada,' said Shatrughan. 'Don't say such things before a battle. It invites bad fate.'

'This is war, Shatrughan. People will die.'

'Yes, but—'

'Anyway, forget all this,' said Lakshman, putting his plate down. He was done with his food. As were his brothers.

Attendants ran up with a water pitcher and a large receptacle. They poured water for each of the royal brothers as they washed their hands in the bowl. Ram, Bharat and Shatrughan took the small towels offered and wiped their hands. Lakshman, however, wiped his hands on his dhoti.

'Lakshmannnn …' said Ram disapprovingly.

'Dadaaa …' said Lakshman jocularly.

The four brothers laughed. And then stood up and moved close, into a circle. Next to the bonfire. As they always did before going to their respective tents. They locked their arms on each other's shoulders and came into a huddle.

Brothers in arms.

Together.

Stronger together.

Nothing could break them. Not the poison of life. Not even the sweet release of death.

'Aaah … others may see four, but I see one.'

The brothers turned to see Naarad standing a short distance away.

'We *are* one,' said Lakshman.

Naarad walked in with a mischievous smile hovering on his face. 'It is interesting how one hears what one wants to hear, regardless of the words spoken.'

'What?!' asked Ram, confused.

'You brothers assumed my meaning; that the four brothers are together, as one. For all you know, maybe I meant that three of you will not survive the war. Only one will. Hence, I see only one.'

'Naaradji,' said Shatrughan, 'your joke is not really appropriate.'

'Appropriate jokes are often not funny.'

'Your joke wasn't funny either,' said Shatrughan.

Naarad laughed. 'Ouch … that was a good one.'

'Naaradji,' said Ram politely, 'is there anything particular you wanted to discuss? Because we were all going to retire to our tents.'

'I have some news.'

'What is it?' asked Bharat.

'I've just received the latest spy report. The Lankans are mobilising. Raavan is performing an astra *puja* in his private temple as well. We should expect them to march out of their fort tomorrow.'

The four brothers glanced at each other, and then back at Naarad.

'It's time.'

Chapter 31

The Outer Lion Gate, at the northern end of the fort, had been flung open two hours after the break of dawn. The massive Lankan army had been marching out for an hour now – over two hundred thousand warriors, comprising the infantry, archers and cavalry. There was a smaller contingent of two hundred warriors in chariots. Powered by two horses, smooth and manoeuvrable on two wheels, large enough to accommodate two people and a mini horde of weapons, with a charioteer to drive it, a chariot afforded a warrior tremendous ability to command the battlefield. Of course, provided the battlefield was suitable for chariots. The smooth and flat field immediately outside Sigiriya was very suitable.

'We will probably take another hour to march out,' said Kumbhakarna. 'And then, one more hour to assemble. We will be ready for battle by the end of the third hour of the second prahar.'

Raavan and Kumbhakarna were mounted on two separate chariots, on the raised plinth at the side of the Outer Lion gate. They were clearly visible to the soldiers marching out. They had no charioteer with them as yet and held the reins of the horses themselves. This was so they could talk freely. Each regiment saluted the Lankan royals as they passed. The two brothers returned the salute.

'Good,' said Raavan, taking a deep breath.

'You seem excited, Dada.'

Raavan turned to Kumbhakarna and smiled. 'Yes. This will be a glorious day.'

Kumbhakarna laughed. 'The gods must be dumbfounded to see someone so eager to die.'

'We are all going to die in any case, Kumbha. What makes life worth living is figuring out what is worth dying for. And then dying for it. Mark my words. This war will be remembered forever. You and I will be remembered forever.'

Another regiment marched past, with perfect military discipline. All the soldiers turned their heads to the right, towards their liege. And roared the Lankan war cry. *'Bhaarat Bhartri Lanka!'*

Lanka, Owner of India!

Raavan and Kumbhakarna raised their right hands high, and repeated the war cry. *'Bhaarat Bhartri Lanka!'*

This had been going on for an hour. But Raavan and Kumbhakarna's enthusiasm had not wavered even once. The mounted soldiers positioned behind Raavan – just out of earshot – had keenly noticed the commitment of their leaders. It inspired them. Soldiers must see their leaders raring to battle. If you have no exposure to military life, you might imagine that soldiers die for abstract ideas like their country, or religion, or simply because it is their job. There is a measure of truth in that, no doubt. But it is not the whole truth. The primary reason why a soldier marches to his death is his faith in his leader. A leader who knows that, ensures that he behaves appropriately.'

Raavan turned to Kumbhakarna. 'So, what surprises are you expecting from Ram today?'

'I don't know,' said Kumbhakarna. 'Our spies have reported nothing out of the ordinary. He has the same divisions in his army as us, though he has around forty thousand lesser infantry. And he has far fewer chariots as well. At least on paper, we are stronger. I suspect we will see some unexpected innovations in the tactics.'

Raavan nodded.

Indrajit and Mareech rode up to the brothers.

'Father,' said Indrajit.

Raavan smiled broadly and his chest puffed up in pride. He looked at his son, the saviour of the Lankan army, who had pre-empted the would-be surprise enemy attack from the west. 'My son ...'

'The Ayodhyans are coming into formation on the open grounds outside. Parallel to our walls. So, when we come into formation opposing them, we will have the Sigiriya walls to our back.'

Raavan frowned. 'Our lines will remain strong. We cannot break.'

'Precisely,' said Indrajit. 'We had hoped to march out early in the day and make our formations, to counter the risk of the Ayodhyans coming into formation perpendicular to our walls. Otherwise, in opposing them, one of our flanks would get hemmed in. But they began getting into their formation earlier than anticipated. And have done exactly what we wanted them to do.'

Mareech made clear the implication. 'Both our flanks remain open. And, our army is much larger. We can outflank and surround them. What is Ram thinking? Why is he playing to our strengths?'

'What do you think he is planning?' asked Raavan.

'I don't know,' Kumbhakarna said. 'But I would expect him to have some trick up his sleeve. He has demonstrated his tactical inventiveness over and over again.' Kumbhakarna turned to Mareech. 'Uncle, you command the right flank. And I will command the left.'

The initial battle plan had put the Lankan royals in the centre. In the thick of battle. And, to direct the war efforts efficiently.

'Are you sure, uncle?' asked Indrajit. 'I could man the left flank. You can stay with father.'

'No,' said Kumbhakarna. 'Let me do it.'

The next regiment passed the Lankan royals and bellowed the Lankan war cry. '*Bhaarat Bhartri Lanka!*'

Raavan, Kumbhakarna, Mareech and Indrajit raised their right hands high and repeated, '*Bhaarat Bhartri Lanka!*'

—JF J5D—

Raavan's battle formation was in the traditional chaturanga arrangement and the divisions were organised separately. The infantry was in the centre, in tight and disciplined lines. The archers were in rows running along the entire front line. They would shoot the initial volleys and then move aside for the infantry charge. The cavalry was at the flanks, ably supported by the fearsome chariot corps. It was a logical formation for a numerically superior army against an opponent with not only fewer infantry soldiers, but a smaller cavalry and chariot corps as well.

They intended to keep the centre stable while building fearsome flanks, with which Raavan's army could surround Ram's forces and decimate them from both sides.

Astute and sensible.

Apparently.

Ram's army was arranged, on the other hand, in a manner that was anything but logical.

A traditional military general would have advised Ram to buttress both his flanks with his cavalry and chariots. And keep the centre strong with a tight infantry configuration. While his flanks would hold against the superior Lankan numbers, the compact central infantry could try to break through the Lankan middle.

That would be the only hope against superior Lankan numbers, especially the advantage of their cavalry and chariot corps.

Hold the flanks, and fight hard to break the centre.

Logical.

Apparently.

Ram's formation did not suggest this strategy at all.

It was a strange formation, and Raavan couldn't understand the rationale behind it.

For the Ayodhyan army had not been arranged by divisions. Instead, the formation was in an unprecedented joint command. Ram's army of one hundred and sixty thousand had been divided into eighty regiments. Each regiment comprised one thousand five hundred infantry soldiers arranged tightly in a phalanx; they had archers embedded within the ranks, and cavalry both in the front and sides. The few phalanxes at the lead had chariots in front. It was evident that each of these regiment commanders had the freedom to attack and defend independently. They had been trained to do so. Ram had, in effect, divided his army into eighty decentralised smaller armies, with a complete complement of divisions within, to mount an attack or even defend independently.

This decentralised formation in an era of set piece battles could be called brave, if one were being polite, and foolhardy, if one were being honest.

Small Ayodhyan cavalries had been placed at the far left and right flanks. But they were clearly not enough to defend against the massive Lankan divisions on the sides.

Quick math would also have revealed that over thirty thousand of Ram's troops had not been arranged on the battlefield. Perhaps they were being held in reserve. At their rear. Within the jungles.

By holding so many soldiers in reserve, Ram had worsened his numerical disadvantage in the battle.

Bizarre.

'What is he doing?' asked Indrajit. 'It is almost as if he is inviting an attack on his flanks.'

Raavan did not speak. He had learnt to not underestimate Ram's strategic brilliance.

'I think he plans to use a flexible charging strategy with this decentralised army. To break through some of our lines in the centre,' continued Indrajit. 'And then pour into the breaches with the rest of his troops. But we will decimate his flanks long before that happens. He has made a mistake. We will nail him for sure.'

'You cannot nail down the sea,' said Raavan. 'Some instinct tells me that attacking his flanks would be a mistake.'

Raavan's instinct was right. Ram's intention *was* to entice the enemy to attack his flanks. For then he would unleash his secret weapons. Weapons hidden in the darkness of the jungle behind his formations. Ram's war elephants.

'But we cannot attack the centre either, father,' said Indrajit. 'His flexible lines will hurt us. Some of those regiments would attack, others would stay behind. And that would break our lines as they charge forward, disturbing our formations. We will get massacred by them in the breaches. It's better for us to keep our infantry stationary and hold off their charge.'

Raavan breathed deeply. A good general is always wary of doing exactly what the enemy wanted.

'We must charge from the flanks,' continued Indrajit. 'That is our only play.'

'No. Send a message to Mareech and Kumbhakarna to hold back. They must not make the first move.'

'Father, we have the advantage. We *must* make the first move.'

Raavan turned to Indrajit. 'The only thing all of you *must* do is follow my orders. Send a message to the flanks. We will not charge. Let Ram make the first move.'

'As you command, father.' Indrajit gestured to his flagbearer to come close. He relayed the order.

Raavan was suddenly distracted by a loud roar from the Ayodhyan ranks in the distance.

Clad in war armour and mounted on his horse, Ram had just ridden to the head of his troops. He was followed by Bharat, Arishtanemi and Lakshman. Hanuman and Angad were hidden in the jungles, in command of the two elephant corps.

Ram raised his right arm high, hand closed in a fist. Acknowledging the wild cheering from the soldiers. Over the last couple of months, Ram had successfully forged the four different armies – the Ayodhyans, Vaanars, Malayaputras and Vayuputras – into one united, disciplined and well-aligned fighting unit.

'Ram!'

'Ram!'

'Ram!'

The cheering was loud and insistent.

'Ram!'

'Ram!'

'Ram!'

'My friends!' roared Ram, his voice ringing in all directions. His arm still raised, he opened his right hand as a signal for silence. 'Hear me, my friends!'

A hushed silence descended upon his army. His followers.

'I have walked with you. I have lived with you. I have spoken with you.' Ram's voice rose now. 'And I have listened to you.'

Bharat looked at the troops. All eyes were pinned in admiration upon his elder brother.

'Many of you have spoken about the reasons for fighting this battle!' Ram's voice was loud and booming. 'Almost all of you think we fight for my wife, Sita!'

Arishtanemi stared at Ram. And smiled a bit. For he guessed what was coming.

'All of you are wrong!' thundered Ram. 'Sita is great beyond measure! She is the Vishnu! I will proudly fight for her! I will willingly die for her!' And then his voice dropped low. 'But I cannot ask that sacrifice of you ...'

The soldiers looked at each other. Confused.

Ram held the pommel horn on his saddle with his left hand, and leaned over from his horse. Bending low. Down to the ground. He picked up some soil in his hand. And then reared up high on his horse. He held the sacred earth aloft. 'We fight for one much greater than my wife! We fight for the greatest Lady we will ever know! We fight for the one that has cradled us from birth! We fight for the one who will cherish our ashes in her bosom when we pass on to the next life! We fight for the mightiest Goddess of them All. We fight for This Land, Our Mother!'

The soldiers bellowed loudly. For one thing united them all. Love. Fierce love. For the one who was Mother to them all.

India.

'Raavan and his army dare to say that they own India! Can a child own his Mother?!'

The soldiers roared in fury, remembering the Lankan war cry.

'Our land was rich once! Our land was peaceful once! But since the Battle of Karachapa, Raavan has ravaged our land!'

Pointing at the Lankans with the fist that held the sacred earth of India, Ram bellowed, 'Those children of Mother India have insulted her! Devastated her! Looted her! We will defeat them! We will restore our precious Mother's glory! For that which is most precious can survive only if there are men willing to die to protect it! Our sacrifice will be a new beginning for This Land, Our Mother!'

Kicking his horse, Ram rode up and down the line, holding his fist high.

'We fight … for This Land, Our Mother!'

Ram's soldiers yelled loudly. A patriotic gush surging through them.

'We will free … This Land, Our Mother!'

The fierce Ayodhyan, Vayuputra, Malayaputra and Vaanar cries reverberated far, beyond the walls of Sigiriya, into the vitals of the city.

'We will honour with our blood … This Land, Our Mother!'

Ram placed the consecrated earth of the motherland in his left palm, pinched some of it with three fingers of his other hand and marked his forehead. From left to right. In three lines. It was the sign of those who were loyal to the Mahadev, Lord

Rudra; a deeply symbolic act. The mark of the Mahadev, made with the sacred earth of the Motherland.

He raised his hand high and roared. *'Jai Maa Bhaarati!'*

Glory to Mother India!

'Jai Maa Bhaarati!' repeated his soldiers.

'Jai Maa Bhaarati!' bellowed Arishtanemi, Bharat and Lakshman.

'Jai Maa Bhaarati!'

Ram, followed by his deputies, rode up and down the line. They repeated the war cry.

'Jai Maa Bhaarati!'

'Jai Maa Bhaarati!'

As the soldiers chanted the war cry, Bharat spurred his horse close to Ram. His face flushed with admiration. 'Not bad, Dada, not bad at all. That was … inspirational.'

Ram looked at his younger brother. And whispered with a smile, *'Janani Janmabhumishcha Swargaadapi Gariyasi.'*

Mother and Motherland are superior to heaven.

Bharat smiled. Leaders delivered speeches to charge and motivate troops. But only a few truly meant the words they uttered. Ram was one of those few. A unique leader of men.

'Now?' asked Arishtanemi.

'Now, we wait for the Lankans to act.'

'Back to positions, Dada?' asked Lakshman.

'Yes,' said Ram. 'Back to positions.'

Arishtanemi saluted Ram and steered his horse towards the left flank of the army. Bharat spurred his horse and galloped to the right flank, while Ram and Lakshman rode to the centre.

And waited.

For the first move from the Lankans.

It would be a long wait.

Chapter 32

'What the hell!' growled an agitated Lakshman, pulling the reins of his horse and turning towards his elder brother.

Thirty minutes had passed since Ram's rousing speech. Raavan had also delivered his address to his soldiers. The Ayodhyan royals had not been able to hear the Lankan king's words from where they were, but they had heard its impact in the loud roars and cheers from the Lankan troops. And after that … absolutely nothing.

The Lankans had simply lingered. Waiting for the Ayodhyans to make the first move.

The line of Lankan archers had fired a few volleys, but they were way out of range. The arrows had fallen harmlessly in the open ground between the two armies.

'Charge, you bloody cowards!' thundered Lakshman.

'Lakshman …' whispered Ram, suggesting calm in his tone rather than words.

Lakshman took a long breath in, and turned to Ram. Not saying anything.

'They are wary,' said Ram. 'They think we have some trick up our angvastram. Which will get triggered the moment they attack our flanks.'

'Should we attack from the centre then?'

Ram paused to think. 'Sometimes a tiny pinprick works better than a mighty cut.'

Lakshman nodded, understanding his brother's mind. Somewhat.

'Send four regiments ...'

'Just four regiments? We have eighty!' said Lakshman, incredulous.

'The idea is to deliver a pinprick, Lakshman,' said Ram. 'Maybe two from Arishtanemiji's flank. And two from Bharat's command.' Ram looked at the sky. And then at the flags tied high on flagpoles at the fort walls behind the Lankan lines. 'The winds are strong. Arrows will not stay on course. Good for us ...'

Lakshman nodded. He turned to his flag bearer, and relayed the orders.

Two regiments each from two ends of the Ayodhya formation marched out simultaneously. One thousand five hundred soldiers in each regiment. Archers embedded within. Chariots at the lead. And cavalry protecting the sides.

It was the slow advance of an orderly army and not the raucous charge of savage rabble. Ram had trained them well. A disciplined march forward was better than wildly tearing ahead and wasting energy. Further, maintaining formation while running at breakneck speed was almost impossible. This army's battle was about maintaining formation and keeping the line. The Ayodhya regiments soon reached midpoint between the two armies. Within the range of arrows. Having reached, they were ordered to halt. The infantry soldiers provided room and the archers nocked arrows onto their bows. As did the chariot-mounted warriors.

'Fire,' the regiment commanders ordered. The arrows were shot. They flew in a high, irregular arc as the strong winds swayed them eastwards. But the Lankan ranks were dense with soldiers. Almost every arrow fell on a Lankan. Many blocked the missiles with their shields. But some got through. Another volley was fired. Same result. And then another volley.

The damage wasn't significant. At most, a little over a hundred from the over two hundred thousand Lankan soldiers were hit. A tiny pinprick. But the Lankan commanders were finding it difficult to control their soldiers from not responding, for the fiery men were straining to charge and wipe out the few Ayodhyans in the middle of the field. Lankan archers did shoot volleys in reply to the Ayodhyans. But there were only two enemy regiments on this flank. A very small target. And the strong winds sent the arrows splaying in all directions. Most Lankan arrows fell on open ground, causing little damage. And the few that did fall on the Ayodhyan regiments were easily blocked by shields.

A bugle was sounded.

The Ayodhyan regiments, both from Arishtanemi's and Bharat's flanks, began retreating. Slowly. Deliberately.

And four other Ayodhyan regiments marched out. The same tactic. The same result. Absolutely no Ayodhyan casualties. A few Lankan casualties.

Another pinprick.

The impact of these repeated pinpricks on the Lankan soldiers was becoming increasingly visible. They were getting provoked. Angry. They wanted to charge. Their Lankan commanders were struggling to hold them back.

The bugle was sounded again. And the Ayodhyan regiments marched back to safety.

And finally, the commander of the Ayodhyan left flank, Arishtanemi, himself rode out, leading two fresh regiments to midfield. The time was right. The two regiments were composed almost entirely of Vayuputra soldiers, and were led by the Malayaputra Arishtanemi. Symbolic of Ram's organisational principle: mix soldiers from different backgrounds and make one united army. And it was poetic that Arishtanemi should lead this final pinprick, for the idea of multiple regiments with joint commands was his.

Arishtanemi positioned his mounted warriors and chariots, along with his infantry regiment, close to the right cavalry and chariot flanks of the Lankan army. This Lankan flank was commanded by Mareech. And this is where Ram's tactics would, at last, bear fruit.

Some Lankan cavalrymen finally lost their patience and thundered out. They knew they could easily wipe out the small Ayodhyan regiment in the middle of the battlefield. The Ayodhyan infantry turned and ran back on spotting the mounted Lankan warriors. At charge-speed. They maintained formation as they ran. The Ayodhyan cavalry and chariots also retreated. But Arishtanemi ensured that they remained behind the running soldiers. As a rear guard to their infantry. Shooting arrows backwards.

More Lankan cavalrymen from Mareech's end broke ranks and galloped. Enticed into the web by the 'cowardly' Ayodhyans who were retreating.

'What the hell are they doing?!' bellowed Raavan at the centre of the Lankan army, when he saw what was happening at the right flank. 'They are thinning out the flanks! Order them to stay back! Send a rider to Mareech immediately!'

But the mounted Lankans at the right flank had committed themselves to the attack. Some more Lankan cavalrymen dashed out. And, most critically, all the Lankan charioteers raced forward. Charging towards the retreating Ayodhyan regiment.

Ram smiled. 'Perfect.' He turned to Lakshman. 'Order the charge of the elephants. From both flanks. Full attack.'

'And what about the twenty reserve infantry regiments?'

'Bring in fifteen. Keep five in reserve, back in the jungle.'

'Okay. I'll order them to follow Angad's elephant corps, and attack from our left flank onto the right flank of the Lankans. That's where we will get maximum impact.'

Ram nodded. *Yes.*

Lakshman quickly relayed the orders, which speedily went down the line through flag signals and bugles.

Even as this played out, more Lankan cavalrymen from Mareech's end hurtled out. Blood lust had overpowered discipline.

At the other end, Kumbhakarna had managed to keep his cavalry in formation. Stationary.

And then came the reverberations.

Like the menacing thunder of oncoming doom.

Boom.

Boom.

Boom.

Boom.

Mareech looked around. As did Kumbhakarna.

The charging Lankan cavalry slowed down. Confused.

Boom.

Boom.

Boom.

Boom.

Like the grim footsteps of death.

Like the very earth was trembling in fear.

Like the menacing voice of wrathful Gods.

It was Raavan who decoded the sounds first. But he couldn't believe it. *Impossible!*

And suddenly, the impossible made itself visible.

The Lankans were stunned into paralysis.

From beyond the edges of the Ayodhyan flanks, war elephants were storming out of the jungle. A corps of one hundred and fifty elephants from the left. And another corps of one hundred and fifty from the right. Charging ahead. Guided expertly by their mahouts in disciplined lines. Trumpeting loudly with their trunks aggressively pointing forward.

Like the messengers of annihilation.

Announcing. Brazenly. That they were coming to kill. And there was nothing anyone could do about it.

A shocked Mareech stared in fear. 'Lord Rudra have mercy ...' But the old warhorse quickly took control. Or at least, tried to. 'Fall in line! Fall in line!'

The few Lankan cavalrymen who had stayed behind tried to rapidly get into formation and fill the gaps. Many of those who had charged recklessly ahead had begun to race back. To reinforce their threatened flanks.

But it was already too late.

'Turn!' roared Angad, from atop the lead elephant, his flag bearer raising the flag to convey the orders clearly.

The Ayodhyan elephants had already charged to the outer edge of the Lankan flank. They traced a gentle curve and turned slowly. With awe-inspiring discipline. Each elephant within its own imaginary lane. No bumping into other elephants. No slowing down. No break in rhythm. It was a manoeuvre they had been trained for repeatedly. And expertly. Under Ram's personal supervision. And then, the gargantuan beasts charged headlong into the Lankan flank cavalry. Not from the front, where stronger resistance was possible. But from the side.

The thinned-out cavalry lines ensured there was little resistance; the chariots that could have slowed them down were gone. The elephants exploded through the Lankan flanks. Barely slowing down, they cut through the formations like hot knife through butter. Crushing the horses and the mounted riders.

Each Ayodhyan elephant was guided by its mahout. Through foot signals on its temples. And three mounted warriors balanced themselves on the howdah tied high on the beast's back. These warriors shot arrows and spears continuously. Their elevated positions ensuring that not a single missile missed its target.

It was carnage.

Within a few minutes, the massive Lankan flank cavalry had been breached. Their formations lay in tatters.

The elephants barely slowed down. They charged on relentlessly. Obliterating all in their paths. Their tusks, sharpened like long swords, slashed soldiers and horses. Viciously. Their trunks flung enemies high in the air. Savagely. Their feet crushed all in their path. Mercilessly.

Arishtanemi ordered the retreating Vayuputra regiments to stop and turn around. The time had come. Time to move in for the kill. They charged towards the Lankans. With Arishtanemi in the lead. Bellowing the war cry of his Vayuputra troops. '*Kalagni Rudra!*'

'*Kalagni Rudra!*' roared many more regiments, and raced down the field. Shooting arrows and thrusting spears at the Lankan cavalrymen who were rushing back to reinforce their decimated flanks.

Caught between the pincer attack of Angad's elephant corps from the side and the charging Ayodhyan regiments of Arishtanemi from the enemy-front, the right cavalry and chariot flank of the Lankan army collapsed completely.

Leaving the field open for the elephants to charge into the infantry ranks. Not from the front from where a modicum of defence would have been possible. But, once again, from the side.

The fifteen reserve regiments of the Ayodhyan army, consisting of over twenty thousand soldiers, charged into the ravages left behind by the elephants corps. Killing all who may have survived.

To the credit of the Lankan infantry, no soldier retreated. Those that weren't crushed to death by the elephants fought the charging Ayodhyans till the end. But it was a lost cause.

They were being massacred. Being thrown into a meat grinder.

And yet, they fought. They died. But not with wounds on their backs, like retreating cowards. They died with their swords in their hands. Like the valiant do.

While Lankans in the right flank were being butchered, on the left flank, with Kumbhakarna in command, the cavalry and chariots held on. Brave and grim. He had already sent a message to his brother Raavan in the centre. A simple message: Retreat before we are all exterminated.

Meanwhile, Kumbhakarna held on.

In a courageous flank-guard struggle.

Refusing to let the elephants pass.

'Their infantry lines are breaking from their right,' said Ram, standing up on his saddle to get a better view.

'We should let loose our infantry, Dada,' suggested Lakshman.

Ram nodded. 'Yes. All in! Full attack!'

Orders were efficiently relayed out.

Bharat ordered all the infantry regiments from the Ayodhyan right flank to charge. While Ram and Lakshman led the regiments from the centre.

All in! Full attack!

The Ayodhyan infantry formations blitzed ahead.

The Lankan infantry ranks were now breaking. And they were falling back. For they had been ordered to do so. Facing two adversary war-elephant corps boring ruthlessly into the sides of their dense formation. Unprepared. It was almost impossible to resist.

Retreat was the only option.

But withdrawing tens of thousands of soldiers through a gate in a fort, while fighting a flank-guard action, presented a massive logistical challenge. Emerging from the fort had taken two hours. They didn't have two hours to pull back. They'd all be dead by then.

It was the bottleneck of all bottlenecks.

Indrajit personally directed the retreat at the gate. The army had to be saved if they hoped to offer battle the next day. Raavan held the front, fighting a brave vanguard action to protect the passage for his retreating troops. But the bravest, most ferocious battle was being fought on the Lankan left flank.

For if that flank broke, it would all be over for the Lankans.

The mercilessly fearsome pachyderms had simply not been able to plough through this flank.

The terrifying war-elephant corps, led by the formidable Hanuman, was fighting a grim and brutal battle here.

No inch was being lost with any ease; every fingerbreadth was being acquired by the Ayodhyans with a king's ransom of blood.

For here, the Ayodhyans faced the most dogged defiance of the day.

For here, the irresistible force of the elephant corps had crashed into an immovable object.

For here, stood the mighty Kumbhakarna.

Chapter 33

'Aim for their eyes!' thundered Kumbhakarna.

An ironical barricade now blocked the Ayodhyan elephant corps led by Hanuman. It was a long, thick line of decimated Lankan chariots, dead horses and the corpses of the massacred charioteers. The elephants couldn't crash through the sharp and mangled metal, mortared together with the gore, flesh and bones of horses and men. The Lankan cavalry, positioned behind the barrier of the battered chariots, was unreachable.

It had been magnificent. The Lankan charioteers had embraced defiant deaths, fighting to the last man and last weapon. And with their sacrifice, they had saved the Lankan cavalry and infantry. It was a resistance that had refused to yield. Even after the end.

The elephants were no longer weapons of war. They were blocked. From ramming with their massive bodies, stabbing with their tusks and thrashing with their trunks. They were now merely carriers of the warriors atop their howdahs. Yes, the mounted Ayodhyans had the advantage of elevation and were shooting arrows and hurling spears. But the distance from the Lankan cavalry made their missiles less effective.

All due to the insurmountable barricade of wrecked chariots.

The Lankan cavalry had not wasted the supreme sacrifice of the charioteers. The horses were held in control behind the safety of the barricades. And rotated regularly in the *Anavarata Taranga Vyuha;* the *strategy of unceasing waves.* Mounted riders shot arrows at the Ayodhyan warriors perched upon the elephant howdahs. On exhausting their missiles or peak strength from the exertions of shooting, the front row of riders slipped back and made room for a fresh line of warriors to ride in and take position. And the assault of arrows would continue. In unceasing waves.

The arrows of the Lankan cavalry were even less effective than that of the Ayodhyans. They were shooting from a lower level and the few arrows that did reach their target mostly injured and did not kill. But the Lankans were not trying to defeat the elephant corps. There were fighting a desperate rear-guard battle to delay the charge of the elephants. Till such time that their infantry had safely retreated behind the Sigiriya walls.

They were not fighting for victory. They were fighting for time.

Having said that, the sheer advantage of height was extracting a bloodied price. Slowly but surely. Kumbhakarna was losing more and more of his cavalrymen to the missiles from the elephant-mounted Ayodhyans. He looked back. Still many infantrymen waiting to retreat through the gates. He had to hold on for some more time. The current strategy was not enough.

And so Kumbhakarna had made a bold decision.

Offence was the best defence.

He would take the battle to the enemy. Not by charging at the elephants. Kumbhakarna was brave. Not stupid.

Instead, he decided to shoot at the elephants and not the Ayodhyans atop them. Target the beasts at their only vulnerable part, if using arrows ...

'Shoot in the eyes of the elephants!' roared Kumbhakarna. Messengers behind him immediately dashed out, rode up and down the Lankan mounted warrior line, and relayed the order in the noise of war.

The Lankan cavalry soldiers changed tack. They began shooting at the elephants now. But the eyes weren't an easy target. The elephants kept moving their heads and flapping their ears. The distance increased the difficulty. The eyes were a tiny target.

Most of the arrows missed.

Then Kumbhakarna decided to show them how it needed to be done.

He steadied his horse, pulled his short-recurved bow forward and nocked an arrow, aiming at an elephant. Focusing on the beast's eye. The cavalry soldiers on both sides provided covering fire. Ensuring that the enemy would not shoot their commander. Kumbhakarna calibrated for the elephant's moving head. He needed to shoot at the spot where the eye would be a split second later. He arched his bow a little higher and gave the arrow the parabolic path to adjust for the height and distance. He pulled the bowstring back to his ear and released the arrow, flicking the fletching as the arrow launched.

The missile flew in a shallow parabolic path – just as Kumbhakarna had planned – and rammed into the left eye of the beast. It cut through the cornea and sank deep into the soft tissue of the vitreous sac. The elephant hollered in agony, jerked its head and stepped back. One Ayodhyan soldier fell off the howdah due to the sudden movement and was crushed underneath his elephant's foot. A deafening roar went up from the Lankans, for they had finally killed one Ayodhyan despite the odds. But it speedily died down. For the elephant did not retreat.

An arrow in the eye of a massive pachyderm is not a fatal wound at all. The Lankans knew this, of course, but had expected the beast to at least pull back. However, the superbly trained war elephant did not. It came back into battle. It picked up the corpse of a Lankan charioteer lying at its feet, with its trunk, and flung it at Kumbhakarna. The body projectile missed Kumbhakarna by a hairbreadth and hit the rider beside him.

And then the elephant held itself back, having received orders from the mahout above. It was stable and stationary again. Letting the warriors atop its howdah do their job: shoot arrows.

Kumbhakarna cursed, clipped his bow on his back and pulled his horse back. These war elephants were unbeatable. They could only be held back, not defeated. He stood on his saddle stirrups and looked at his rear formations. The infantry behind the Lankan cavalry was beginning to move back to safety. The retreat march was finally reaching this end of the Lankan infantry lines. Indrajit was managing the gates well.

Half an hour more … We'll save them. We'll fight again tomorrow.

'A little while more, lads!' roared Kumbhakarna, keeping up the spirit of his men. 'We'll save our boys. Hang in there! Keep shooting!'

The order for the next change was relayed out. The front line of the Lankan cavalry retreated, to be replaced by the next batch of mounted warriors. And the fresh soldiers began firing arrows once again.

Kumbhakarna looked towards the Ayodhyan command. Towards Hanuman. And was surprised to find his opponent missing.

Where is Lord Hanuman?

The Ayodhyans were also following the Anavarata Taranga Vyuha. Like the Lankans. Moving back the front line of war elephants every ten minutes and replacing them with a fresh line of warriors. But Hanuman, just like Kumbhakarna, had never retreated. Through the last hour of pitched battle, he had remained unmoving. Up in front.

A good field commander should always be right up front. Where he is needed: to direct the war effort, to rally his troops and inspire them.

He would never retreat. Unless he is seriously injured. Or if he is—

And it suddenly struck Kumbhakarna.

He pulled his horse farther back, stood up on the saddle stirrups and stared into the distance. Far to the left. Towards the Sigiriyan walls. At the gap in the lines. For, obviously, when the Lankans had formed for battle, they had kept some space between themselves and the fort walls. To allow for the movement of medical corps and relief supplies.

Oh Lord Rudra!

No soldier ever attacked the medical corps and relief supply regiments. They were not armed. Assaulting them was against the rules of war. It was *adharma*. Neither the Lankans nor the Ayodhyans would break this rule.

But the medical corps and relief supplies regiments had already retreated. That land was empty. Nothing there to stop the adversary.

The Ayodhyan war elephants could smash through from that point, outflank the Lankan cavalry, and go straight for the infantry behind them. If they made it through, hundreds, maybe thousands of Lankan infantry soldiers would be killed within a very short while. It would be like the massacre at the right flank.

'Upon me!' thundered Kumbhakarna to the mounted warriors behind him.

He turned his horse and raced towards the walls. A squadron of fifty cavalrymen galloped after him. Riding hard.

'Faster!'

Kumbhakarna feared the worst.

'Faster!'

They rode at breakneck speed and soon arrived at the end of the cavalry lines. Kumbhakarna circled the warriors and turned his horse. Towards the front line.

And he saw them.

A boundary line of twenty horses to his right, one in front of the other, facing away from Kumbhakarna. Each horse marked the ground like a stake at the left end of the line and stretched to the right. It was a part of the Lankan cavalry formation fighting the Ayodhyans. Beyond the horses in the distance was the barricade of destroyed Lankan chariots. And farther still, a long way off, was a thick border of five war elephants, one in front of the other, all facing in the direction of Kumbhakarna, each war elephant manning the left-most edge of the elephantry formations that stretched to the right. And beyond that boundary line of the elephantry formation, far into the distance, Kumbhakarna saw some elephants turn in.

Lord Hanuman.

It was too far. It was only a silhouette. But Kumbhakarna knew in his heart. It was Hanuman.

This was it.

This was the end.

Kumbhakarna took a deep breath.

This was a channel of death.

With the Sigiriya walls to the left of him. And a boundary defined by the Lankan cavalry, destroyed chariots and Ayodhyan war elephants to the right, stretching into the distance.

At the end of the channel, seven hundred metres away, a contingent of Malayaputra war elephants, led by Hanuman. Taking formation for a charge.

Nothing between the two opposing forces. Just open land. Broad enough for two elephants to charge abreast from the Ayodhyan side. And three horses, abreast, from the Lankan side.

Kumbhakarna instinctively knew he couldn't allow the enemy elephants to cross the line of mangled and destroyed chariots. For they would plough through his cavalry from the side.

Only one thing would hold the elephants back – if one of them lay on the ground. Elephants never step on corpses of their own. Everyone knew that.

A seven-hundred-metre-long open-ground channel.

Fort walls to the left. Beasts and destroyed chariots to the right.

The mission was clear.

The elephants had to be stopped.

The first few elephants had to be killed.

Quickly.

The mission was clear.

For it was a suicide mission.

And Kumbhakarna, valiant Kumbhakarna, did not hesitate. Not for a moment.

He drew his sword and held it high. His brave cavalry and experienced warriors, all knew exactly what they were charging into. They took formation behind Kumbhakarna. Three abreast.

Stretching back to sixteen lines. Two riders took position on either side of Kumbhakarna.

The rider to the left of the Lankan prince spoke. 'Fighting alongside you has been my life's honour, Lord Kumbhakarna.'

Kumbhakarna looked at him and smiled. 'I'll see you on the other side, my friend.'

The soldier smiled and nodded.

Kumbhakarna looked at his courageous fifty and thundered, 'We must kill the first two elephants! More, if we can! We have to!'

'Yes, Lord!' roared his soldiers.

Kumbhakarna faced the Malayaputra elephants. He swung his sword down and pointed forward, towards his adversaries. And roared, '*Bhaarat Bhartri Lanka!*'

'*Bhaarat Bhartri Lanka!*'

And the valiant Lankans charged. Galloping hard. Galloping strong. Galloping to their deaths.

At the other end of the channel, Hanuman was atop the lead elephant. Even from that distance, he could see the giant form of Kumbhakarna, on his massive steed, charging towards them in a storm of dust. He should have been surprised that the Lankan prince had deduced the Ayodhyan tactic. But he wasn't. He knew Kumbhakarna's genius at battle. He also knew – oh, he knew so well – Kumbhakarna's raw courage. For Hanuman had once saved his life. And, now, it had fallen upon him to take it away.

Fate.

So, there he was, the mighty Vayuputra, beholding his Lankan friend charging bravely towards him. To what was certain death.

Magnificent ...

He turned to his warriors. They knew what had to be done. What they had to do. They had been briefed.

Hanuman raised his spear high above his head. And bellowed the war cry of his Malayaputra soldiers. A Vayuputra, honouring the Malayaputra ways. '*Jai Parshu Ram!*'

Glory to Lord Parshu Ram.

'*Jai Parshu Ram!*' roared the Malayaputras behind him. 'Attack!'

The elephants charged, the very earth beneath their feet trembling with their mighty strides.

The elephants were stronger. But the horses were quicker. They passed the Lankan cavalrymen to the right faster than the time it took for the elephants to pass the Ayodhyan elephantry formations.

Soon the adversaries were sandwiched between the Sigiriya walls and the battered chariot barricades. They raced towards each other.

The Malayaputras atop the elephants began to fire arrows. Three warriors on each elephant. With the advantage of height. A lot of arrows were fired. Too many Lankan cavalrymen were hit. But no slowing down. They kept coming. Riding hard.

'For Lanka!' roared Kumbhakarna as he neared the charging elephants, spurring his horse to a manic speed.

'For Mother India!' bellowed Hanuman from the other end. He hurled his spear at the Lankan next to Kumbhakarna. The missile rammed into the Lankan with brutal force, propelling him backwards off his horse and under the feet of the horse behind. But no horse slowed down. Including the one that raced without its rider now.

Hanuman's elephant swung its mighty trunk at Kumbhakarna; an immense whip moving at a fearsome speed. The prince of Lanka ducked and swerved to the right. The trunk lashed into the Lankan soldier riding to left of Kumbhakarna, flinging the rider towards the fort walls. His head bludgeoned into the wall and shattered like a melon, giving him the blessing of instant death. The horse came under the feet of the charging elephant, neighing desperately even as it was crushed.

Meanwhile, Kumbhakarna had swerved between the first two elephants at the Ayodhyan front line. He held his sword out in his right hand. Gripping it strong and steady, his muscled arm flexing fiercely as he passed the elephant to the right of the one carrying Hanuman. The elephant's trunk whizzed above Kumbhakarna's head. A miss. Kumbhakarna's sword viciously slashed into the right front leg of the beast. From the side. It sliced through the gargantuan digitorum lateralis and digitorum communis muscles. Amazingly, Kumbhakarna did not lose his hold on the sword; it dug farther into the elephant's front leg, cutting the carpi ulnaris muscles, both the extensor and the flexor. It was but a micro-moment. Kumbhakarna passed by as blood burst out in a shower of red. But he wasn't done. He slashed again, savagely, as he passed the right rear leg, cleaving the massive digitorum, peroneus and soleus muscles.

The beast was roaring in pain now. It collapsed, its front and rear right legs rendered useless. Blood was spraying in a flood. The howdah toppled over and the three Malayaputra archers crashed into the mangled chariots to the left of them. The mahout was crushed under his own elephant. Kumbhakarna immediately pulled the reins of his horse and turned around, barely missing the tusk of an elephant charging on the second line.

As Kumbhakarna charged back towards the elephant that he had just felled, the warriors on the elephants behind him began shooting arrows at him. Kumbhakarna swerved his body to the left and right as he rode, avoiding the missiles by a whisker. But only just. He was flirting with his fate ... And the law of numbers always overrides fate ... There were just too many arrows ... Three of them finally hit. Kumbhakarna's body arched forward as the arrows slammed into his back with brutal force. But he did not slow down. He swerved to his right. Towards Hanuman's elephant. It was charging towards the second line of Lankan cavalrymen ahead. Kumbhakarna stretched out his sword hand and attempted to slice the left rear leg of Hanuman's elephant.

But the elephant he had attacked earlier, grievously wounded and lying on the ground, had fight left in him. You can bring a good elephant down, but it is not easy to kill it. The beast lay on the ground, blood jetting out of the massive wounds on its legs, roaring in fury. It swung its massive trunk. Weak, and yet, it carried punch. It brushed Kumbhakarna's horse. The stallion lost its footing momentarily, and Kumbhakarna's strike on Hanuman's elephant lost its bite. The sword sliced into the elephant's rear left leg and got buried in the flesh as Kumbhakarna lost his grip on the blade.

The prince of Lanka immediately reached to his side and pulled out another sword. Simultaneously, two more Malayaputra arrows hit him from behind; one punched into his thigh, and the other pierced his left shoulder. He roared with rage, ignoring the searing pain. He extended his sword arm again. Hanuman's elephant slowed a bit, turned its head and swung its trunk out viciously. The prince of Lanka ducked and lashed out with his sword, cutting into the elephant's front left leg. But it was a weaker strike. Though it cut through the thick hide and drew blood from the muscles and tissue, it was not incapacitating.

The Lankans on the other side were raining arrows at the Malayaputras in a high loop, hoping to slow down the unstoppable elephants.

Kumbhakarna's horse had galloped ahead. He pulled the reins and turned it around again. He was bang in front of Hanuman's elephant now. Hanuman hurled a spear at Kumbhakarna. He ducked again. But the missile hit the outgrowth, that was like an extra arm, on his left shoulder. This was a spear flung by the mighty Hanuman himself. Robust and strong, it sliced through, severing the small extra arm cleanly.

Arrow wounds all over. Spears buried into limbs. This was agony beyond endurance for an ordinary human being. But Kumbhakarna was no ordinary human being. He barely flinched and swung at the elephant's trunk with his sword.

The elephant smoothly moved its trunk aside and stabbed with its mighty tusks, which were the size of long-swords. They were sharpened at the point-edge. One tusk gored Kumbhakarna's horse, ramming into its viscera. The horse hollered in desperate pain even as Kumbhakarna quickly pulled his feet out of the stirrup. The elephant trumpeted ferociously as it swung its head, carrying the horse with its mighty tusk and flinging it away. Like a rag doll. Kumbhakarna had, meanwhile, jumped off his horse, rolled on the ground and come to his feet. Right in front of the now almost stationary elephant.

'Come on!' hollered Kumbhakarna at the elephant. 'Do your worst!'

Arrows were shot from atop the elephant, but the Lankans behind gave covering fire. Only two hit Kumbhakarna. One slammed into his left arm. The other pounded into his chest. But he was beyond noticing, or even caring about his numerous wounds.

The elephant swung its tusks but the nimble-footed Kumbhakarna, despite his massive size and his wounds, dodged the blow.

Or at least it appeared that he had.

For elephants are not like horses. They are not dumb beasts. They are menacingly intelligent.

The stab with the tusks was just a feint. The actual blow was with the trunk.

As Kumbhakarna sprang to the side, the elephant's trunk veered in and wrapped around the Lankan's legs.

The trunk of an elephant has no bones. Instead, it has forty thousand powerful muscles, more than sixty times the entire count of muscles in a human body. An elephant's trunk has the power to crush, swing hard, thrash and bang down. And yet, it also has the delicate dexterity to lift a feather from the ground.

The beast swung its trunk high, carrying the gargantuan Kumbhakarna up. Hanging upside down. It was planning to pound the prince of Lanka down into the ground, smack on his head. And it would all be over.

A feint, followed by the main blow.

The elephant is a menacingly intelligent animal.

But there is one animal even more menacingly intelligent: man.

The strength of an elephant's trunk is also its weakness. So many muscles. It also means much more vascularity. And more vascularity means much more blood flow.

Kumbhakarna roared loudly and crunched his massive stomach, swinging his shoulders up as he swivelled high. Dangling off the elephant's trunk. He flexed his mighty shoulders and slashed hard with his long sword. Hacking through the trunk of the pachyderm, severing it cleanly.

The elephant howled in frenzied agony as blood burst from its sundered trunk. Moving with the motion of the trunk that had been swinging him rapidly higher, Kumbhakarna flew in the air and crashed to the ground, landing on his right shoulder. The shoulder joint smashed to smithereens. As the Lankan prince bounced onto his back, the buried arrows burst through and emerged from his chest, slicing his vital organs. Blood pumped out of the gashing wound on his shoulder where the small extra arm had been severed and from the numerous arrow wounds on his body.

Meanwhile, the elephant collapsed. It had lost too much blood from its severed trunk. But its descent was slow. Deliberate. Ensuring that its mahout remained unharmed. Hanuman and the warriors dismounted quickly from the howdah atop the grievously injured elephant.

Arrows were still falling like missile showers. From both the Ayodhyan and Lankan ends. Two arrows walloped into the prone Kumbhakarna. Inflicting two more punctures. Piercing his massive abdomen.

'STOP!' Hanuman commanded, raising his hand. 'Ceasefire!'

The fight was over. The Lankan infantry behind the cavalry had escaped to safety behind the walls of Sigiriya. Kumbhakarna's courageous last stand had saved a significant portion of the Lankan army.

The Malayaputras immediately followed the order of their commander. Putting their weapons down. Within a flash, the Lankan arrows also stopped.

Hanuman looked at the prince of Lanka. His friend. Lying on the ground. A few short steps away.

Kumbhakarna's broken body was twisted into inhuman angles. He struggled to lift his head. He saw one elephant on the right, bleeding from its severely injured legs, thrashing about in pain with its mahout crushed underneath. Another elephant lay to the left, blood spurting like a fountain from its severed trunk; in its dying throes, its mahout holding the pachyderm's head, crying. Like a man mourning the imminent death of his brother.

Two elephants. On the ground. The charge had been stopped. He rolled his eyes and looked at the back. Practically the entire Lankan cavalry contingent that had followed him into this courageous charge had been decimated. They lay on the ground, felled by the arrows and spears of the Ayodhyan elephantry division.

They had died, but they had fulfilled their mission.

They had died. And saved the lives of their comrades behind them.

I will see you soon, my brothers.

'My friend …'

Kumbhakarna turned. And saw Hanuman standing over him. Tears in his eyes.

The mighty Kumbhakarna smiled. Weakly. 'Lord … Hanuman …'

Hanuman went down on one knee and held Kumbhakarna's hand gently. 'I'm sorry … I'm so sorry …'

Kumbhakarna shook his head slightly and laughed. 'You did your duty … my friend … And I did mine …'

Hanuman's tears flowed.

'You saved … my life once … you had the right … to take it now … the accounts are settled … As they should be …'

'You are a noble man, Prince Kumbhakarna. A good man …' Hanuman sensitively did not complete his statement. *A good man on the wrong side.*

Kumbhakarna tried to lift his head again. Hanuman helped him and placed his head on his lap.

Kumbhakarna looked at the heroic elephant. His last battle. The beast was bleeding slowly to death from the massive gaping wound on its cleanly hacked trunk. 'That beast … is noble … Put him down with grace … Lord Hanuman … put him down … with me …'

'We will …'

Hanuman looked at the elephant. And then back at his friend, Kumbhakarna.

A beast. And a human. But common in their fate.

Tragic males. Both.

The beast. That had been abandoned by its mother, its sisters, its lovers ... when the matriarchal clan had no further use of it.

The man. Hated by the world simply because of the way he looked. And for the crimes of his elder brother.

Both lonely. Both angry. Suppressed anger. Both courageous. Both ... noble.

Both deeply in love with their brothers.

The elephant with its brother, the mahout. And Kumbhakarna with his brother, Raavan.

Both saved by their brothers.

The elephant by the mahout, who gave it purpose when it was alone. Kumbhakarna by Raavan, who saved his brother's life at birth.

Both used by their brothers.

The elephant, used by its mahout for his own glory in war. Kumbhakarna, forced into a lifetime of managing his brother's actions.

Hanuman looked at the mahout, leaning against the elephant's head. Desperately crying. The elephant was bending its head. Almost as though, even in its dying throes, it was trying to console its mahout.

Love beyond measure.

'He loved me ... the most ...' whispered Kumbhakarna.

Hanuman looked down at his friend.

'Give him ... nobility in his death ...'

Hanuman's heart felt heavy. Even in his last moments, Kumbhakarna was thinking about his *elder brother,* Raavan.

His *dada*. His blessing. His curse.

'I fight under the banner of Ram,' said Hanuman. 'We will be noble, my friend. You know that.'

Kumbhakarna nodded. 'Goodbye ... my friend ...'

'I will see you soon on the other side, my brother,' whispered Hanuman.

Kumbhakarna's eyes twinkled. 'Take your time ...'

Hanuman laughed softly.

Kumbhakarna smiled. He then looked at the elephant again; the beast was bleeding to death. Slowly. He bowed his head with respect towards the magnificent fighter, a worthy adversary. And then, Kumbhakarna allowed his last breath to slip out softly.

Hanuman's tears spilled out in a stronger flood now. He embraced his friend. And then gently put his head back on the ground.

The mighty Vayuputra stood up tall, drawing his sword and holding it high. So that all, both friend and foe, could see him clearly. He then swung the sword down and pushed it, tip first, into the ground. And then went down on one knee. And bowed his head.

Showing respect to an extraordinary enemy.

And all the soldiers present, both Lankans and Ayodhyans, went down on one knee.

As good soldiers do. When a noble warrior dies.

A great warrior is neither an enemy nor a friend. He is just a great warrior.

The elephant and Kumbhakarna.

Both lonely and tragic.

Both had been blessed with what such males deeply hanker for.

A good death.

Chapter 34

A little after noon, during the third prahar, Ram stood quietly at the feet of Kumbhakarna's body.

The day's battle had been called to a close, though the sun remained high in the sky. There had been a little over two hours of fighting. It had devastated a majority of the Lankan army.

Lankan corpses were being carried back by tearful relatives. The funeral ceremonies would be conducted in the no man's land between the outer and inner fort walls of Sigiriya. There was enough open land to conduct the mass cremations that would be required. The rituals would be conducted in accordance with Vedic precepts. The injured were being cared for by Lankan doctors. Ram had offered his army's doctors as well. They were working in tandem with Lankans, tending to the their wounded. A proper count of the casualties had not been conducted as yet. But the figures would run into many tens of thousands for the Lankans. And perhaps a few hundreds, for the Ayodhyans.

The Ayodhyan elephants had wrecked the Lankan battle plans.

'What a man ...' said Ram, looking down at the corpse of Kumbhakarna. 'I wish that fate had blessed him with a different family ...'

Standing next to Ram, Hanuman had just described the entire battle that had taken place there, and the way Kumbhakarna had saved this section of the Lankan army.

Ram went down on one knee, pulled his *angvastram* off his shoulder and placed it across the body of Kumbhakarna. Covering his torso, up to his knees. His face was left uncovered. The Suryavanshi symbol of the sun, with its rays streaming out in all directions, was emblazoned on the cloth.

Ram's angvastram covering Kumbhakarna's corpse.

A mark of respect.

Marking Kumbhakarna as one of his own.

There was some noise behind them. Ram turned to see Raavan and Indrajit. On a single chariot. Both injured in battle. Raavan injured more than his son. For he had led the gritty vanguard action to stop the Ayodhyan infantry from breaking through till his own infantry had retreated.

Raavan had not taken off his leather-coated metallic battle armour. His left arm was in a makeshift sling made of cloth. Two arrow-stumps lay buried in his left biceps. The shafts had been broken off and some herbal paste was packed around the wound. Quick battlefield first aid. The blood around his numerous wounds had congealed, leaving thick red streaks that ran down the side of his head and both his arms. He limped, favouring his right side. Clearly his right leg had suffered a serious injury, but it wasn't an open wound. No remnants of blood on his dhoti. His right eye had been pierced with shrapnel. It was evident that he would not be able to use that eye anymore, no matter how talented the surgeon.

Raavan cut a grisly figure.

But the indescribable pain on his face was not caused by any of these wounds.

The weapons could not have done what the sight of the corpse of his younger brother had achieved.

Raavan did not let a tear escape. No show of weakness in the presence of the enemy. Not in front of Ram. Never.

Six Lankan soldiers rushed forward. Quickly, but gently, they lifted Kumbhakarna's mangled body and placed it on a stretcher. They carried him to Raavan. The king of Lanka stared unblinkingly at his brother's face. Kumbhakarna's last expression, the one that his immortal soul would record as the residue of this life's final thought, was not the agony of immense pain but the smile of happiness. Like he had shared an easy moment with a friend.

The king of Lanka turned and cast a look at Hanuman. For Hanuman would have been the last man Kumbhakarna saw. Without saying anything, Raavan looked away.

Hanuman also remained silent. He brought his hands together into a namaste and bowed his head low in respect to the corpse of Kumbhakarna.

The king of Lanka tenderly touched his younger brother's face. He ran his hand along the cheeks, then up the forehead and through the hair. Staring at Kumbhakarna. A forlorn expression on his face.

But he did not cry. He kept his sorrow bottled up within his soul. There would be time to release it. Later.

He took a deep breath, and composed himself.

He looked at the Suryavanshi-inscribed angvastram of Ram on his brother's body. And then turned to the king of Ayodhya.

Raavan whispered, 'Thank you.'

Ram bowed his head and said, politely, 'Your brother was a brave warrior. He has earned the respect of his adversaries. May Lord Yama guide him across the Vaitarni. May his songs be sung forever.'

Raavan smiled slightly, though with his wounds it appeared more like a grimace. *You don't measure your worth only with the love in the eyes of your friends. You also measure it with the admiration in the eyes of your enemies.*

Raavan glanced at the gates and then back at Ram. He repeated. 'Thank you.'

Raavan had just thanked Ram for not chasing his army into the city. Which he could have done through the open gates, while the Lankans had retreated. Had Ram done that, he could have finished the war today itself. But a good general knows that once an enemy army enters a city during battle, there is no telling what will happen. It is very difficult for the general to control the troops. There are no formations. Chains of command can break down. Street battles between adversary forces cause a lot of collateral damage. Fighting could have broken out between the Ayodhyan army and the Sigiriya citizens, and many thousands of unarmed civilians could have been killed. An enemy army should enter a city only as a last resort; only if the defender army is not coming out to offer battle.

Ram had behaved with *dharma*. And Raavan had had the grace to recognise it.

The king of Ayodhya nodded once, acknowledging Raavan's gratitude.

'We …' Raavan hesitated.

'Yes, King Raavan?' asked Ram.

'Lord Ram, we have different traditions in our community of Brahmins. We do two separate funerals. We make a straw replica of the body with a facial death mask made in the exact likeness to the last expression of the deceased. It is then cremated. The body itself is not cremated, but buried. Close to the birthplace, where the umbilical cord of the individual was once buried. We bury the body along with a few objects that were important to the passed soul in this life. And, if he died in battle, we keep some remnant of the enemy or weapon that caused his death, within the burial chamber.'

'I know the tradition,' said Ram. 'Lord Hanuman told me about your community's rituals. We will send a tusk of the elephant he battled at the end to you. Bury the tusk of the noble beast with your brother. It will honour our brave elephant as well.'

Queen Sita was right about this man … He will make a good Vishnu …

Raavan couldn't move his left arm freely, with the arrow shafts buried in his biceps. So, he pulled his right hand to his chest and bowed his head. 'Thank you.'

Ram brought his hands together into a *namaste*.

Raavan turned around and limped back to his chariot, followed by Indrajit. Kumbhakarna's body was placed in the chariot next to Raavan's. The king of Lanka glanced back at Ram, and then turned, to be driven away from the battlefield.

'Do you think he will surrender now?' asked Hanuman.

Ram shrugged. 'I don't know.'

'I estimate that he's lost at least half his army. And most of his cavalry and chariot corps. Two of his best commanders, Kumbhakarna and Mareech, are dead. He cannot carry on the fight. He should see that for his own good. The battle is as good as over.'

But a battle is never over till it's over.

Raavan's son Indrajit was not one to surrender easily.

He had a plan. And he had given the orders already.

—— ⅃⸀ ⅃⸵⸠ ——

'They should be cremated with full honours,' said Ram. 'Just like our soldiers.'

The two elephants that had died in the battle had been moved on giant rollers, pulled by elephants, to the outskirts of the Ayodhyan camp. Once there, all the elephants, even those not part of this particular corps, had come up and paid their respects. One by one, the elephants had slowly walked up to the two corpses, stretched their trunks and, with deep deference, gently touched the foreheads of their fallen comrades. They had walked around the corpses reverentially and then trudged away. Without looking back. The Ayodhyans waited patiently till the last elephant completed the ceremony. Animals have as much right to their rituals as humans have to theirs. Funeral pyres glowed in the distance, where the Ayodhyan departed were being consigned to the great God Agni, the messenger between human and divine orders. Priests were softly chanting Sanskrit hymns from the Garuda Purana. The sounds wafted in the air, infusing the atmosphere with poignant dignity.

'Yes, of course, Dada,' said Bharat. 'But first, the tusks.'

Ram nodded.

Removing tusks from a dead elephant is painstaking work. Stripped to the waist, men had been working for some time, methodically prying the skin and flesh around the base of the tusks. And cutting it out.

Hanuman stood on the other side of Ram. He turned as he heard footsteps. As did Lakshman and Shatrughan.

Arishtanemi, Vibhishan and Naarad walked up.

'We just received the spy reports,' said Arishtanemi. 'I'm afraid there is bad news.'

'Bad news?!' asked Bharat, surprised. 'Are they not surrendering?'

The casualties had been tallied. Three hundred and six Ayodhyan soldiers had died in action. The fatalities on the Lankan side brooked no comparison. Over seventy thousand infantrymen were dead. Another forty thousand seriously injured, unlikely to be fit for battle the next day. The cavalry and chariot corps were practically wiped out. Those that had survived owed their lives to the lionhearted last stand of Kumbhakarna and his cavalry. The Lankans were down to ninety thousand soldiers now, with almost no cavalry to reinforce their flanks. The Ayodhyans, on the other hand, still had nearly one hundred and sixty thousand soldiers and almost all of their cavalry and elephantry.

'No, they are not,' answered Arishtanemi. 'But that is not the bad news we bring.'

'Careful ...' Naarad suddenly called out to the soldiers working on removing the tusks.

Everyone turned to look.

The soldiers were now at the most delicate part of the operation. Through meticulous and careful axe strokes, they were chipping away at the bone around the roots of the tusks. One careless tap could damage or crack the tusks. But they clearly knew what they were doing. They didn't deign to reply to Naarad.

'How can there be bad news?' asked Lakshman, bringing the conversation back on track. 'Half their army is destroyed, thanks to our elephants. And we will destroy the other half tomorrow. Our elephants will finish the job.'

'The bad news is that our elephants cannot fly,' said Naarad. Shatrughan frowned. 'What?! Please be clear, Naaradji.'

'Indrajit is loading the Pushpak Vimaan with fuel. And weapons. I have heard that he intends to use it in the battle tomorrow.'

Bharat frowned. 'That's ridiculous. The Pushpak Vimaan is not a weapon of war.'

'Indrajit did not receive that memo,' said Naarad, sardonic as usual. 'He plans to fly low over our army tomorrow, raining arrows, spears and burning oil upon our troops. The only good news is that the vimaan has a very small door; the rest of it is tightly sealed. So, they will not have more than two warriors shooting at us at a time.'

Ram looked up at the sky. 'A flying ship, firing weapons … That's a formidable adversary. They can break our infantry formations. They can also wear our elephantry and cavalry down.'

'Precisely,' said Naarad.

They heard loud grunts from the soldiers and turned to look once again. The bones around the base of a tusk had been chipped away now. Four soldiers carefully pulled the tusk out of its bony canal and lay it on the ground. Clearly, it was extremely heavy. One man squatted over the tusk and skilfully sliced and freed the long strobile nerves and tissue from the hollow base of the tusk. The white viscous fibres slithered out with a plop. Two soldiers walked up with jars of water and began to wash the tusk, cleaning it thoroughly of blood and tissue; both, of enemies stabbed with that tusk by the elephant, and of the elephant itself.

'Vibhishan,' said Naarad, as he turned to the Lankan prince, 'I'm sure you have given some thought to the solution.'

'The same thought that must have occurred to you, I think.'

'Akampana?'

Vibhishan nodded.

'Who is Akampana?' asked Shatrughan.

'One of Raavan dada's oldest allies,' answered Vibhishan. 'Raavan Dada began his career in piracy on Akampana's ship. Now, Akampana looks after the royal finances and accounts.'

'How can he help us with the Pushpak Vimaan?' asked Lakshman. 'Will he refuse to clear the bills for the vimaan's fuel?'

Naarad laughed. 'You are finally learning the art of humour, Prince Lakshman.'

Bharat laughed too. 'Coming back to the point,' he said, 'how can Lord Akampana help us?'

'The vimaan is very difficult to fly,' said Vibhishan. 'They have very few pilots. And the pilots were also soldiers. They fought in the battle today. They didn't survive.'

'And Akampana can fly the vimaan?'

'Yes. Among the senior officers and royalty, only Kumbhakarna Dada and Akampana knew how to fly the vimaan. So, now, there is only Akampana ...'

Bharat observed Vibhishan keenly. The Lankan prince was least perturbed by the fact that his elder brother had been killed today. *Strange family ...*

He looked at Ram. Who was probably thinking the same thing.

Ram spoke up. 'And if Minister Akampana is on our side, he can, at the right time ...'

'Precisely.'

The soldiers were now packing the massive ivory tusk in a large cloth. They knew it was to be sent to Raavan, inside Sigiriya.

'But why will he help us?' Bharat asked Vibhishan. 'What is his angle in this?'

It was Naarad who answered. 'The thing with Akampana is this: he was born crying. And he never stopped.'

Bharat laughed. 'That's a good one, Naaradji. But it's not an answer to my question.'

'Akampana is always worried about what can go wrong,' said Vibhishan. 'I have never known a more pessimistic man. And the mood in the Lankan camp today would be that everything has gone wrong. That they will almost certainly lose it all tomorrow. Even an honourable defeat may be difficult. Akampana would want to keep his options open.'

'Hmm, then let's contact him,' said Ram. 'Prince Vibhishan, what do you need from us?'

'What can I offer him?'

'Whatever you feel appropriate. I trust you. Naaradji can also go with you to help in the negotiations.'

Vibhishan nodded. 'I will bring him to our side, King Ram.'

— JF J,5D —

'We need a back-up plan,' said Ram.

The four brothers were sitting together for a late lunch in Ram's tent. Their wounds had been washed and dressed. Their bodies freshly bathed and oiled.

'Yes,' said Lakshman. 'I'm not sure Vibhishan will succeed.'

'I think Dada doesn't trust Prince Vibhishan completely,' said Bharat. He knew that Ram's conduct suggested that he trusted his followers completely. But both of them had also set up a very efficient and discreet spy system within the army. To ensure that they were aware of the exact goings-on among their troops. They wouldn't allow anyone to do to them what

Vibhishan had done to Lanka. Don't just look at your enemies without, also focus on the traitors within, Ram had told Bharat once.

'I don't trust him completely either,' said Shatrughan. 'A traitor to his family will also be a traitor to his friends if it suits him.'

'Anyway,' said Ram, 'this is not about Prince Vibhishan. This is about the Pushpak Vimaan. If Prince Indrajit uses the vimaan well, he will devastate and scatter our infantry formations. Imagine arrows and fire raining down on us from the skies. Imagine the tremendous roar of the vimaan rotors, and the impact it will have on our elephants. They might run in panic, causing devastation among our own soldiers. Hanumanji and Angad are sure that the mahouts will be able to control the elephants, but the risk to the infantry remains. It's critical that we have a back-up plan, just in case Minister Akampana doesn't deliver.'

Bharat nodded. 'Agreed.'

'So, this is what we will do ...' said Ram, leaning close to his brothers.

— Jᖴ ᒐᢖD —

The massively muscled Lakshman stood tall atop the elephant howdah, his feet shoulder-width apart. He gripped the triceps muscle of his left arm above the elbow with his right hand. Holding the grip, he pulled the left arm across his chest. He felt the stretch on his left shoulder and sighed in pleasure as his muscles relaxed, stimulating increased blood flow. Better circulation would aid oxygen availability and rid the muscles of lactic acid accumulation, reducing the likelihood of cramping.

He then reversed the hold and stretched his right shoulder. Sighing once again.

'Enough, already!' grumbled Bharat, from atop another elephant howdah to the side of Lakshman's pachyderm. 'I've finished my stretches.'

Lakshman turned to Bharat, and with complete insouciance, answered, 'Dada, please understand … More muscles. Longer stretches.'

Bharat raised an eyebrow, a crooked smile playing on his face. He had a pretty impressive physique as well. By most standards. At five feet, ten inches tall, he was well built through regular exercise and a good diet. But Lakshman was a good one foot taller at six feet, ten inches, and built like a bull. Some battles are best left unfought. 'All right, all right … Let's get started now.'

Lakshman grinned and picked up a spear from the weapons hold. He held it high above his right shoulder. His grip, perfect; the spear shaft flat on the palm of his hand, between the index and middle finger, the thumb pointing backward, while the rest of the fingers faced the other direction. He placed his right leg back, his foot perpendicular to his body. The left leg was up front, the foot pointing forward. Left arm raised high, elbow straight and rigid, palm facing down. The body was twisted slightly to the right, to give the required momentum to the throw. Back arched. Eyes towards the sky.

'Release!' ordered Lakshman loudly.

A captured white-throated needletail bird was released from a treetop. The bird was perfect for the task. Bred in Central Asia, it wintered in the Indian subcontinent and was among the fastest flying creatures. The needletail had a length of just twenty centimetres and a wingspan of forty-five. It provided a very small, fast-moving target.

Perfect.

Throw ... thought Bharat.

But Lakshman waited. Letting the bird soar higher. Farther away. Raising the challenge. Literally.

Throw, Lakshman ...

Just when it appeared that the bird was getting away, Lakshman whipped his body to the left, putting the fearsome power of his formidable shoulder and back into the throw. He flung the spear, spurring its momentum with a flick of his wrist and fingers. The spear shot up high with awe-inspiring force and speed. It appeared headed slightly ahead of the flight path of the bird. But Lakshman's instincts had calculated the increasing acceleration of the swift bird with precision.

The missile walloped ferociously into the needletail, its sharp metallic head slicing the bird into two. The spear soared farther ahead, barely slowing down. Blood sprayed like a cosmic jet and coloured the sky with a speck of red as the bisected body of the bird fell to the earth in two neatly cleaved halves.

Lakshman pulled his hands together into a namaste and bowed to the bird, seeking forgiveness for what had to be done.

'Woah ...' said Bharat.

Lakshman looked at his brother and smiled jauntily.

Bharat nodded, his lip curled up on one side as if an acknowledgement was being prised out. But a compliment was due. 'Not bad ... Not bad at all ...'

Lakshman laughed. 'Not bad? That was awesome, Dada ...'

'Yes, it was,' laughed Bharat. 'That was awesome.'

'Your turn.'

Bharat stretched again. And prepared himself. The next bird was released. Bharat flung his spear with perfect timing. Earlier. At a lower height. Less flashy. But it hit the bird and killed it instantly.

'That too was awesome, Dada!' said Lakshman.

'Only twenty more birds to practice on,' said Bharat.

Ram had suggested that they not overdo it. It was important that they not strain their muscles. But the brothers had decided that 'practice makes perfect'.

Picking up another spear, Lakshman called out, 'Next ...'

Ram and Shatrughan were busy with other things. Ram was training his infantry on new formations, preparing for the Pushpak Vimaan attacks. And Shatrughan was designing and fabricating some extra-protective gear for the elephants and horses. Gear that Ram believed would be critical for battle the next day.

Chapter 35

'If only he had listened to me, none of this would have happened ...' cried Kaikesi, Raavan's mother. She was with her half-daughter Shurpanakha, standing in one corner of the royal hospital chamber.

Kaikesi had come back to Sigiriya from Gokarna and had been provided safe passage through the Ayodhyan siege, as per Ram's orders. She was in the hospital now, mourning the passing of her favourite son, Kumbhakarna, and her brother, Mareech.

The ostensible reason for her return was her desire to morally support her sons in this war. But Raavan knew better. She was here to torture him. One last time.

He overheard his mother's apparently whispered words and ignored them. He knew in his heart that she had deliberately ensured that he heard her.

She lived the good life, feeding off his success. And yet, she ill-treated him the most.

But he didn't want to waste his time on her. His attention was focused on the one who he knew he had ill-treated.

Kumbhakarna's body lay on top of the operation table in the centre. It was already exhibiting signs of rigor mortis. Raavan held his brother's right hand, the fingers stiff and unbending. The extremities of the body become rigid first.

The royal physician was making the death mask, even though this was not, technically, a medical process. To start with, the physician had applied grease to the face and facial hair. This was to prevent the hair from sticking to the plaster. Then plaster was carefully layered upon the face to capture every single detail.

As the plaster was applied, Kumbhakarna's face was progressively hidden behind a white gooey cover. Kaikesi began to wail even more loudly, beating her chest and tearing out her hair. 'I can't even see my son anymore! I can't even see my son anymore!' Kaikesi lamented theatrically, apparently losing her ability to breathe as well. She was panting desperately now.

The physician stopped and turned to his attendant, signalling him to go check on the queen mother. Raavan stopped them with a slight hand gesture. 'Focus on my brother,' growled Raavan softly, straining to control the expletives that he wanted to hurl at his mother. His navel had been hurting excruciatingly for the last few hours. It was unbearable now.

The physician got back to work on Kumbhakarna. He smeared more and more layers of plaster. The more the layers, the stronger the cast. While it normally took an hour or two for the plaster to dry into a cast mould, the Lankan physicians had developed a new formulation that dried in fifteen to twenty minutes.

For Raavan, it was fifteen to twenty minutes with his mother's howling lamentations in the background. Finally, he turned to her. 'Why don't you ... Why don't you wait with Mareech uncle's body? His death mask has already been prepared. And the physicians are—'

'You want to make me see my brother's body again?' screeched Kaikesi. 'Have you even seen what the elephants did to his body?! There was almost nothing left after they trampled him to death! Just the head and some parts of the torso!' Kaikesi took a break from her screaming and began to sob loudly again. And in between her wailing and bawling, she managed to shriek some more. 'I will ... I will die if I have to ... have to ... see Mareech Dada again! Are you trying to ... kill me, Raavan?! Why do you ... hate me so much?! I am your mother!!'

Kaikesi dramatically began beating her chest. Banging her hands against the wall. Cursing her fate.

Raavan tried to control himself. His navel ached desperately. 'Then why don't you wait in your chambers, mother? I will call you when Kumbhakarna's death mask is ready.'

'I am not leaving!' hollered Kaikesi angrily.

'Please ...' said Raavan, holding his head. 'I have just lost ... Please ... Don't irritate me.'

'It was because of you that he died! You caused this war! I have lost my good son because of you!'

Raavan would have so loved to draw his sword on his mother. But he knew that Kumbhakarna's soul was around. His brother wouldn't approve of even a rude word thrown at their mother. Raavan turned to Shurpanakha. Normally, she would have rushed to obey an order, even an implied and silent one. But she just stood there. Disdain on her face.

Perhaps she thinks Vibhishan is already king in my stead.

Raavan turned to his guards. 'Please escort the queen mother to her chambers.'

Kaikesi did not fight the guards. But she did keep muttering loudly as she walked out. Complaining that her good son was gone because of the curse that had afflicted her womb sixty-one years ago. Shurpanakha followed her half-mother out of the room, glaring at Raavan.

The royal physician looked down. Too embarrassed to glance at his king.

Raavan looked at the gooey white plaster that concealed his brother's face. He clung to Kumbhakarna's hand.

There was nothing to do now but wait.

His left arm was cramping. It was in a sling. The arrow heads had been removed, antiseptic ointment applied and *guduchi* stitches sown. The shrapnel from his right eye had been removed and the wound had been cleaned and bandaged. Numerous other wounds all over his body had also been medicated and bandaged. And he had been given herbal infusions to rebuild his strength. The battle would, after all, resume the next day.

The doctors had advised some rest. Raavan couldn't do that. He had to be there for his brother. He had often ill-treated Kumbhakarna when he was alive. He had to make up for it now.

'It's time, my lord,' said the physician.

Raavan looked at the prahar lamp clock. And realised that twenty minutes had passed. 'All right. Go ahead.'

The mould had hardened well. It simply came off Kumbhakarna's face with a pop. The physician cleaned the inner side of the mould with a soft felt cloth, while an assistant cleaned Kumbhakarna's face. All traces of plaster and grease were removed. The physician, meanwhile, started pouring liquid molten wax into the mould.

Raavan looked at him, puzzled.

'This is just for back-up, my lord,' explained the physician. 'A copy of the mould in wax. In case, we need to use it later. We will use the same mould to make a bronze death mask of Prince Kumbhakarna. It will be ready by late tonight.'

'Please make two bronze death masks,' said Raavan.

This was against the standard rituals. Only one death mask was supposed to be made. But the physician wasn't about to argue with his liege. 'Of course, my lord.'

Raavan continued to hold his brother's hand.

'Do we …' asked the physician carefully. 'I mean the body.'

'Not here,' said Raavan. 'We will not bury Kumbhakarna here. We will bury him back in my homeland. Close to where we both were born.'

'All right, my lord. Then what do we do with …'

'You will create a freezing room. You will preserve my brother's body.'

'Yes, my lord.'

'And …'

The physician waited. Surprised at Raavan's hesitation.

'And,' continued Raavan, 'if either Indrajit or I die, you will keep our bodies here in frozen condition. They will be taken home for burial when appropriate. You will also create two bronze death masks for each of us. You will receive your orders from one who will understand my desire.'

The physician suddenly straightened up. 'You will win tomorrow, my lord! We will mutilate the corpses of your deplorable enemies and then—'

'Just shut up and do what I am telling you to do,' growled Raavan, irritated.

'Yes, my lord.'

— Jᖴ ⅃5D —

Sita looked up as she heard the rustle of the leaves.

It was late in the evening, and she was sitting in the veranda of her cottage within the Ashok Vatika. Chanting to the

Mother Goddess, with a rosary of one hundred and eight beads. Chanting for the protection of her husband and his army.

She saw Raavan at the edge of the clearing. On a wheelchair, being pushed by a soldier. His left arm was in a sling. A bandage was tied across his right eye, and also around multiple other wounds on his body. He was followed by a bodyguard platoon of twenty soldiers. Sita looked behind Raavan. No Kumbhakarna.

Oh Lord Rudra … Have mercy …

Despite knowing that he fought on the side of her husband's enemies, despite knowing that this day would come, her heart felt burdened with grief. She mourned for the gentle giant.

Kumbhakarna.

He was a hero. A hero on the wrong side. A hero who fought for *adharma*. But a hero, nonetheless.

In a war, no one side has a monopoly on heroes.

Raavan was wheeled to Sita's presence. With a wave of his hand, he dismissed his guards. They walked back to the treeline, well out of ear shot.

'I'm so sorry …' said Sita, her eyes moist, her hands folded together into a namaste in honour of the departed soul.

'I should have died before him …' said Raavan. 'He was a better man than me …'

'Perhaps this, too, is your burden to bear.'

Raavan shook his head. 'No … Truthfully, I was a burden on him … Always … He is free of me now …'

Sita didn't respond. But she knew in her heart that Raavan was right.

Raavan looked around him. 'I still feel his presence … As if his soul watches over me.'

'How did he go?' asked Sita.

'Like the courageous warrior that he was …'

And Sita listened as Raavan described the Battle of the Left Flank. She was awestruck by the astounding courage of Kumbhakarna. At the same time, though, she was also amazed by her husband's brilliant strategy and Hanuman's battle tactics.

'Kumbhakarnaji died a warrior's death,' said Sita, once Raavan completed the tale. 'He will be honoured by the ancestors in *pitralok* when his soul crosses the Vaitarni River.'

Vedic people believed that, after death, the soul of the deceased remained on earth for thirteen days, till the funeral rites of the body it inhabited were completed. And then the soul crossed the mythical Vaitarni River to the *land of the ancestors, pitralok*. *Pitralok* was beyond the constraints of time and space. Three generations of ancestors remained in *pitralok*. And generations beyond either came back to earth for their next life, or attained *moksha, liberation from the cycle of rebirths*.

'I'll be with him soon …'

Sita looked at Raavan's wheelchair, a quizzical expression on her face.

'I will fight tomorrow,' said Raavan, clarifying. 'My right leg is injured, but I am able to walk. This is only a precaution my doctors insisted upon. So that my legs have a chance to recuperate.'

Sita nodded. Still quiet.

'You were right,' said Raavan. 'Your husband is a brilliant general.'

'He is.'

'And a good leader. He has forged four disparate armies into one tight fighting unit.'

'Hmm.'

'My son, Indrajit, is trying his best. He does not surrender easily. He has had a brilliant idea. Let's see …'

Sita nodded. 'Let's see …'

Raavan took a deep breath. He reached into a side pocket in his wheelchair and pulled out Kumbhakarna's death mask. Sita arose and accepted the death mask from Raavan. With both hands. Respectfully.

She stared at the mask. It had recorded for posterity the final moment of Kumbhakarna's life. Suffused not by pain but happiness.

Many incarnations go by before one is blessed with a death that makes a soul smile.

'It was Hanuman ...' said Raavan. 'He was there ... At the final moment ... With Kumbha ... Whatever they said to each other – I don't know, but my brother left with peace. And happiness.'

Sita bowed her head in respect to the death mask.

'We have distinct ceremonies in our sub-community of Brahmins,' said Raavan.

'Yes. I am aware of that. Kumbhakarnaji had told me.'

'The ...' Raavan struggled with his words.

Sita waited. Silently.

'The straw replica of Kumbha's body is ready for cremation. And his corpse remains in the Sigiriya royal hospital ... In frozen condition.'

Sita knew what she would have to do. But she waited for Raavan to spell it out.

'I've given instructions that my body should also be treated the same way ... Hopefully, Indrajit will live ... But if not, his body will also ... Once I am dead, and if Indrajit also dies, can you ensure that all our bodies are buried in the land where we were born? It's a village close to Yamunaji. Far to the north. It's called—'

'Sinauli,' said Sita, completing Raavan's sentence. 'I know. Kumbhakarnaji told me.'

'Also, my uncle Mareech … He was a good man … His corpse remains in refrigeration in the royal hospital as well. If his body can also be …'

'I will ensure it.'

'Thank you. I don't care what is done with the rest of the royal family.'

'We fight under the banner of Ram. All non-combatants will be treated well.'

Raavan laughed softly. 'Feel free to treat the rest of my royal family well. But don't trust them. Except my wife, Mandodari. She's a hard nut, but she is a good woman.'

Sita nodded.

Just then it began to drizzle. Some soldiers silently ran up and fixed an umbrella into a cupped cavity on Raavan's wheelchair. They gave an umbrella to Sita as well. And then, just as silently, they retreated to the treeline.

Raavan tilted the umbrella with his left hand and turned his face up. He let the rain drops moisten his face. He looked down and readjusted the umbrella before the bandage over his right eye could become wet.

'I will be with her soon,' said Raavan, smiling slightly, rubbing his face.

Sita smiled too.

It was time to go. Just one last thing left to do. Raavan took a deep breath and touched his gold chain. He unclipped the clasp and removed his pendant. The pendant made from Vedavati's finger-bones.

'What are you doing?' asked Sita, raising her hands in a gesture of denial.

Raavan stared at Sita. He held the pendant in his hands. 'To you and me, these are the relics of a Goddess. To anyone else, they are just bones. You should keep it.'

'I have one already,' said Sita, holding her mother's bone pendant. It hung on a black thread around her neck. 'You still need her.'

'I am going to her in any case,' smiled Raavan.

'Don't just go to her. Go with her.'

Raavan smiled.

'Whenever you pass to the other side—'

Raavan interrupted Sita. 'It will probably be tomorrow.'

Sita ignored Raavan's interruption. 'Whenever you pass to the other side, it will be my personal responsibility to ensure that this finger pendant is with you in your burial chamber.'

Raavan took a deep breath, his eyes moistening. Only a little.

'Tears can fester inside the body,' said Sita. 'There is no dishonour in letting them flow.'

'The tears will, anyway, get hidden in the rain ...' Raavan smiled, wiping his left, good eye. 'My grief and anger will die with my death. I will be free. I will be healed.'

The pain in Raavan's navel had reduced. The thought of the release of death helped.

'You are healed when you remember rather than relive. For then you can smile with your heart...'

'Hmm ... Then I can smile with my heart ...' Raavan fixed Vedavati's pendant back on his gold chain. 'Don't forget your promise to me. I need her help in my burial chamber.'

'I will not forget.'

'Well, then ... there is nothing more to be said,' said Raavan. 'Except, farewell ...'

'Farewell, noble princess. You will always be a Vishnu to me.'

'Farewell, brave king.'

—Jf J5D—

'It's not over,' said Akampana firmly. 'Prince Indrajit can turn things around.'

'Then why have you agreed to meet us here?' asked Naarad. 'There is nothing to talk about.'

Vibhishan and Naarad had made their way stealthily to Sigiriya's outskirts on the southern side, far from the Ayodhya war camp. Akampana had joined them there, using one of the tiny secret tunnels through the walls; the tunnels that smugglers normally utilised during peace time to avoid customs duties at the city gates. The trio had met beyond the open land surrounding the outer walls, within the forest treeline, far from prying eyes. Though the moonless night ensured that even if prying eyes were on the lookout, there was little they would see.

'Then I should leave,' said Akampana, always on edge.

'Calm down, my friend,' said Vibhishan, reaching out and holding Akampana by the shoulders.

Vibhishan cast a stern, reproachful look at Naarad, apparently admonishing him. Only apparently though. They were playing the traditional good cop–bad cop routine. A nervous Akampana had to be cajoled into this.

'What do you want, Vibhishan?' asked Akampana.

'You are intelligent enough to know what we want,' said Vibhishan. 'I don't need to spell it out.'

'If I refuse to fly the vimaan, I will be executed.'

'But we are not asking you to not fly it.'

Akampana frowned. Then his eyes opened wide as he understood what they were planning. 'Are you mad? That is impossible.'

'You don't worry about what is impossible and what is not,' said Naarad. 'Leave that to us. Are you in or are you out?'

'There is no way you will succeed. Do you know how fast the Pushpak Vimaan moves? It is impossible for any of you to—'

'Good for you then,' interrupted Naarad. 'You will become the hero who helped Indrajit defeat the Ayodhyans. The rewards will be great.'

Akampana didn't say anything, but his indecision was writ large on his face.

Vibhishan said, 'My friend, you face no risk. You have been given the greatest privilege that anyone caught between two warring sides can receive. You can play both sides. And whichever side wins, you will be their hero.'

'But this is impossible, I tell you,' said Akampana. 'The vimaan moves too fast. And the door is too small. Arrows will be useless, due to the distance as well as the solid armour of Prince Indrajit. It has to be a—'

'Leave that to us, my friend,' interrupted Vibhishan, as he pointed to a spot on the map he was holding. 'Just fly the vimaan close to the treeline at this point. With the door facing the forest. Do that once. Just once.'

Akampana remained silent. Staring at the map. Shaking his head.

'Akampana?' asked Vibhishan.

Akampana looked at Vibhishan and Naarad. 'This is impossible. No one can fling a spear that far into the distance with accuracy. You can either get accuracy or distance. You cannot get both.'

'Thank you for the spear-throwing lesson,' said Naarad. 'Now, are we doing this or not?'

'Akampana,' said Vibhishan, his voice calm and gentle. 'You know that, even with the Pushpak Vimaan, Indrajit can only delay the inevitable. We have the elephants, Lanka doesn't. We have a large cavalry, Lanka doesn't any more. And we have more infantry than Lanka. We will win. It's a matter of time. And I will become the king of Lanka when the war is over. It's not a question of if, but when. It's just about cutting Lanka's losses now. The longer the war takes, the more Lanka will lose. You know that. You support us now, and I will remember what you did for us.'

'So, what will it be, Akampana?' asked Naarad.

Akampana nodded briefly. And then turned and ran. Quickly. Towards the outer wall of Sigiriya.

Chapter 36

Indrajit was waiting patiently. Sitting on the ground. He knew his mother. She could not be disturbed during her meditation. Never.

Mandodari sat in the lotus position on the terrace outside her simple hut. Mandodari's simple hut, made of wood and stone. A home for an ascetic. It was a short distance away from the monolith, Lion's Rock, upon which stood Raavan's fabulously opulent palace complex. It was within the garden complex that surrounded Lion's Rock, guarded by fierce Lankan soldiers. Except for that tiny surrender to the requirements of security, Mandodari had refused to compromise on her choice of life. She had steadfastly spurned the life of luxuries that, she said, had been paid for by crimes and piracy. By *adharma*.

She was very clear: if I live a life of luxuries provided by my husband's life of crime, then I am a partner in his crime. If the tree is poisonous, the fruit of that tree will be poisonous as well.

A simple maxim. But it took a woman of Mandodari's clear conscience to put it into practice.

She wore a simple, saffron coloured cotton *dhoti*, blouse and angvastram. Saffron, the colour of *sanyasins, women hermits,* who had detached themselves from the world. A woman of average height, she was fair-skinned and slightly overweight. Her straight brown hair was combed back fastidiously and tied into a plait. Her nails were cut short and her hands were hard and calloused as she had refused all personal staff, preferring to look after her home by herself. A gentle smile played on her face always, hinting at a life lived in consonance with dharma. Nothing about her physical appearance conveyed her steely character. Except her eyes. Her dark, strong-willed, captivating eyes that revealed her unbending, righteous spirit.

The eyes were closed right now.

Indrajit recalled a conversation with his mother. He was sixteen at the time.

'Life, at its core, is very simple, my son,' Mandodari had said. *'We build complicated nonsense around it to avoid looking at the simple truth. Maybe because the truth troubles us. Maybe because the truth makes us unhappy. And so, we waste our lives living a lie.'*

Indrajit had said nothing. Just listened quietly. He had recently found out about Vedavati, the Kanyakumari; apparently, the love of his father's life. It had redeemed his father in his eyes, somehow. A father he had despised earlier for his debauchery and life of excess.

He was shocked to discover that his mother already knew about Vedavati.

'You live in the fond hope, my son, that there is some good in your father. Like your uncle Kumbhakarna does. You uncle is a good man, who is wasting his life living a lie. The lie that your father could ever have been a good man. Do you think your father would have been different had the Kanyakumari lived here with us in Lanka, rather than in the Land of our Ancestors?'

Indrajit had nodded. 'I think he could have been a better man, Maa.'

'No,' Mandodari had answered. 'It's the nature of the beast. Your father would have behaved himself for a while. A short while … to impress the Kanyakumari. But his innate nature would have ultimately prevailed. The Kanyakumari, Vedavatiji, was lucky that she passed away before she could be disappointed by Raavan. Otherwise disappointment would have been inevitable. The true nature of the beast, ultimately, always prevails.'

Indrajit had shifted uncomfortably. Like any good son, he wished to love his father. Even if his father gave him no cause for it. And he was clinging, with fond hope, to the one thing that indicated to him that his father was more than just a cruel, selfish, debauched pirate. An extremely capable pirate, with fearsome intelligence and extraordinary talent. But a pirate, nonetheless.

'My son,' Mandodari had continued, 'it is said that power corrupts, and absolute power corrupts absolutely. It is not so simple. Power doesn't corrupt, it simply unveils. The hidden character of a man remains what it is. Whether in power or not. Power just brings it all out in the open. Why? Because a powerful man thinks he can get away with it. You will be a king someday. And a king must always see things for what they are, in all their ugly truth, rather than what he would like them to be. The delusional view should be left to fools in universities; let them formulate air-headed theories. Kings and administrators need to live in the real world. That is the only way they can actually do their jobs. So many silly fallacies and maxims float in this world. Like 'All people are decent at their core'. Or 'All religions are the same and none of them preach hatred'. Or 'All cultures are worthy of respect'. The truth is ugly. All people are not fundamentally decent. Some are actually good, and some are actually bad. All religions are not the same, and some do preach hatred. Just read their scriptures. Some cultures are better than others. That is reality. Strip the nonsense away and have the

courage to see the simple truth. Remember, life is not complicated. It is simple. We make it complicated to avoid seeing the simple truths that trouble us. Don't we?'

'Yes, Maa.'

'And you have to understand the truth about your father and yourself. You will be a warrior when you grow up. In many aspects you already are.'

'Yes, Maa.'

'Warriors are so male. With all their masculine glory and also its hideousness. Some willing to sacrifice their lives to protect the weak. And others willing to kill and rob to get what they desire. We – the ordinary people – we cannot have a normal relationship with warriors. We either admire them beyond limits or despise them so much that we cannot even bear to see them exist. We either worship them like Warrior-Gods or despise them like Warrior-Devils. There is no middle ground.'

Indrajit remained silent.

'You will be a God, my son. You will not be like your father. You will conduct yourself in a manner that is worthy of admiration.'

'Yes, Maa,' said Indrajit, out loud.

Mandodari opened her eyes. And smiled, seeing her son. 'When did you come, my child? Have you been waiting long?'

Indrajit shook his head. 'Not too long, Maa.'

Mandodari patted Indrajit's hand gently.

'Maa, Kumbhakarna uncle …'

'I know. I was praying for him …' said Mandodari. 'He was a good man. A dharmic man. I prayed that the wheel of *dharma* would bless him with an easier life the next time. He deserves it.'

Indrajit nodded. 'And also …'

'Yes, I prayed for your Mareech grand-uncle as well. He was loyal to the family. Always. He saved your father's and Kumbhakarna uncle's lives many times. Om *Shanti*.'

The Vedic Indians acknowledged a soul's journey as it leaves a body with two words: Om *Shanti*. Thereby wishing for *peace*, and, hopefully, moksha for the departed soul.

'Om *Shanti*,' repeated Indrajit.

Mandodari waited silently for her son to bring up what he wanted to speak about.

'Maa …'

Mandodari waited.

'Tomorrow is a difficult day. We have lost most of our commanders today. Practically, all our cavalry. More than half our infantry. Our army is, I think, almost permanently broken.'

Mandodari continued to wait for Indrajit to arrive at his question.

'I am attempting something unorthodox tomorrow,' said Indrajit. 'I don't know if it will succeed.'

'The Pushpak Vimaan?'

'Yes.'

'I think you could succeed.'

'Really?!' Indrajit was surprised.

'What is your definition of success in this battle?'

'Defeating the Ayodhyans.'

Mandodari remained silent. But her eyes clearly conveyed that she didn't think that was likely.

'What would you call success?' asked Indrajit.

'Peace.'

'Why will the Ayodhyans give us the option of peace? They have us outmanoeuvred.'

'King Ram will … once your father is dead.'

'Maaaa …' Indrajit knew that his mother detested his father. But to speak so casually of his death, in the middle of a battle.

'I am only speaking the truth to you, my child.'

Indrajit didn't respond.

'Once your father dies, only you will be left. Offer peace to King Ram then. He will accept.'

'Why would he?'

'Do you remember that we had spoken about two types of warriors? Many years ago?'

'Yes, Maa. The Warrior-God and the Warrior-Devil.'

'Yes. The Warrior-Gods fight to protect that which is precious. And the Warrior-Devils kill to loot that which is precious. You are a Warrior-God. As is King Ram, from what I have heard. There is much that Lanka can learn from him. How to mould an army, for instance, into one that fights for Good, rather than one that plunders kingdoms, rapes women and murders innocents. But, also, there is much that King Ram can learn from Lanka. How to not destroy their *trader* class, for example; for destroying your *Vaishya* community only guarantees poverty for everyone, as the Sapt Sindhu kings have done. Once your father is gone, King Ram will accept peace. Trust me.'

'But Maa, what I have …'

'But peace must be attained from a position of strength, Indrajit,' interrupted Mandodari. 'Not from weakness. The Lankans have lost too much today. You can balance that by causing some losses in the Ayodhyan forces with your Pushpak Vimaan. And hope that your father dies tomorrow. No peace is possible till he is alive.'

'Maaaaa …' Indrajit's eyes conveyed his disapproval.

'I will only think of what is good for our land, not what is good for your father. Only the nation matters, Indrajit. Only the nation is *most precious. Desh sarvopari.*'

Indrajit didn't say anything.

'Also, don't waste time trying to kill their infantry soldiers tomorrow,' Mandodari continued. 'You cannot kill that many by firing arrows and throwing spears from the narrow door of the Pushpak Vimaan.'

'Then what should I do?'

'Go for their main strength.'

'Their elephants?' asked Indrajit, flummoxed.

'Yes.'

'What can I do to armoured elephants with spears and arrows? I will not cause enough damage.'

'You cannot do much to elephants, sure,' said Mandodari. 'But you can do a lot to those who control the elephants.'

Indrajit smiled at the simple brilliance of the idea.

'I have always wondered, Maa,' said Indrajit. 'How come you know so much about everything? Including even the art of war?'

Mandodari smiled. 'Life is all about learning how to live, my son. As Seneca – the great intellectual living far to our west – once said, *As long as you live, keep learning how to live.*''

Indrajit smiled. 'Only the Gods know what role you may yet play for the good of others and for our motherland, Maa.'

Mandodari leaned over and kissed her son's forehead. 'The only role that I wish to play, my child, is that of a proud mother. The proud mother of a magnificent man.'

— J⁺ ⫫⑃D —

'Is it hurting?' asked Shatrughan.

Lakshman and Shatrughan were sitting outside Shatrughan's tent. They were eating together. A camp doctor had massaged Lakshman's strained shoulder with a mixture of mahanarayan and ashwagandha oil. And then wrapped it tight with a warm cloth.

'No,' answered Lakshman. 'It's not hurting. Just a bit strained with the practice this afternoon. I want it to remain strong tomorrow.'

'Hmm … Do you think the battle will end tomorrow?'

'Let's see … I will be surprised if it does. The Lankans won't surrender so easily. Where are the dadas?'

'Both have gone towards the city walls. Some war strategy, I guess.'

—JF JᵣɔD—

'I think the war will end tomorrow if we can neutralise the Pushpak Vimaan,' said Ram.

'I agree,' said Bharat. 'They will have no other move left.'

'Either Lakshman or you must get him.'

'We will, Dada.'

'They will be better prepared for our elephants tomorrow,' said Ram. 'Shatrughan has quickly got some extra armour manufactured for our elephants.'

'I have seen that. I've asked both Hanumanji and Angad to ensure that all our elephants are covered with the extra armour.'

'Hmm …'

'This is hardly a reason to delay dinner, Dada,' said Bharat. 'Why have you brought me here?'

'Because if the war ends tomorrow, we need to be clear on how we intend to manage the peace. Especially how our army will enter the city. We cannot allow even a single instance of looting or random killing.'

'I agree. For we may need Lanka as an ally for our future battles.'

'Correct.'

'So, what's your plan?' asked Bharat.

Chapter 37

The second day of the Battle of Sigiriya dawned.

The Lankan troops had made their formations outside the walls again. The militias belonging to the Gokarna business guilds had slipped away the previous evening, using an old contractual clause, which stated that the guilds have the right to recall their soldiers if their own security was at risk. The result was that the Lankan infantry numbers were further reduced from ninety thousand to only sixty-five thousand.

An army built on promises of plunder and wealth suffers desertions at the first sign of serious trouble. On the other hand, an army built on the far more precious emotion of patriotism will fight to the last man.

Ideas are more powerful than wealth and weapons. Few get this. And those who do, rule the world.

Most of Raavan's great generals, along with the cavalry and chariot corps, had been killed in battle the previous day. And his best general still alive, Indrajit, was in the city. With the

Pushpak Vimaan. Raavan had one other good general, the ruthless but efficient Prahast. And his brigade-level officers were also still available. Supported by them, he was supervising the infantry formations now. He had a plan for the Ayodhyan elephant corps. It wasn't about killing the elephants, for that was almost impossible now. This was a survival plan. While Indrajit carried out his aerial attack and damage the heart of the Ayodhyan lines.

Raavan's left bicep had been washed with ointments and then wrapped tight with a thick cloth bandage. It allowed for some movement of the damaged muscles. The left arm had been tied to the shield. He would use it as defence. He wore an eye patch to cover his surgically removed right eye; it had had to be removed or it would have turned septic. And he rode on his horse, to avoid putting weight on his injured right leg. The talented physicians of Lanka had given Raavan energy-enhancing infusions. They lent him the vigour he required to fight hard, and more importantly, to supervise the battle. Raavan had refused the painkillers. They would have dulled his faculties.

Physical pain can break a weak mind. But it has value to a mind that is strong. For it can bring focus.

While Raavan was readying his troop formation, at the other end of the field Ram, aided ably by his generals, was supervising the arrangement of his army divisions.

'When do you think Indrajit will fly in?' asked Arishtanemi, who by now had enormous respect for Ram's brilliant battle tactics.

'I am assuming he is unaware that we know about his plans with the vimaan,' said Ram, 'so, I think he'll come in late. When we have committed our infantry and are charging ahead.

Which is why our infantry must not move. We must draw Indrajit towards us. For only then will our trap work.'

'Only elephants, cavalry and chariots then,' said Angad, who was on the other side of Ram.

'Yes,' confirmed Ram. 'And, Lord Hanuman …'

'Yes, King Ram,' answered Hanuman.

'You know what you have to do.'

Hanuman looked towards the jungles. Behind the right flank. Where Bharat and Lakshman waited. In hiding. On two elephants. Hanuman had to lead Indrajit into the trap. His role was the riskiest in the battle plan. And, hence, the most glorious.

'I'll handle it,' said Hanuman. 'I'll draw Prince Indrajit towards the jungles.'

'And my brothers won't miss.'

'I know they won't.'

Ram nodded and reached out with both his hands. Hanuman held Ram at the forearms.

'Go with Lord Rudra,' said Ram.

'Go with Lord Parshu Ram,' answered Hanuman.

Then Ram extended his hands towards Angad. But Angad stepped forward and embraced Ram. The king of Ayodhya smiled and warmly hugged Angad. 'You destroyed many Lankans yesterday. Today is the day we end it all.'

'We will, Lord Ram,' Angad said, smiling.

Hanuman and Angad saluted Ram and left to take up position at the head of their respective elephant corps.

Arishtanemi and Ram mounted their horses. And rode to the front lines.

'Oh hell,' whispered Arishtanemi, pulling his horse up.

Ram looked at Arishtanemi. And then up towards the sky.

'Oh man …'

It had started raining close to the city walls. Upon the Lankan formation. But the clouds were moving. It was only a matter of time ...

'This island gets rain practically all year round,' said Arishtanemi. 'How the hell do they plan proper battles?'

And, just then, the rain began pelting down over the Ayodhyan formations as well.

Rain – especially the heavy rain that fell on the Indian subcontinent – made war exceptionally difficult. It drenched the ground, which made the movement of chariot wheels arduous. Chariots were all about speed and manoeuvrability. They had little role to play if they were bogged down in wet mud.

Raavan had no chariot corps left. Ram did.

Rain also made bowstrings soggy. It was difficult to shoot arrows using a dank string. And even if a talented archer managed to do so, the range was heavily compromised.

Raavan had a much smaller archer corps left with him. Ram had a full complement of archer corps.

Rain would mitigate some of Raavan's main weaknesses, and weaken some of Ram's key strengths.

Apparently.

'This is bad news,' said Arishtanemi.

'No ... I think the rain is good news,' answered Ram.

Arishtanemi turned to Ram. Confused. 'Are you thinking of our elephant corps?'

Rain or sunshine made no difference to the elephants. They could move even through marshy terrain. Elephants were known to swim when needed. Damp ground would not slow them down.

The rain would not notably diminish the effectiveness of Ram's elephant corps.

'No ... Not our elephants. Though they can still cause some serious devastation. The real benefit of the rain lies somewhere else.'

'Tell me.' Arishtanemi was really confused now.

'We need the rains to help us make them commit to the Pushpak Vimaan strategy,' said Ram.

Arishtanemi waited for Ram to explain.

'King Raavan and Prince Indrajit are talented generals. We must not underestimate them. They know that we have one hundred and sixty thousand troops and that they have only sixty-five thousand. We have a full chariot and cavalry corps. They have practically none. And we also have the elephant corps. And if, despite all this, we do not launch a full-scale attack, it would make them suspicious. They would suspect that we know about their plans with the Pushpak Vimaan. And they may then change their strategy.'

Arishtanemi smiled. The hallmark of a great general is the ability to read the mind of his enemy. 'So, we now have an apparently good reason to not charge in a full-scale attack? Without raising their suspicions. It is the rains after all!'

'Precisely,' said Ram. 'And if we don't charge with all our troops, then we are not vulnerable to the vimaan. Remember, this battle ends only when we take away the Pushpak Vimaan factor.'

'Do you think they will retreat behind their walls and wait for tomorrow?'

'No. King Raavan will lose even more men to desertion tonight. It will end today. Either way.'

Arishtanemi looked at the Lankan formations. They were ready. And waiting. The rain had slowed down a bit. It wasn't raining cats and dogs anymore. Just kittens and puppies.

'So, what are your orders?' asked Arishtanemi.

Ram touched his chin thoughtfully. 'Only our elephants. The rest will hold back.'

Arishtanemi turned to relay the orders.

'Just an echelon, Arishtanemiji,' added Ram.

An echelon would mean fifty elephants. A third of a single elephant corp.

A light attack. Not meant to cause serious damage. Just to provoke a response.

'Yes, my lord,' answered Arishtanemi.

In no time, fifty elephants thundered out from the Ayodhya ranks. The elephants were trumpeting loudly, their trunks thrust forward. Some archers atop the elephant howdahs began firing arrows as they neared the Lankan infantry lines. But the distance and their soggy bowstrings ensured that they did not cause too much damage.

The inadequacy in the arrows could be more than adequately compensated by the rumbling mass of elephant feet, though. For soldiers could be crushed to death under their weight.

Or so was the plan.

But Raavan was not out of tricks yet.

'Break formations!' ordered Raavan.

And, at an unbelievable speed, the Lankan lines reformed. Across the formations, soldiers moved quickly sidewards and five lines merged into one. This was done within a few minutes. Rapid speed. It had been practised repeatedly the previous evening, within the city walls.

The result was spectacular. A dense traditional *chaturanga* formation of Lankan infantry in two hundred lines seamlessly recoalesced to just forty lines, with massive open lanes in between.

A dense formation of soldiers would have been perfect for the elephants. A target-rich environment. Like the previous day.

Just crash through and stamp the Lankans in massive numbers. The resultant stampede would add to the mayhem.

Now, there was empty ground in thirty-nine broad lanes, with soldiers lined up in single-file on either side. All of a sudden.

The mahouts could have attempted to crash into the single files of Lankan soldiers, in a zig-zag manner. But that was risky. A golden rule in elephant charges: keep the elephants in their lane. For there is only one thing that can bring down an elephant quickly. Another elephant.

The risk of elephants running zigzag was that they would crash into each other. The entire Ayodhyan elephantry charge could collapse.

The elephant mahouts had no choice. They had to rush into the open lanes. And hope that the Ayodhyan soldiers atop the howdahs would kill as many Lankans on-ground as possible. With their spears and arrows.

But the bowstrings were wet. The arrows were not effective.

The elements seemed to be helping Raavan today.

The Ayodhyan warriors flung spears at the Lankans. They killed a few. But the bigger hope was to get them to break formation in panic. The Lankans though, in an awesome display of discipline, and despite the great fear of elephants stampeding so close to them, remained in formation. They stood firm.

And then Raavan unleashed his secret weapon.

Long axes.

Essentially, they were spears, with the pointed blade at the top edge replaced with an axe head. An axe head with a wickedly sharp metallic bit.

Raavan had learnt from the Battle of the Left Flank the previous day. Kumbhakarna had brought down two elephants. By slicing the legs and incapacitating the beasts.

The Lankan soldiers along the lines lifted the long axes which had been lying on the ground, undetected. And simply held them up. Intending to slice through as many elephant legs as possible. And bring them down.

But if Raavan had a secret weapon, then Ram had a secret shield!

Unfortunately for Raavan, Ram too had studied Kumbhakarna's tactics. And had quickly put Shatrughan to work, designing and fabricating a leather armour which ran down the outer side of the elephants' legs.

Most of the axe thrusts were ineffective.

Two struck through and drew blood. But not enough to bring down the pachyderms. The elephants swung their trunks in rage and swatted the axes away.

'There is no damage being caused, my lord,' said Arishtanemi. 'To them or to us. It's a stalemate.'

'We wait,' answered Ram.

'Why don't we send out a few infantry battalions?'

'No. We wait.'

'But …'

Arishtanemi stopped speaking when he heard the sound. The unmistakeable sound.

Whump! Whump!

Whump! Whump!

He looked at Ram.

Ram nodded. 'Finally …' He turned to his flagbearer. 'Message for Hanumanji … The Pushpak Vimaan is coming …'

The message was relayed quickly to the right flank.

Meanwhile, all the faces of the Ayodhyan infantry were turned towards the sky.

Whump! Whump!

A roar went up from the Lankans. Their champion was coming!

War elephants, like most beasts of war, are trained for loud battle noise. Even so, the thundering blast of the flying machine was alarming. Some elephants charging down the Lankan ranks stopped in their tracks. The expert mahouts started turning the elephants around. To get them to retreat, even as they whispered calming messages to them, through signals from their feet on the beasts' temples.

And then …

The vimaan swiftly emerged from high above the fort walls. Like the sudden appearance of a demonic monster. Colossal. Shaped like an inverted cone that gently tapered upwards. The massive main rotor at the top of the cone rotating rhythmically, like the giant slices of a mammoth sword. There were many small manoeuvring rotors close to the broad base, which controlled directional movement. They were whirring smoothly. The portholes at the base of the vimaan were sealed with thick glass, soldiers clearly visible behind them. The main door was ajar. Two warriors plainly outlined against the opening. One of them was the prince of Lanka. Indrajit. Dressed in black dhoti, tied tight in the military style. A sleeveless armour covered his torso. A bow in his left hand. A rope tied around his waist, which was hooked farther inside the vimaan; to ensure that he did not topple out with any sudden movement.

He turned around and shouted an order to the pilot. Akampana.

The vimaan dipped lower. Bearing down quickly upon the enemy.

Whump!

Whump!

Whump!

Whump!

Raavan looked at the vimaan. 'Go get them, son!'

Across the battlefield, Ram bellowed his order. 'Cover!'

Orders were rapidly relayed out through flag signals,

The infantry had been trained well, the previous day. They quickly held up their massive shields. Laid them flat above their heads. Each soldier's shield partially covered the soldier ahead and behind him. Within seconds, the Ayodhyan infantry regiments looked, from the air, like massive turtles: the hard shell made from many shields. Protecting the soldiers from assaults from the sky. They were metallic shields, coated with leather. Strong. Waterproof. Providing protection against arrows, spears and even burning oil.

Indrajit looked at the Lankan standing beside him and laughed. 'The Ayodhyans expect us to attack their infantry!'

The Lankan laughed along with his prince.

Ram had prepared for an attack that wasn't coming.

Indrajit was not about to have his soldiers pour burning oil on the infantry. That would have efficiently killed many hundreds of Ayodhyan soldiers. But it was fraught with risk for the Lankan soldiers within the vimaan as well. A flying vehicle making sudden movements *and* woodfires with tubs of boiling oil within ... Not a good combination. The oil could very easily spill on the Lankans within the vimaan. The fire itself could spread within the flying vehicle.

No. Not burning oil. Instead, Indrajit had listened to his smartest advisor. His mother.

He wasn't going for his enemy's weakest link. He was going for their strongest.

Jiujitsu.

The vimaan turned suddenly. Away from the infantry at the centre. Towards the left flank.

It took but a moment for Ram to understand what his enemy planned to do.

'Lord Rudra have mercy …'

'What do we do, Lord?' asked Arishtanemi.

The vimaan was approaching the left-flank elephant corps, commanded by Angad, the hero of the previous day.

'You have the command, Arishtanemiji!' roared Ram.

'What?!' asked Aristhanemi. And then he understood. 'No, Lord Ram! Don't!'

But Ram was already riding towards the left flank. Galloping hard. Into the mouth of danger.

Arishtanemi immediately controlled his emotions. Ram had to do what he must. And he had to do the same. He turned towards his flagbearer with brisk commands for the infantry. 'Hold formations! We don't break!'

Arishtanemi's job was to hold the infantry and prevent panic. If it came down to it, they would fight the Lankan infantry soldiers to the finish. But Ram had to stop the vimaan before that. Or contain the damage it would wreak.

Ram was riding hard. Spurring his horse forward. Followed closely by his personal bodyguard.

But the vimaan was a demonic machine of fearsome ability. No horse could match it for speed. It was already hovering over the left-flank elephant corps. Indrajit and the Lankan beside him had begun their attack. Spears. And poisoned arrows shot from bows with strings that had remained dry within the vimaan. Other soldiers were showering stones from behind Indrajit. Stones falling from that height, powered by vicious warriors and the pull of gravity, were lethal missiles that killed on impact.

Spears. Arrows. Stones.

Targeted. Surgical. Brutally effective.

He had listened to his brilliant mother.

Strike the enemy's strength. Strike the elephants. Not directly. But through their mahouts.

It was very difficult to target mahouts from the ground, because of their elevation and heavy armour. But from the altitude of the flying Pushpak Vimaan, they were sitting ducks. And without the mahouts, the elephants were as good as useless; like the Pushpak Vimaan would be without any rotors to guide it. The elephants would either be paralysed without instructions from a trusted source, or run amuck with grief for their slain mahouts.

'Prince Angad!' thundered Ram from a distance. 'Hold!'

But Angad had already been struck. A stone had fallen on him, hard. On his head. His metal helmet had prevented a head injury that would have killed him. But it had rendered him unconscious. Twenty mahouts had already been killed or knocked out cold. Most elephants were standing still. Not knowing what to do, as the instructions, conveyed through the feet of the mahouts on their temples, had suddenly stopped. It was only a matter of time before some elephant lost his self-control and reacted angrily to the death of his mahout. For most elephants looked up to mahouts like their elder brothers.

If even one elephant reacted with rage and rampaged, the others would follow suit. And the only ones who would die in this melee would be the soldiers around them. Ayodhyans.

This would be fratricide.

The elephants that had destroyed the Lankans the previous day could very well hurt the Ayodhyans today.

Jiujitsu.

Using your opponent's strength against him.

Indrajit was turning the battle single-handedly. Or so it seemed.

The strategy intrinsic to Jiujitsu can be countered in only one way. The opponent steps back and does not strike. If your strength is going to be used against you, then you stand down and don't use your strength.

Ram was galloping hard. And as he reached the elephantry corps, finally, an elephant became hysterical.

It was Angad's elephant. The lead elephant. As it saw its mahout fall to the ground, two arrows buried deep in his throat, the beast bellowed in rage. Emotions had clouded the thinking of an intelligent animal. It raised its trunk and trumpeted ferociously at the Pushpak Vimaan. And charged towards its shadow. Other elephants followed. Frenzied. Incensed.

Some Ayodhyan soldiers on the elephant's path were trampled to death.

This would very soon turn into a stampede.

'No, my lord!' screamed a worried bodyguard, as he saw Ram racing towards the lead elephant, not slowing down at all.

Meanwhile, Indrajit turned and shouted to Akampana at the flight controls, making sure his voice carried over the roar of the vimaan motors. 'Towards the other flank! Quickly!'

As Akampana worked the controls to turn the vehicle, Indrajit looked at the Lankan beside him. 'Our task here is done. The elephants will do our job for us. We have to get to the elephants on the right flank before they retreat.'

The Ayodhyan infantry formations next to the left-flank elephantry were breaking, as soldiers tried to avoid getting trampled. Ram raced towards the lead elephant. If he managed to control it, the other beasts behind would also calm down.

Ram pulled his feet out of the stirrups, jumped up and crouched on top of the saddle. He transferred the reins, placing them between his teeth. Still expertly guiding the horse towards the rampaging elephant. As he neared, he swerved the horse to the side, leveraged himself with his upper limbs and stood up on the saddle. The elephant was chasing the vimaan, its eyes pinned on the object in the sky. It did not notice the horse galloping up to it. Ram guided the horse close to the elephant's right, and, in an awe-inspiring feat of athleticism, coupled with a super-human sense of timing, sprung from the saddle. He landed on the elephant's massive tusk, used it as leverage, and vaulted up. Onto the top of the elephant's head. All in a moment. The elephant sensed a presence on itself. It raised its trunk in fury, but stopped as the scent of the human being was familiar. And dear.

There was trust.

Suddenly the elephant felt a gentle and controlled pressure on its temples. From Ram's feet.

Calm down.

I'm here.

Slow down.

And the beast listened. It started slowing down.

Calm down ...

The elephant listened to the familiar.

It listened to its elder brother.

Ram had spent the last many months not just acquainting himself with most of his soldiers but also with each elephant. They trusted him. They listened to him.

Calm down ...

Slow down ...

After a few seconds, the lead elephant came to a halt. And so did the elephants behind it.

The Ayodhyan infantry soldiers roared in triumph. Their king had saved them. But their king was not roaring. He was staring into the distance. Towards the right flank.

'Hanumanji ...' Ram whispered. 'Take them towards the jungle ...'

On the right flank, Hanuman and his elephant corps were in full retreat. Hurtling back towards the forest.

'Lower!' roared Indrajit, shouting at Akampana. He knew that the vimaan was still too high for their missiles to be effective.

The elephants of the right flank were racing hard. Towards the trees. Most of them would enter the jungle soon. And would then be protected from arrows and spears by the tree tops.

'Lower, Akampanaji!'

Akampana turned to look at Indrajit. At the door. And took a deep breath.

I am only following orders. The other soldiers will back me up.

He expertly lowered the vimaan. Much lower than he should have. And boosted the rear directional motors. Turning the doorway towards the jungle. Slowly.

Just a few moments more, and the target would be presented. Perfectly.

Now, you Ayodhyans do your thing ...

And the main Ayodhyan, who had to do his thing, was ready.

Lakshman was not wearing his armour. It would hamper his ability to fling the spear to his farthest limit. He saw the vimaan nearing and ordered his mahout to move his elephant forward. Out of the tree cover.

'Lakshman! Wait!' shouted Bharat, who was on an elephant to the left of Lakshman's.

The vimaan still wasn't in perfect position. But the deafening din of the vimaan's motors meant that Lakshman didn't hear his brother. He held his spear up and took position. Feet spread apart. Backfoot perpendicular. Left arm raised high. The spear shaft flat on the palm of his right hand, between the index and middle finger, the thumb pointing back, and the rest of the fingers facing the other direction. Breathing steady and rhythmic. Eyes pinned on the vimaan door.

Meanwhile, within the vimaan, the Lankan beside Indrajit spoke loudly, pointing with his left hand, 'My lord! That is the prince of Ayodhya, Lakshman! Kill him!'

Indrajit whipped his body to the right, changing the planned direction of his shot, and released his arrow.

At that same moment, Lakshman flung the spear high. With all his might. Aiming unerringly for Indrajit.

A sudden gust of air turbulence made the vimaan shift a degree.

'Lakshman!' roared Bharat, as he saw the arrow swooping in.

Lakshman's spear missed. Due to the slight movement of the vimaan. But Indrajit's arrow did not miss. It slammed into Lakshman's chest. Brutally. Cutting through knotted layers of bull-like muscle, piercing through a rib, puncturing the right lung. Striking deep into the body of the mighty Lakshman. He fell back in the howdah. Blood burst forth from his chest.

'Lakshmaaaaan!' howled Bharat. 'Noooo!'

The vimaan continued turning slightly. And began to rise.

Bharat already had a spear in his hand. He looked up and hurled it hard. His instinct guiding the aim.

The vimaan was moving higher. It was already beyond the limit of Bharat's throwing range. But this thrust of the spear was not just powered by muscle, bone and training. It was also powered by the furious rage of a protective elder brother.

The spear sped high, piercing through the air like lightning.

Indrajit was exulting at the sight of Lakshman lying prone in his howdah. He knew how close the four royal brothers were. This would devastate them all. As the vimaan turned, another elephant came into view. The prince of Lanka reached for an arrow from his quiver. But the warrior atop the howdah was bent forward, his arm hanging down, as if he had just flung a spear. Before Indrajit could piece together this information, the missile flung by Bharat pounded into his chest. The spear had serrated edges along a ridiculously sharp blade point. And it was propelled to a manic speed. It crashed through his armour, tore through his ribs, and burst out from his back. Slicing his right lung asunder. Indrajit swayed for a moment. The pain had immobilised him. And then he fell forward. Out, from the open vimaan door. He fell like a stone, the descent picking up force, powered by gravity. Till the rope that had been tied around his waist and hooked to the vimaan halted his fall mid-air. But the sudden jerk also broke his back and neck. Killing him instantly.

Hanuman, farther out to right, at the edge of the jungle line, looked at the vimaan. Indrajit's body was dangling below it. The rope was tied around his waist, his torso twisted at an odd angle from his legs. His head hung askew from his broken neck. His body was skewered by the spear.

'Lakshmaannn!' cried Bharat, as his elephant rushed towards Lakshman's mount.

Meanwhile, the vimaan had begun its descent onto the open ground. Akampana was bringing it down. Slowly. Careful to ensure that the vimaan did not land on the swinging corpse of Indrajit.

The prince of Lanka was a true warrior. He deserved not to have his corpse crushed under a machine.

'Dismount!' Hanuman ordered his elephant corps soldiers. 'Rush into the vimaan. Arrest them all! No killing!'

Chapter 38

'Dada …' whispered Bharat, tears flooding his eyes.

The white flag of Shantidevi, the Goddess of Peace, had been raised as soon as the Pushpak Vimaan had landed on the ground. A temporary truce had been declared.

Messengers had been sent to Raavan, carrying news of his son's death.

Ram had rushed to the right flank. Close to the jungle edge, where the vimaan had been forced to land. Hanuman and his troops had already disarmed and arrested the Lankan soldiers inside the Pushpak Vimaan. Akampana stood in front, his hands tied behind him. Indrajit's body had been freed from the rope tied around his waist, and his corpse had been laid, sideways, on a piece of cloth on the ground. With respect.

This was Ram's army. Their conduct was dharmic, even with their enemies.

Ram and Bharat were down on their knees. Bharat cradled Lakshman's head on his lap. Their giant young brother lay unconscious. His torso was smeared with congealed blood. Some quick battlefield first aid had been performed. The shaft of the arrow had been broken. But the arrowhead and point remained buried deep in Lakshman's right lung. The physician had put ointments around the wound to stem the bleeding. And an apparatus on Lakshman's nose to help him breathe.

Ram placed his hand on Bharat's shoulder and turned to the physician. His face was lined with pain, but he held himself strong. An emotionally devastated elder brother is of no use during a younger brother's crisis. Only someone who remains calm and focused can pull his brother out of an emergency situation.

'What can you do, doctor?' asked Ram.

'He is breathing, great king,' said the doctor. 'He is alive. I can perform a surgery and remove the arrow. But the surgery itself ...'

'What about the surgery?' asked Bharat.

'My lords, this is a poisoned arrow. A very specific poison. It temporarily paralyses the muscles around the wound. Even more, surgically removing the arrowhead can trigger the worst effects of the poison. It will kill Prince Lakshman within a few minutes ... But if we don't do anything, then ...'

The doctor was sensitive enough not to complete the statement. For they truly were in the horns of a dilemma. If the doctor left the arrowhead inside, the wound would turn septic and Lakshman would die a slow, excruciatingly painful death over a few days. But if the doctor surgically removed the arrow, then the poison would get triggered and the Ayodhyan prince would die within a few minutes. In simple terms, a surgery would be merciful and spare him the pain.

But Ram and Bharat were not the kind of brothers who would give up.

'There must be something you can do, doctor,' said Bharat, for he knew the miracles that were possible in the traditional Indian form of medicine. '*Ayurveda* has an answer to everything.'

'There is something that can help, my lords. But it is almost impossible to get the medicine.'

'Nothing is impossible,' said Ram. 'What do you need?'

'I will need three particular herbs. Vishalyakarani, Saavarnyakarani and Samdhaani. And the branches of the Sanjeevani tree.'

'Oh no ...' whispered Bharat. He knew that these herbs and tree were found in the Himalayas. Far to the north. Too far.

'It's not as far as you think, Lord Bharat. They have been transplanted in very limited quantities in the southern mountains. The closest hillside where these herbs are available is the Dronagiri mountain, in the campus of the Mahodayapuram university, in the land of Kerala. But even that is too far. For it is impossible to transport Lord Lakshman there without triggering the poison. We cannot move him too much, and we certainly cannot transport him over a long distance.'

'But why do you need to move him? I don't understand. Don't you have the medicines here?'

'We have the branches of the Sanjeevani tree. But the three herbs of Vishalyakarani, Saavarnyakarani and Samdhaani must be used within half an hour of being plucked from the soil. So, the surgery has to be done at Mahodayapuram itself. That is the conundrum. It is impossible to bring the medicine here. And we cannot move him. We are stuck between a rock and a hard place. There are no options.'

Ram and Bharat looked at each other. They both had the same thought.

If Lakshman cannot go to the mountain, then the mountain's treasures must be brought to Lakshman.

'The Pushpak Vimaan ...' said Bharat.

Ram looked at Akampana, standing in the distance.

—— JƮ ᒐ5ᗡ——

The vimaan was commandeered by Ram. Akampana had agreed to fly it. The Lankan minister was happy to curry favour with the Ayodhyan royals, as the war was as good as over. Hanuman was to lead the mission, accompanied by Shatrughan and one hundred Ayodhyan soldiers. Three doctors were a part of the team as well. Their role was to ensure that the right herbs were collected in the proper manner. The Dronagiri mountain was only a half-hour flight away. So, they hoped to be back very soon.

A makeshift bed had been made on the battleground itself and Lakshman had been placed on it. Prince Angad, who had recovered substantially but was still weak, also rested on a bed nearby, the doctors carefully monitoring for signs of concussion. The medicine men hovered around the two royals, ensuring that no further harm came to them.

Meanwhile, physicians had set up a field hospital behind the Ayodhyan lines and were taking care of the wounded.

There was a sudden commotion at the thunderous sound of galloping horses approaching in a storm of dust. Ram and Bharat turned to look while Arishtanemi closed in, next to them, protectively.

It was Raavan.

He swayed over the saddle and a bodyguard helped him dismount. His haggard face had aged a decade within a few hours. There were only two men that he had truly loved. Ever. The first had died the previous day. And he was about to see the corpse of the second.

There was a time when he would have gruffly pushed aside a helping hand. But now, he allowed his bodyguard to hold his elbow, as he stumbled towards the king of Ayodhya.

'King Raavan,' said Ram as he came to his feet, politely folding his hands into a namaste. 'My sincere condolences. Your son fought fiercely. Like the warrior that he was. He made his ancestors proud today.'

Raavan folded his hands into a namaste. 'Lord Ram ... Where ...'

Ram took Raavan by the arm and gently led him forward. They were enemies, but Ram was a follower of the Vedic code of conduct. The path of *dharma*. There is a protocol to be honoured, a grace to be maintained, even in enmity.

Ram led Raavan to where Indrajit's body lay, guarded by Ayodhyan soldiers. They were followed by Raavan's bodyguards.

The king of Ayodhya nodded to his soldiers. They saluted smartly and stepped aside.

A strangled cry escaped from Raavan's mouth as he saw the broken body of his son. He fell to his knees. Tears streamed down his face. His soul was crushed. He couldn't take it anymore. If the Gods had to bear witness, they would think that this was the final tragedy that would break Raavan's dogged, pig-headed spirit. This was the straw that would finally break the beast's back.

Indrajit was lying on his side. He was placed with honour on a large piece of cloth bearing the Suryavanshi symbol. The shaft of the spear, buried deep in Indrajit's chest, had been cut with care. The main foreshaft remained buried in his lungs and heart. The pointed, serrated blade that had run through him and burst from his back, remained where it was. Thick blood had congealed around the blade and hardwood support. His head had been carefully put back in place, but it was obvious that the neck was broken. The skull was clearly detached from the cervical vertebrae. The Ayodhyans had placed Indrajit's legs back in position as well. The rope that was tied around his waist had been cut and removed. But it was still apparent that the base of the torso and the legs were at an unnatural angle to each other. The pelvic girdle, which held the torso in place, had not just fractured when the rope had broken Indrajit's fall, it had cleaved apart, shattering into four pieces.

No father should have to see his son this way. No father should see his son this way.

There is no glory in war. Only pain and devastation. Bhasa – the greatest Sanskrit playwright of antiquity – had written, this war-ground is actually a sacrificial ground, where dead warriors are the sacrificial victims, war cries are the mantras, dead elephants are the altar, arrows are the sacrificial grass, and hatred and enmity are the burning fire.

But one among them was willing to give up hatred and enmity.

Ram walked up to the kneeling Raavan and gently touched his shoulder. 'I am so sorry, King Raavan. He was a brave man ... your son.'

Raavan was staring at his son's beautiful face. Indrajit had inherited his looks. And without the pockmarks that had ravaged Raavan's visage, he was handsome. Raavan knew his son represented the best that he could ever have been. For Indrajit was a combination of his father's physical appearance and fearsome capability, and his wife's unblemished character. Raavan was being forced to witness the death of someone who embodied the best he could have been.

'I will have my men help you take Prince Indrajit's body back into Sigiriya,' said Ram. 'To carry out the funeral ceremonies that you must. We honour him. We will continue to honour him.'

Raavan didn't turn to look at Ram. He was frozen, his eyes pinned unblinkingly on his son. Tears surged down his face. Squeezing out the remains of his soul, to be burned in the heat of the sun.

Honour ... Knowledge ... Wealth ... Dignity ... Dharma ... All nonsense...

Raavan stopped crying. He wiped the tears off his face. And looked up. The rain clouds had retreated. Revealing a sullen sun. Burning bright. Scorching all below it. Proud of its immense power. The clouds, swollen with their droplets of tear-like rain, may hide it at times. But the sun will, ultimately, emerge. It will. It will conquer the clouds. And burn those who challenge it. Why? Because that is what the sun does.

Power ... That is all there is ... Power ... Demonstrating your power ... Crushing others with your power ... Making them cower with your power ...

Raavan stared at the sun. Still a few hours away from its highest point for the day. There was life left in the sun. More life for today. It hadn't begun its descent. Not yet. Not yet.

The sun still had more to burn of itself. It still had more to burn of others.

Raavan brushed Ram's gentle hand off his shoulder and stood up abruptly. The pain in his right leg was forgotten. He turned around and looked at his enemy. Proud unbending face. Defiant reckless eye.

'Duel of Indra,' whispered Raavan.

'What?' asked a flummoxed Ram. He thought he hadn't heard right.

'I challenge you to the Duel of Indra!' barked Raavan. Loudly, so that all around could hear him.

Ram stared at Raavan. Eyes steady. Face calm. But Bharat could feel his brother's rage in the slightly clenched muscles of his arms.

Ram had been decent. Ram had been gracious. Ram had been dharmic.

But Ram had made the cardinal mistake of most gracious people. They expect grace in return.

'Dada ...' whispered Bharat.

He knew what his elder brother would do. What his brother would be honour-bound to do. He had to dissuade Ram. There was no need for this duel. They had won already. The Lankans were defeated. Pragmatic Bharat understood this. But before he could say anything more, Ram raised his hand for quiet.

And then, staring at Raavan, in a voice that was eerily calm, Ram said, 'I accept. Duel of Indra. In the centre of the battlefield. Fourth hour of the third prahar, today.'

Duel of Indra. Fight to the death.

— ᒍᖴ ᑕᖽᕍ —

Raavan stood quietly. Holding Indrajit's hand. Just like he had held Kumbhakarna's the previous day. Letting the physician do his work. Making the death mask. An image of Indrajit's last expression, the one that would be recorded for posterity in a bronze mask.

It was an expression of *veera ras*. The *emotion of courage and triumph*. He had nearly turned the battle single-handedly. Stopped only by the courage and brilliance of Ram and Bharat. History would record, in glowing words, Indrajit's lionhearted defence of his land and his father. A brave last stand in the face of defeat.

'My lord…' whispered the physician. He knew that Raavan would be fighting a duel in a few hours. He wanted his lord and master to rest. 'Do you need a chair? Should I ask for some herbal infusions for you?'

'Just do your job,' growled Raavan. 'Make sure my son's death mask is perfect.'

'Yes, my lord.'

Ram had not allowed the Lankan army to return to Sigiriya. He had insisted that Raavan order his troops to disarm and remain outside the fort walls, in the open ground. They were detained and surrounded by the Ayodhyan army. Raavan had been allowed to go back into the city with the corpse of his son and a hundred bodyguards. Not one warrior more.

Ram had ensured that, if he won the duel and ordered a victory march into Sigiriya to take control of the city, there would be no street-by-street resistance. He would restore order in Sigiriya immediately and cleanly.

Ram had accepted the challenge of the Duel of Indra. But he was putting only himself in harm's way. He was not about to make a move that would damage his army later.

There is a difference between being noble and being stupid. Ram was certainly not stupid.

'My lord?' The physician asked for permission to pour the plaster on Indrajit's face. Raavan would not then be able to see his son's visage anymore.

Raavan remained quiet. He could not tear his eyes away from his son's warrior countenance. *I'll be with you soon, my boy.*

He ran his fingers through his son's hair. *But I will leave this world like you did … In a blaze of glory … I will go like the sun …*

For the sun does not go quietly into the night. As he sets, he rages. He turns the sky into vivid colours of orange and purple as he burns everything around him with his fury.

I will not go quietly. I will go in a blaze of glory ...

'My lord?' asked the physician once again.

Raavan was about to answer when he stopped. A sound at the door. Someone had entered the royal hospital chamber. Raavan turned and looked.

Mandodari.

'Please wait,' said Mandodari, politely and softly.

This was the first time she had entered the palace complex in nearly two decades. The ever-present, sage-like gentle smile on her face was missing. Her dark, captivating eyes normally revealed her unbending and righteous spirit; now, it was a window into a person who was broken and bereft.

She stood there.

Looking at her son.

Her pride and joy.

Her finest accomplishment.

Her sun and moon.

Her refuge from the misery caused by the husband she had been cursed with.

Gone.

Mandodari staggered to the corpse of Indrajit as Raavan stepped back quietly.

The one woman – besides Vedavati – whose moral force Raavan acknowledged, was his wife Mandodari. But he had never loved Mandodari. There was space in his heart only for Vedavati. If he was honest with himself, though, he would accept that in the dark suppressed corners of his heart, he was afraid of Mandodari.

The queen of Lanka reached Indrajit and gently touched her son's face. She did not utter a sound. No crying. She did not allow the tears to slip past. Her eyes had imprisoned grief which ached to burst forth from her soul now.

She would not cry. Not in front of Raavan. Not in front of her husband.

'I'm so sorry, Mandodari …' whispered Raavan, speaking to her for the first time in many years. 'He died like a hero … He was one of the finest ever … A better man than me …'

Mandodari did not look at Raavan. She had eyes only for her son.

'I …'

Mandodari ignored her husband.

'I am fighting a duel with King Ram in a few hours. I will … This will probably be the last time that you and I …'

Mandodari did not say anything.

'I am sorry for everything …'

Mandodari remained silent. Focused on her son. Only on her son. Gently running her hands over his face.

'I will be with our son soon … I will go with my head held high.'

Mandodari looked at Raavan. And whispered, 'The only thing you will be holding high is what you have always held high – your ego.'

Raavan took a sharp short breath. Anger coursed through his veins. He wanted to shout curses and expletives at his wife. But he could not. Not in front of his son. For he knew … He knew that his son had worshipped Mandodari like a Goddess.

Raavan bent down, kissed Indrajit's forehead, turned around and stormed out of the chamber.

Mandodari held her son's hands. And finally allowed her tears to pour out in a flood. Crying bitterly.

A mother who had lost her son. Her magnificent son.

A mother who had lost everything. All that she was left with was her life.

Life. Vicious life. Lucky are those who escape early. The others are kept around long enough to suffer more.

I am sorry that I couldn't protect you from him, my son. I am sorry that I couldn't protect you from your father.

Chapter 39

The ground for the duel was prepared strictly according to the rules prescribed by Lord Indra himself. A circle had been carefully drawn, with the field shaped into a circular net made of the ground's clay, the chords stretching wide and half buried into the ground. The Indrajal. The net of Indra. The ground for the Duel of Indra.

All the measurements within Indra's net were deeply symbolic. The radius of the circular ground was exactly 10.185 metres. The circumference then was sixty-four metres, a number sacred to Lord Indra. At the vertexes of the 'chords of the circular net' at the boundary, along the perimeter of the circle, were bows of the colour of a rainbow. The *Indradhanush*. Literally, *Indra's bow*. But, also, a word that meant *rainbow*.

The symbolic meaning of the ground's design was steeped in esoteric mystique.

The Atharva Veda describes Indra's Net as a deeply philosophical metaphor representing the universe as a web of interconnectedness and interdependence. The entire universe as a whole remains in balance and all the vertexes of the universe are either positive or negative reflections. All the positives and negatives combine to make the *zero principle* or *shunyata*. It's not exactly zero, for the universe is not actually in complete balance, but that is not important here. And, the logical corollary to shunyata is *pratityasamutpada*, or *dependent origination*, like the seven colours of the rainbow, the *Indradhanush*, originating from white light.

In the simple words of the warrior, it can be stated that in order to remove the effect we must first remove the cause. To remove the seven colours we must remove white light. To end the enmity, one of the foes must die.

So, when soldiers say that entering Indra's Net ends enmities, they are correct. Without the enemy, there is no enmity.

Ram and Raavan waited on opposite ends of the circle. Facing each other. Their seconds stood behind them. Bharat with Ram. Prahast with Raavan.

Hanuman and Shatrughan had returned with the Vishalyakarani, Saavarnyakarani and Samdhaani herbs, carefully carried in large pots filled with the soil of Dronagiri mountain. The herbs were alive when plucked off the plants by doctors at the battleground outside Sigiriya. Lakshman's surgery had been conducted and he was on his way to recovery. The herbs had helped Angad's recovery from concussion as well. They had also helped heal Angad's fractured leg.

Ram's mind was at rest. His brothers were safe. He was free to put his own life at risk. He was ready for the duel.

The priestess of the temple dedicated to Lord Indra emerged from the gates of the city of Sigiriya. She was followed by an assistant carrying a large plate. They moved ceremonially to the centre of the ground. The heart of Indra's Net. The assistant's plate held a conch shell, a small seven-coloured bow, a tiny net, a hook, and the vajra – a thunderbolt-shaped knife. Symbols of Lord Indra, the great conqueror.

No one knew the original name or antecedents of the priestess of Lord Indra. As tradition dictated, she had come from the sacred mountain valley of Kashmir. Like all the priestesses before her. The Lankans knew her only by her title: Indrani.

The priestess picked up the *shankh – conch shell –* from the plate and brought it to her lips. She took a deep breath and blew into it strongly. The deep resonance of the conch shell reverberated like streams of sonic consciousness over the teeming audience that had gathered to witness this duel. A duel that people knew would be the greatest in the century, if not the millennium. A hush descended like an invisible cloak on all.

The Indrani delicately picked up a copper ewer with her left hand. She poured water from it and washed the conch shell, nestled in the palm of her right hand. After placing the shankh back on the plate, she poured the rest of the water, via the palm of her right hand, onto the ground. She performed the ritual three times.

She then spoke in a loud, clear voice. 'May the heroic Indra, the wielder of the mighty vajra, the slayer of the heinous dragon Vritra, the splitter of immortal mountains, bless the soul of the two duellists.'

'*Om Indraya Namah!*' chorused Ram and Raavan.

I bow to Lord Indra.

'*Om Indraya Namah!*' repeated all who stood there.

The Indrani turned to Bharat. 'You second the duellist who was thrown the challenge. By the immutable laws of Lord Indra, he has the right to choose the weapon of combat. What say you?'

Bharat stepped up to Ram. 'Dada?'

Ram didn't hesitate for a second. He whispered, 'The sword. No armour.'

Bharat hesitated. He expected nothing less than honourable behaviour from his brother but had hoped nevertheless that Ram would be practical. Nope. His brother had chosen honour over pragmatism. Ram's favourite weapon was the bow. He was the most skilled archer alive. But Raavan's left arm was injured. Everyone knew that. The king of Lanka would not be able to wield a bow well. It would not be a fair fight.

Dharma dictates that a warrior must defeat his enemy fair and square. Ram had chosen *dharma*.

But Ram was enraged as well. A righteous rage. For his hand of grace and dharma had been rejected by Raavan. Hence, no armour.

The battle would be brutal.

Dharmic goodness, without the power of righteous indignation, can be weak. Ram had chosen goodness, but he had rejected weakness.

Bharat looked at the priestess and announced, in a loud clear voice, 'My warrior brother Ram has chosen. With Lord Indra's permission, he chooses a sword as a weapon. With one condition. No armour.'

The audience audibly gasped with surprise. Ram had given away his tactical advantage by not choosing bow and arrow. The soldiers, men among men, warriors all, acknowledged the honour in Ram's choice. Even the Lankan soldiers were constrained to admit within their hearts: Ram is a warrior of the noble code.

The Indrani smiled slightly. Impressed. She understood well what the weapon of choice meant. She turned to Prahast, the second of Raavan. 'What say you?'

Prahast was a warrior of the ignoble code. He could not believe his master's luck. Without even checking with Raavan, he answered. 'My warrior brother Raavan has chosen. With Lord Indra's permission, he accepts the choice of a sword as the weapon. And also accepts the condition of no armour.'

The Indrani turned to the audience. 'So let it be recorded.'

Prahast meanwhile edged up to Raavan and whispered, 'What luck, my king! Your opponent is a moralising moron! You will defeat him easily!'

Raavan did not say anything. He continued to stare at Ram. But his mind was haunted by Mandodari. And her last words.

The Indrani glanced at Ram and Raavan. 'Enter the Indra's Net.'

The warriors bent and touched the boundary with their right hands, and then brought their hands to their foreheads in reverence. Offering respect and obeisance to the ground on which the duel would take place. Then they entered in unison, whispering the words, '*Om Indraya Namah.*'

Raavan looked at the sun, still thinking of Mandodari as he walked to the centre. Towards the priestess of Lord Indra. Ram was looking directly at Raavan as he walked with calm self-assuredness, as if to defeat and bend the very earth under his gait. They stood on either side of the Indrani, and waited.

The priestess of Lord Indra announced in a thunderous voice, 'Dying wishes!'

This was a tradition of the Duel of Indra. Both warriors handed a written list of dying wishes to the opponent. The champion who won and lived was duty-bound to honour and fulfil the dying wishes of the duellist he had killed.

This was the law.

Raavan pulled out his list from his cummerbund and handed it over with his right hand to the Indrani. Respectfully.

As did Ram. The priestess of Lord Indra studied the dying wishes. None broke the rules and conventions of what could be demanded. She handed over Raavan's dying wish list to Ram. And Ram's to Raavan.

The warriors read the demands.

Ram had asked Raavan to not hurt his wife, his brothers, any soldier in his army, or the people of his land. Raavan must honour all these wishes if Ram died. That was it. A simple list. Simple direct men place simple direct demands.

Complicated men, on the other hand, place complicated demands. The first in a long list from Raavan: that Vibhishan would not be made king of all Lanka. The second in the list: the corpses of Raavan, Kumbhakarna and Indrajit would be given full royal burials by Ram, near the ground where the umbilical cords of the three Lankans were buried. Helpfully, Raavan had named the place. Sinauli. Third in the list: that the straw bodies of the three Lankan royals, along with the death mask, would be cremated in Lanka, again by Ram. Fourth in the list: that Ram personally fund and maintain a hospital in Vaidyanath. He had written the address of the hospital. And, fifth in the list: that his pendant be handed to the Vishnu, Sita.

Ram looked up from the list and saw the single finger-bone pendant that hung on a gold chain around Raavan's neck.

Strange request.

But Ram set all deeper thought of the requests aside. A warrior should not allow himself to be distracted before a battle. He looked back at the list. And read on.

Sixth in the list: hand over his musical instruments to Annapoorna Devi. Ram knew of Annapoorna Devi, the brilliant musician who lived in Agastyakootam, the capital of the Malayaputras. Seventh in the list: Raavan's books should be handed over to Ram's youngest brother, Shatrughan.

Ram felt a lump in his throat. Genuinely surprised by this demand. But he did not allow a change of expression. He read on.

The eighth in the list of demands: that if and when the story of Ram and Sita was ever written, Raavan would not be erased from the tale.

And finally, the ninth in the list, clearly added later, in a fast scrawl: Mandodari, wife of Raavan, would not be allowed to live in Sigiriya.

Ram had no choice. He had to agree to carry out all the demands. It was the rule of the Duel of Indra.

He looked at the Indrani and nodded.

'Now, the blood oath,' said the Indrani.

The priestess of Lord Indra picked up the thunderbolt-shaped knife – the vajra – and handed it to Ram. He pricked his thumb and let a few drops of blood fall on the bow of Indra. He then smeared the bow with his blood in one strong action. The Indrani took the knife from Ram and handed it to Raavan. He repeated the blood oath.

The Indrani raised the tiny, delicate replica of Indra's bow, smeared now with the blood of Ram and Raavan, and spoke in a booming voice belying her petite stature. 'The duellists have taken the blood oath of Indra's Net. They will honour the dying wishes of their defeated opponent.'

This oath was not to be taken lightly. For the thunderbolt of Lord Indra strikes dead the one who breaks this blood oath. There was a more practical reason to not break this pledge as well: a true disciple of Lord Indra, from any corner of the world, was honour-bound to kill the winner who broke the blood oath of Indra's Net.

The seconds briskly walked up and took the pieces of paper from the two duellists.

The opening rituals concluded, the Indrani, accompanied by her assistant, walked out ceremonially from the field. Ram and Raavan stood with their heads bowed in her direction.

Then the duellists turned to each other. Ram drew his sword and held it out, straight. He waited for Raavan to tap it with his sword.

A tradition. Before the duel began.

The swords should tap each other and whisper, before the murderous argument began.

Ram believed in tradition. This was an honourable one.

Raavan drew his sword and sneered at Ram. He stepped back jauntily. Without tapping his opponent's blade.

Ram drew a short angry breath and also stepped back. He walked a short distance away, turned around and stood in the orthodox sword-fighter stance. Feet spread out shoulder width. Left leg slightly forward, right slightly back. Body twisted sideways, offering a narrower target to the opponent.

Ram wore a coarse white dhoti and saffron cummerbund, tied tight in the military style. It offered his legs ease of movement. His left hand held the shield close to the body, angled towards the opponent. His right hand gripped the sword and was held high. The blade rested on top of the shield. He did not intend to tire the right, killer arm. Not yet.

Raavan stood at a distance. He wore a violet-coloured silk dhoti, a colour-dye only royalty could afford. He had on a pink cummerbund. Tied tight in military style. His right eye was covered by an eye patch. His right leg seemed to be moving smoothly; the magic of talented Lankan doctors.

He stood straight, his full body confronting his opponent. Both shield and sword were held low. Raavan was arrogantly offering his entire body as target. Challenging his opponent: Come and get me, if you dare.

Raavan's navel though, covered by the cummerbund, was throbbing with the familiar dull pain again. There was nothing that the doctors could do about it. Ever present, it was often forgotten and in the background. But sometimes it surged in intensity. To remind Raavan of its existence. A mark of his *Nagahood*. A recorder and reminder of the tragedy that his life had been. A signal that told him he had suffered yet another blow.

Mandodari.

She always hated me.

'Let the duel begin!' ordered the Indrani loudly from outside the circle.

Ram waited. Breathing smoothly. Focused.

Raavan seemed distracted. He glanced at the sun and stretched his shoulder.

Ram was too experienced a swordsman to be deceived by this schoolboy trick. His attention was directed on Raavan's eye. The eye moves before the body does.

Suddenly Raavan darted forward, leading with his left leg. Using a powerful pumping action from his right calf muscles to spring ahead. At a speed and pace that seemed preternatural, especially for one over sixty years old!

A flicker of surprise flashed on Ram's face as Raavan was suddenly upon him. The king of Lanka violently swung a standard up-down blow, using his great height and bulk to effective advantage. Ram swiftly raised his shield high and blocked the blow. The sound of hard metallic blade striking shield echoed through the air. The blow had jarred Ram's defensive shield arm. He ducked low, avoiding Raavan's follow-up slash from high on the left, and darted forward. He turned around after a couple of steps. In position again.

Raavan whirled around to face Ram.

Grinning. Eyes gleaming.

Not so old after all ...

I've still got it, young man ...

Raavan was bulky in musculature and a good three inches taller than Ram. He remained in situ. Hips bent slightly, letting more of his weight fall on his left leg. Shield down. Sword held to the side. Haughty and cocky. Daring the younger, leaner, shorter man to charge.

Ram also remained in situ. He would not be triggered. Shield held up. Close to the body. In the orthodox standard position. Sword resting on top of the shield. Elbow high. No strain on the fighting right arm. Breathing calmly.

Raavan charged. Swinging hard from the right, and then from the left. Ram kept his shield up, but at an angle, deflecting Raavan's blows rather than arresting them head-on. Letting Raavan complete his swings. One more blow from Raavan. Ram deflected it easily. The force of Raavan's strike kept his sword in motion, heading away from his body. And Ram found an opening. He stabbed forward.

But Raavan, too, was an experienced warrior.

He swerved to the side and deftly avoided the blow. And then thrust his shield forward, like a boxer jabbing with his left arm. It hit Ram's face. Hard.

Ram stepped back. Holding his shield up in defence.

Raavan grinned broadly. He was enjoying this. The sun had more to rise. The sun had more to burn.

An ugly blue splotch rapidly formed on Ram's right cheek. He did not flinch. He did not reach up to touch the bruise with his hand.

Never show your pain. Not to an enemy. That is the way of warriors.

Raavan paced around. Staring at Ram. Swinging his sword in small circles. Taunting the king of Ayodhya to charge.

Ram remained steady. In the standard fighting stance.

Raavan charged again, swinging his sword with frenzied aggression. From the left. Then the right. Ram moved back, step by step. Defending against the strokes with his shield and then his sword. Ram knew what was coming. But he could not predict the when.

And then it came. Earlier than Ram had expected.

Raavan should have waited till Ram had been pushed to the edge of Indra's Net. Stepping out of the boundary would have nullified the duel and called for the execution of the loser. Ram's freedom of movement would have been constrained at the boundary.

But Raavan moved early.

The king of Lanka had been pushing the king of Ayodhya back with his ferociously brutal blows. Repeatedly. And Ram's shield and sword were held high to defend himself. Raavan suddenly pushed his shield forward in a jab, intending to block Ram's field of vision and swiftly stab with his sword. Aiming low. Going for the abdomen. Using the monstrous power of his bulk for what would have been a devastating strike.

But Ram was no amateur. He was expecting this. And with a body that was leaner and more flexible, he had options that Raavan did not possess. For the bulkier a body, the less flexible it is. A biological fact.

Ram twisted his body and pirouetted sidewards, letting Raavan's sword glance the side of his torso, inflicting a minor cut. But Ram was a genius swordsman. In the same movement he swung his sword from behind, extending his flexible shoulder more than one would have assumed possible. With the added momentum of the pirouette that he had just executed, the sword careened out from behind him in a savage swinging cut. Raavan was focused on his forward stab, his shield held high. He did not notice the brutal slash coming towards his abdomen.

The blade cut deep, tearing across Raavan's abdomen. In the same smooth movement, Ram moved a few steps ahead and then whirled around. Steady. His shield held high. His sword, stained now with Raavan's blood, resting on top of his shield. Left foot forward. Right foot at the back. Breathing calm and rhythmic. Standard orthodox fighting position.

The audience — men of war — held their breath. This was awe-inspiring sword skills on display.

Raavan shifted weight and faced Ram. His gaze fell on the insignificant snip he had inflicted on Ram's torso. And then he looked down. At the savage cut across his abdomen. Blood dripped freely from the wound.

Raavan looked at Ram, raised his eyebrows cockily and smiled. He nodded. Acknowledging a strike of exceptional skill by his enemy.

Ram's eyes remained steady. No loss of focus. No acknowledgment of Raavan's appreciation. He did not glance once at the wound he had inflicted. Or, the ugly purple outgrowth on Raavan's navel, which now lay exposed as the cummerbund had come loose. Most people had a morbid fascination with Naga deformities and couldn't help but look. Again and again. But not Ram. His eyes were fixed upon Raavan's eye.

Raavan began moving to the right, edging slowly towards the centre. Staring at Ram with menace.

Ram followed. Moving slowly. Deliberately. Never off balance. He kept pace with his opponent.

Raavan suddenly charged again. Ram was in mid-step, moving to the left to keep pace with Raavan. He dug his right foot into the ground, flexed his muscles and held his shield and sword in readiness to tackle Raavan's assault. Swords brutally thumped on shields. The warriors held each other in a tackle. Their swords and shields pushed into each other. Raavan was bulkier. He should have pushed the leaner Ram back. But he was also older. And, more importantly, injured. The cut on his abdomen was deep.

A few moments in this stalemate and then Raavan disengaged and stepped back. To a safe distance. He held his shield high. Defensively. And rested his sword blade on top of the shield. In the classic sword-fighter pose for the first time in the duel. Staring at Ram. Breathing deeply and hurriedly.

Ram instantly knew. Now was the time. Now was the time to charge.

'Ayodhyatah Vijetaarah!' roared Ram, and charged forward. *The conquerors from the unconquerable city.*

Ram swung his sword in pitilessly. Incessantly. From the left and right. He kept his brutal strikes at mid-body level. He used his shield like a battering weapon. He forced Raavan to step back. The Lankan's shield was held high as he tottered at an unnatural angle. And then steadied. Ram kept advancing. Subtly moving to his left. He was forcing Raavan to put more weight on his injured right leg. And, also, moving in the direction in which the Lankan's vision was impaired by his patch-covered right eye.

Raavan knew he was being pushed to the edge of Indra's Net. He could not continue to step back. He suddenly swung in hard from the right. It was the rage of the cornered. As Ram was also committed to charging forward, Raavan pushed back hard with his shield. Ram thumped back brutally and appeared to slip. Raavan saw a golden opportunity. He roared triumphantly, dropped his shield, held his sword with both his hands and swung in viciously. A back-hand strike. From an unexpected angle.

And the trap was shut. The victim ensnared.

Ram had feinted the slip. It was a bluff. With his left foot dug in deep, he now expertly angled his shield, allowing Raavan's blade to glide off without aggressively blocking it. Raavan's fearsome momentum from the brutal strike made his body turn. Ram moved like lightning. The opening emerged precisely as Ram had expected and the king of Ayodhya did not lose the moment. He stabbed forward ferociously.

The sword tore into Raavan's abdomen remorselessly. It encountered no resistance. It sliced his Naga purple-coloured outgrowth into half and then cut deep inside, cleaving the intestines, liver and kidney. Ram gave no quarter. He rammed forward, using the full weight of his shoulder and back. The blade burst forth from Raavan's back, having ripped through all in its path.

Ram the warrior was ruthless when the need arose. But he was not cruel. He pulled out his sword instantly. But moved it to the right as he did so. The sharp edge of the sword transversely cut through the ganglia near Raavan's spinal cord. Ensuring no further pain.

Raavan's sword dropped from his hands as he fell on his knees. He looked down. Blood was pouring out of the massive wound on his abdomen, almost like a small fountain. But he felt no pain. He looked at his gaping injury with detached wonder. Was this his body? Shouldn't he be feeling some pain?

He fell on the ground. Down on his back.

Vedavati … I'm coming …

Ram stepped up, bent over and straightened Raavan's legs. With the severed spinal cord, Raavan had no control over his lower body anymore.

A small gesture. But one that was noticed by all who had gathered. And a single thought passed through the many minds. *Ram is a noble warrior.*

Ram went down on a knee, dug his sword into the soft ground and waited next to Raavan's head. 'Tell me when ...'

Raavan was breathing slowly. Eyes drooping.

'Not yet ...' whispered Raavan.

Ram waited.

Raavan reached up to his neck, yanked at the gold chain and removed Vedavati's finger. He held it tight in his bloodied right hand. He took a few long, gentle breaths. Firing energy into his body. He looked at Ram. 'I ... I never touched your wife ...'

Ram's eyes were expressionless. No pity. No anger either. 'She wouldn't let you touch her. She is Sita. She is the Vishnu. She is too powerful for you.'

Raavan smiled slightly. 'No ... You don't understand ... I loved her mother ...'

Ram frowned. Genuinely confused now.

Raavan opened his palm, letting Ram see the finger bone, the phalanges carefully fastened with gold links. 'I return to this Goddess now ...'

Raavan paused for breath and then continued. 'After I am gone ... give this finger to Vedavati's daughter ... Sita ... She will know what to do with it...'

Ram nodded.

'My death will give rise to the legend of Ram ... Maybe that was my purpose ... For Light is the child of Darkness ...'

Ram chose to keep quiet again. He didn't agree with Raavan. But he had the grace to not argue with a dying man.

Raavan took a deep breath. 'I am ready ...'

Ram looked at Raavan's sword. It lay in the distance. Warriors that worshipped Lord Indra believed they should die holding their weapon in their fighting hand. 'Would you like to hold your sword?'

Raavan smiled. 'Your wife is right ... You are a good man ...'

Ram paused. He appreciated this first sign of grace from Raavan. He repeated his question, softer this time. 'King Raavan, do you want to hold your sword?'

'No … I am holding what I want. The only thing I ever truly needed … Vedavati's hand ….

Ram held his breath for a moment. A man who loved a woman so magnificently could not have been all bad. Maybe there was some good in him … Maybe …

'Go in peace, King Raavan,' whispered Ram.

Ram picked up his sword and held it vertically. He brought the tip of the sword to Raavan's chest. Just above his heart. He looked at Raavan's eye for confirmation. And Raavan smiled. For he was about to see her again.

Vedavati …

Ram pushed the sword in swiftly. It sliced easily through the sheath and muscles, gliding between the bones of the rib cage, finding the heart and cleaving through it. In one quick merciful strike. Ram was a skilled warrior.

Raavan's heart ripped apart and blood burst forth, offering his soul the path to escape. And the love that had been caged inside, till it had turned malignant, was released. Into the cosmos beyond this petty world. Where malignancy does not survive in the radiant sheen of the spirit.

His soul rushed out. Carrying the memory that was important. The only memory that was important.

Vedavati.

Chapter 40

Late in the evening, Ram stood in the Ashok Vatika. At the edge of the clearing. Staring at the central hut.

She was inside. His Sita was inside.

Events had moved quickly after Raavan's death. Ram had ordered that Raavan's corpse be treated with utmost respect. Along with his brothers and key generals, he had carried Raavan's body to his palace. The death mask was being made. Some in Ram's army felt this was unnecessary and according excessive respect to an enemy. But Ram had silenced them by quoting Lord Indra himself: *Maranaantaani Vairani. Enmity ends with death*.

The disarmed Lankan army had been stationed outside the city, with Ayodhyan soldiers standing guard. A contingent of Ram's army had entered Sigiriya and flag-marched along the main streets, to ensure that there was no lawlessness. The Lankan citizens remained orderly, though fearful of their fate.

Having rapidly ensured that there was no chaos in the city, Ram had rushed to Ashok Vatika. He had fulfilled what his head had dictated were the duties of a victorious commander. Now, finally, he was listening to the insistent calls of his forlorn heart. A husband had arrived to meet his beloved wife. After a separation that had been too long.

'Wait here, please,' whispered Ram to the men with him, and then he walked towards the hut.

Ram's bodyguard soldiers stood silent at the edge of the clearing. Bharat and Shatrughan, his brothers, followed at a discreet distance. Lakshman was still recuperating from his surgery. He had been transferred to the royal hospital of Sigiriya.

Ram stopped just outside the hut. He looked at the cane chairs and table on the veranda. Beyond the furniture was the open door that led into the simple dwelling that had been his wife's prison for many months.

He breathed in deeply. Slowing his wildly beating heart.

Sita.

He climbed up the three stairs and walked towards the door.

'Sita …'

And then he stopped.

For his life, his Sita, had just appeared at the doorway of the hut. Clad in a white dhoti and a white blouse, a saffron-coloured angvastram hung from her right shoulder. She held a golden *puja thali* with both her hands. On it was placed a small earthen-lamp, some grains of rice, a pinch of saffron powder and a small bowl of water. She beheld her victorious husband, eyes brimming with pride, a smile infused with love.

Ram remained where he was standing. That was the tradition.

Sita walked up to him and circled the *puja* plate, clock-wise, around Ram's face. Three times. Lord Agni, the God of Fire, bore witness that her husband had come back to her in triumph.

The conquering hero from the unconquerable city.

She dipped her fingers in the small bowl of water and then the grains of rice. They stuck to her fingers. She pressed the grains on Ram's forehead. The rice grains plastered themselves between his eyes. She then pressed the saffron powder with her moistened ring finger and smeared it on Ram's forehead. In a neat vertical line.

Following ancient tradition then, she repeated the proud words of Ayodhyan queens as they welcomed their conquering husbands back home. 'May the news of your great victory travel on the back of every single ray of the mighty Sun God and reach every corner of the universe that they fall upon.'

'*Jai Surya Dev*,' said Ram, hailing the patron God of his dynasty, the Suryavanshis.

Glory to the Sun God.

'*Jai Surya Dev*,' repeated Sita.

Ram took the *puja* plate from his wife's hands and placed it on the table. And he reached for her. She melted into his arms. As he melted into hers.

It had been many months. It had been a lifetime.

Dhyaus, the Sky God, had no reason to be blue anymore. And had taken on a saintly saffron hue. Surya, the Sun God, was still emanating strong light, but had gently reduced his heat at this late evening hour. Chandra, the Moon God, had come in early, despite the night sky being some time away... For Chandra, the amorous divinity, is forever enchanted by passion. Vayu, the Wind God, blew tenderly across the verdant gardens, spreading the fragrance of love. And Prithvee, the Earth Goddess, serenely cradled her warrior daughter Sita and the victorious descendant of the solar dynasty, Ram. As they held each other.

It had been many months. It had been a lifetime.

The ancients say that young love is like coal. It burns brightly and with passion. Alas, it does not last often. But when subjected to pressure – immense pressure – it transforms into a diamond. A love that is strong – strongest – in this world. Ram and Sita ... Their love had been strengthened by the heat and pressure of grief. By the burden of separation. Nothing could break it now. Nothing.

If the universe spreads to infinity in every direction, then where is the centre? Is it even possible to find a centre within infinity? Wise men say that your centre is where you stand. Spiritually wise men say that the true centre is where your true love stands.

Ram and Sita had found their true centres. Once again.

'I love you, my princess,' whispered Ram.

'I love you, my heart,' said Sita.

Ashok Vatika, the garden with *No Grief*, had truly, become Ashok.

—JF J5D—

It was well into the next day. The third hour of the second prahar. And the sun was nearing its daily peak.

Ram and Sita had attended to pressing matters of city administration. And then had visited the Lankan queen, Mandodari. As they had been advised to do by Vashishtha. For Mandodari was not just a queen. Respected by rishis and rishikas around the Indian subcontinent, she was one of the foremost scholars of the Vedic path.

Ram and Sita waited outside the open door of the simple hut that was home to the queen of Lanka. Vashishtha walked in alone.

Bharat had wisely not accompanied his brother and sister-in-law on this visit. He had killed Mandodari's son. It would not be proper for her to see him. Not so soon.

'Mandodariji,' said Vashishtha, holding his hands together in a namaste. He went down on his knees by her side and said, gently, 'You have a lot to do in life. Much more to give to Mother India. You cannot ... You cannot go ...'

Mandodari lay on a simple straw mat on the ground. She had made the decision to undertake the ancient Dharmic tradition of *Praayopaveshan*; *lying down until death*. In the colloquial Prakrit tongue of the masses, *Praayopaveshan* was known as *Santhara*. Having undertaken this vow, one voluntarily fasted to death by gradually reducing the intake of food and liquids. Spiritually, it represents thinning the human body and its passions when a soul decides that its karma in this life is over and it must move on.

Mandodari had decided that there was nothing more for her to do in this life. Vashishtha disagreed with her.

'Vashishthaji,' said Mandodari, with her ever-present soft smile, and also the radiant spirit of one moving on the noble path of *Santhara*. 'I have given all that I had. Now it falls upon you to guide those who must lead Mother India to a purposeful path. My time is done. My karma is done.'

Sita walked quietly into the hut. She went down on her knees, touched Mandodari's feet and spoke. 'I am too small to open my mouth in the presence of masters such as you and Guru Vashishtha. But, Guru Mandodari, if I may say something ...'

'Of course, my child,' said Mandodari.

'The paralysis caused by grief does not mean that one's karma is over,' said Sita. 'All it means is that one is paralysed by grief. Which is perfectly understandable. But this paralysis will end. For change and movement are the very essences of life. We must not give in to grief.'

Mandodari smiled. 'No, my child. Do not devalue grief. It can bring clarity to the mind. My mind is clear. Remember the words of Sikhi Buddha: Grief is the ultimate reality of the universe.'

'That is true, Mandodariji,' said Sita, 'but only from the prism of the universe. From a different prism, that of human beings, grief is merely love that is aching to be expressed. Grief is dammed up love. It arises when love is blocked, like the waters of a dam. Grief is made of feelings that have nowhere to go; because the one you ache to express your love to, is gone ...'

Mandodari remained silent. Her eyes were moist. With dammed up love.

Sita continued, her fingers clutching the pendant hanging around her neck. Her mother's finger. 'I know what you are going through, Guru Mandodari. Love needs to flow, for it is the energy of youth and life in a soul. Love should not be static, for then it becomes disconsolate. When you lose the one you love, when there is nobody to give love to, then love ripens into grief. Grief is disheartened love, Guru Mandodari. Grief is love that has been bound by depression. Grief is not having the one you want to give love to. Not having the one who will accept your love ... I did not get to meet the one I wanted to give love to ... My birth mother ... I lost the one I had given love to ... My adoptive mother ... But I have someone else now. Someone who makes me complete.' Sita looked at Ram, who stood silently in the doorway. 'I waited, I opened my heart, and my grief did go ...'

Mandodari took a deep breath. She struggled to hold back tears that insistently begged to flow from her soul. For she had so much more love to give. So much more love to give to her son. Indrajit.

'Give your love to me, my mother,' said Ram.

Mandodari looked at Ram. And the tears burst forth. She sobbed aloud.

Ram walked up to the queen of Lanka and went down on his knees. 'Give your love to me, Maa. I promise you, I will be a good son. I vow that me and my brothers – all my followers – will honour Indrajit and Kumbhakarnaji every year. Till the end of time. That is my Dashrath vow.'

The Dashrath vow. An open-ended promise that could never be broken. No matter what the circumstances. No matter what the time. No matter what the space.

Mandodari reached out and gently stroked Ram's cheek. Like a mother soothing her child. Her tears fell strong. They cleansed.

'Everyone suffers, Mandodariji,' said Vashishtha. 'Nobody escapes suffering. That is the reality of life. But the suffering of the selfish is different from the suffering of the noble. The selfish wallow in their misery, they whine, want attention, want others to empathise and console. They are convinced of their sense of victimhood. The noble, on the other hand, do not view themselves as victims. They make it their life's mission to reduce the suffering of others. The noble want that nobody else should suffer the way they suffered. The way the one they loved, suffered. The suffering of the selfish harms the world. The suffering of the noble makes the world a better place.'

Mandodari was quiet. But her eyes reflected a new understanding. Vashishtha's words were getting through.

'Stay in this world, Mandodariji. Make it a better place.'

—— ᒍᖴ ᒲᢖᗞ ——

Three of the four brothers and Sita were glued to the glass-encased porthole windows, gazing at their home. Their lovely home. Shatrughan, the fourth brother, was reading a book.

The Pushpak Vimaan hovered over the vast Grand Canal that encircled the mighty fort walls of Ayodhya. It had been built a few centuries ago, during the reign of Emperor Ayutayus. Engineered by efficiently drawing in the waters of the Sarayu River, the Grand Canal's dimensions were almost other worldly. It stretched for over fifty kilometres and circumnavigated the third and outermost wall of the city of Ayodhya. Enormous in breadth as well, it extended to about two-and-a-half kilometres across the banks. It was breathtaking. And for Ram, Sita and Lakshman, the view was ethereal. Indescribable. They had last set eyes upon this magnificent view over fourteen years ago.

Surya, the Sun God, was slowly calling it a day. It was late in the evening. The citizens of Ayodhya, though, were celebrating with verve. Every home was lined with lamps—inside, on the thresholds, the verandas, and also their roofs and terrace edges. The ramparts of the three fort walls had been meticulously skirted with lamps, alight and ablaze. The air was rife with the sound and light of fireworks, firing without a break in all the various gardens of the city.

Their king and queen were returning. Ram and Sita were coming home.

It was a special day in an auspicious period. The third of a traditional five-day celebration that commemorated events for most dharmic paths: the Mother Goddess, the Mahadevs, the Vishnus, Jain Tirthankaras, Sikhi Buddha; all celebrated since ancient times. Now onwards, there would be one more. Forever. The legend of Ram and Sita was grafted on to this bouquet. The Ayodhyans did not know it then, but they had established a resplendent tradition for their people, their land, their culture.

For all time to come. For this was the day of the first Diwali. And as long as India would breathe, it would mark this day with pomp and pageantry.

Ram held Sita's hand as they both looked at their city. With awe and wonder. And hearts bursting with love.

'Urmila is waiting for you at the palace, Lakshman,' said Bharat.

Lakshman looked at his brother and smiled warmly. He hadn't seen his wife in fourteen years. He couldn't wait to see her again.

Ram had ensured that he had honoured all the vows he had made to Raavan on the day of the Duel of Indra.

The straw body-replicas of Raavan, Kumbhakarna and Indrajit were embellished with their death masks and consigned to the holy flames on cremation pyres by Ram. Their corpses were buried with full royal honours at the site where their umbilical cords had been laid to rest upon their births: Sinauli. Ram had handed over Vedavati's finger relic – given to him by Raavan before he died – to Sita. Sita had interred the relic with Raavan's body in his burial chamber. The king of Lanka did go into pitralok holding Vedavati's hand. Mareech, Raavan's uncle, had also been buried in Sinauli.

Ram had made a promise: that he would repeat the ritual of cremating the bodies of his three enemies on the anniversary of Indrajit's death; the tenth day of Shukla paksh in the month of Ashwin. Year after year. His brothers reminded him that he had given his word to Mandodari for only honouring Kumbhakarna and Indrajit thus. Why include Raavan? With his typical grace, Ram had repeated: *Maranaantaani Vairani.*

Ram had used his personal funds to create an endowment for the hospital in Vadiyanath, named after Vedavati. It met all the expenses of the hospital.

Raavan's musical instruments were taken to Agastyakootam by Arishtanemi and handed over to Annapoorna Devi. The collection of instruments included the Raavanhatha, invented by the talented Raavan. All his books were given to the one who would appreciate them the most: Shatrughan. In fact, he was reading one right now, immune to the commotion all around.

One dying wish of Raavan's had been particularly difficult to implement. For he had demanded that Vibhishan not be made the king of Lanka. However, Ram had already given his word of honour to Vibhishan that he would be enthroned. Ram would never break his promise. But what do you do when two promises stand in contradiction to each other?

The ever-pragmatic Bharat had found a solution. With the creative verbal skill of a lawyer, he had pointed out that Raavan had only demanded that Vibhishan not be made the king of *all* Lanka. So, they had partitioned Lanka. The coastal city of Gokarna and its surrounding regions were made an independent republic, to be administered by its entrepreneurial guilds and citizens in the democratic traditions established by the Shakyas, Vajjis and others in the Sapt Sindhu. Lanka was reduced to Sigiriya and the island's west coast. And Vibhishan was crowned the king of this truncated region. Hence, with Bharat's ingenuity, Ram had kept his word of honour given to Vibhishan, while also upholding the vow made to Raavan at the Duel of Indra.

Raavan's hastily written last dying wish, too, had been honoured. Mandodari did not wish to stay in Lanka anymore. She sat now in the Pushpak Vimaan, in deep conversation with Vashishtha at the back.

'The only dying wish of Raavan that you have not honoured yet, Dada,' said Bharat, 'is ensuring that he is woven into the story of Bhabhi and you!'

Sita laughed. 'Trust Raavanji and his ego, to even demand something like this.'

Ram looked at Sita, the daughter of Vedavati. His eyes fell upon the finger bone pendant hanging around her neck. The mark of Vedavati, Sita's birth mother. He smiled. 'It was his right to demand anything. But this is not in my hands. It's up to the storytellers.'

'Then he will certainly be woven in!' said Bharat, grinning. 'Flawed, doomed characters are terrible to live with. But are wonderful to read about. Storytellers hunt for such characters with the ardency of a lost ship searching for land!'

Ram, Sita, Bharat and Lakshman laughed.

An announcement informed them that the vimaan would soon be landing. The brothers and Sita got back to their seats and clasped their seat belts.

'Who do you think will attack us first?' Bharat asked Ram and Sita.

'Why will anyone attack us now?' asked Lakshman.

'Raavan was not the real enemy, Lakshman,' said Bharat. 'He was just a stepping stone. His defeat gave the Vishnu ...' Bharat stopped, and then pointed at both Ram and Sita, before continuing, 'the *Vishnus*, the aura they need, to do the more important task.'

'What more important task?'

'Their real mission: reviving Mother India. They are not just the Vishnus for Ayodhya, but for India. The whole of India. And it will be a long struggle. We will hurt many vested interests among the ruling classes.'

'I'm sure we can build allies among the nobility,' said Ram.

'I'm sure we can,' said Sita. 'But even the allies will turn against us when we work for the people. Old feudal interests are rarely aligned with those of the common people.'

'It will be a struggle,' said Ram. 'Maybe a long struggle. But we will prevail. For the good of Mother India.'

'Hmm,' said Sita. 'There's so much more that we have to do.'

'And there will be a lot more for the storytellers to record!' Bharat laughed.

Shatrughan smiled and quoted from the book he was reading. '*Kathaa adyaapi avashishtaa re vayasya.*'

It was old Sanskrit. *The story is not yet over, my friend!*

There was laughter all around.

'Well said, Shatrughan!' said Ram. 'The story is not yet over.'

'But for now, we rest,' said Sita. 'This may not be the climactic end, but it certainly is a good penultimate end!'

—JF J,5D—

Annapoorna put the Raavanhatha aside.

Vishwamitra blinked away his tears. The raga had touched his heart and then plunged deep into his soul, bringing to life emotions from lifetimes ago. Annapoorna had played the complex Raga *Malkauns* on as modest an instrument as the Raavanhatha. 'Only someone with your divine skill can play the *Malkauns* on this simple instrument, Annapoornaji. You truly have Goddess Saraswati's blessings.'

Vishwamitra and Annapoorna were at the Hall of Hundred Pillars at the ParshuRamEshwar temple in Agastyakootam. She had stepped out of her house. For, with the death of Raavan, her vow had expired as well. She could leave her home now. And Vishwamitra had delighted her with the gifts that Arishtanemi had come bearing: the musical instruments of Raavan himself.

'It is the magic of the instrument, Guruji,' said Annapoorna. 'It may look simple, but the Raavanhatha has the musical cadence of Raavan's divine talents. He was the one truly blessed by *Goddess Saraswati*, not me.'

Vishwamitra smiled and brought his hands together into a namaste. 'Well, whoever may have been blessed by the great *Goddess of Knowledge*, it is I who have truly felt bliss listening to this raga on the Raavanhatha.'

Annapoorna folded her hands into a *namaste* and smiled. She looked to her right, towards the citizens of Agastyakootam who waited outside the temple. Arishtanemi stood among them. They too had heard the loud timbre of her instrument clearly. And enjoyed the raga she had just played. But they did not hear the words that were exchanged between Vishwamitra and her. They were spoken softly. She looked at the Malayaputra chief. 'What are you planning, Guruji?'

'I don't understand your question, Annapoornaji.'

'I am well aware of the manner in which news of Sita reached Raavan's ears, Guruji,' said Annapoorna, smiling. 'And I did play along. For I do owe you for giving me refuge when I had nowhere else to go. Among the foremost rules of *dharma* is to remember the debt we owe to those who help us.'

Vishwamitra paused for a moment, almost as if he was evaluating how much he could trust Annapoorna. Having made a decision, he spoke. 'What did you think of Raavan?'

'A talented fool. The Almighty gave awesome capabilities to one whose character was incapable of handling it. His talents were not a blessing to him; they were his curse. But all said and done, I believe there was some good in him.'

'Hmm … And what do you think of Ram?'

'A good man. He is noble. So noble, that it's difficult to believe he is real.'

Vishwamitra's expression remained deadpan. 'Hmm.'

'And Raavan is dead.'

'Yes, Raavan is dead.'

'So, what are you planning, Guruji?'

'Divodas thinks he is in control now.'

Annapoorna knew enough about Vishwamitra's life to know that Divodas was the *gurukul* name of his childhood friend who was now his greatest foe, Vashishtha. 'And he's not?'

'No, he's not.'

'Why do you say that?' asked Annapoorna, intrigued.

'Firstly, I have planted someone right in the heart of Ayodhya. Mrigasya of the Bheda family.'

Annapoorna was shocked. She didn't know this. 'Is Mrigasya a Bheda?'

'Yes. And, more importantly, Divodas only has his precious Ram and the kingdom of Ayodhya. I have ten kings with me.'

Annapoorna leaned forward and listened keenly to Vishwamitra's plan.

— JF J5D —

'There will be a period of peace, I suspect,' said Mandodari. 'But it won't be long-lasting.'

'No, it will not be a long peace,' agreed Vashishtha. 'A long peace only happens after a war to end all wars … After a war that settles issues in such a comprehensive manner that the losing elite accepts their fate.'

It was early in the morning after the first Diwali and Vashishtha and Mandodari had walked to the Grand Canal for their morning *puja*. Having completed the ritual, they asked their bodyguards to wait at a distance and strolled along the majestic terrace that ran along the inner banks of the Grand Canal.

'A war to end all wars,' said Mandodari. 'Yes, there lies the difference between wars and wealth.'

Vashishtha looked at her, intrigued.

'I had read this statement in a book, long ago,' said Mandodari. 'Written by a philosopher far to our west, called Schopenhauer. "Wealth is like sea water; the more we drink, the thirstier we become," he had written.'

Vashishtha laughed softly. 'That is true.'

'And that's where war is different. The more war there is, the more people grow tired of it. Excessive warring creates conditions for a long period of peace. Peace that will last at least a few generations.'

'True ...'

'And, a new social order emerges only when the elite of the old social order surrenders completely.'

'And that has not happened ... The old elite is still strong in India. They have to be defeated comprehensively. They have to be afraid of the new elite. Only then will they accept the new order. For fear is the mother of love. But we are not there yet.'

'Yes ... we are not there yet. But once they are defeated completely, and accept the new ways, we have two fine leaders who will create that new social order.'

'Three, come to think of it.'

'Three?'

'Yes. Ram, Sita and Bharat ... Sudas, Bhoomi and Vasu.'

'Those were their *gurukul* names?' asked Mandodari.

'Yes,' answered Vashishtha. 'We have our trinity. Our new trinity.'

'Hmm. And they will create a new order. They will restore Mother India's glory.' Mandodari looked at Vashishtha and smiled, her eyes twinkling. 'Though we still have to win the war to end all wars.'

'Oh, we will. The Gods are with us. And our three heroes will certainly create a *Land of Pure Life*.'

'*Meluha* is the name they have decided upon, haven't they?'

'Yes, that's the name. And to help them build that perfect empire is the last goal and purpose of my life. That will be my final journey. The last story to be written. Once it is recorded, my life's purpose will be complete. I can go in peace ... I will go in peace ... The last story in this long chain ... The story of the Rise of Meluha.'

... to be continued.

Other Titles by Amish

The Shiva Trilogy

The fastest-selling book series in the history of Indian publishing

THE IMMORTALS OF MELUHA

(Book 1 of the Trilogy)

1900 BC. What modern Indians mistakenly call the Indus Valley Civilisation, the inhabitants of that period knew as the land of Meluha – a near perfect empire created many centuries earlier by Lord Ram. Now their primary river Saraswati is drying, and they face terrorist attacks from their enemies from the east. Will their prophesied hero, the Neelkanth, emerge to destroy evil?

THE SECRET OF THE NAGAS

(Book 2 of the Trilogy)

The sinister Naga warrior has killed his friend Brahaspati and now stalks his wife Sati. Shiva, who is the prophesied destroyer of evil, will not rest till he finds his demonic adversary. His thirst for revenge will lead him to the door of the Nagas, the serpent people. Fierce battles will be fought and unbelievable secrets revealed in the second part of the Shiva trilogy.

THE OATH OF THE VAYUPUTRAS

(Book 3 of the Trilogy)

Shiva reaches the Naga capital, Panchavati, and prepares for a holy war against his true enemy. The Neelkanth must not fail, no matter what the cost. In his desperation, he reaches out to the Vayuputras. Will he succeed? And what will be the real cost of battling Evil? Read the concluding part of this bestselling series to find out.

The Ram Chandra Series

The second fastest-selling book series in the history of Indian publishing

RAM – SCION OF IKSHVAKU
(Book 1 of the Series)

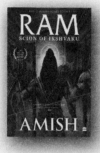

He loves his country and he stands alone for the law. His band of brothers, his wife, Sita and the fight against the darkness of chaos. He is Prince Ram. Will he rise above the taint that others heap on him? Will his love for Sita sustain him through his struggle? Will he defeat the demon Raavan who destroyed his childhood? Will he fulfil the destiny of the Vishnu? Begin an epic journey with Amish's latest: the Ram Chandra Series.

SITA – WARRIOR OF MITHILA
(Book 2 of the Series)

An abandoned baby is found in a field. She is adopted by the ruler of Mithila, a powerless kingdom, ignored by all. Nobody believes this child will amount to much. But they are wrong. For she is no ordinary girl. She is Sita. Through an innovative multi-linear narrative, Amish takes you deeper into the epic world of the Ram Chandra Series.

RAAVAN – ENEMY OF ARYAVARTA
(Book 3 of the Series)

Raavan is determined to be a giant among men, to conquer, plunder, and seize the greatness that he thinks is his right. He is a man of contrasts, of brutal violence and scholarly knowledge. A man who will love without reward and kill without remorse. In this, the third book in the Ram Chandra series, Amish sheds light on Raavan, the king of Lanka. Is he the greatest villain in history or just a man in a dark place, all the time?

Indic Chronicles

LEGEND OF SUHELDEV

Repeated attacks by Mahmud of Ghazni have weakened India's northern regions. Then the Turks raid and destroy one of the holiest temples in the land: the magnificent Lord Shiva temple at Somnath. At this most desperate of times, a warrior rises to defend the nation. King Suheldev—fierce rebel, charismatic leader, inclusive patriot. Read this epic adventure of courage and heroism that recounts the story of that lionhearted warrior and the magnificent Battle of Bahraich.

Non-fiction

IMMORTAL INDIA

Explore India with the country's storyteller, Amish, who helps you understand it like never before, through a series of sharp articles, nuanced speeches and intelligent debates. In *Immortal India*, Amish lays out the vast landscape of an ancient culture with a fascinatingly modern outlook.

DHARMA – DECODING THE EIP ICS FOR A MEANINGFUL LIFE

In this genre-bending book, the first of a series, Amish and Bhavna dive into the priceless treasure trove of the ancient Indian epics, as well as the vast and complex universe of Amish's Meluha, to explore some of the key concepts of Indian philosophy. Within this book are answers to our many philosophical questions, offered through simple and wise interpretations of our favourite stories.

INDIA, 3400 BCE.

KEKAYA

Indraprastha

Beas

Ravi

Sutlej

Yamuna

Sarayu

Ayodhya

KOSALA

Mithila

VIDEHA

Gandaki

Kosi

Brahmaputra

Saraswati

Chambal

Karachapa

Drishad

Saraswati Course

Narmada

DAKSHIN
KOSALA

Mahanadi

Ulaka Lake

Panchavati

Mandak
Forest

Krishna

Kishkindha

Tungabhadra

Western Sea

Eastern Sea

N

Kaveri

Agastyakootam

Ram Setu

Gokarna

Sigiriya
Lanka

● RIVERS

● PLACES

● KINGDOMS

'NOT TO SCALE'